SUNNY
ROLLS THE DICE

JENNIFER L. HOLM & MATTHEW HOLM
WITH COLOR BY LARK PIEN

graphix

AN IMPRINT OF

■SCHOLASTIC

Library of Congress data available

ISBN 978-1-338-23315-5 (hardcover)
ISBN 978-1-338-23314-8 (paperback)

10 9 8 7 6 5 4 3 2 1   19 20 21 22 23

Printed in China 62
First edition, October 2019
Edited by David Levithan
Lettering by Fawn Lau
Color by Lark Pien
Book design by Phil Falco
Publisher: David Saylor

To Jon, Sean, Brian, Chris,
and all the other boys on the
block who played D&D with us

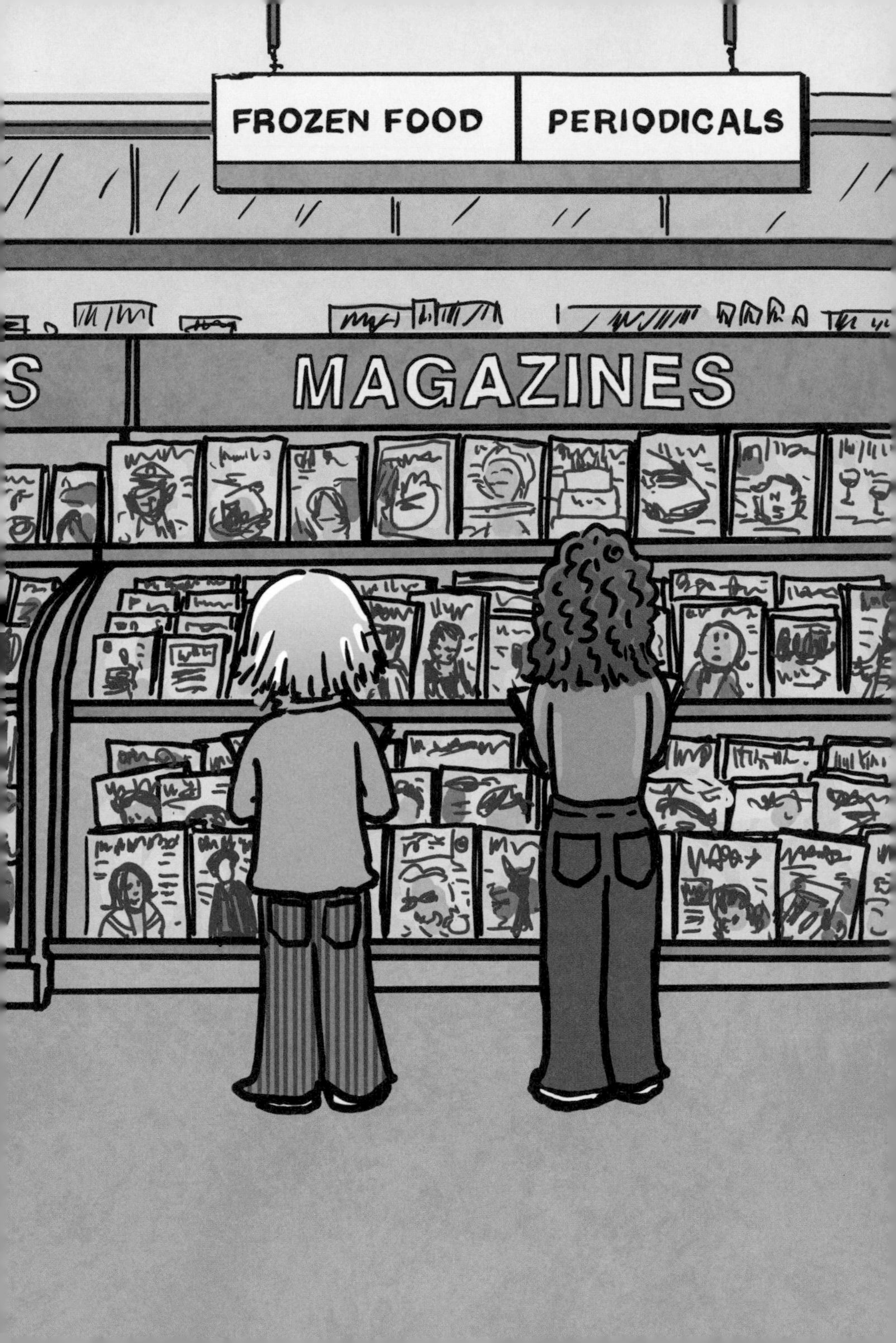
FROZEN FOOD
PERIODICALS
MAGAZINES

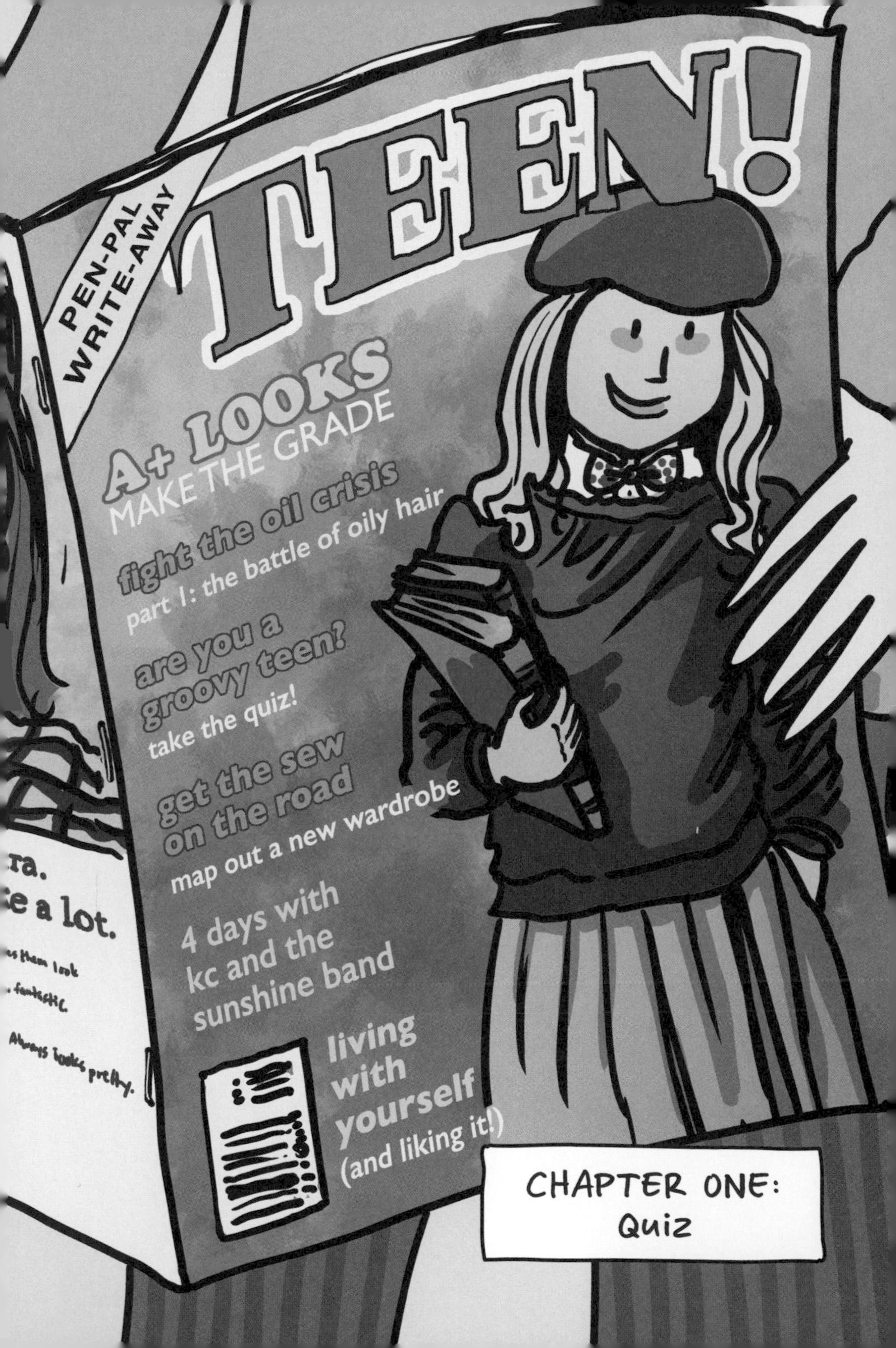
TEEN!
PEN-PAL WRITE-AWAY
A+ LOOKS
MAKE THE GRADE
fight the oil crisis
part 1: the battle of oily hair
are you a groovy teen?
take the quiz!
get the sew on the road
map out a new wardrobe
4 days with kc and the sunshine band
living with yourself (and liking it!)
Always looks pretty.
CHAPTER ONE:
Quiz

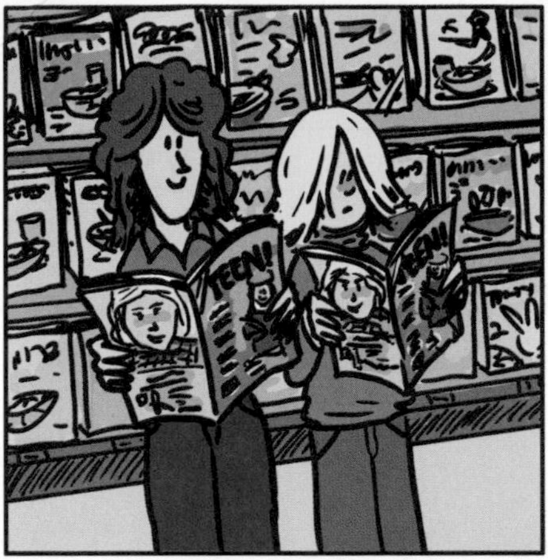
TEEN!

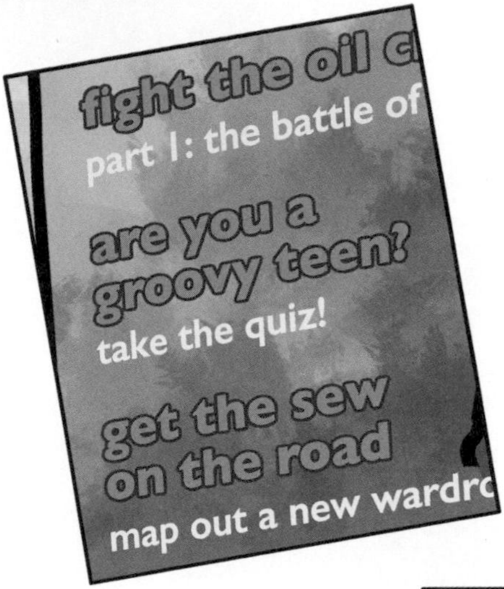
fight the oil cr
part 1: the battle of
are you a
groovy teen?
take the quiz!
get the sew
on the road
map out a new wardro

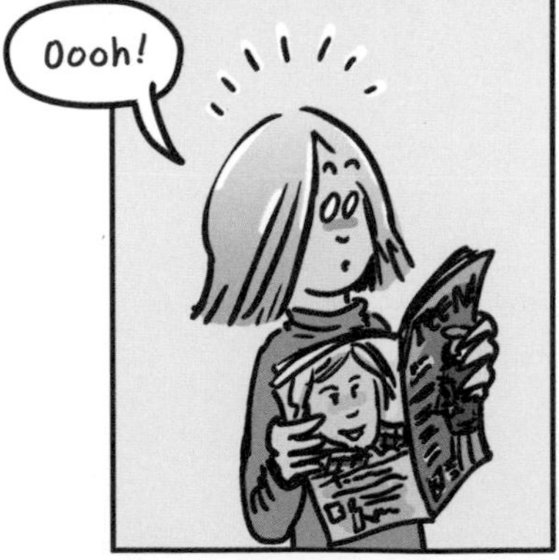
Oooh!

Do you have groovy STYLE?

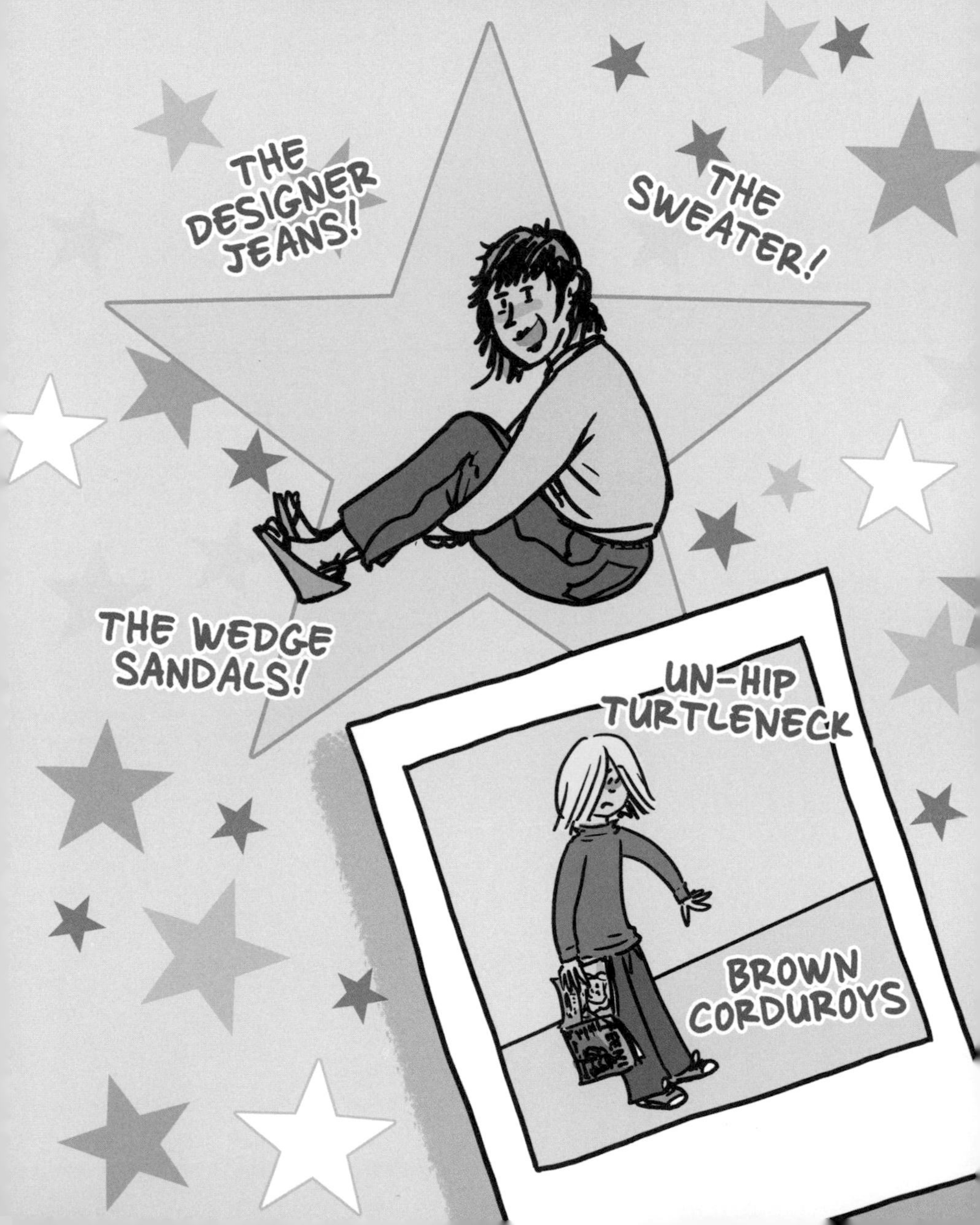
THE DESIGNER JEANS!
THE SWEATER!
THE WEDGE SANDALS!
UN-HIP TURTLENECK
BROWN CORDUROYS

Do you have groovy HAIR?

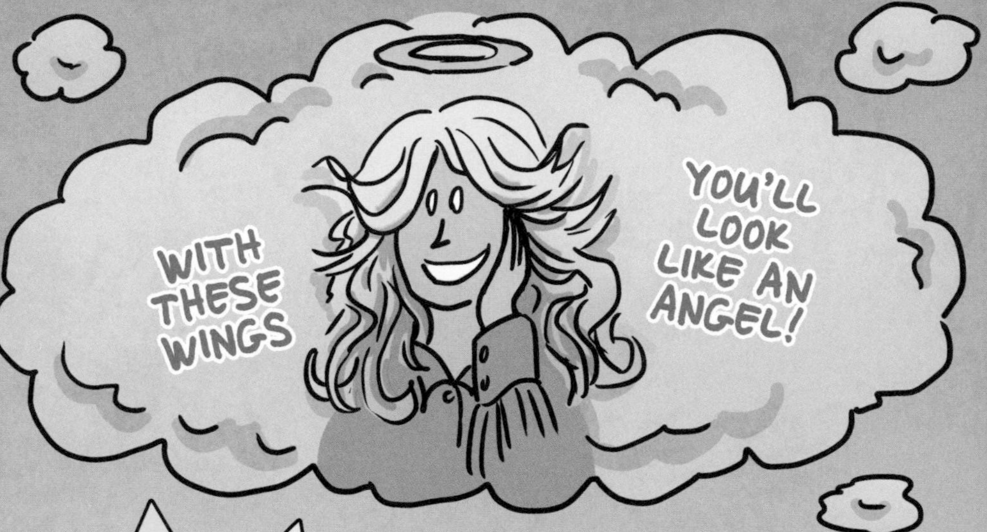
WITH THESE WINGS
YOU'LL LOOK LIKE AN ANGEL!

HAIR HINT:
FOR SUNNY STREAKS, SQUEEZE SOME LEMON JUICE ON YOUR HAIR AND SIT IN THE SUN!

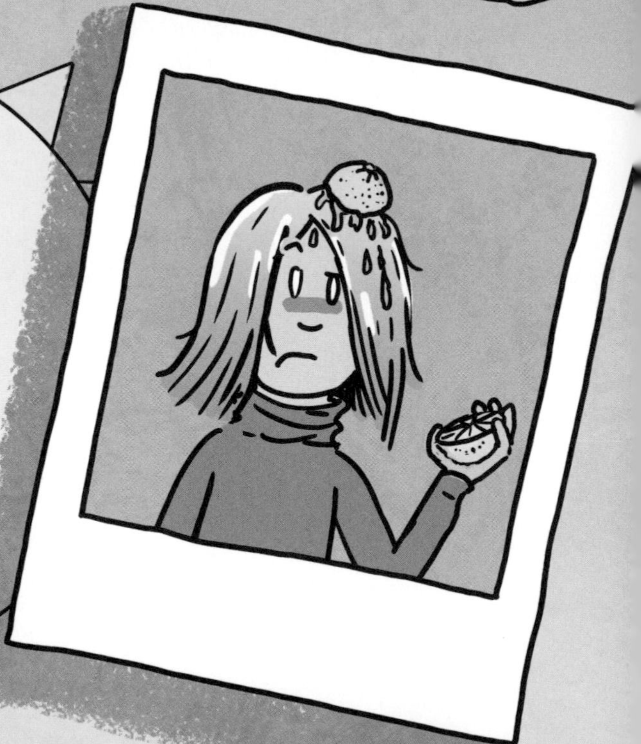

Do you have a groovy ROOM?

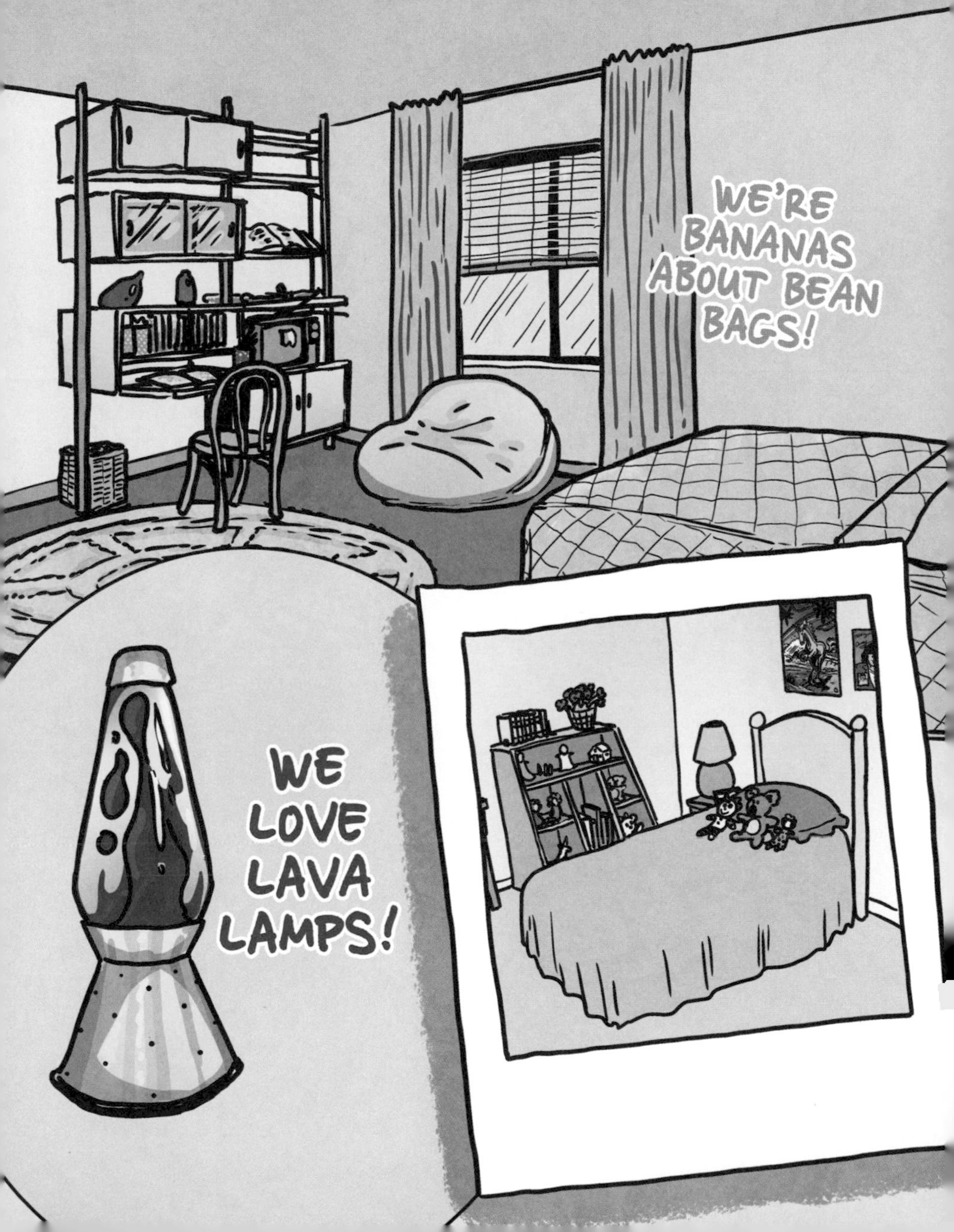
WE'RE BANANAS ABOUT BEAN BAGS!
WE LOVE LAVA LAMPS!

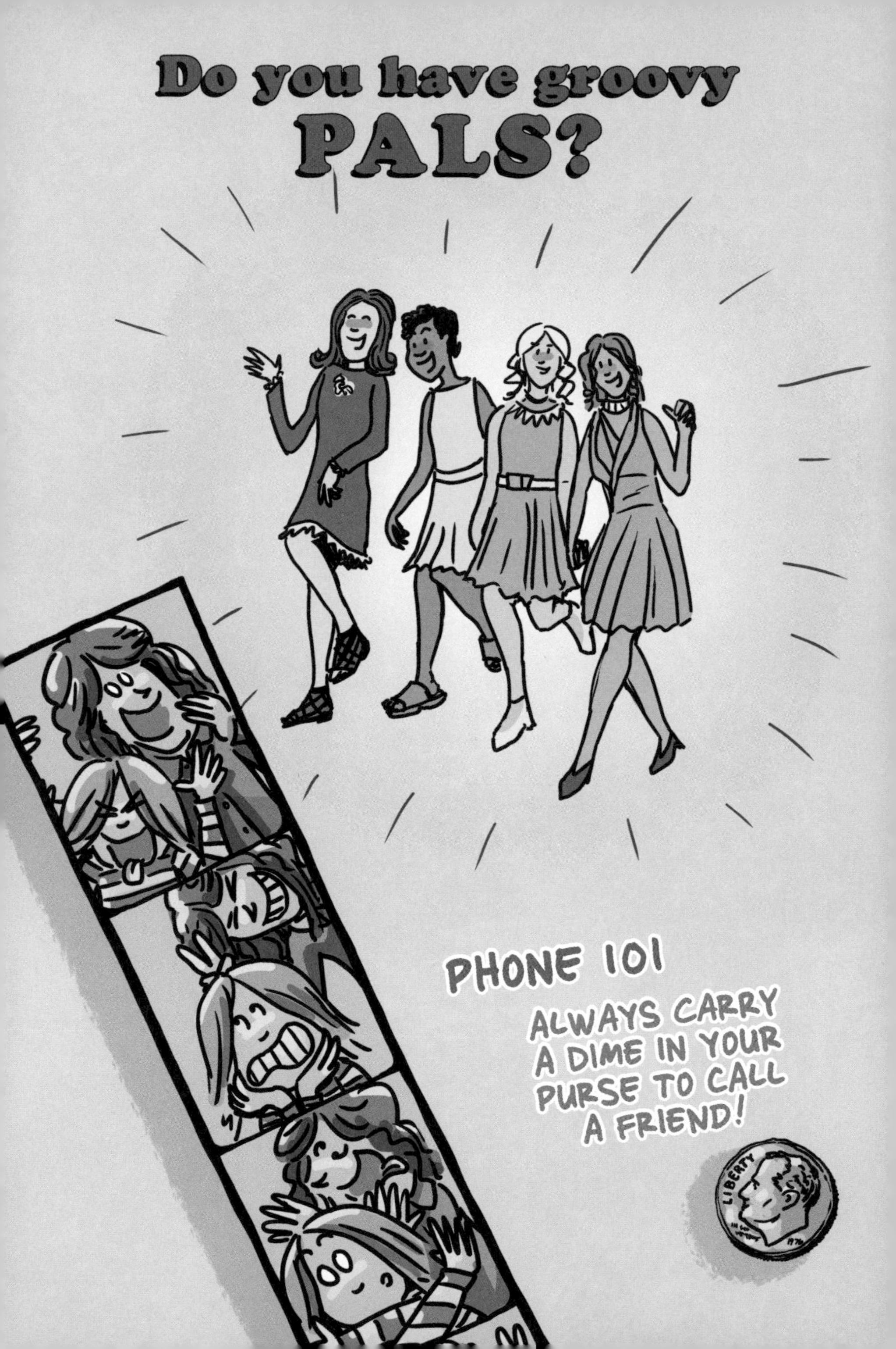
Do you have groovy PALS?
PHONE 101
ALWAYS CARRY A DIME IN YOUR PURSE TO CALL A FRIEND!
LIBERTY

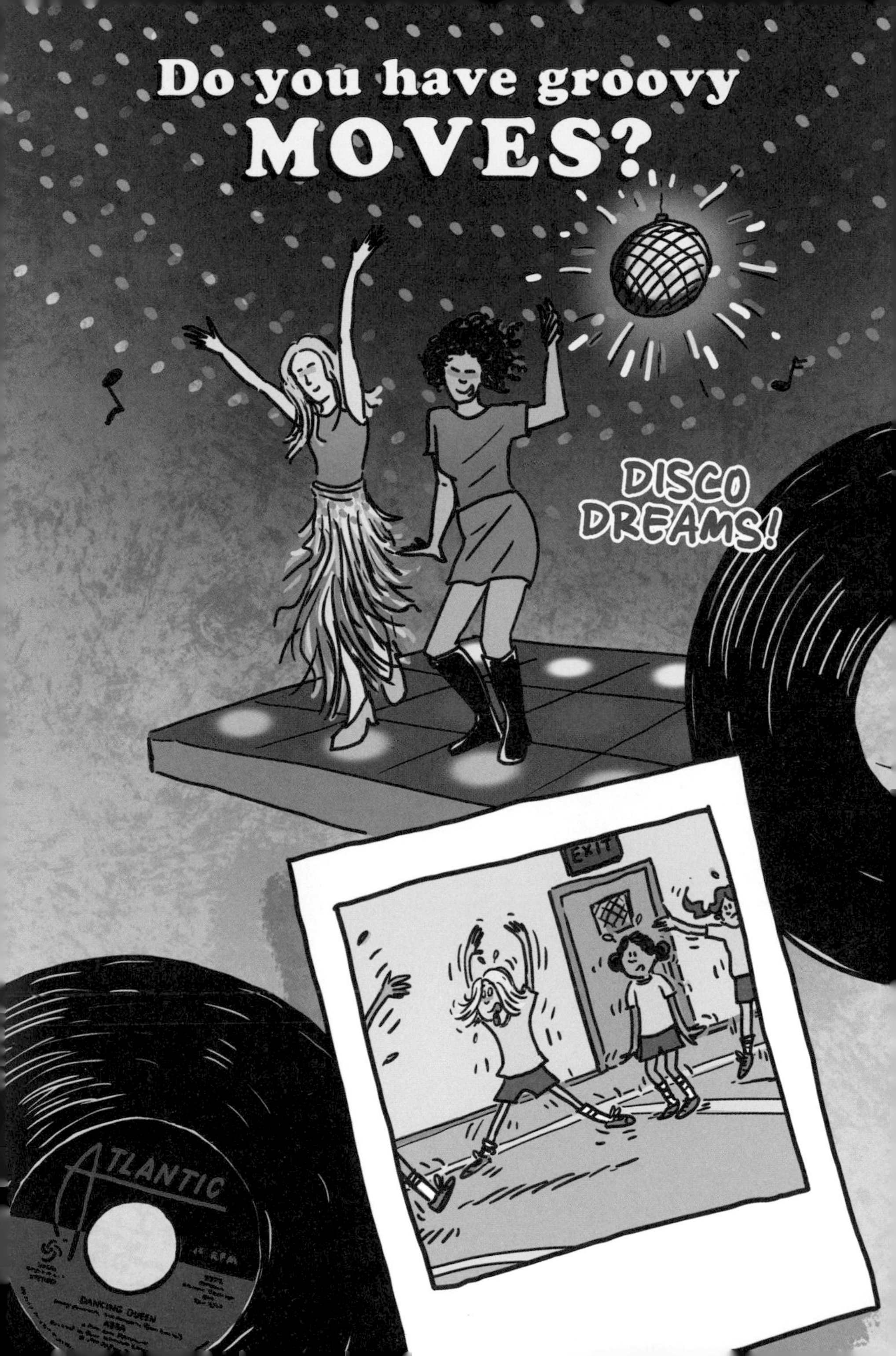
Do you have groovy
MOVES?
DISCO
DREAMS!
EXIT
ATLANTIC
DANCING QUEEN
ABBA

Do you have a groovy GUY?

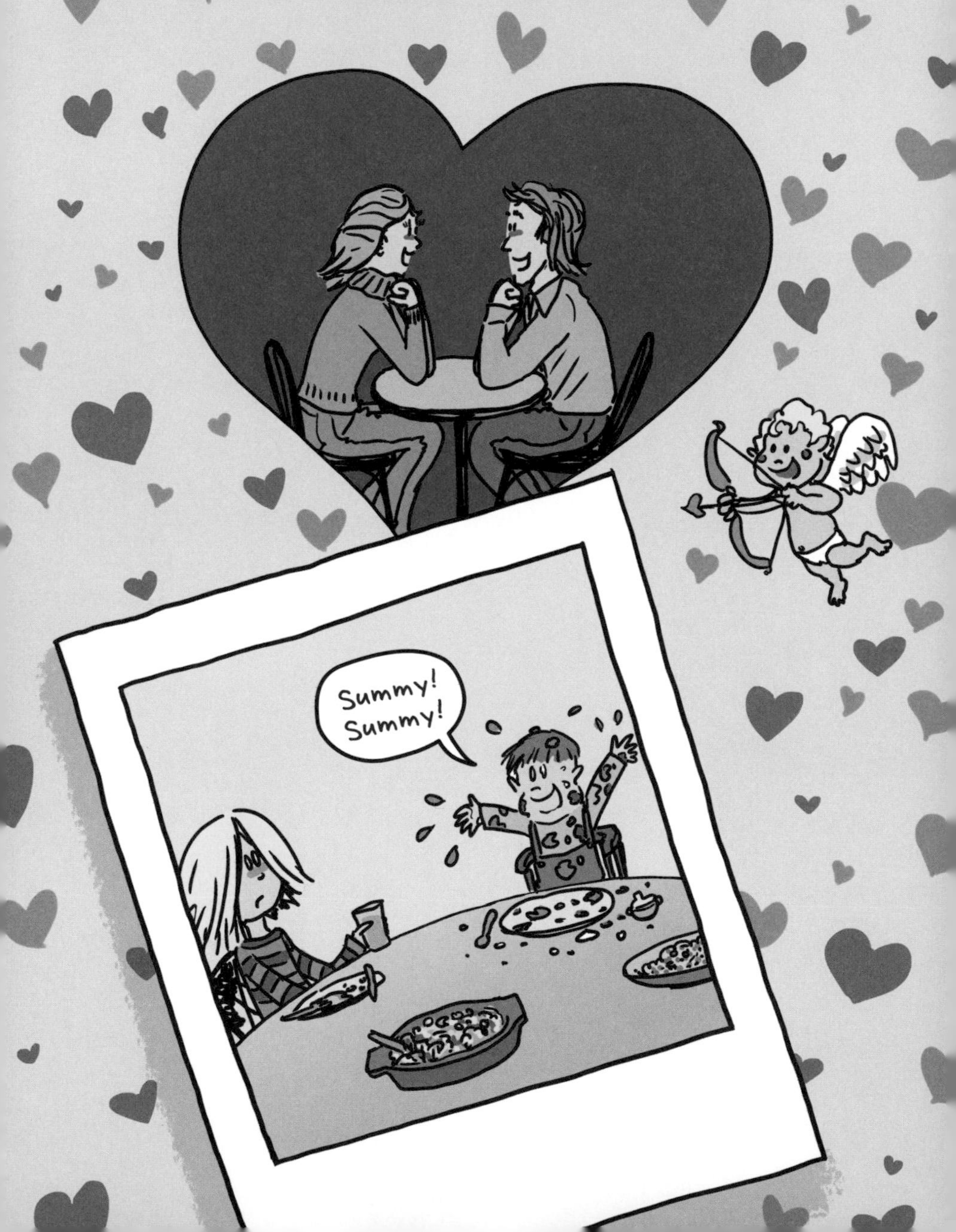
Summy!
Summy!

NOW TALLY YOUR SCORE!

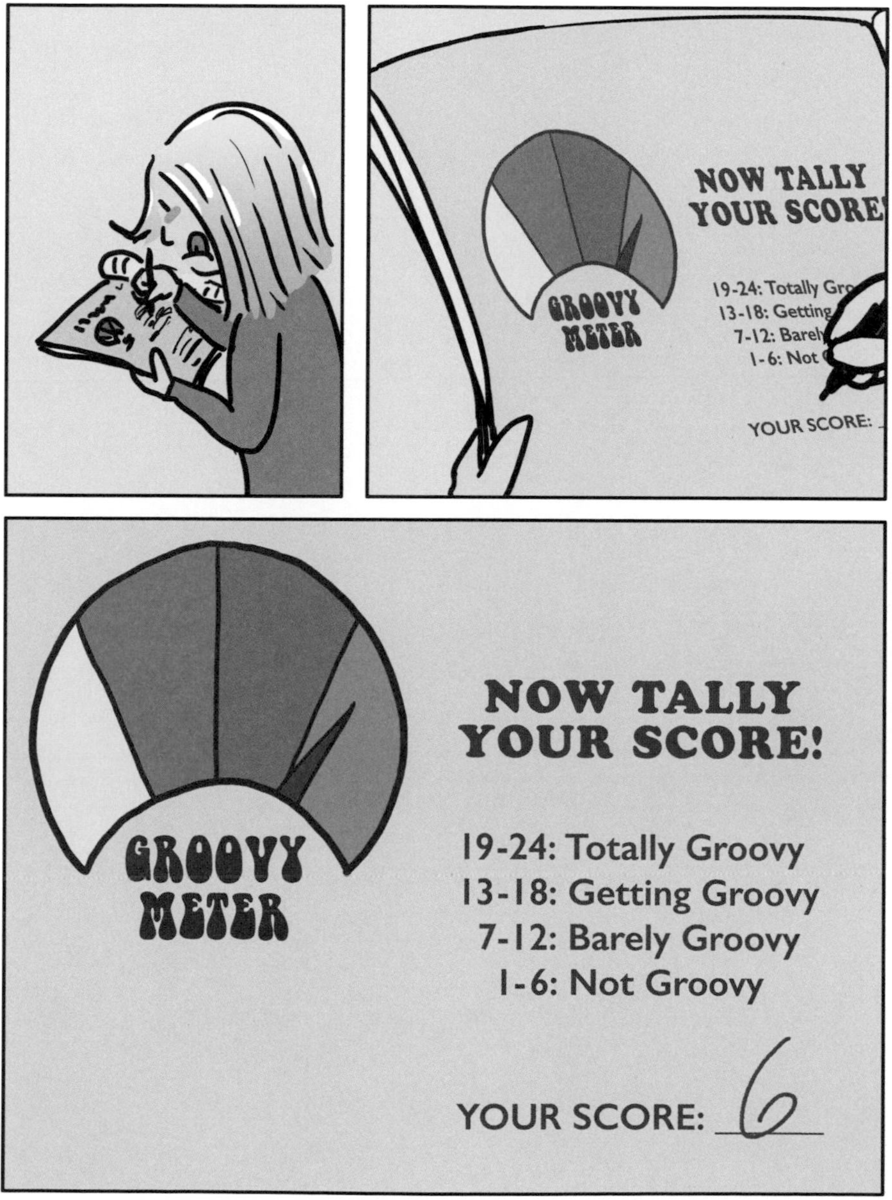
NOW TALLY
YOUR SCORE
GROOVY
METER
YOUR SCORE:
GROOVY
METER
NOW TALLY
YOUR SCORE!
19-24: Totally Groovy
13-18: Getting Groovy
7-12: Barely Groovy
1-6: Not Groovy
YOUR SCORE: 6

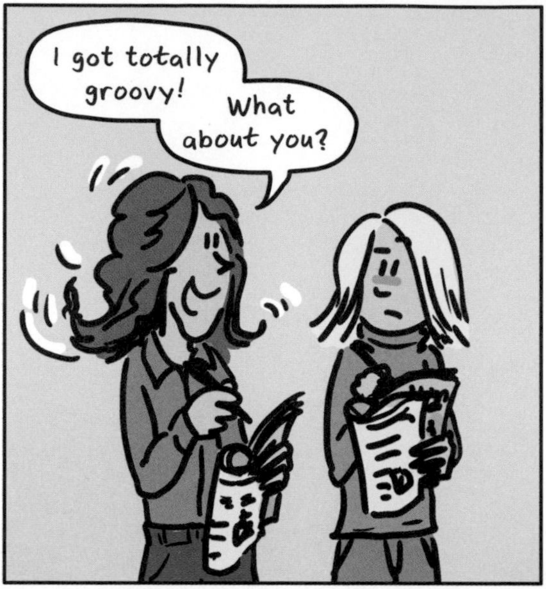
I got totally groovy!
What about you?

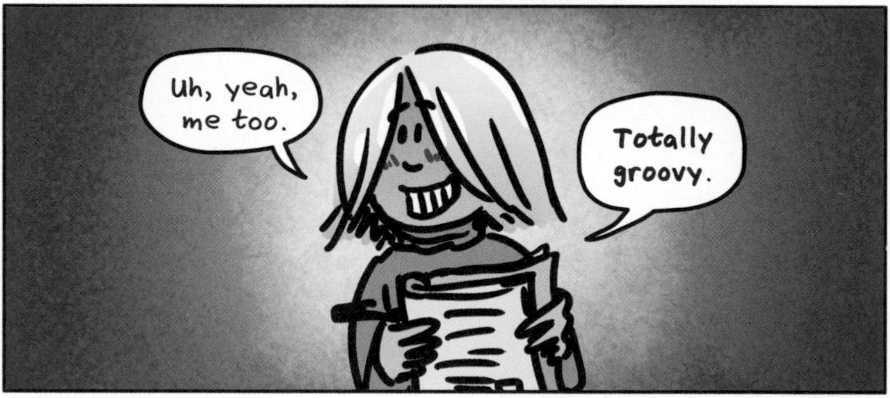
Uh, yeah, me too.
Totally groovy.

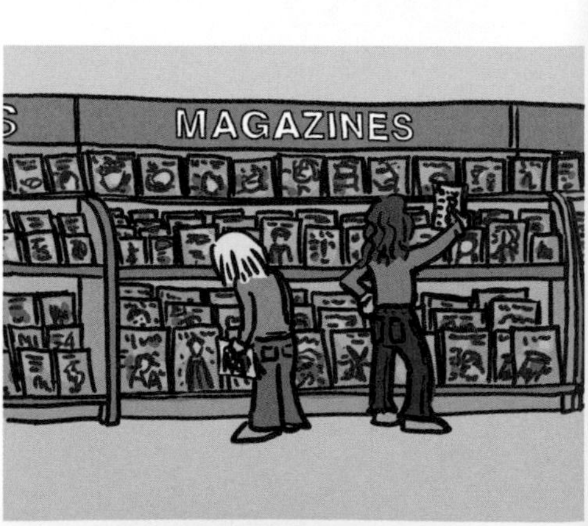
MAGAZINES

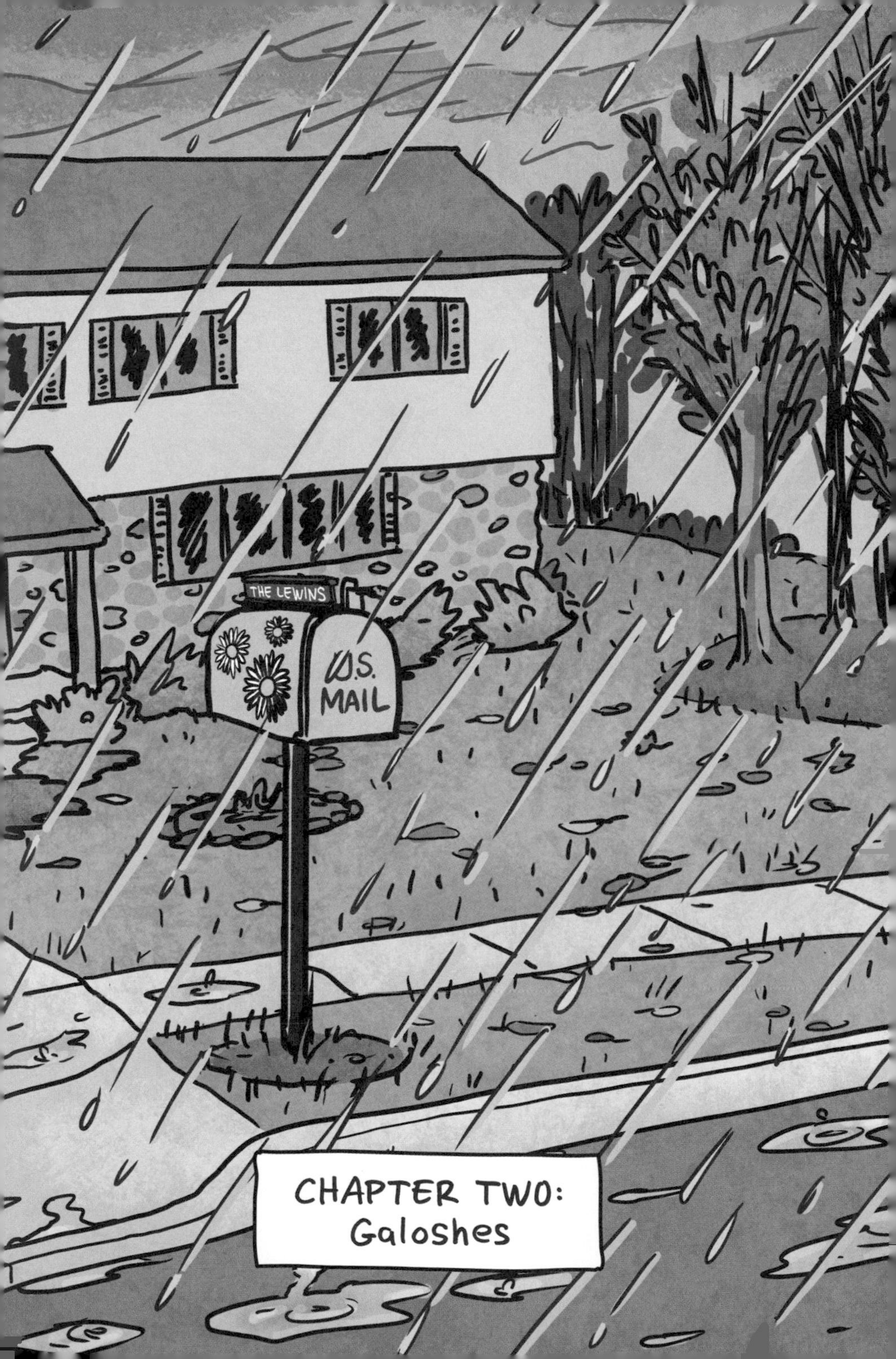
THE LEWINS
U.S.
MAIL
CHAPTER TWO:
Galoshes

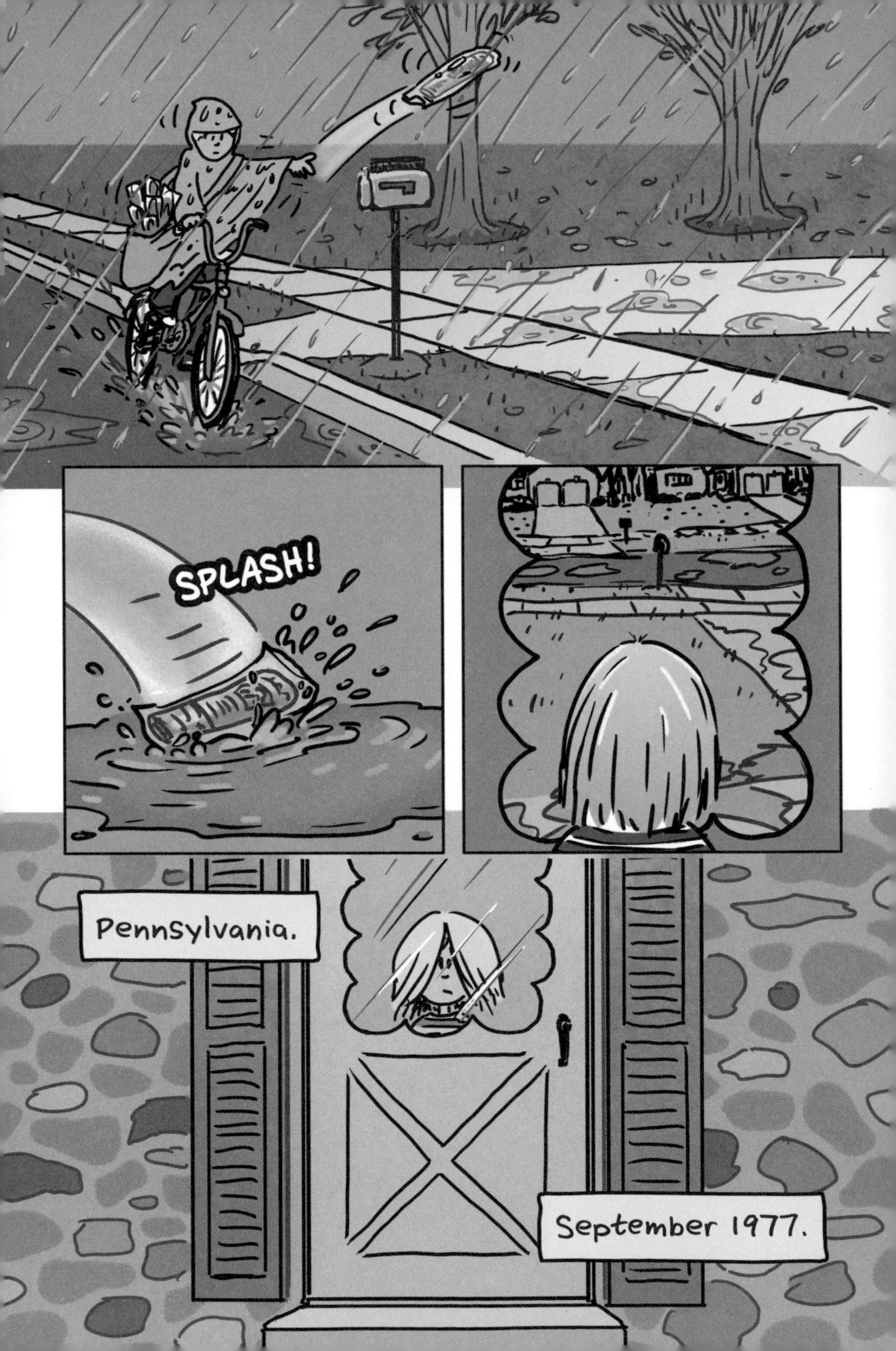
SPLASH!
Pennsylvania.
September 1977.

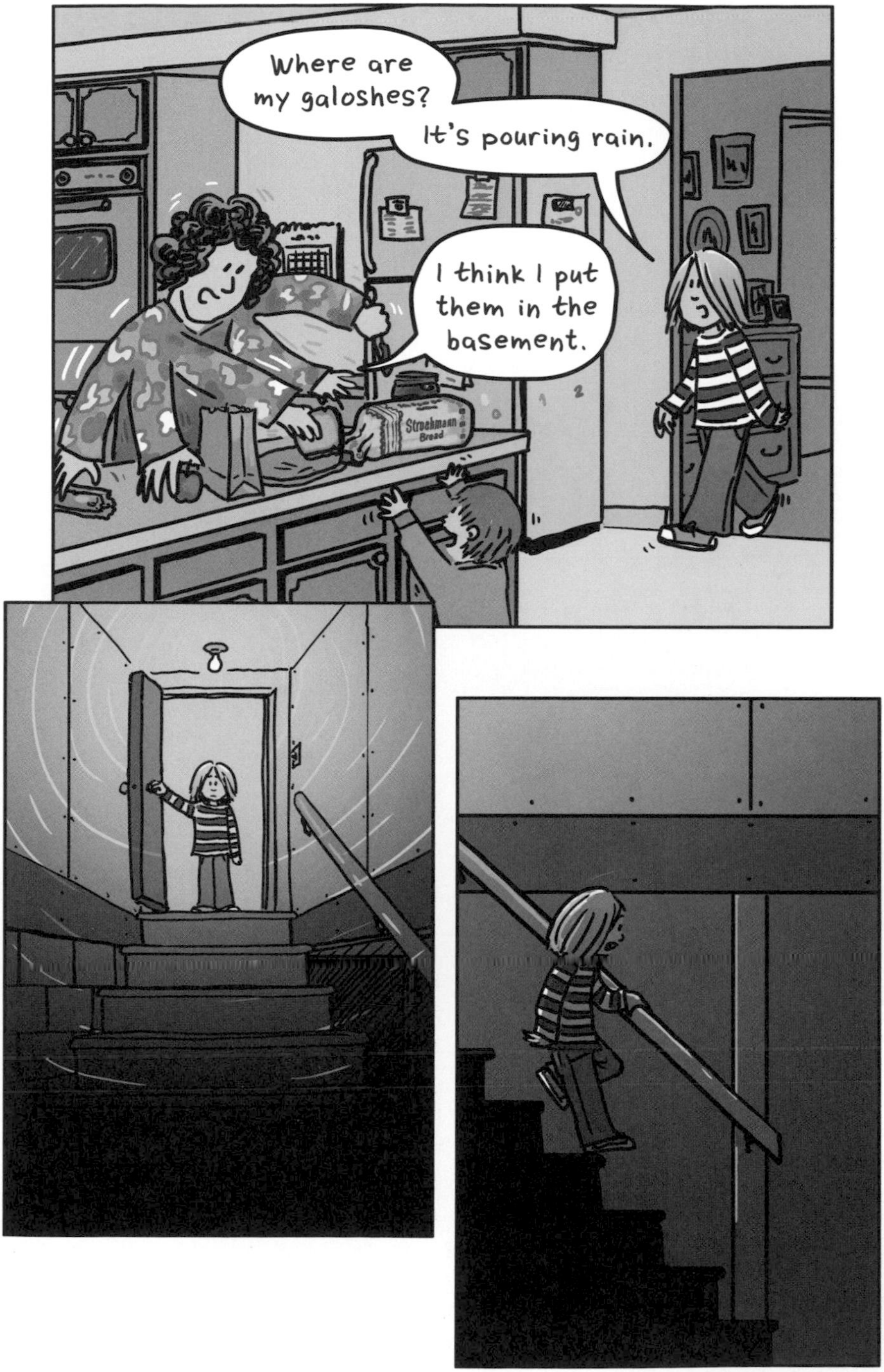
Where are my galoshes?
It's pouring rain.
I think I put them in the basement.
Stroehmann Bread

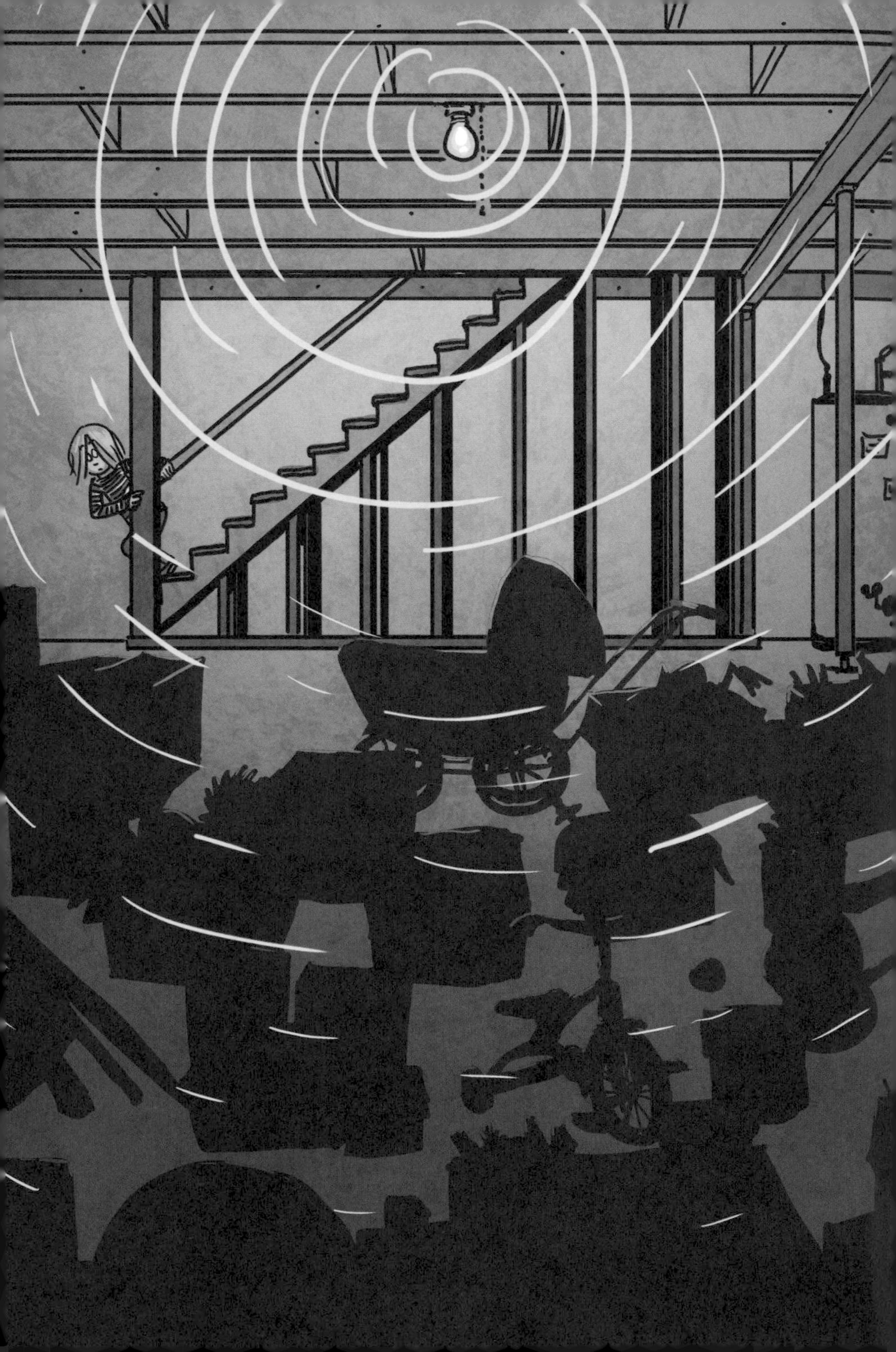

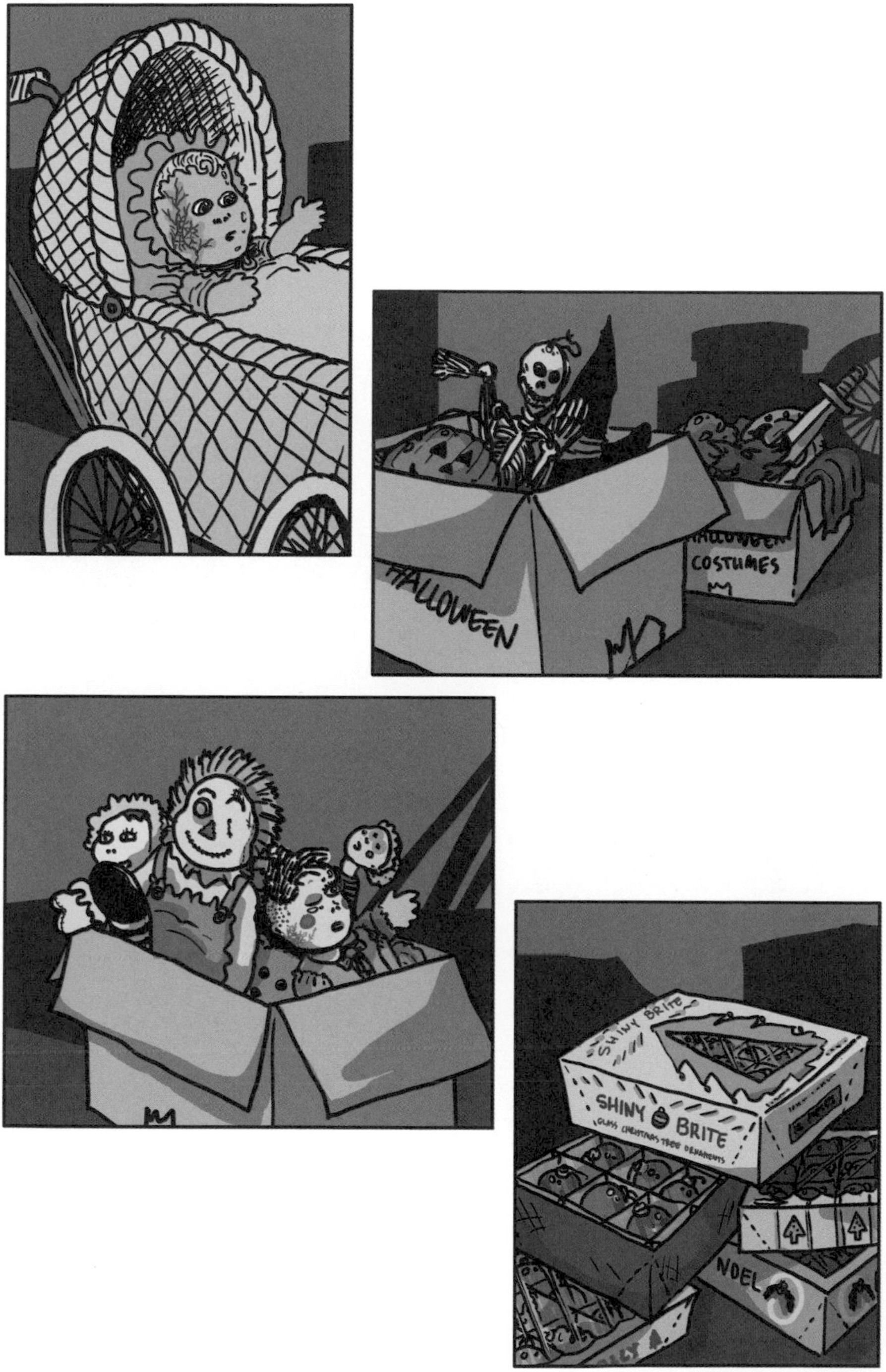
HALLOWEEN
COSTUMES
SHINY BRITE
SHINY BRITE
GLASS CHRISTMAS TREE ORNAMENTS
NOEL

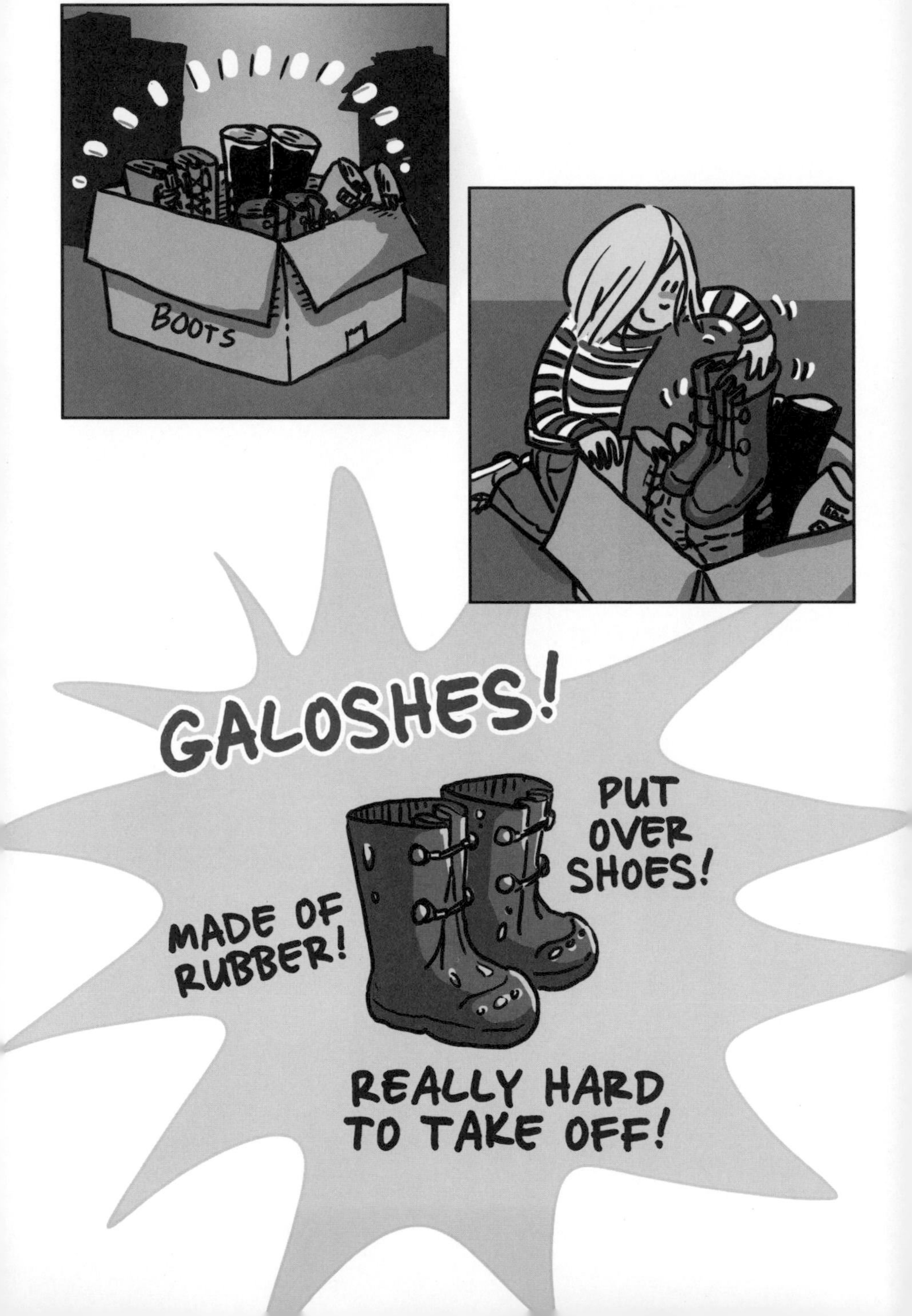
BOOTS
GALOSHES!
PUT OVER SHOES!
MADE OF RUBBER!
REALLY HARD TO TAKE OFF!

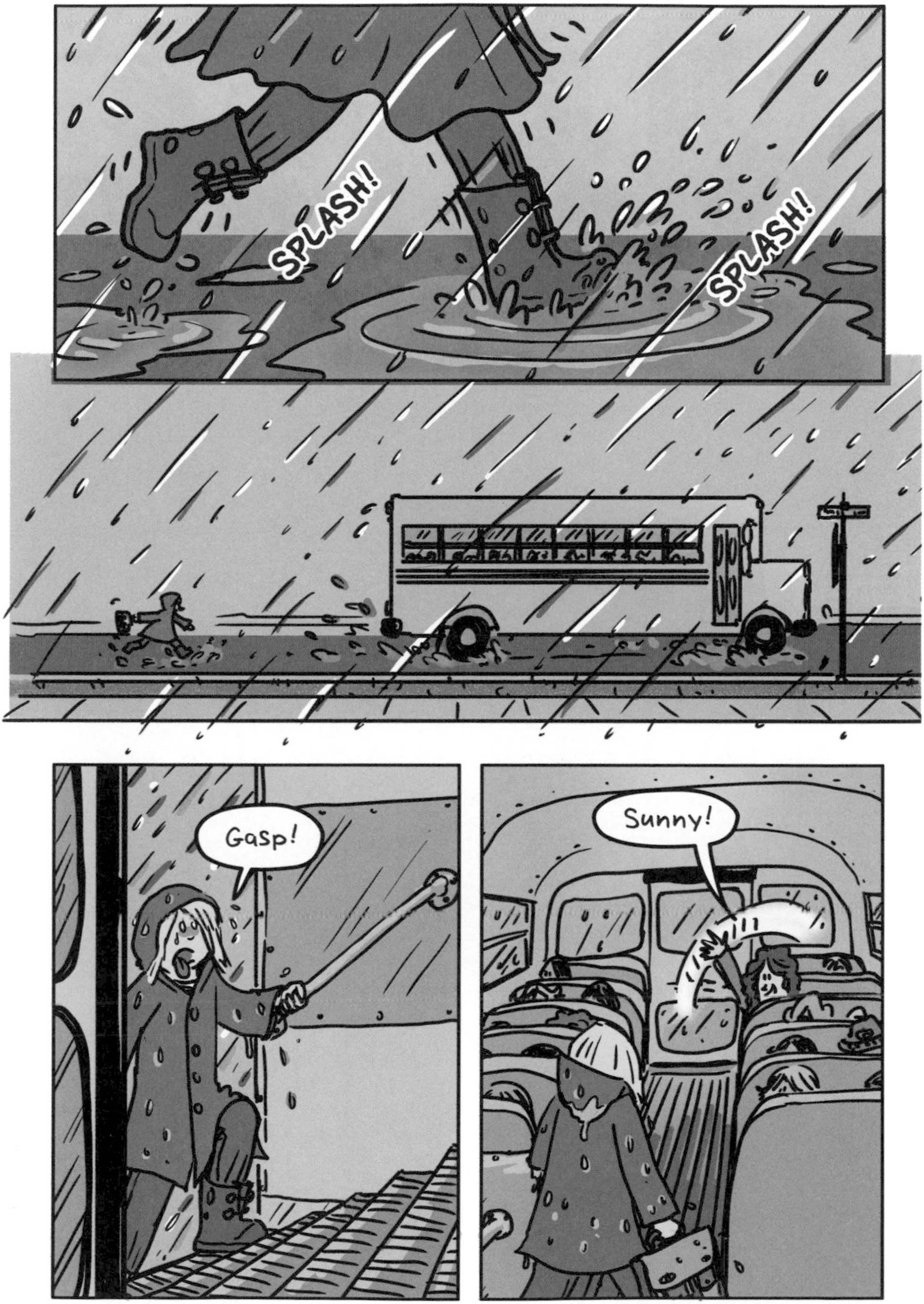
SPLASH!
SPLASH!
Gasp!
Sunny!

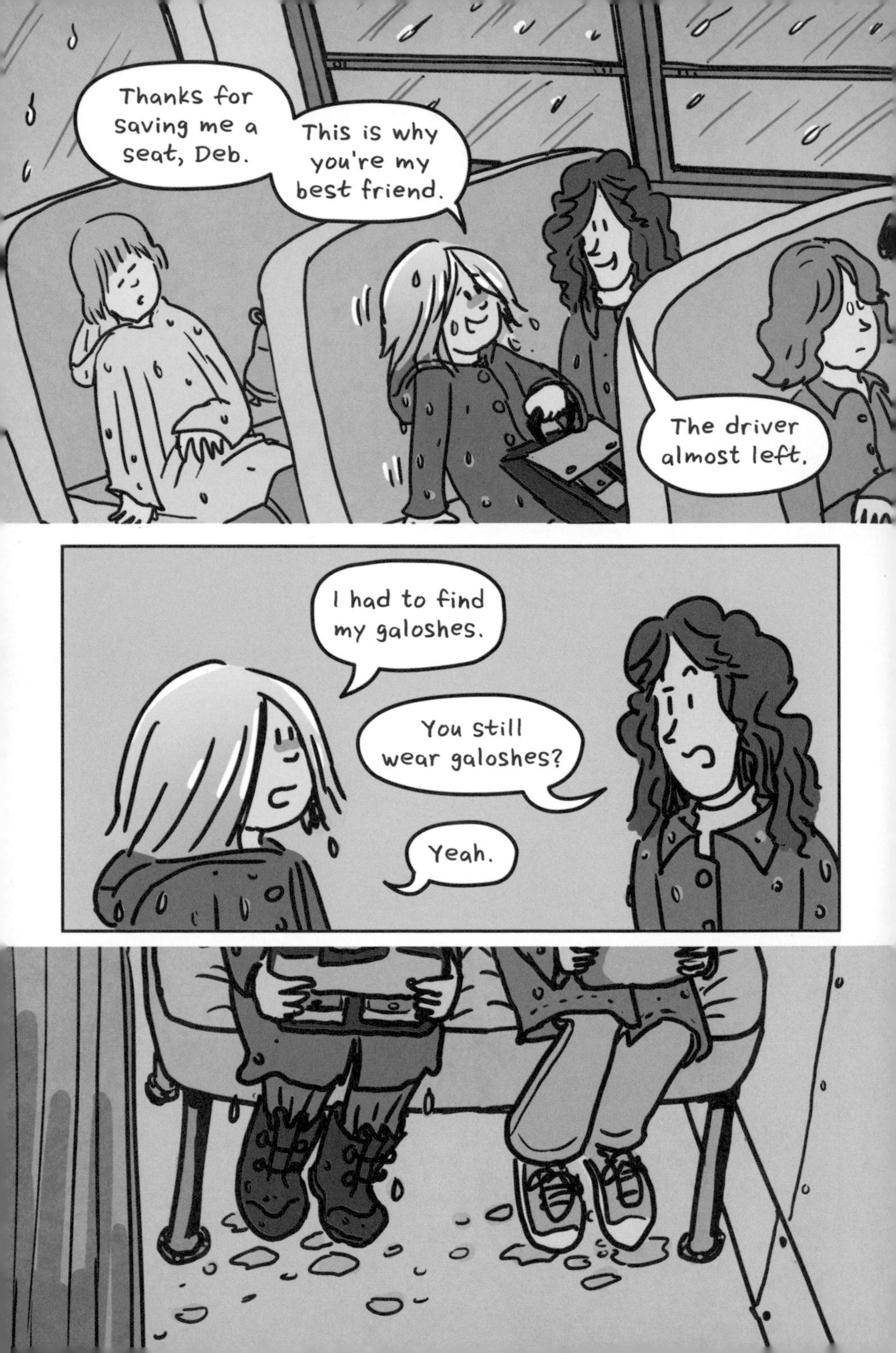
Thanks for saving me a seat, Deb.
This is why you're my best friend.
The driver almost left.
I had to find my galoshes.
You still wear galoshes?
Yeah.

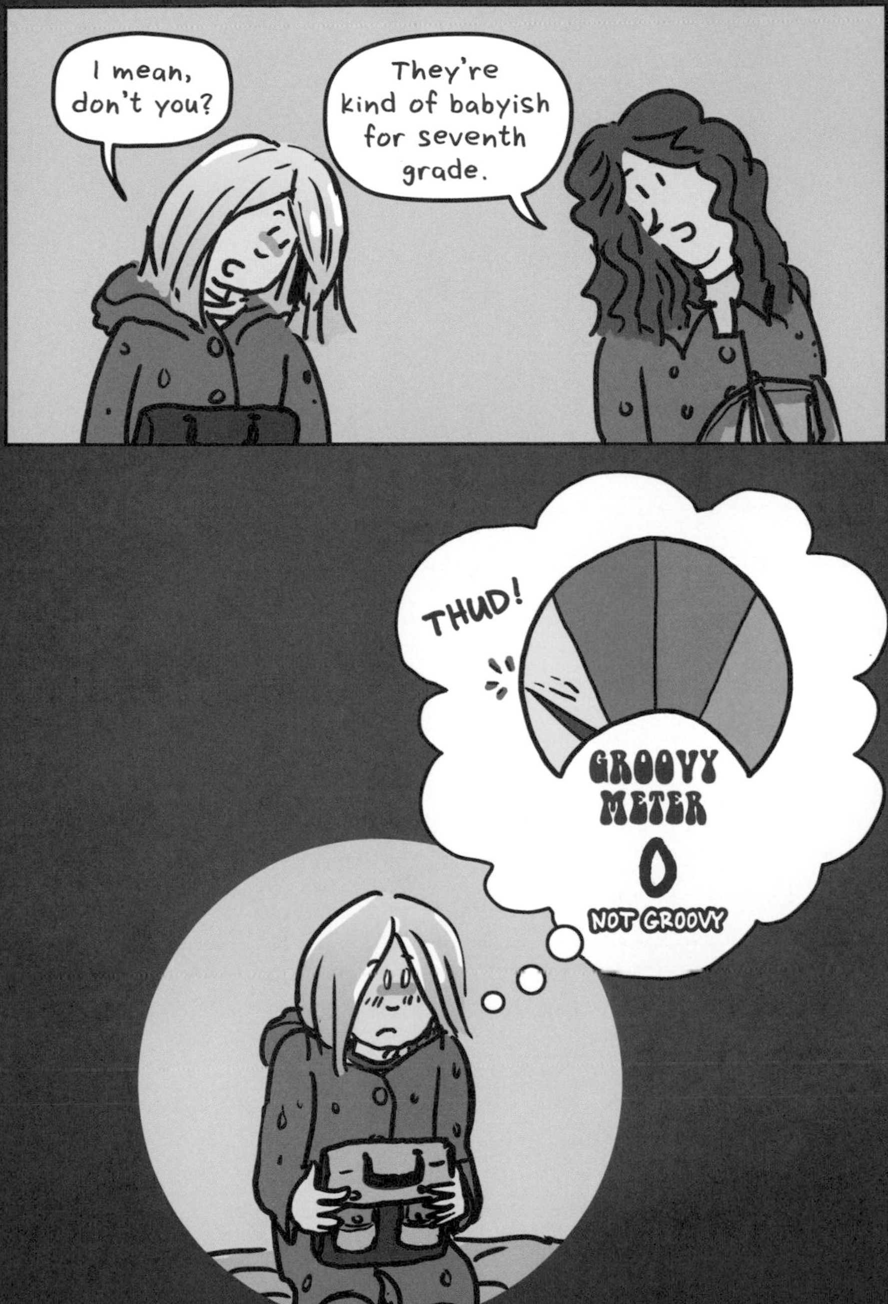
I mean, don't you?
They're kind of babyish for seventh grade.
THUD!
GROOVY METER
0
NOT GROOVY

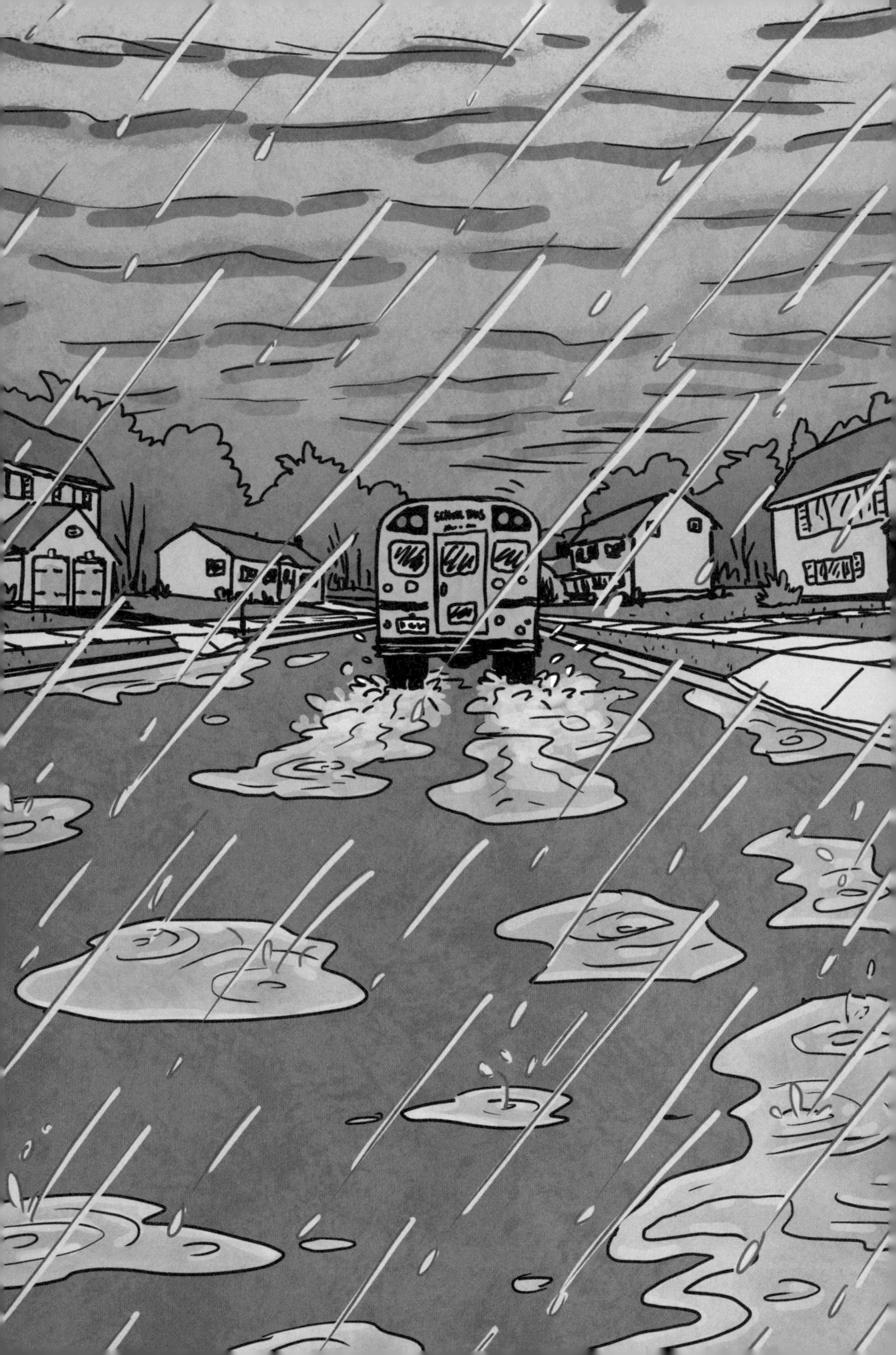
SCHOOL BUS

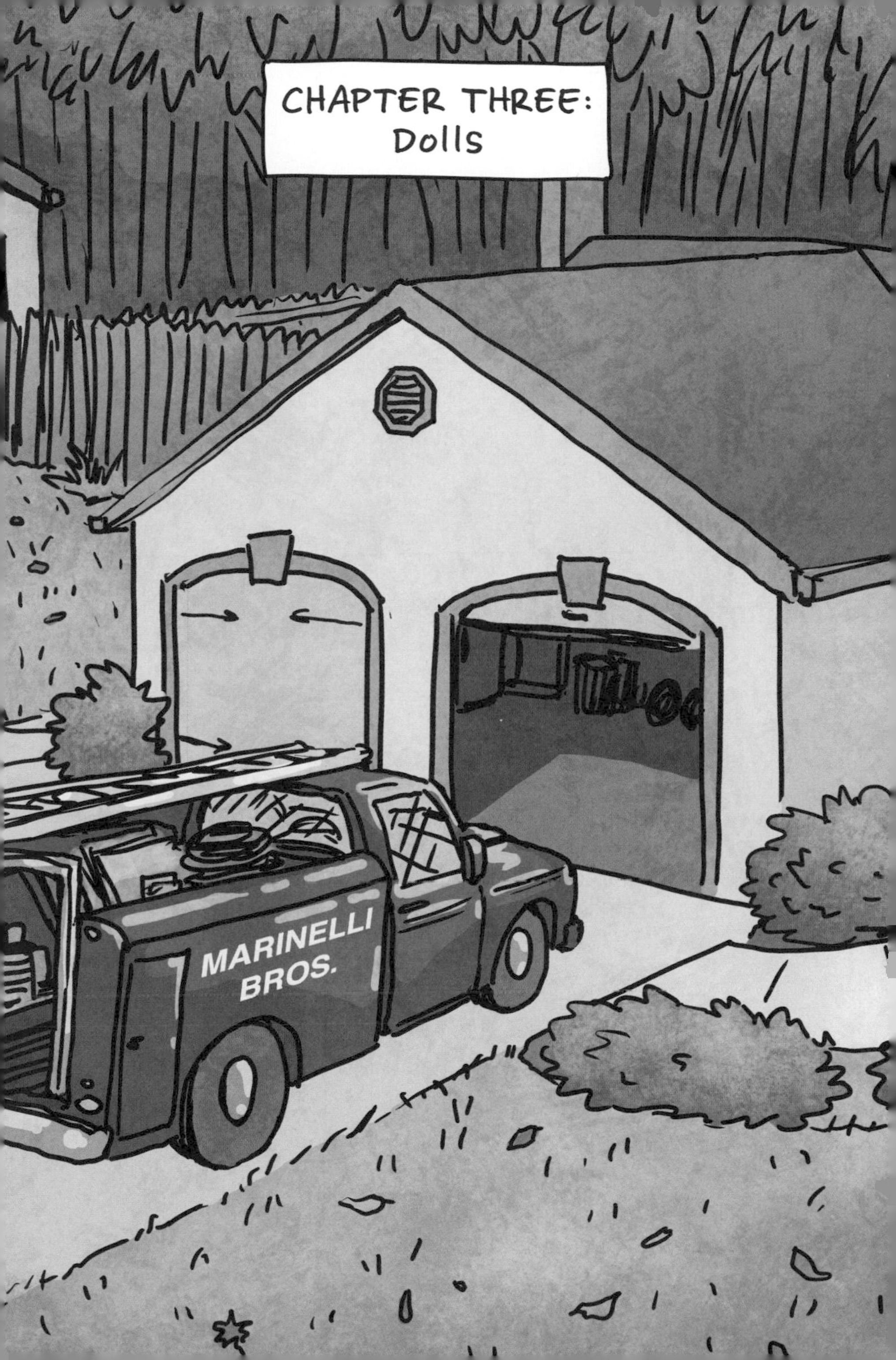
CHAPTER THREE:
Dolls
MARINELLI
BROS.

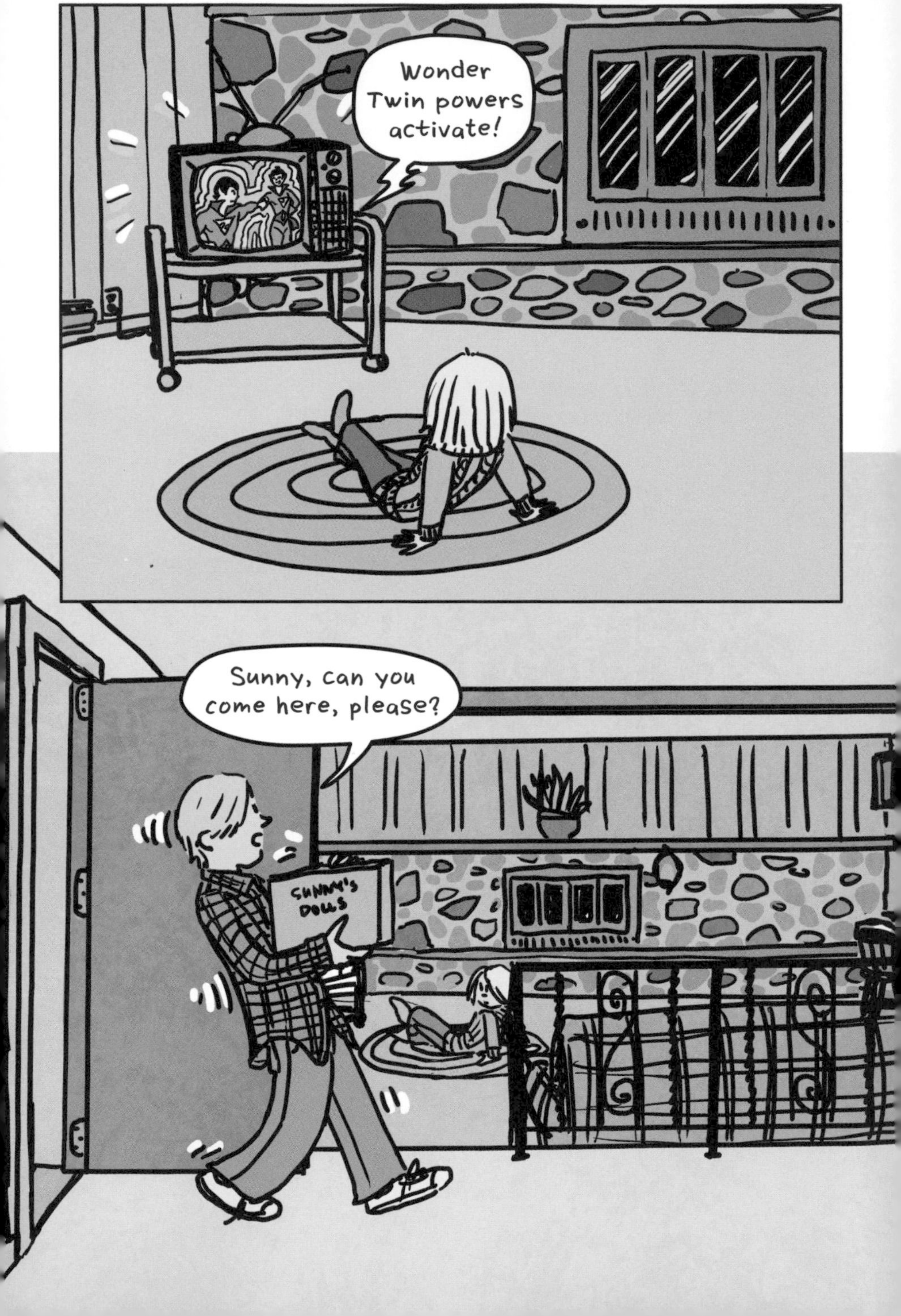
Wonder Twin powers activate!
Sunny, can you come here, please?
SUNNY'S DOLLS

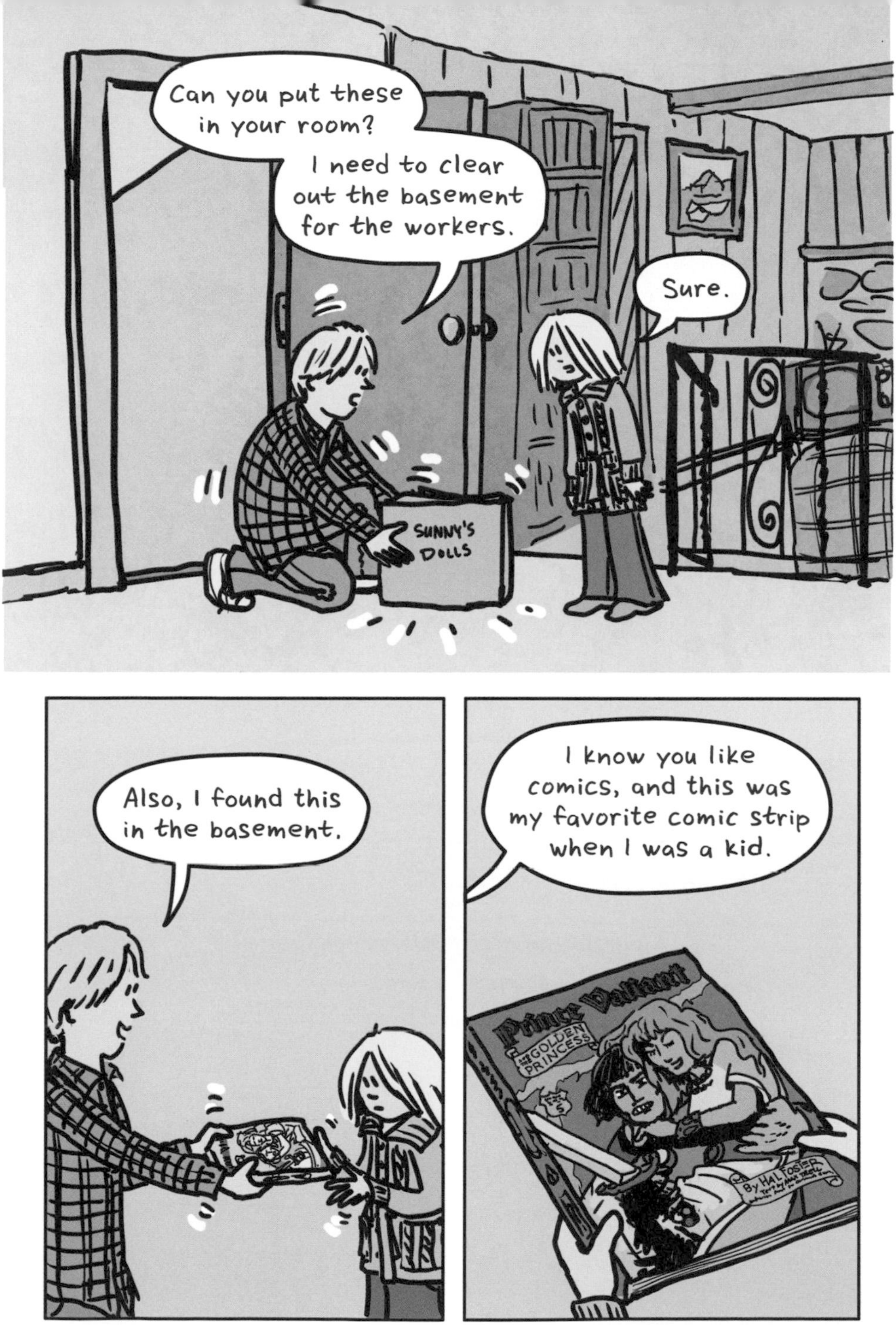
Can you put these in your room?
I need to clear out the basement for the workers.
Sure.
SUNNY'S DOLLS
Also, I found this in the basement.
I know you like comics, and this was my favorite comic strip when I was a kid.
Prince Valiant
GOLDEN PRINCESS
By HAL FOSTER

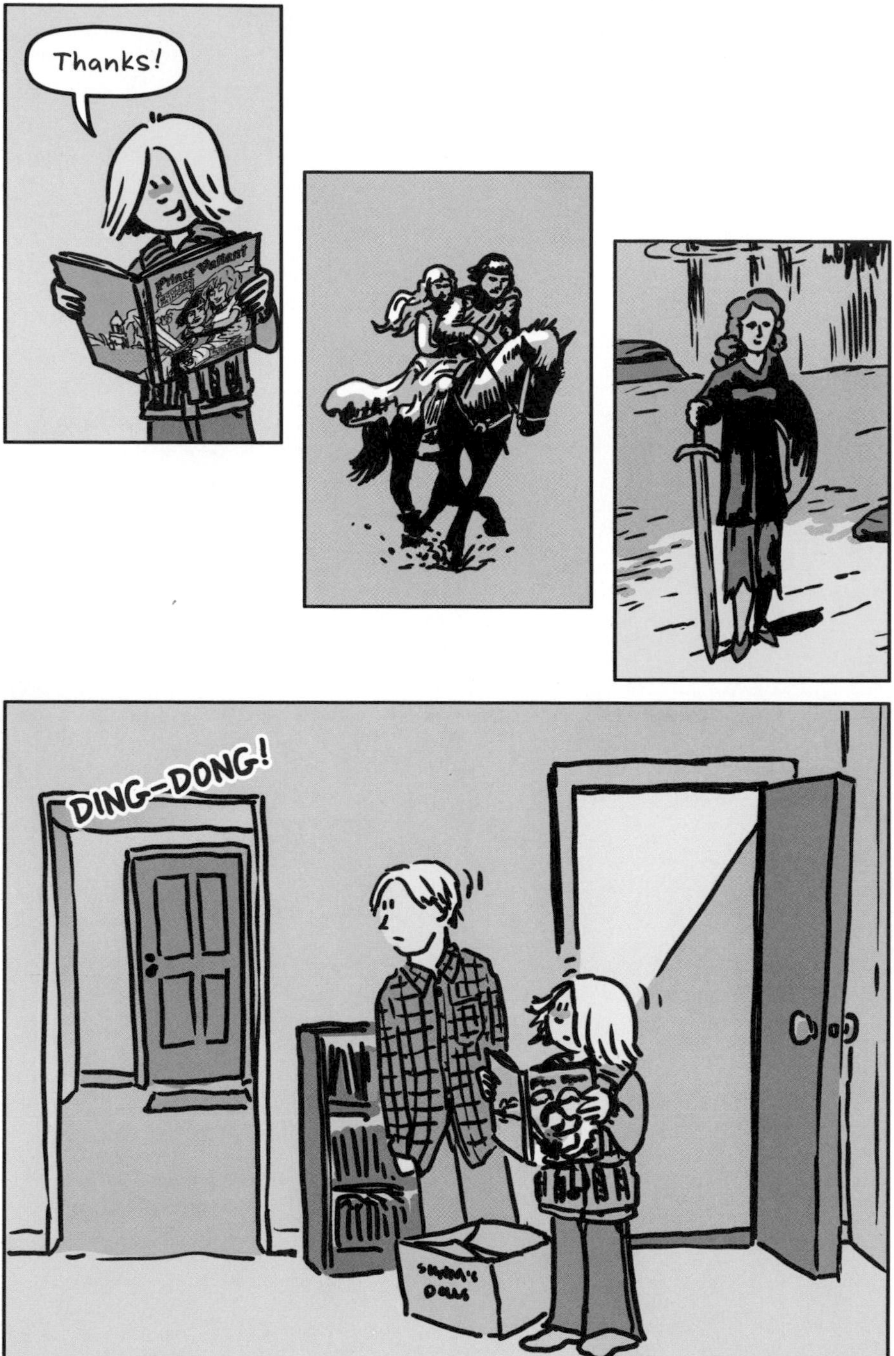
Thanks!
Prince Valiant
DING-DONG!

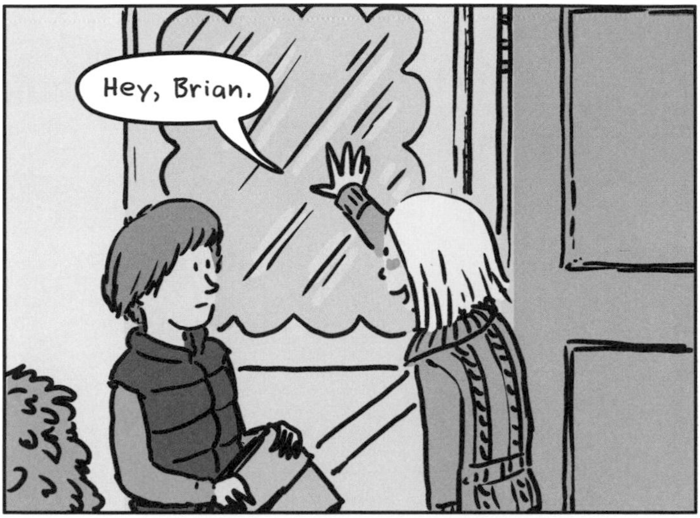
Hey, Brian.

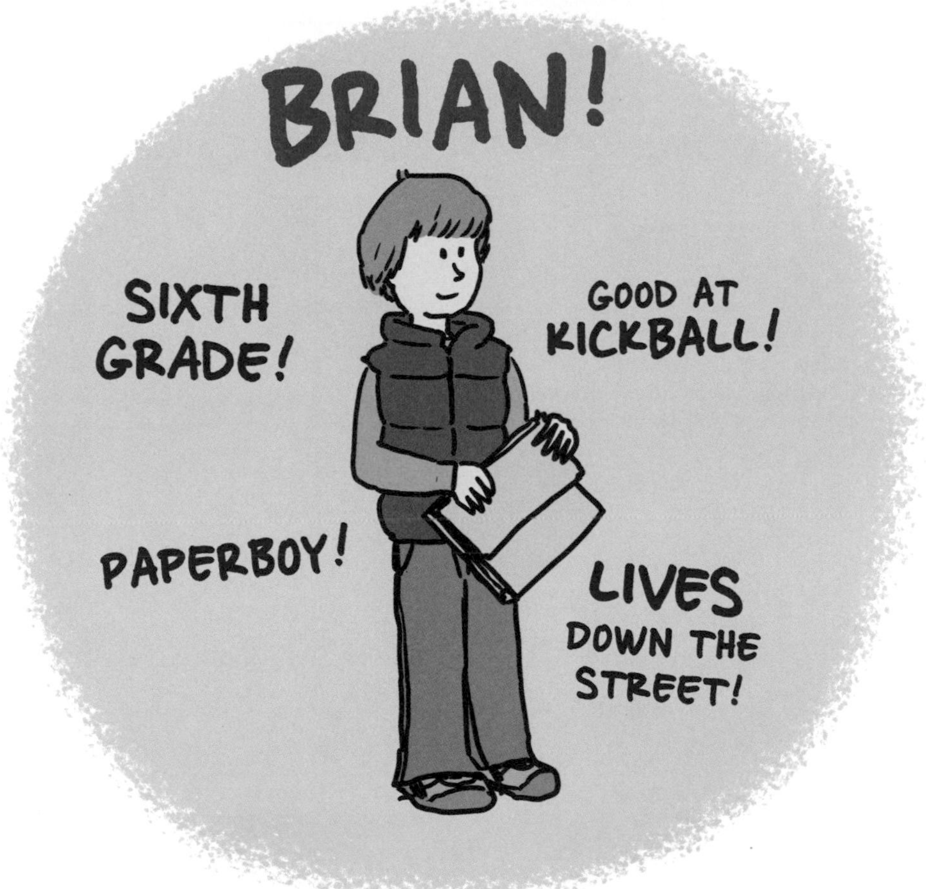
BRIAN!
SIXTH GRADE!
GOOD AT KICKBALL!
PAPERBOY!
LIVES DOWN THE STREET!

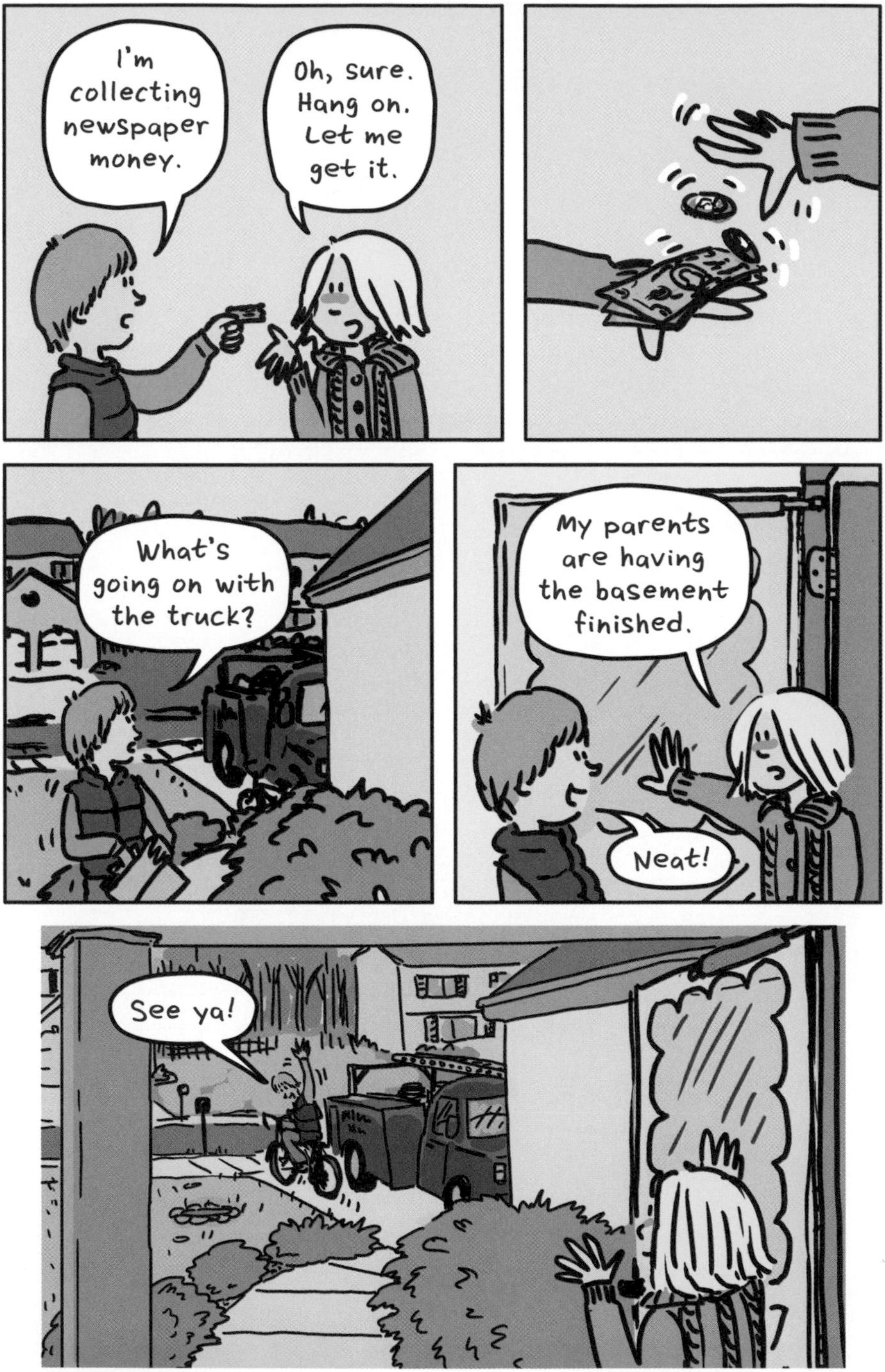
I'm collecting newspaper money.
Oh, sure. Hang on. Let me get it.
What's going on with the truck?
My parents are having the basement finished.
Neat!
See ya!

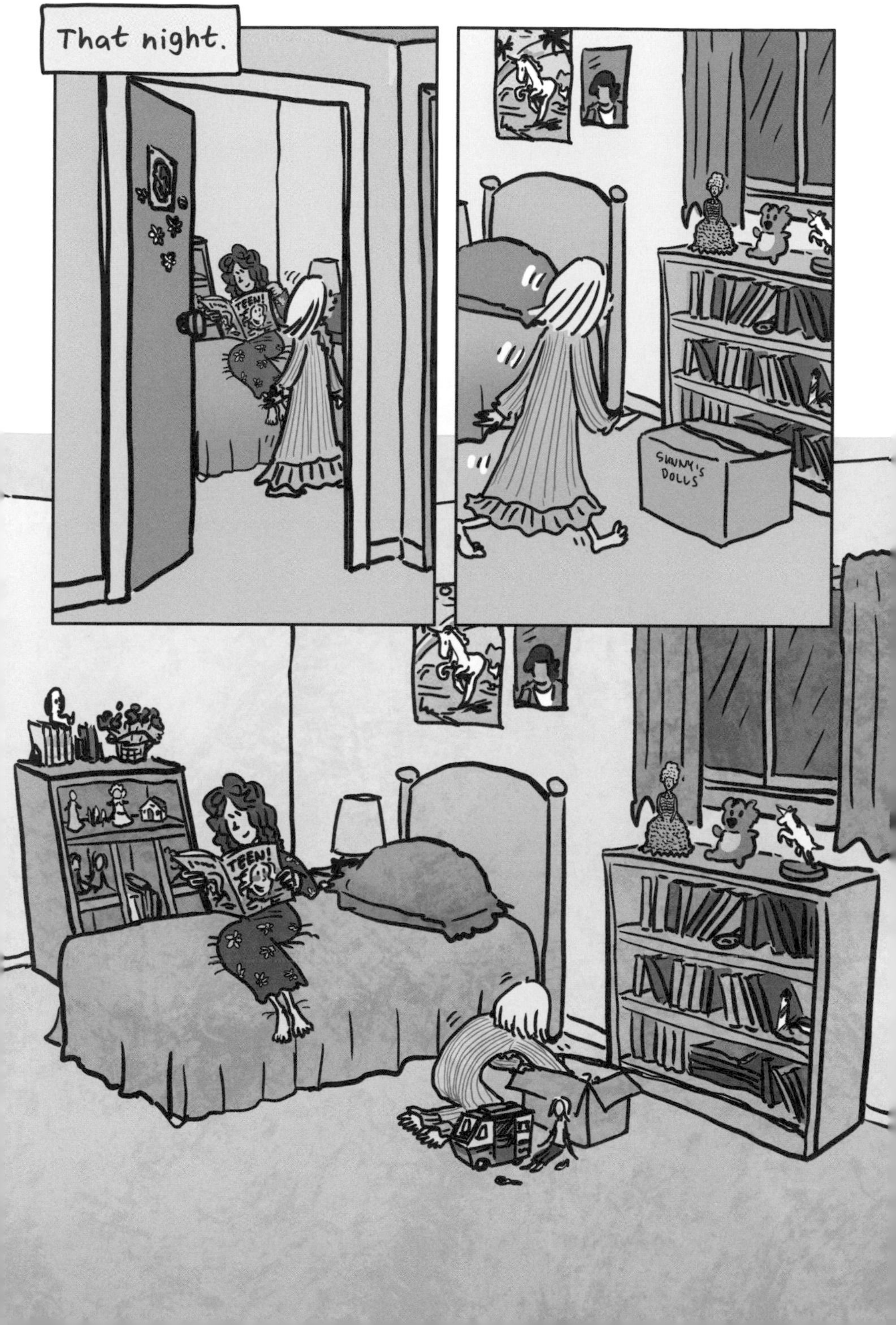
That night.
TEEN!
SUNNY'S DOLLS
TEEN!

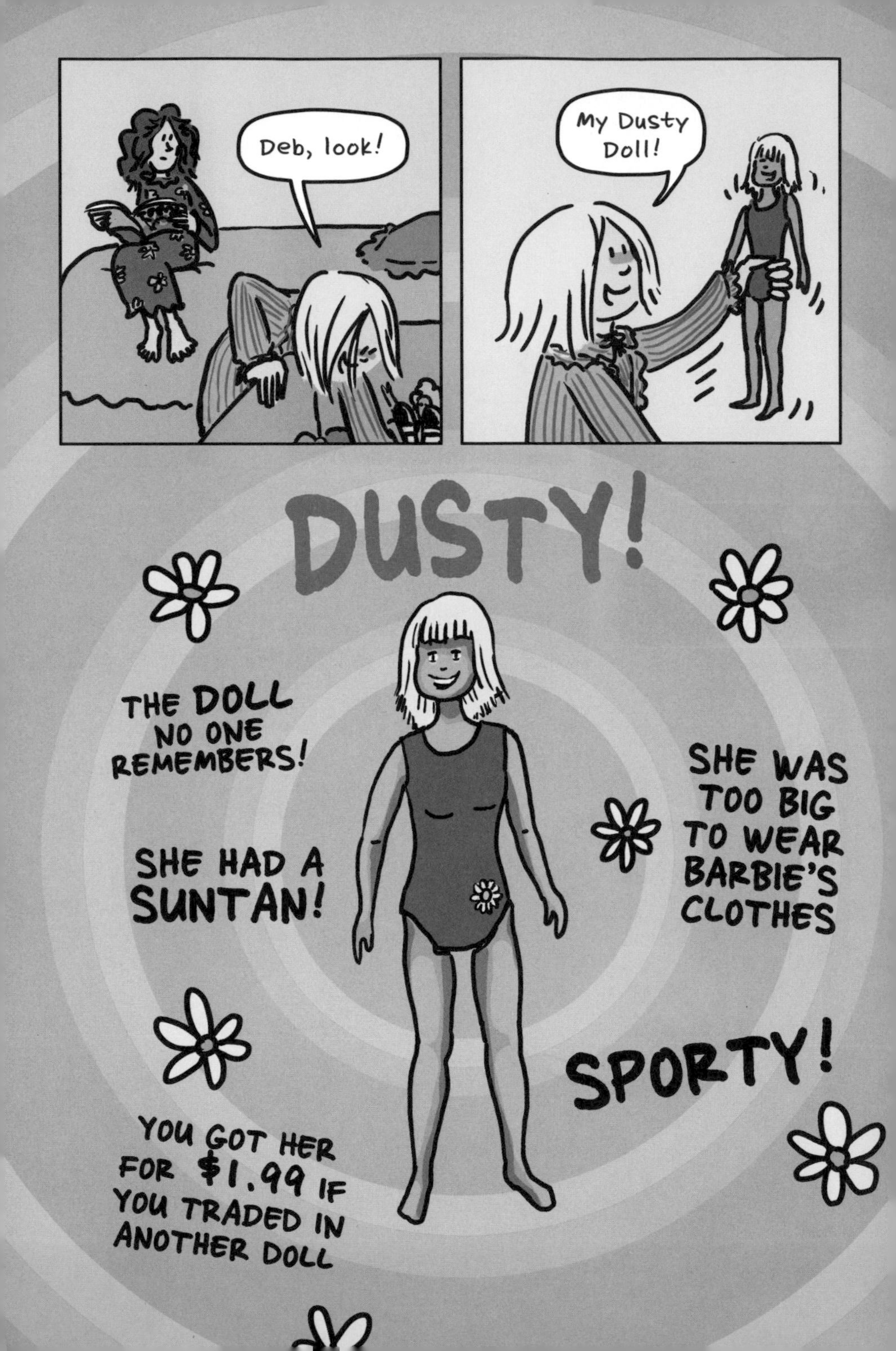
Deb, look!
My Dusty Doll!
DUSTY!
THE DOLL NO ONE REMEMBERS!
SHE WAS TOO BIG TO WEAR BARBIE'S CLOTHES
SHE HAD A SUNTAN!
SPORTY!
YOU GOT HER FOR $1.99 IF YOU TRADED IN ANOTHER DOLL

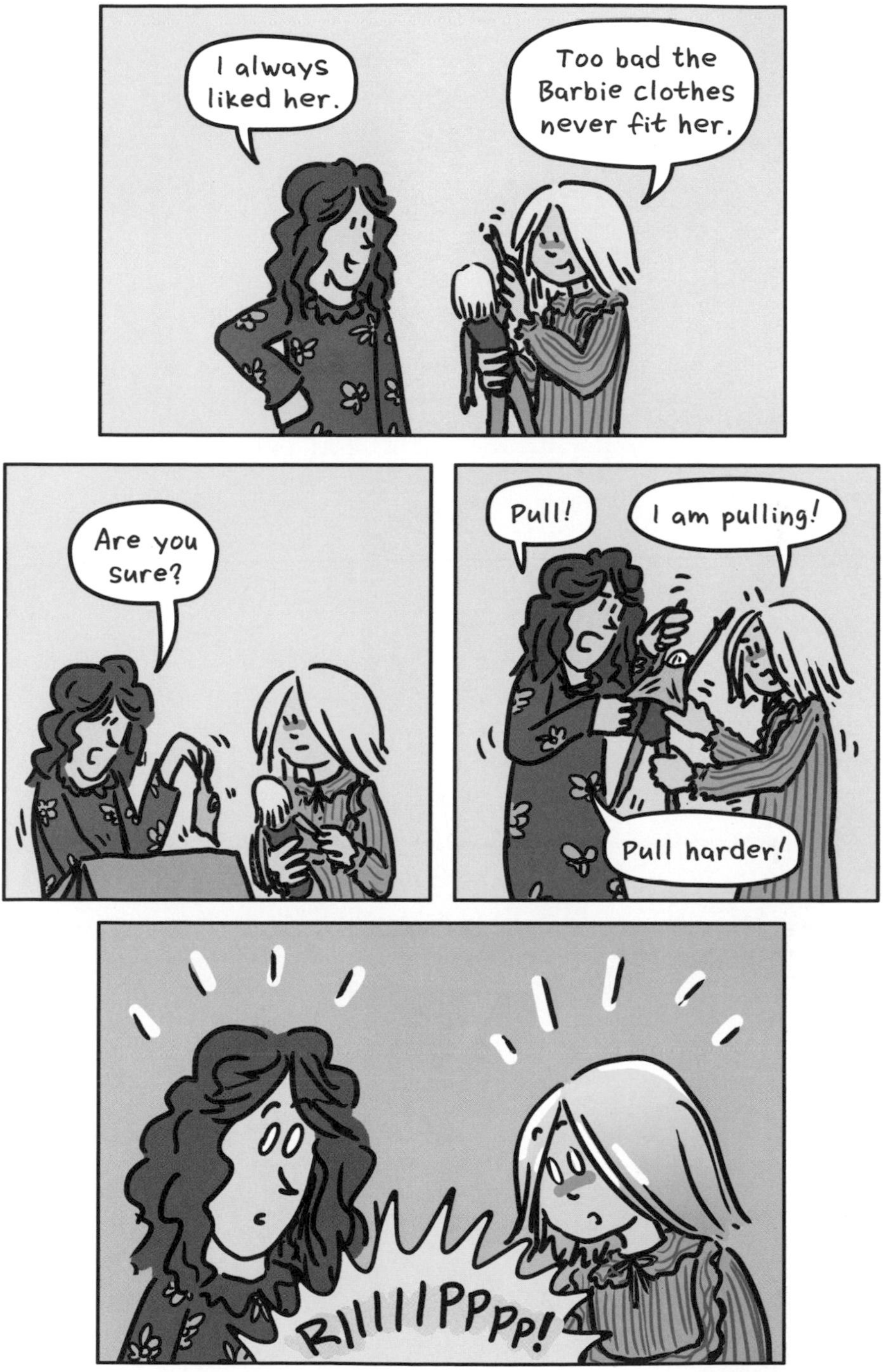
I always liked her.
Too bad the Barbie clothes never fit her.
Are you sure?
Pull!
I am pulling!
Pull harder!
RIIIIIPPPP!

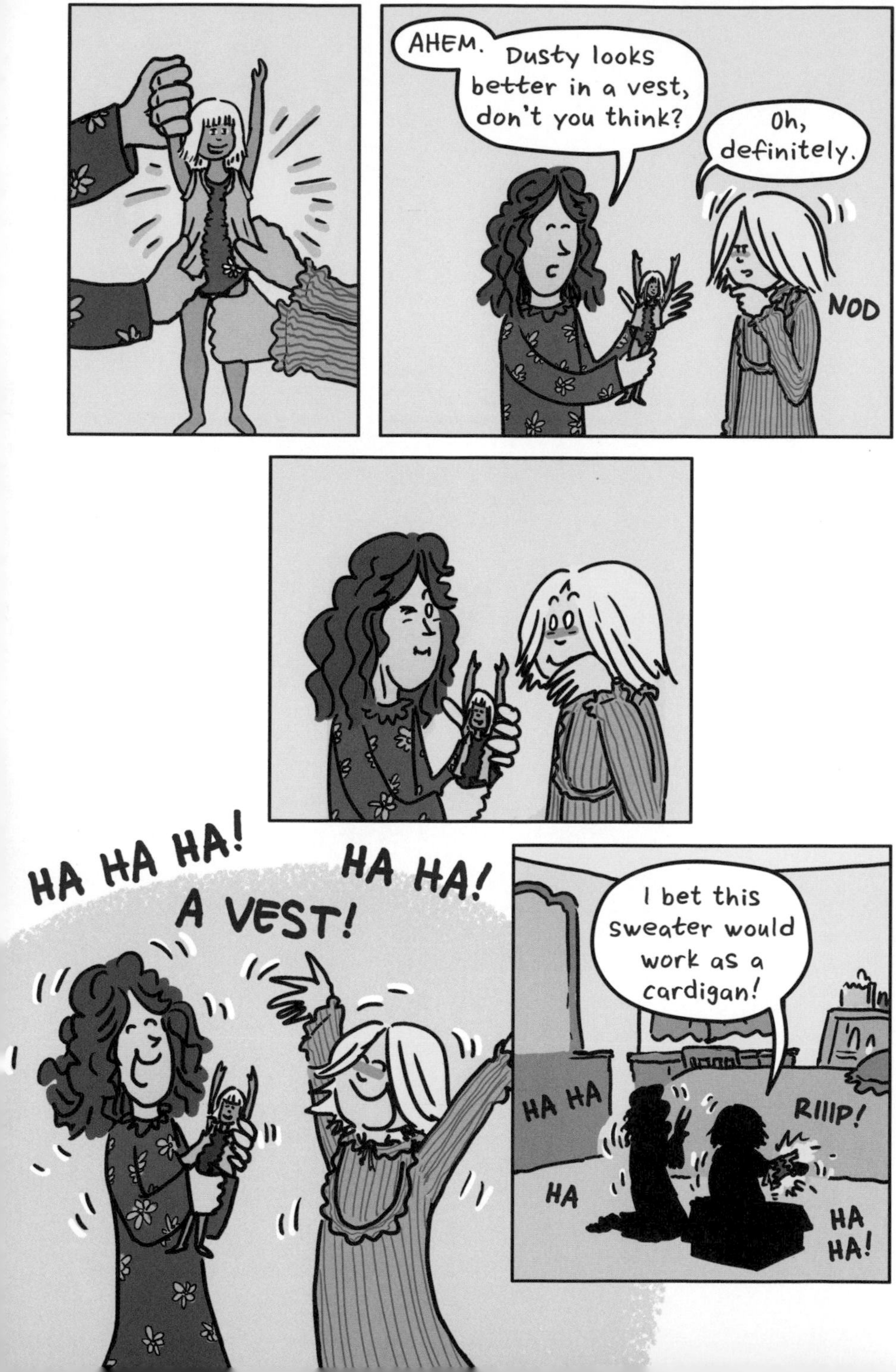
AHEM.
Dusty looks better in a vest, don't you think?
Oh, definitely.
NOD
HA HA HA!
A VEST!
HA HA!
I bet this sweater would work as a cardigan!
HA HA
RIIIP!
HA
HA HA!

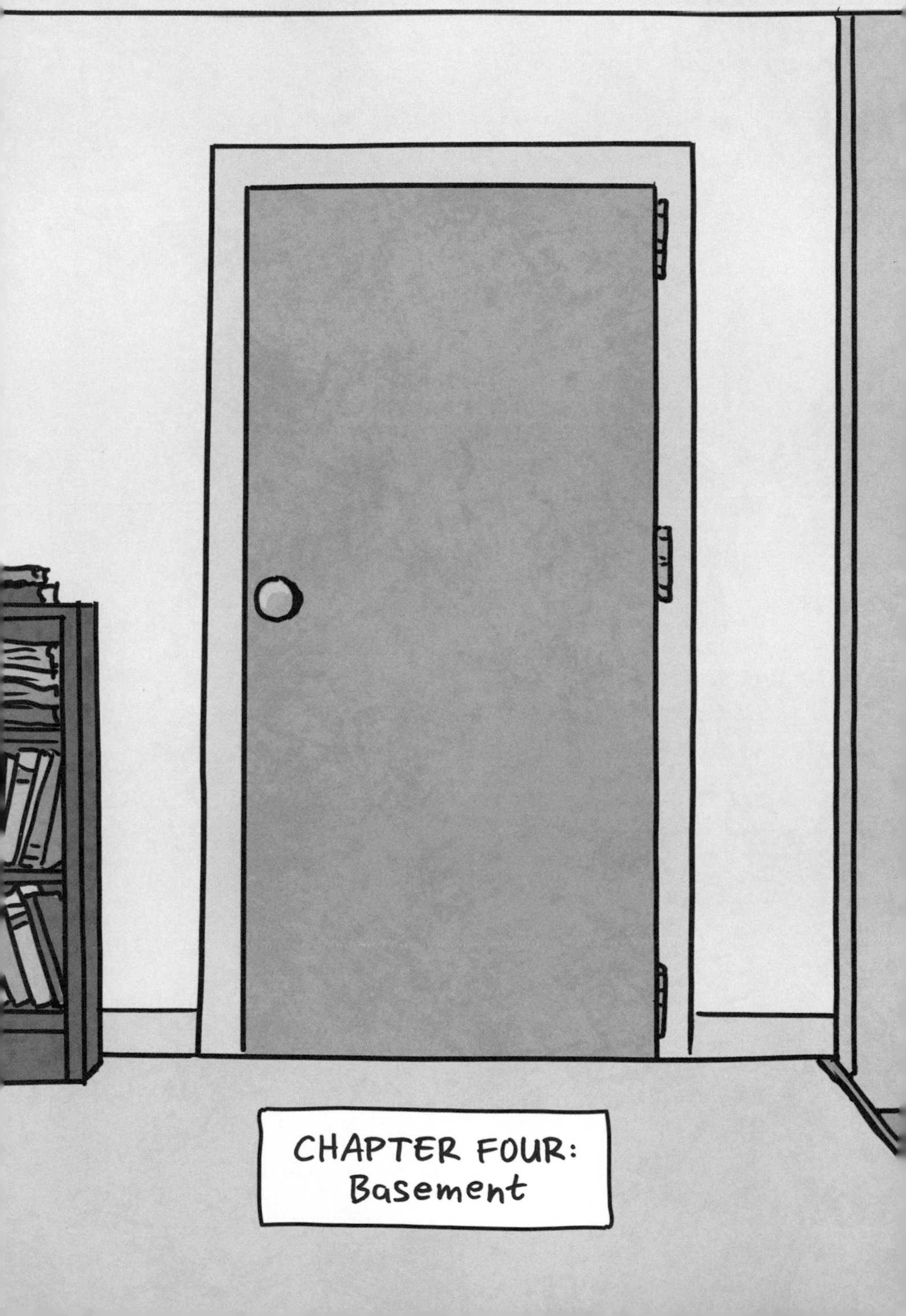
CHAPTER FOUR:
Basement

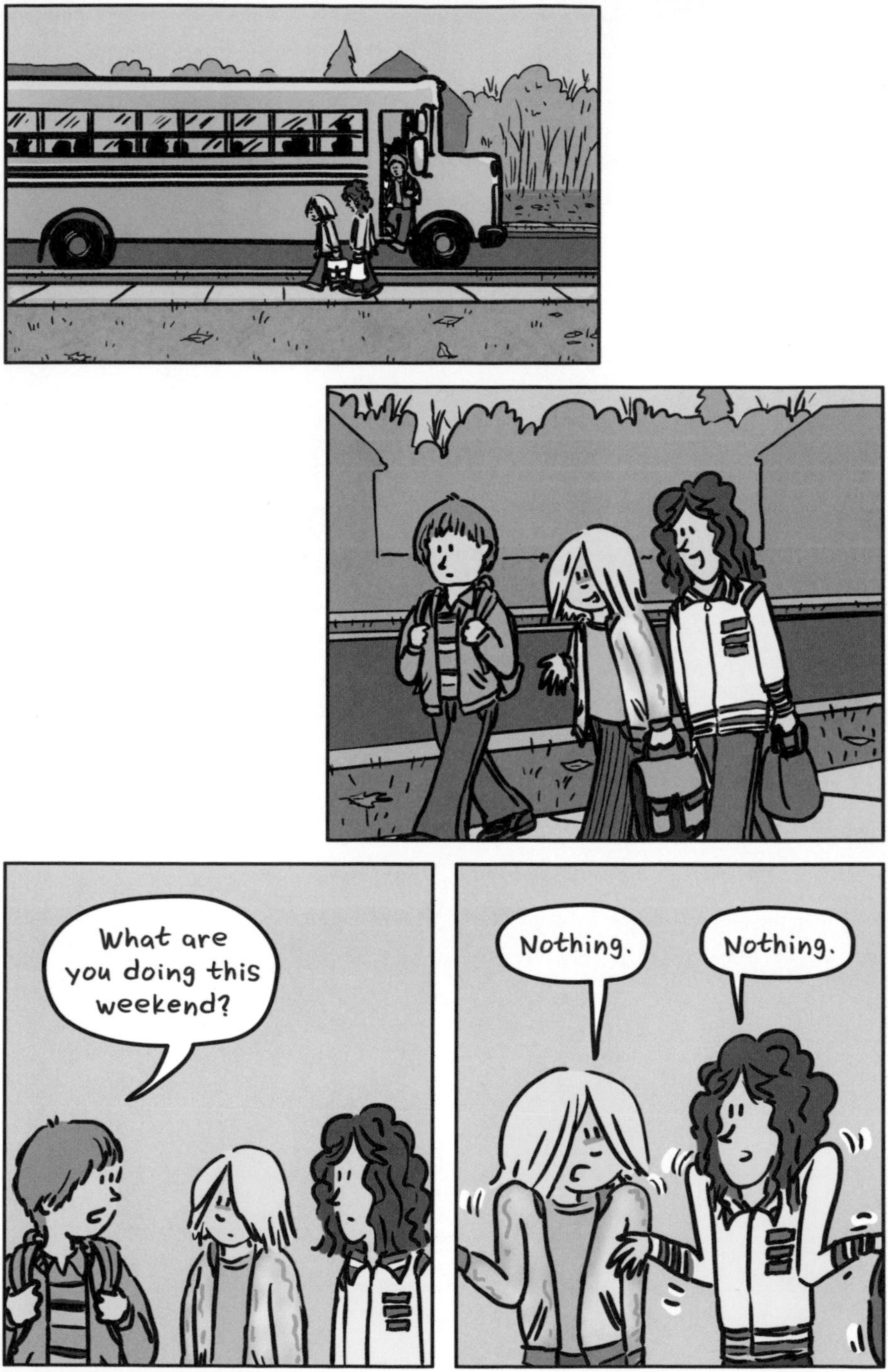
What are you doing this weekend?
Nothing.
Nothing.

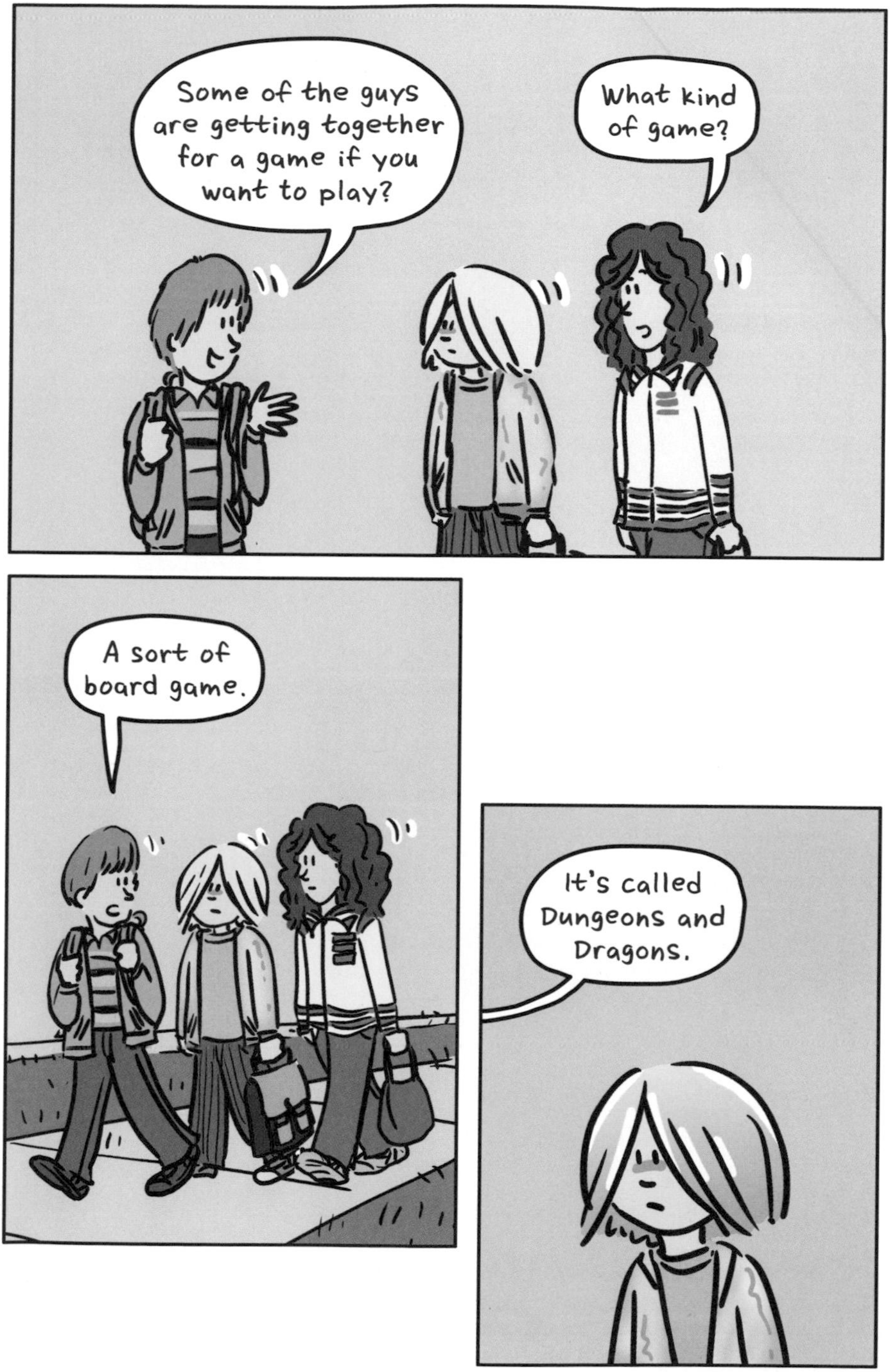
Some of the guys are getting together for a game if you want to play?
What kind of game?
A sort of board game.
It's called Dungeons and Dragons.

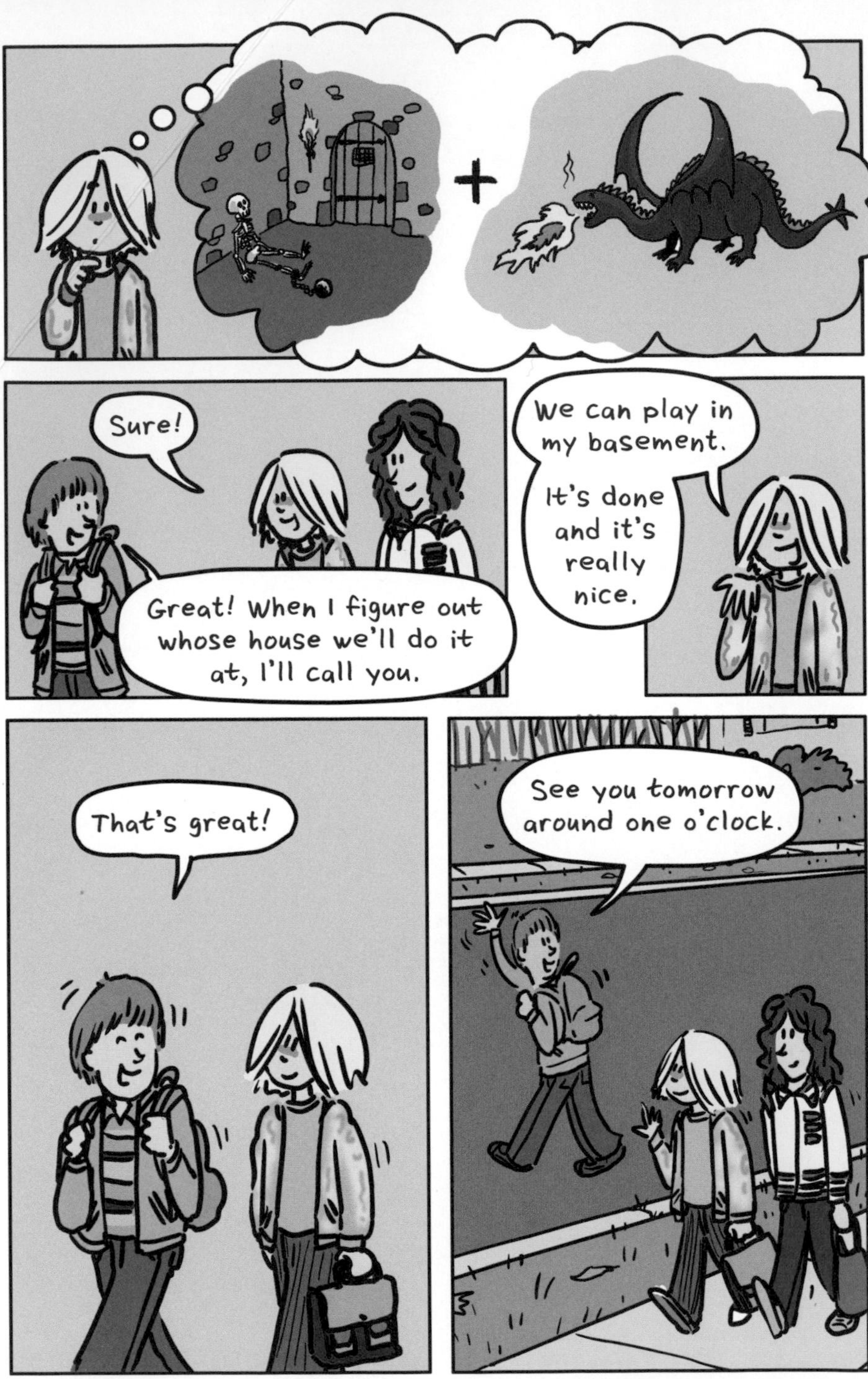
Sure!
Great! When I figure out whose house we'll do it at, I'll call you.
We can play in my basement.
It's done and it's really nice.
That's great!
See you tomorrow around one o'clock.

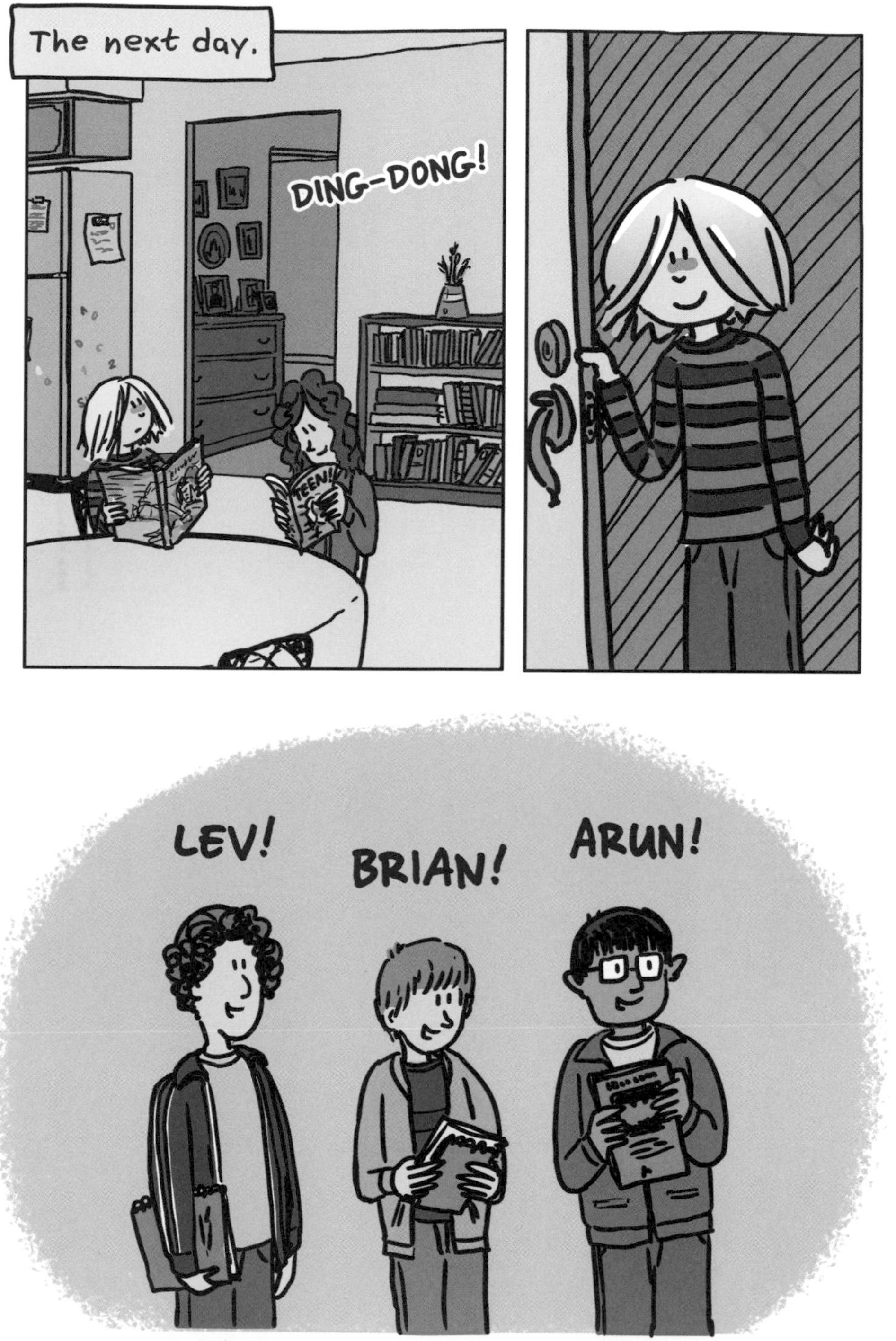
The next day.
DING-DONG!
TEEN!
LEV!
BRIAN!
ARUN!

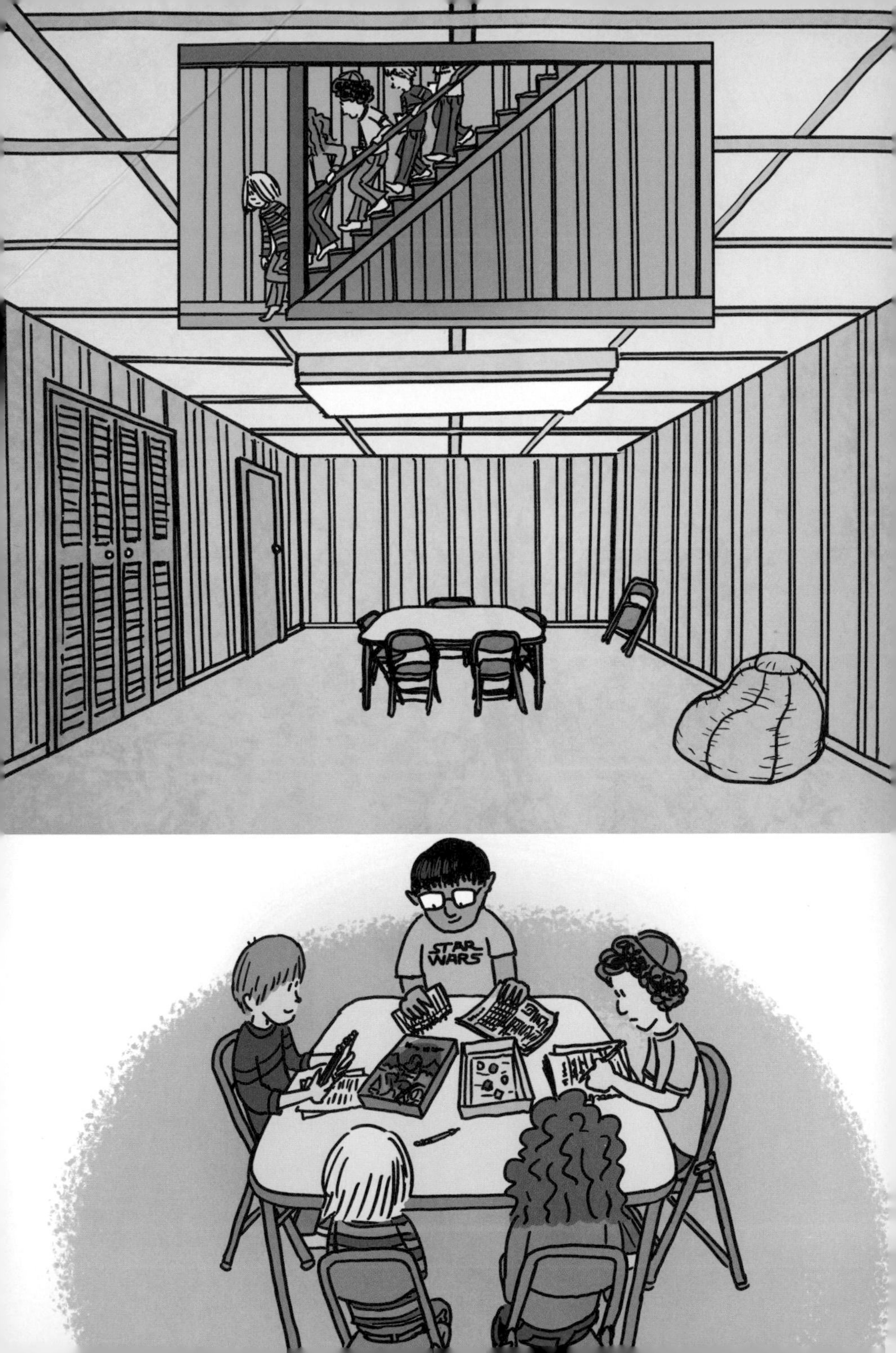
STAR WARS

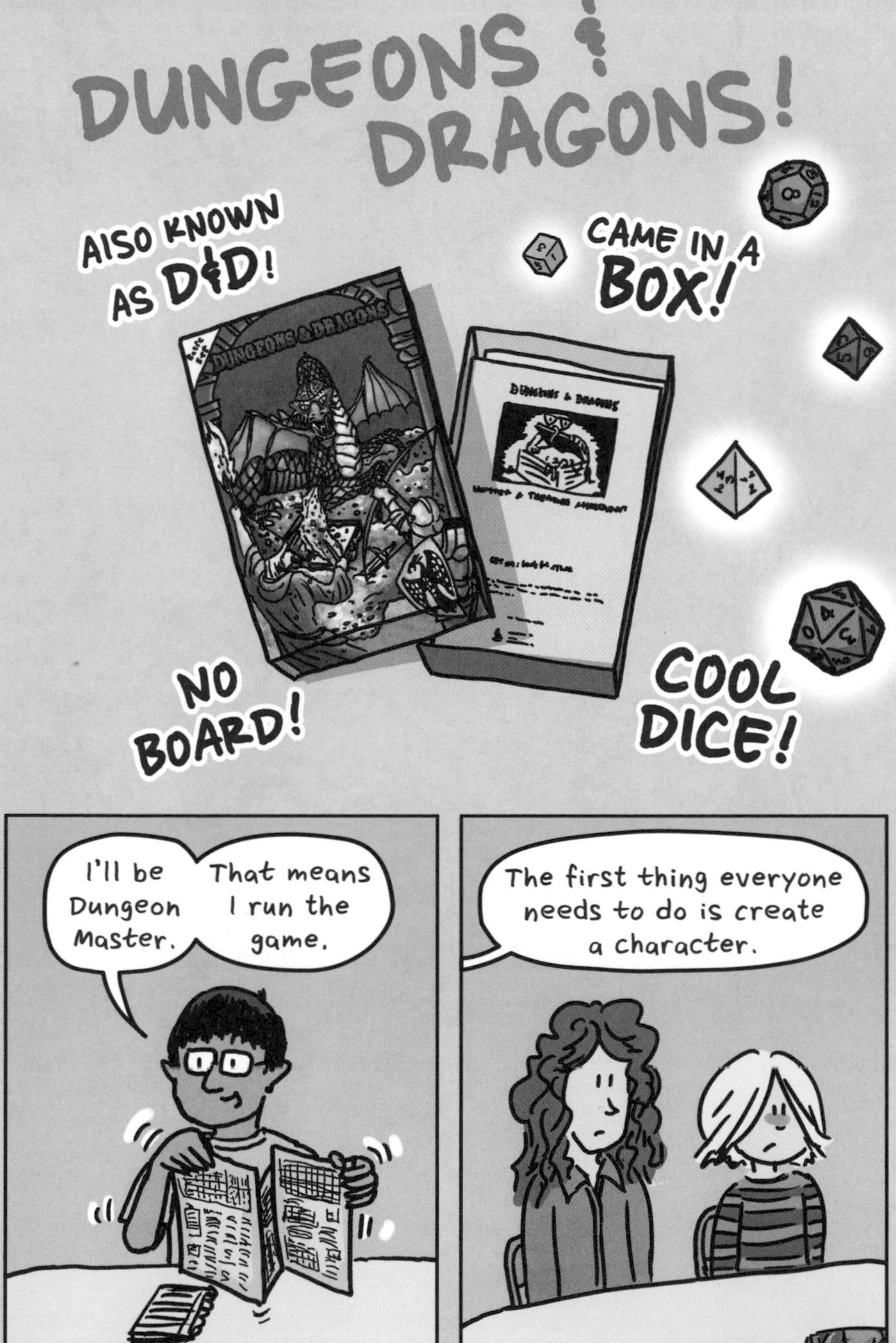
DUNGEONS & DRAGONS!
AlSO KNOWN AS D&D!
CAME IN A BOX!
DUNGEONS & DRAGONS
NO BOARD!
COOL DICE!
I'll be Dungeon Master.
That means I run the game.
The first thing everyone needs to do is create a character.

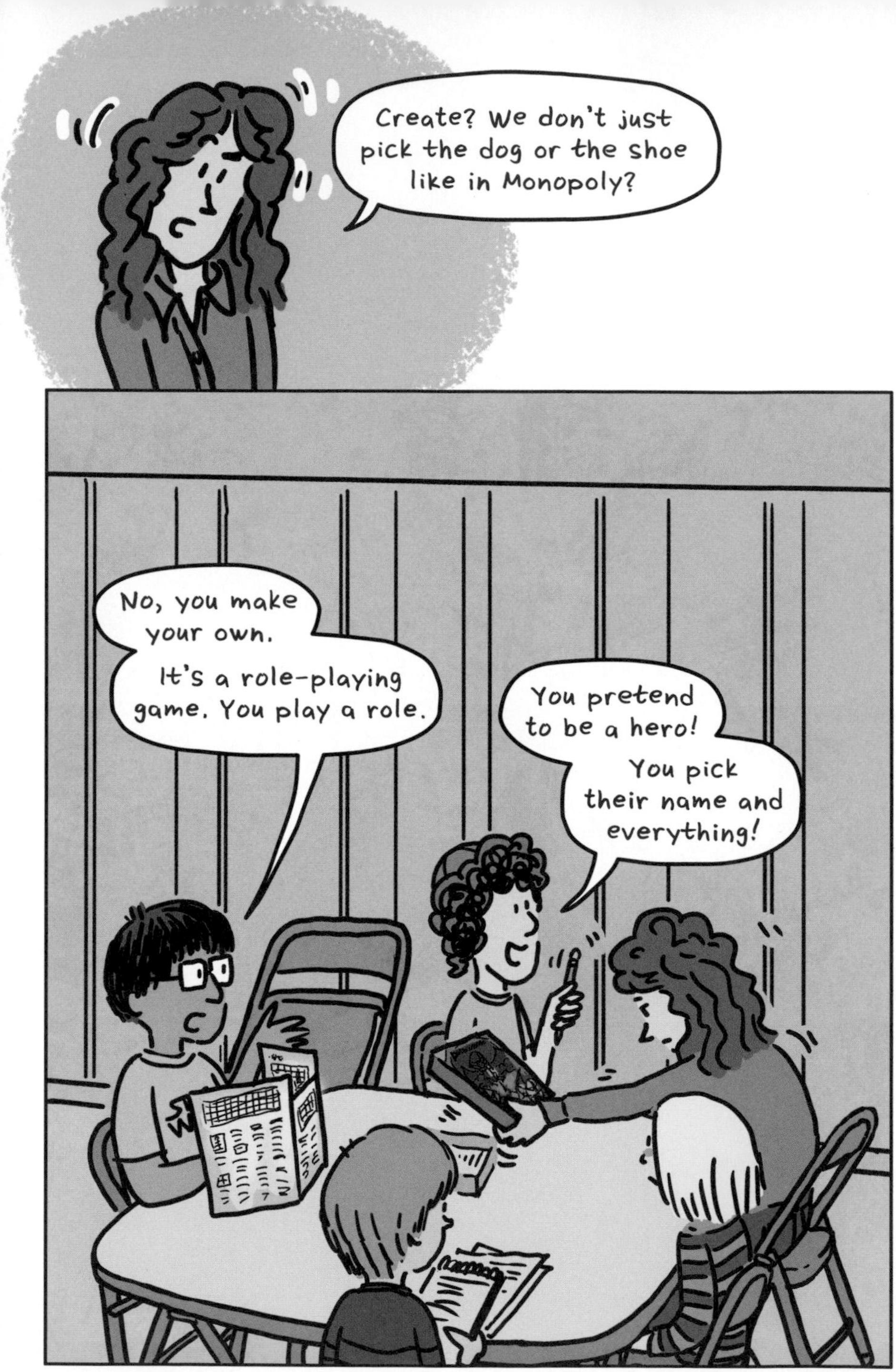
Create? We don't just pick the dog or the shoe like in Monopoly?
No, you make your own.
It's a role-playing game. You play a role.
You pretend to be a hero!
You pick their name and everything!

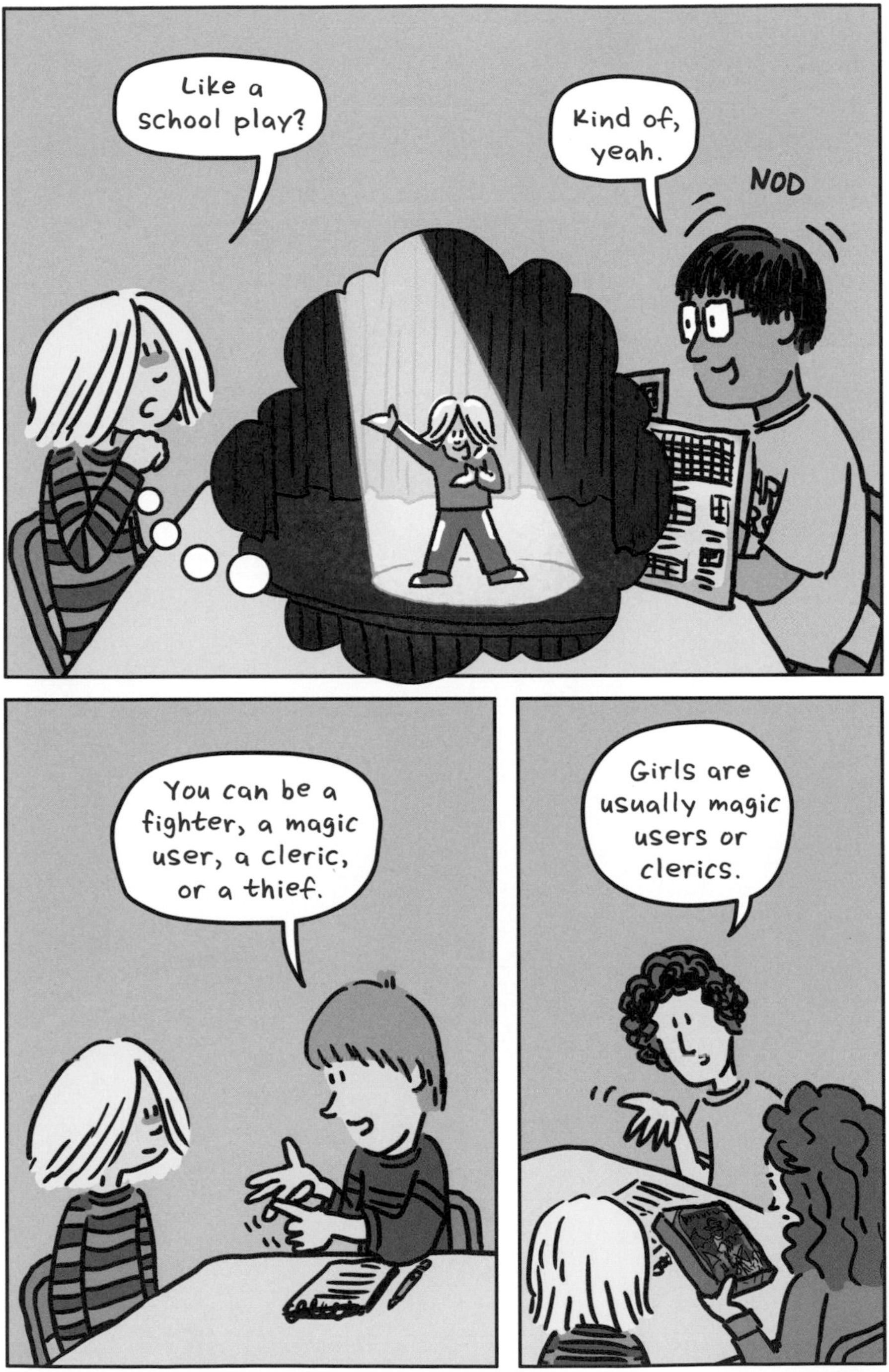
Like a school play?
Kind of, yeah.
NOD
You can be a fighter, a magic user, a cleric, or a thief.
Girls are usually magic users or clerics.

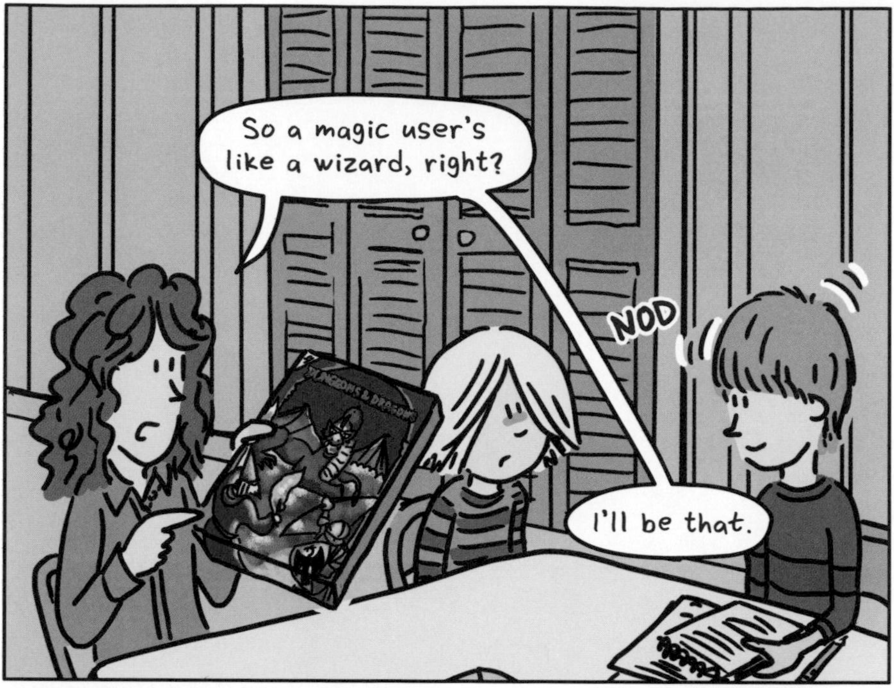
So a magic user's like a wizard, right?
DUNGEONS & DRAGONS
NOD
I'll be that.

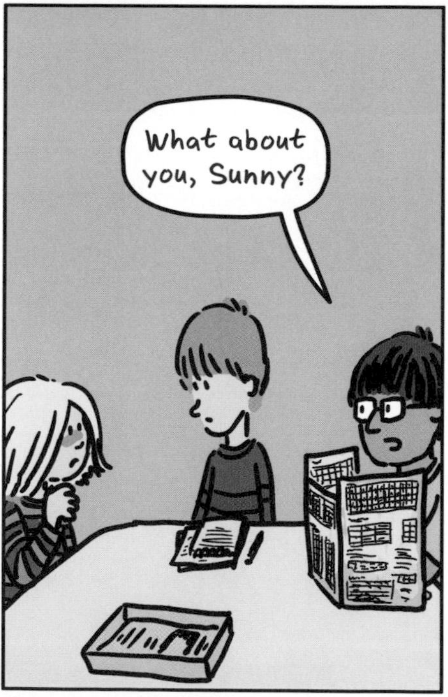
What about you, Sunny?

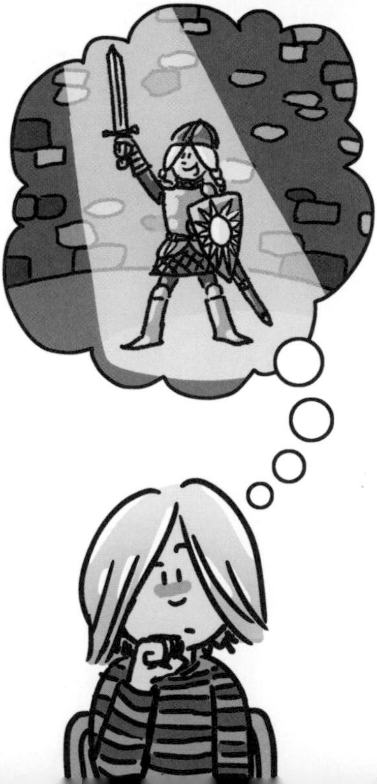

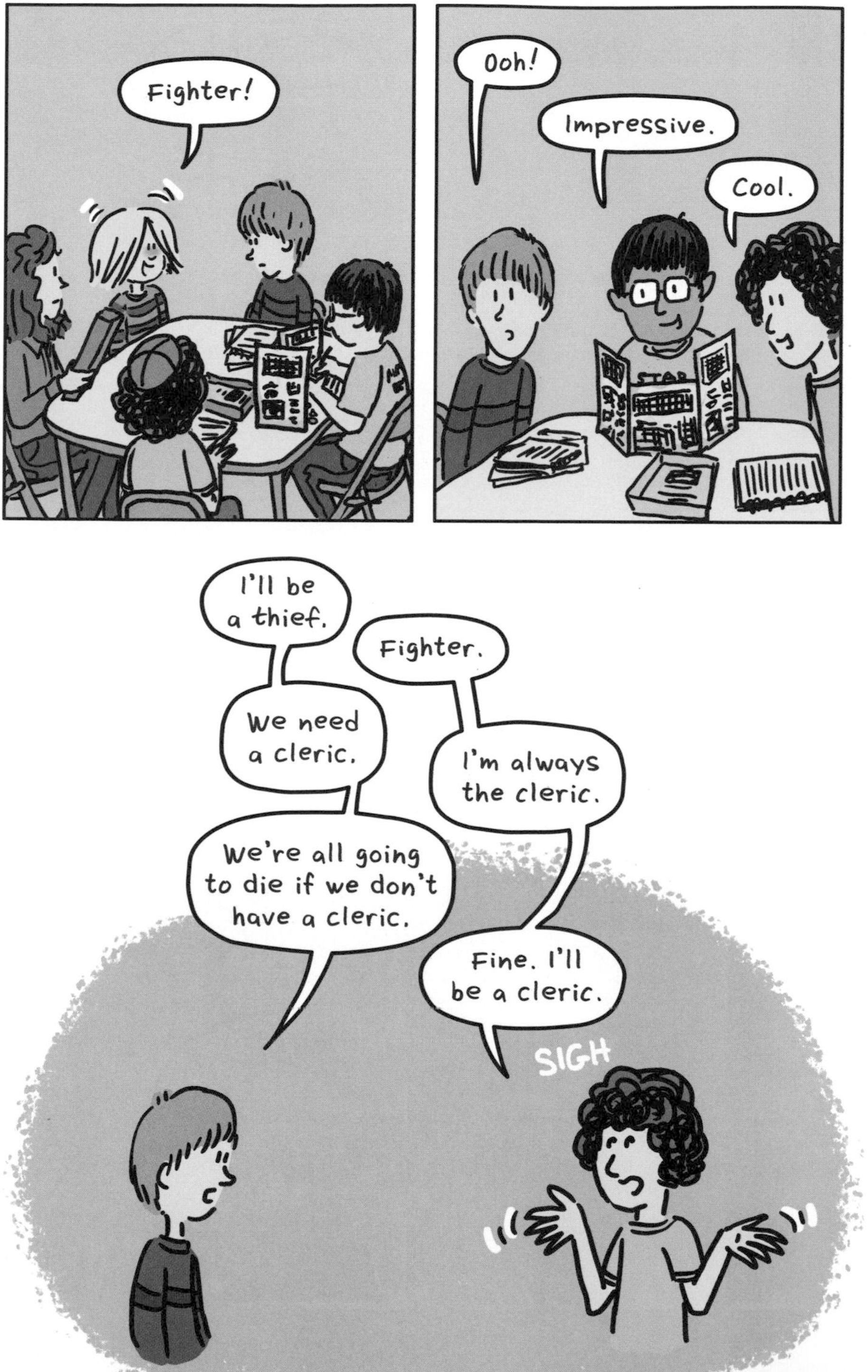
Fighter!
Ooh!
Impressive.
Cool.
I'll be a thief.
Fighter.
We need a cleric.
I'm always the cleric.
We're all going to die if we don't have a cleric.
Fine. I'll be a cleric.
SIGH

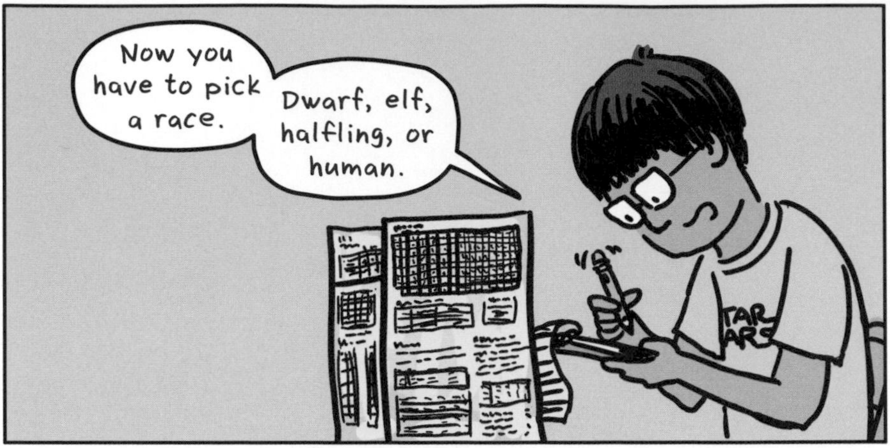
Now you have to pick a race.
Dwarf, elf, halfling, or human.
STAR WARS

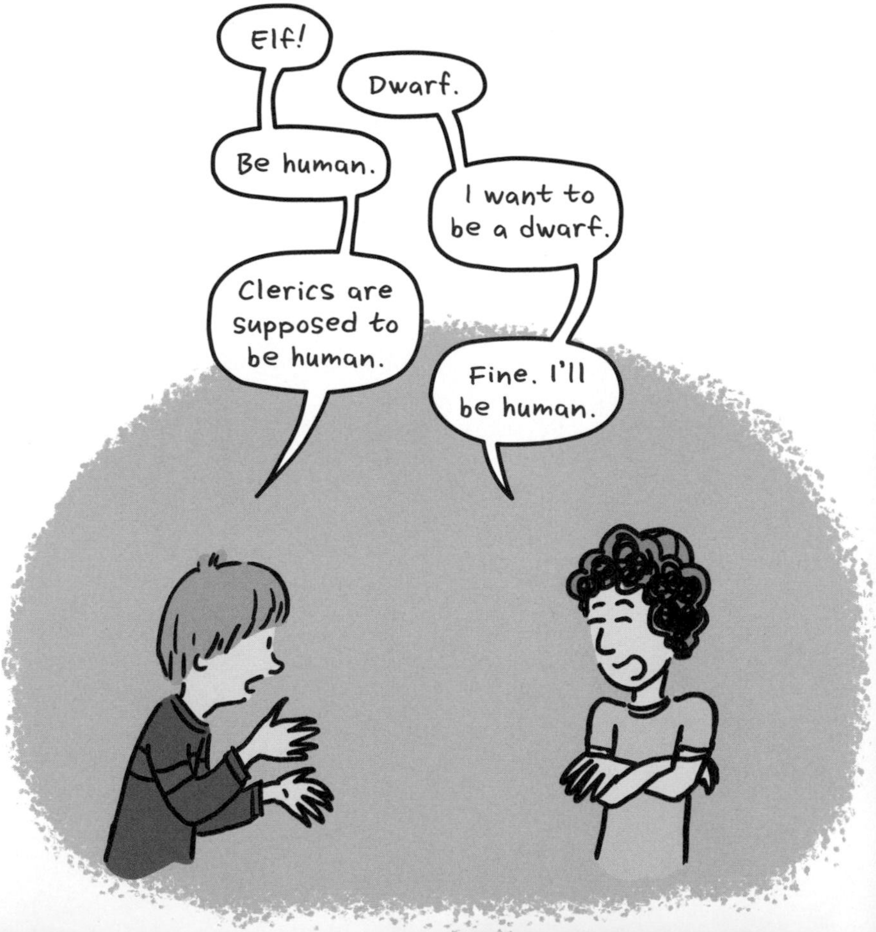
Elf!
Dwarf.
Be human.
I want to be a dwarf.
Clerics are supposed to be human.
Fine. I'll be human.

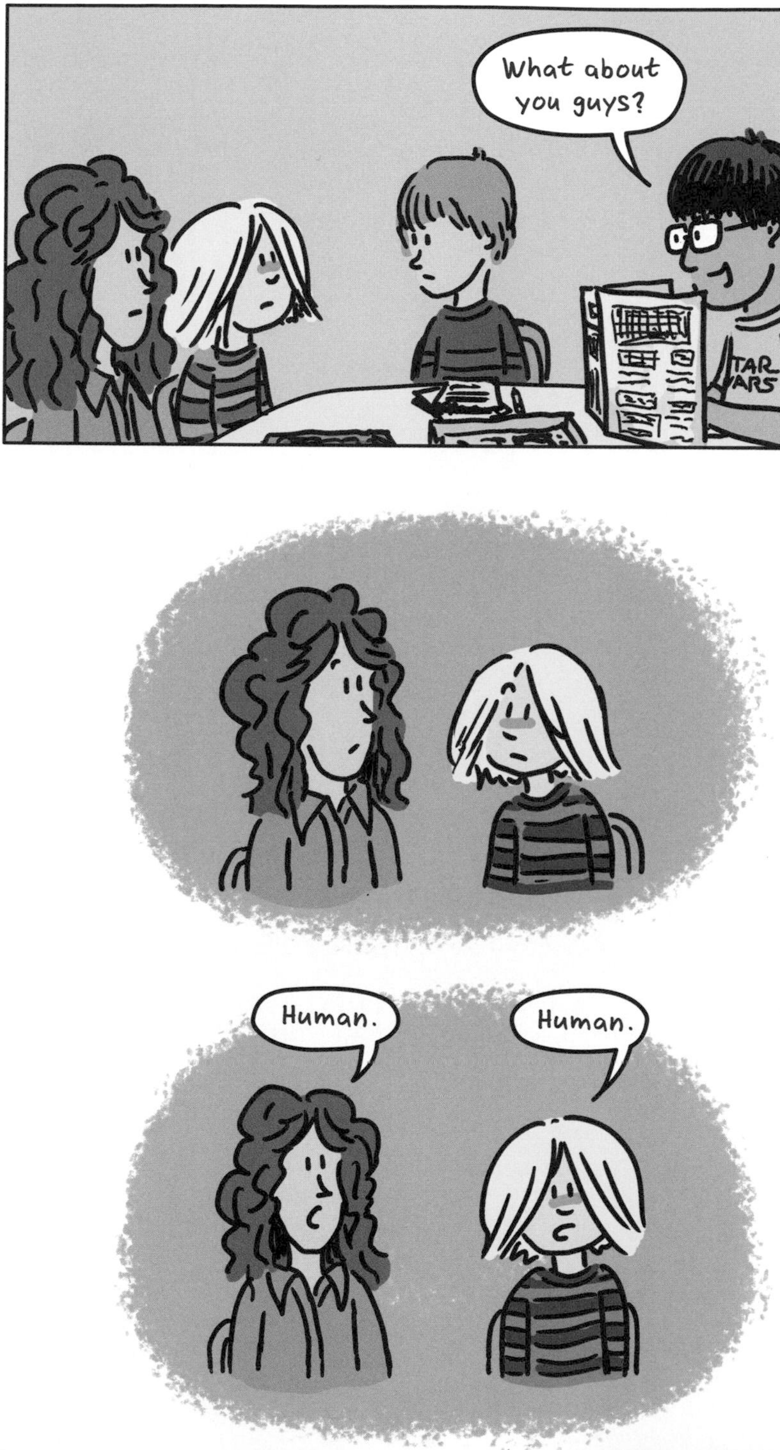
What about you guys?
STAR WARS
Human.
Human.

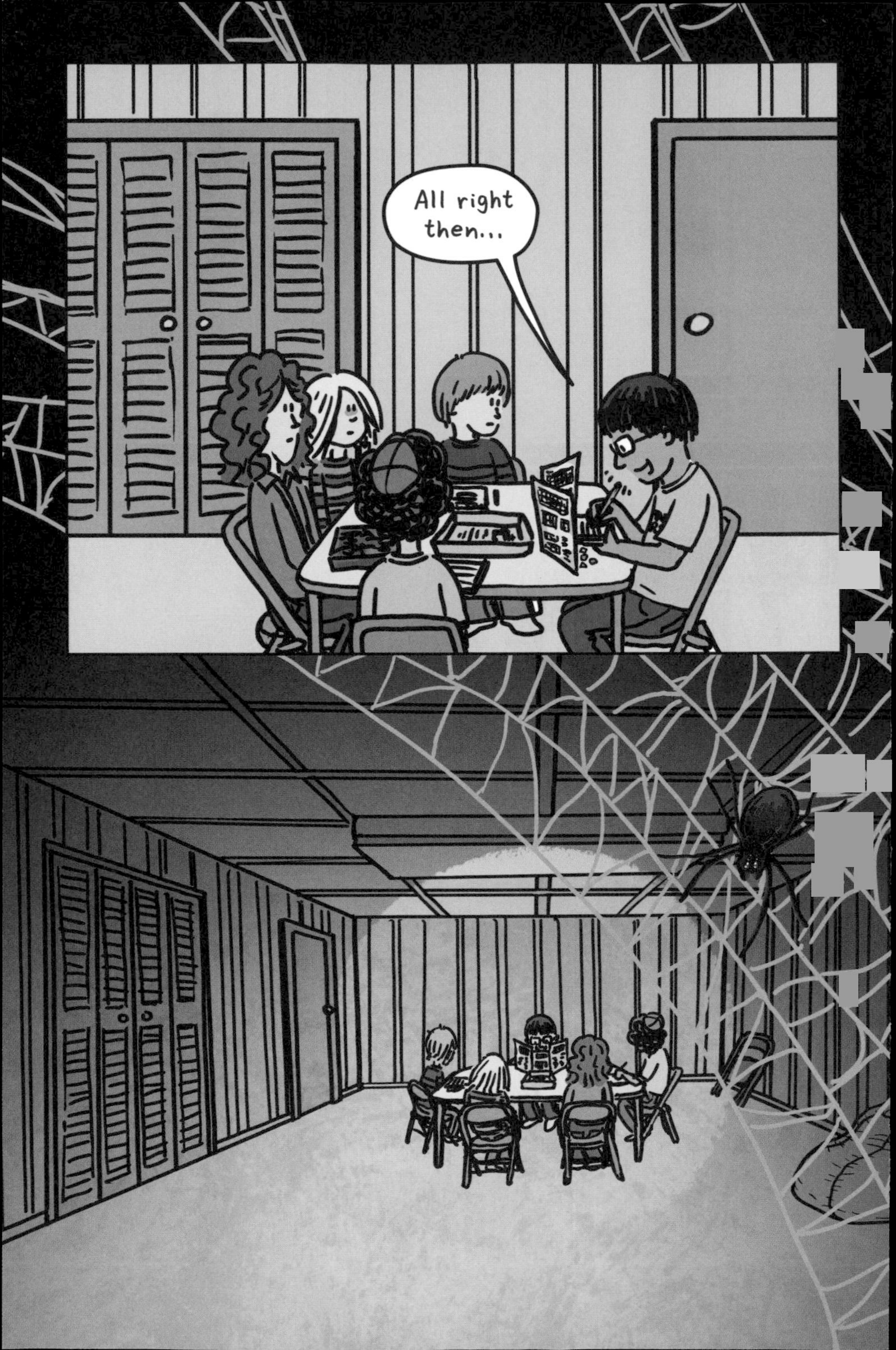
All right then...

CHAPTER FIVE:
Giant Spider

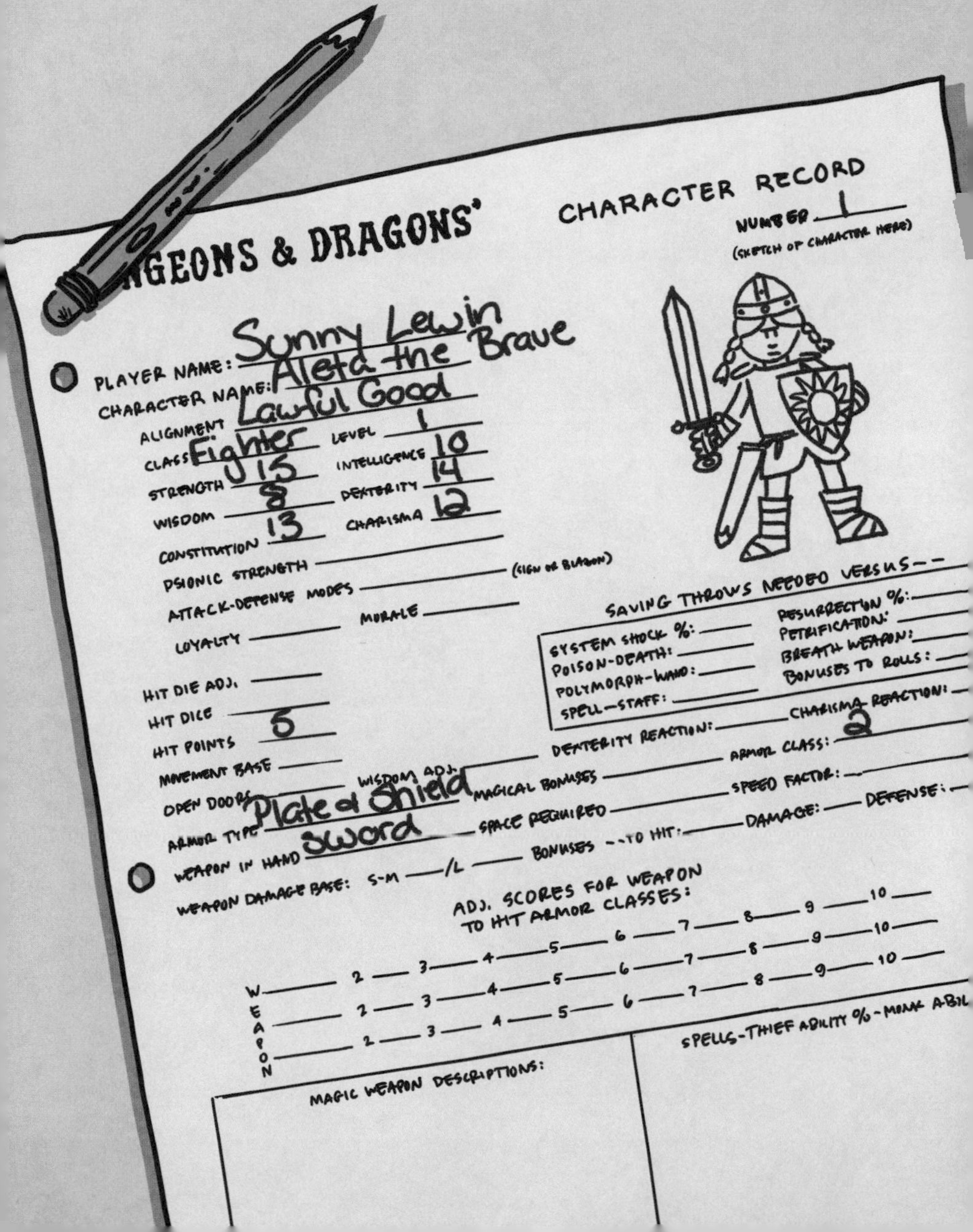
NGEONS & DRAGONS®
CHARACTER RECORD
NUMBER 1
(SKETCH OF CHARACTER HERE)
PLAYER NAME: Sunny Lewin
CHARACTER NAME: Aleta the Brave
ALIGNMENT Lawful Good
CLASS Fighter
LEVEL 1
STRENGTH 15
INTELLIGENCE 10
WISDOM 8
DEXTERITY 14
CHARISMA 12
CONSTITUTION 13
PSIONIC STRENGTH
ATTACK-DEFENSE MODES
(SIGN OR BLAZON)
LOYALTY
MORALE
SAVING THROWS NEEDED VERSUS--
SYSTEM SHOCK %:
POISON-DEATH:
POLYMORPH-WAND:
SPELL-STAFF:
RESURRECTION %:
PETRIFICATION:
BREATH WEAPON:
BONUSES TO ROLLS:
HIT DIE ADJ.
HIT DICE
HIT POINTS 5
CHARISMA REACTION: 2
DEXTERITY REACTION:
MOVEMENT BASE
ARMOR CLASS:
WISDOM ADJ.
OPEN DOORS
MAGICAL BONUSES
SPEED FACTOR:
ARMOR TYPE Plate & Shield
SPACE REQUIRED
DAMAGE:
DEFENSE:
WEAPON IN HAND Sword
BONUSES --TO HIT:
WEAPON DAMAGE BASE: S-M /L
ADJ. SCORES FOR WEAPON TO HIT ARMOR CLASSES:
WEAPON
SPELLS-THIEF ABILITY %-MONK ABIL
MAGIC WEAPON DESCRIPTIONS:

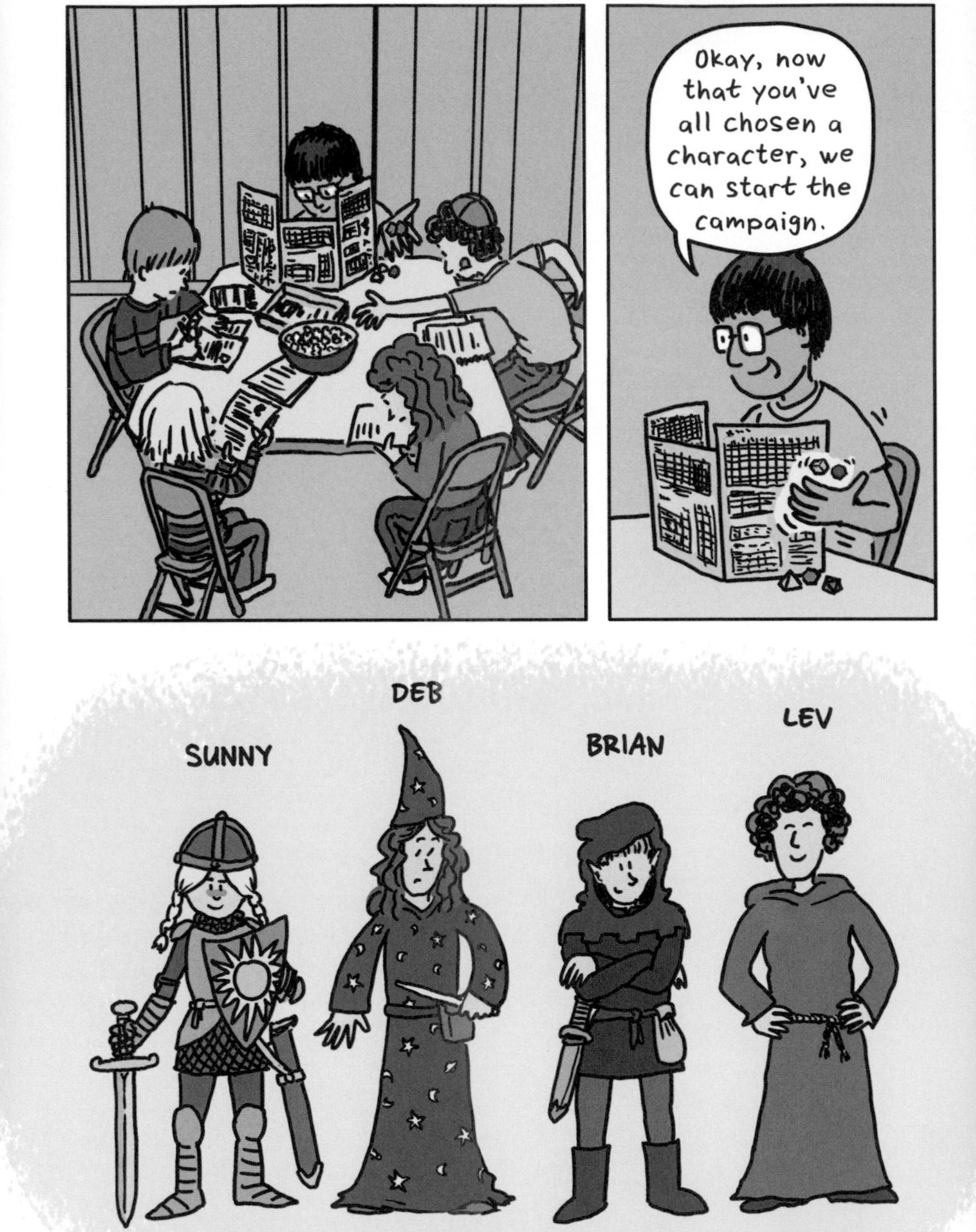
Okay, now that you've all chosen a character, we can start the campaign.
DEB
SUNNY
BRIAN
LEV
FIGHTER!
MAGIC USER!
THIEF!
CLERIC!

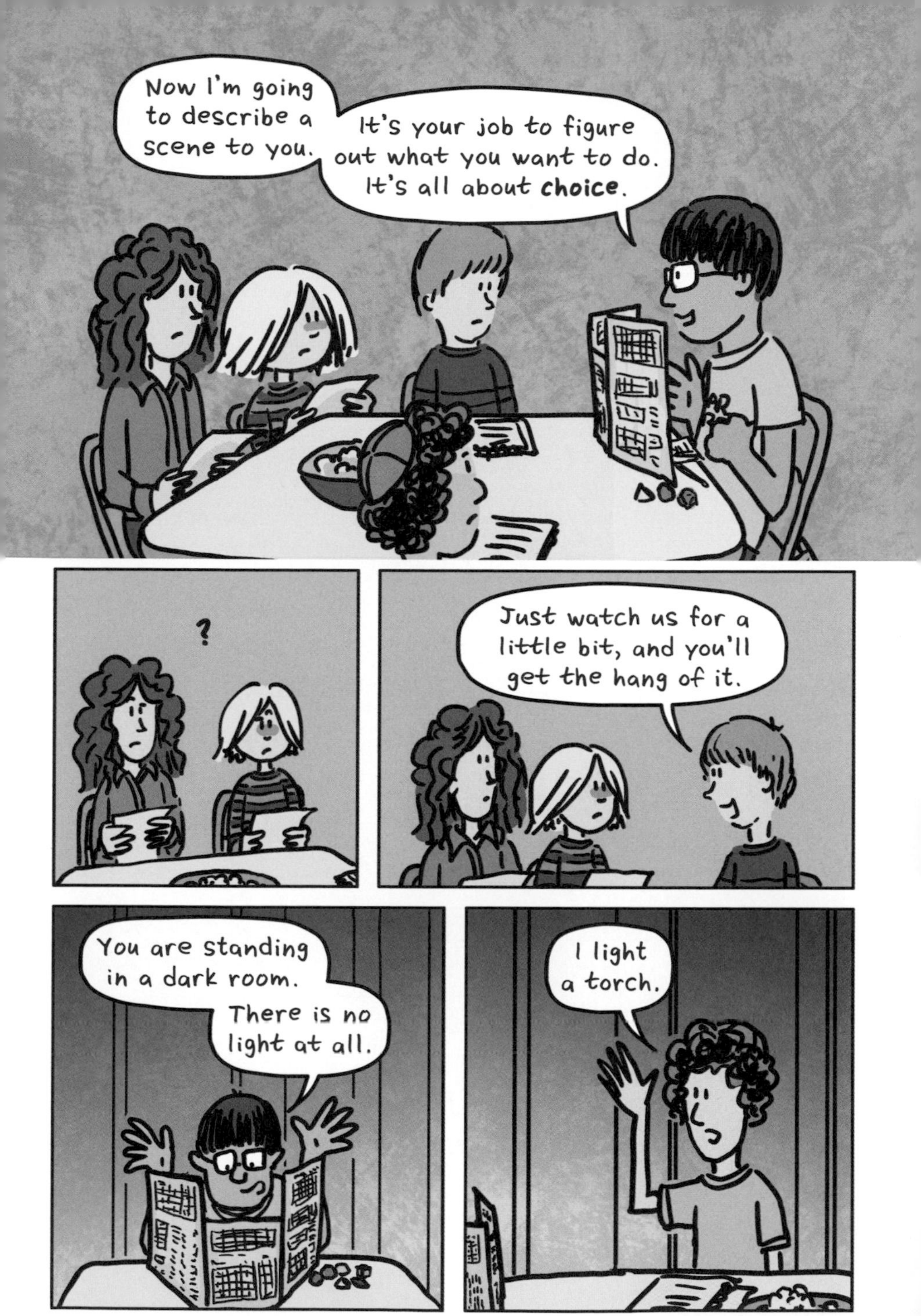
Now I'm going to describe a scene to you.
It's your job to figure out what you want to do. It's all about **choice**.
?
Just watch us for a little bit, and you'll get the hang of it.
You are standing in a dark room.
There is no light at all.
I light a torch.

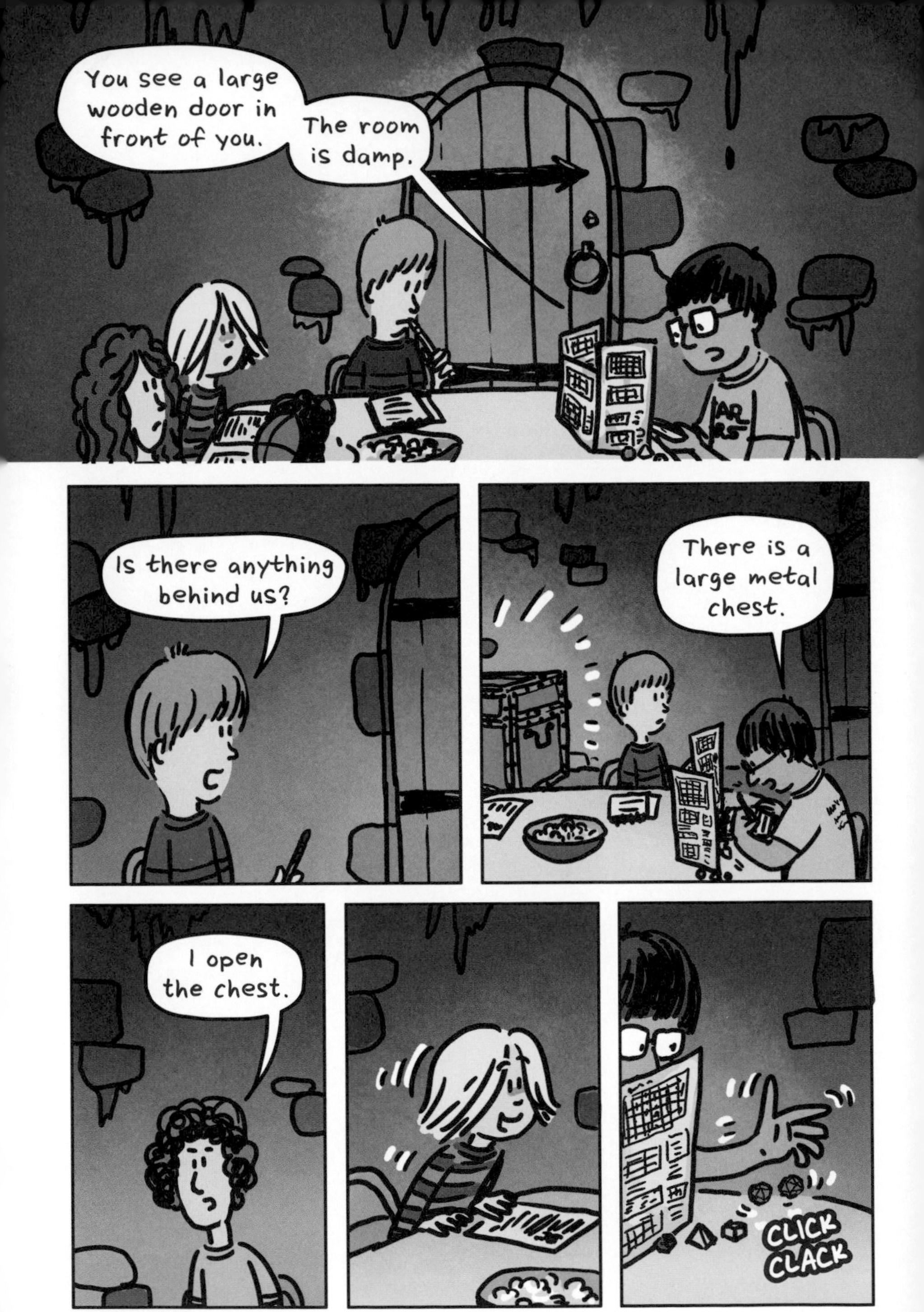

You see a large wooden door in front of you.
The room is damp.
Is there anything behind us?
There is a large metal chest.
I open the chest.
CLICK CLACK

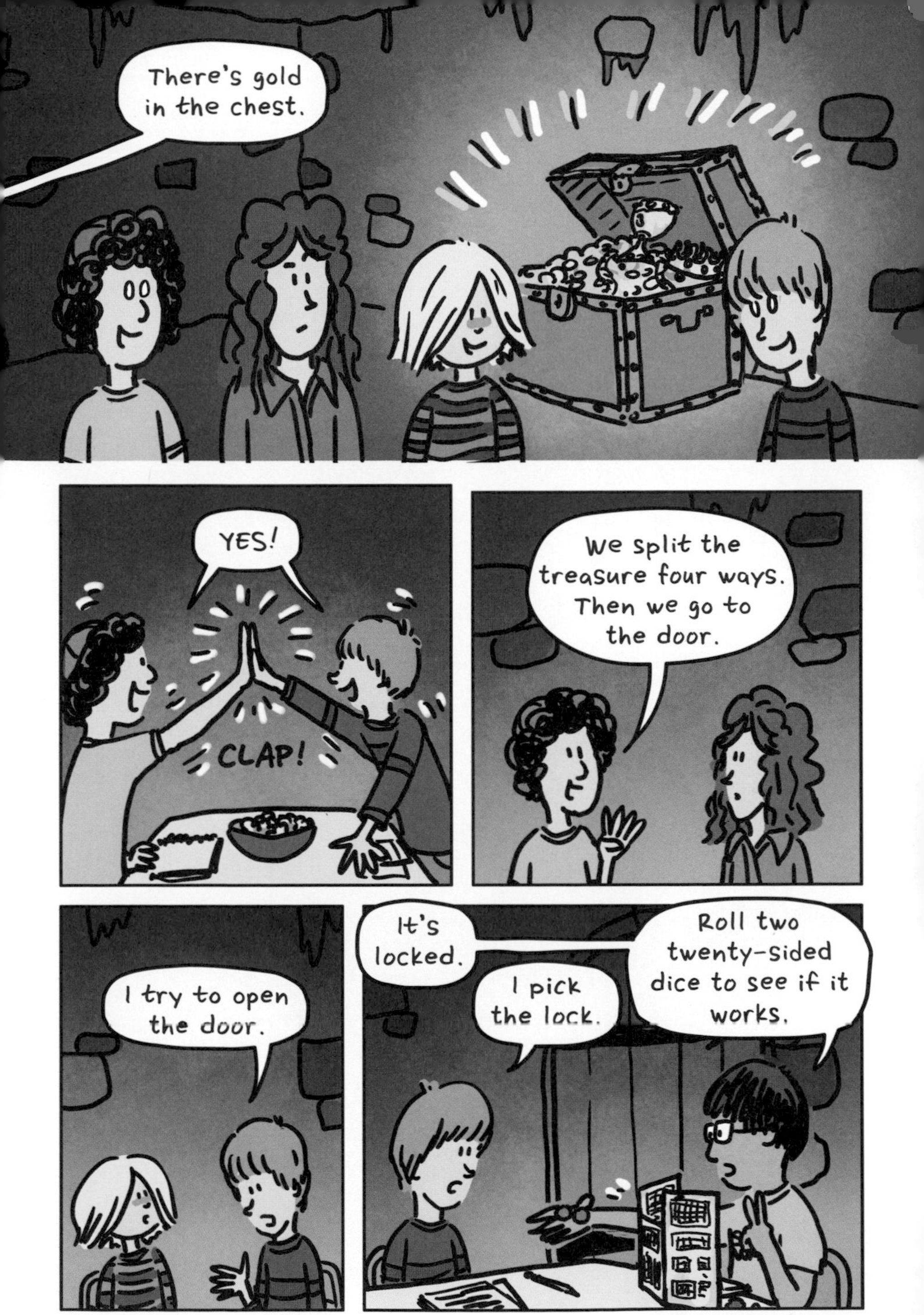
There's gold in the chest.
YES!
CLAP!
We split the treasure four ways. Then we go to the door.
I try to open the door.
It's locked.
I pick the lock.
Roll two twenty-sided dice to see if it works.

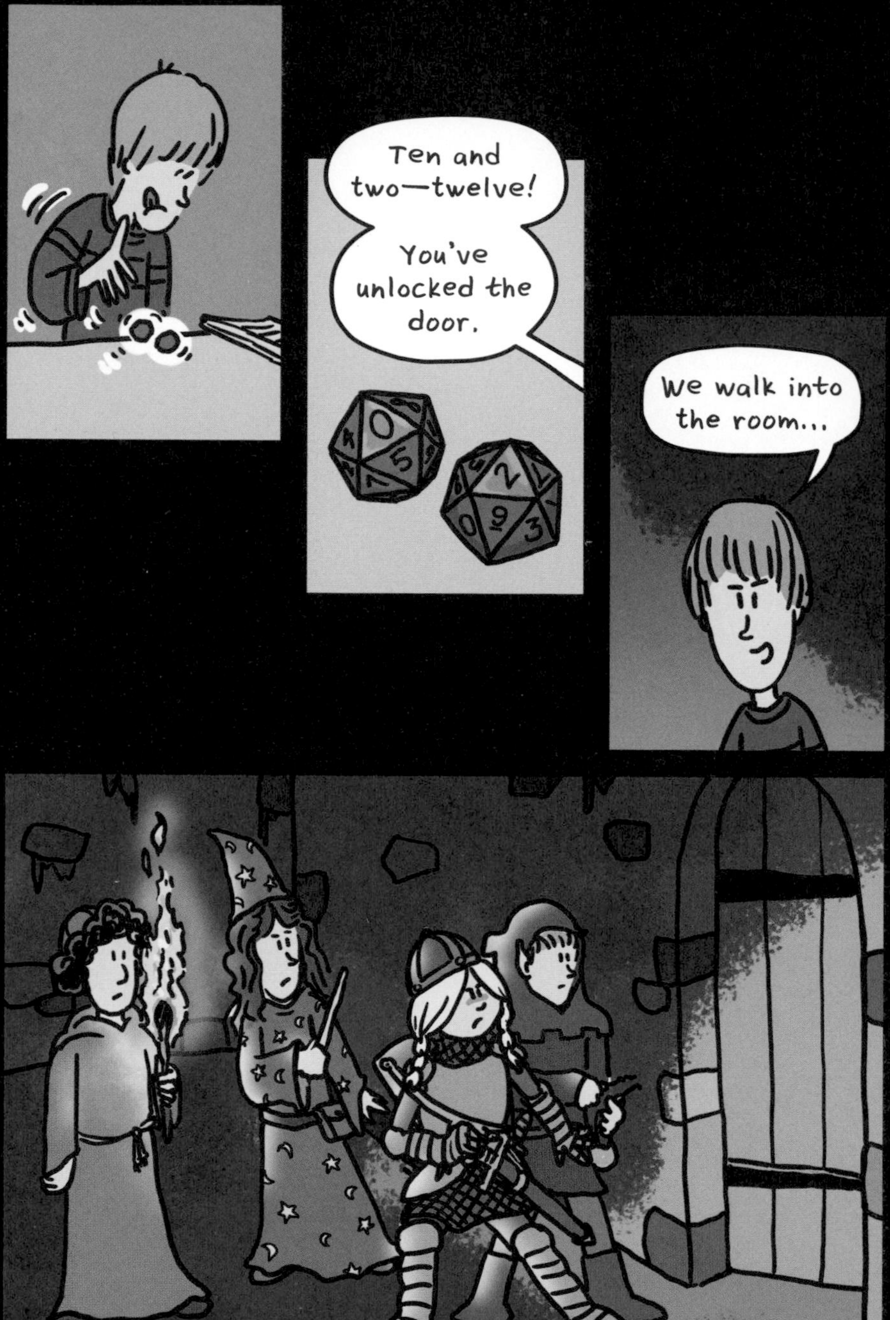

Ten and two—twelve!
You've unlocked the door.
We walk into the room...

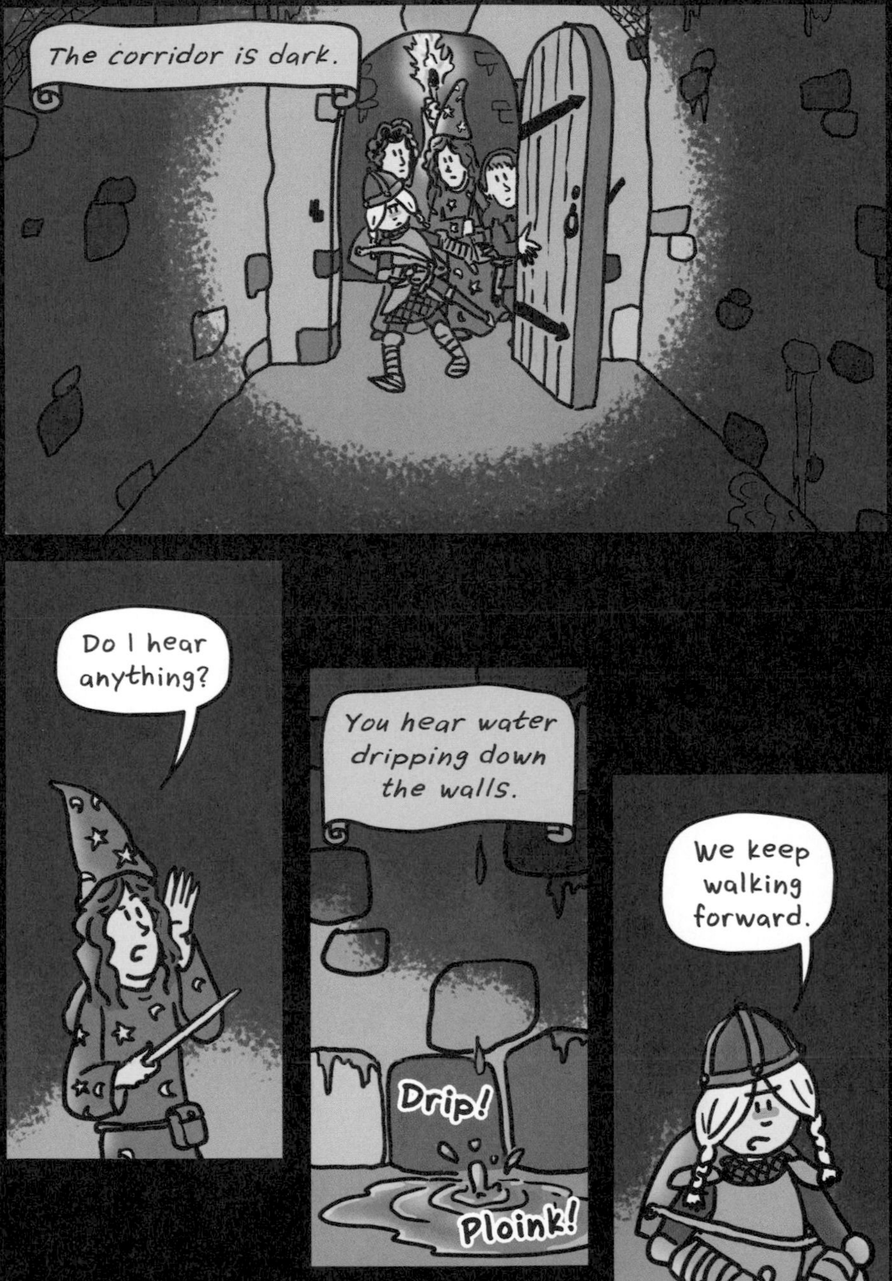
The corridor is dark.
Do I hear anything?
You hear water dripping down the walls.
Drip!
Ploink!
We keep walking forward.

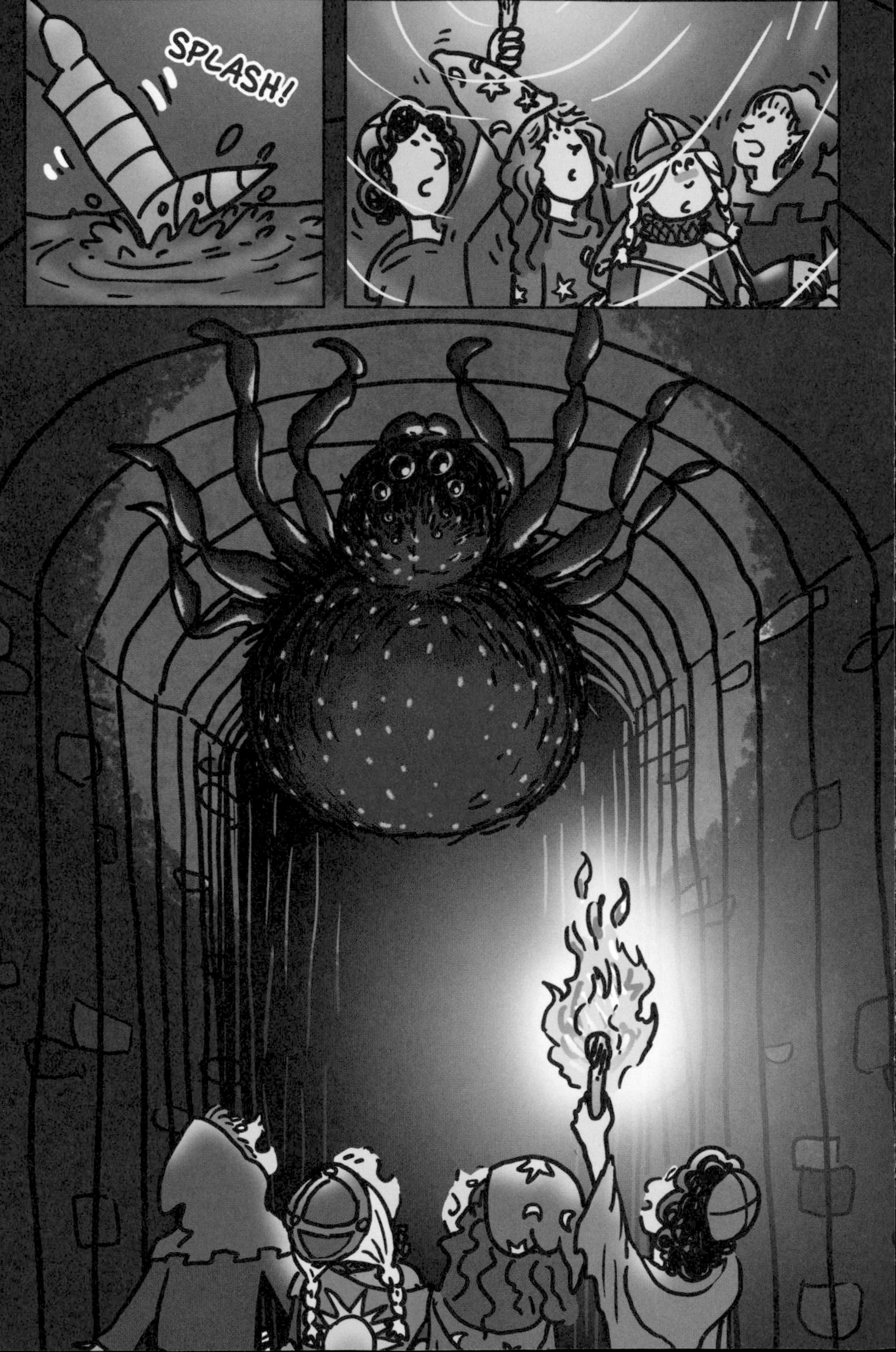
SPLASH!

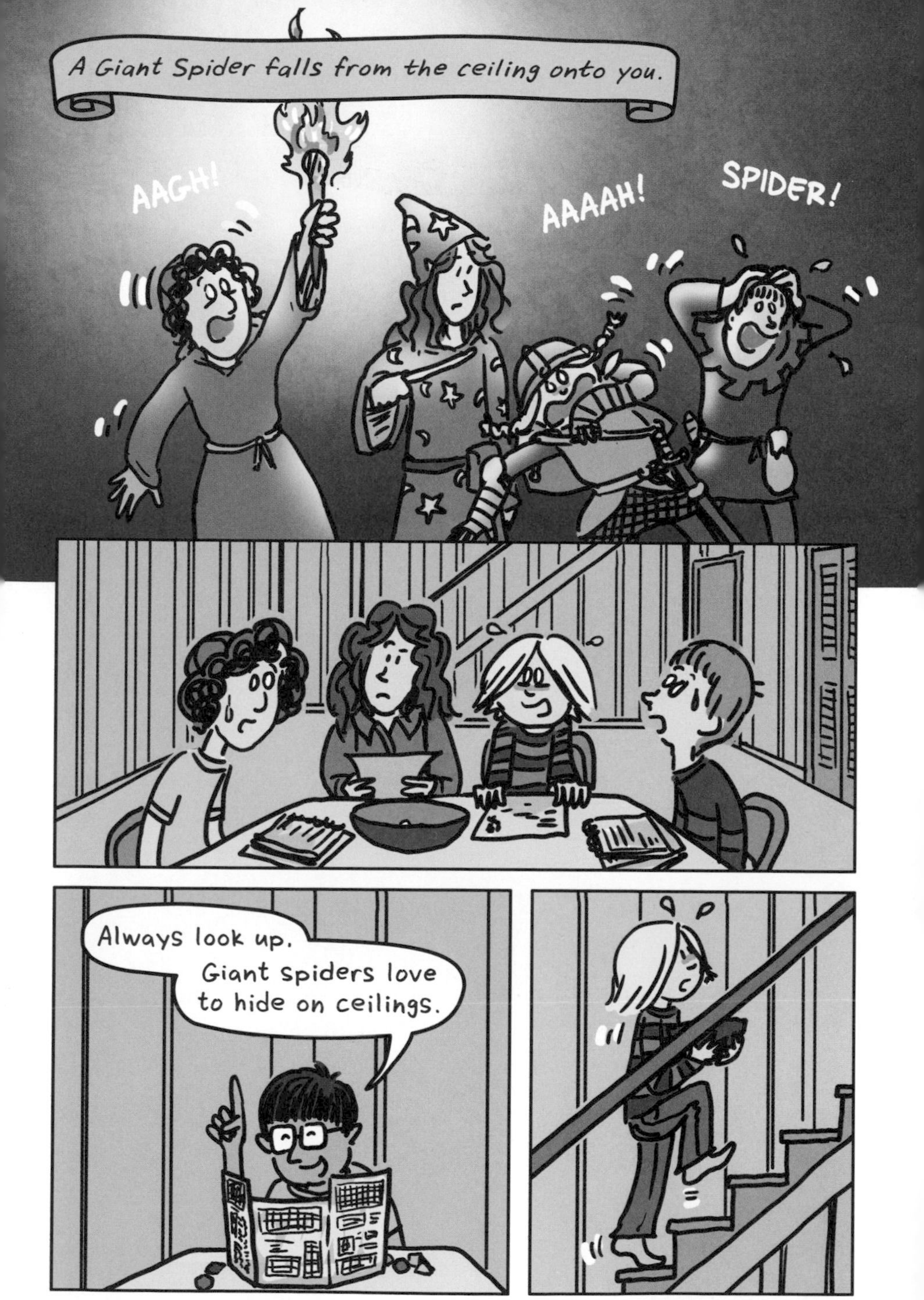

A Giant Spider falls from the ceiling onto you.
AAGH!
AAAAH!
SPIDER!
Always look up.
Giant spiders love to hide on ceilings.

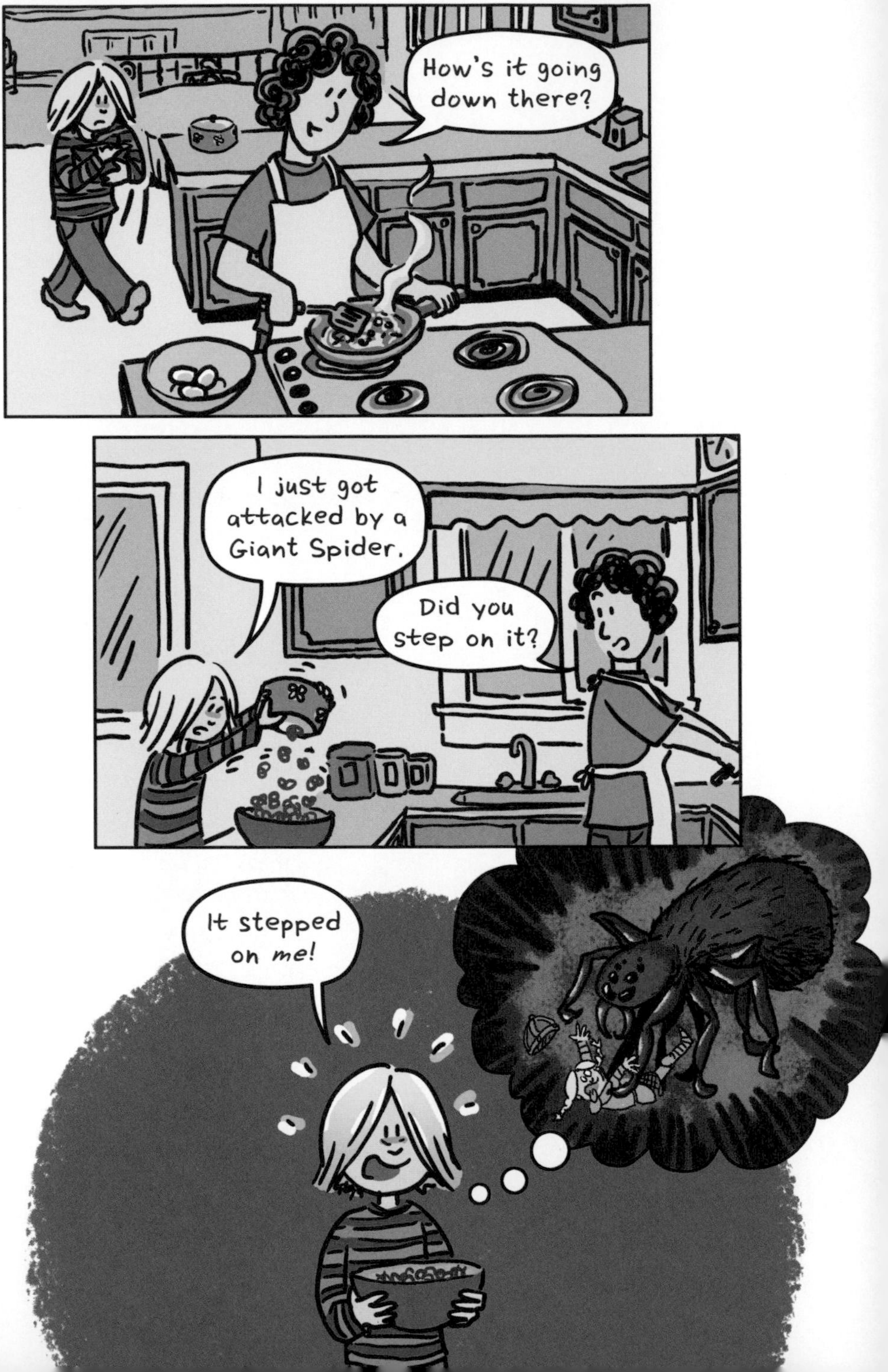
How's it going down there?
I just got attacked by a Giant Spider.
Did you step on it?
It stepped on *me*!

CHAPTER SIX: Biology

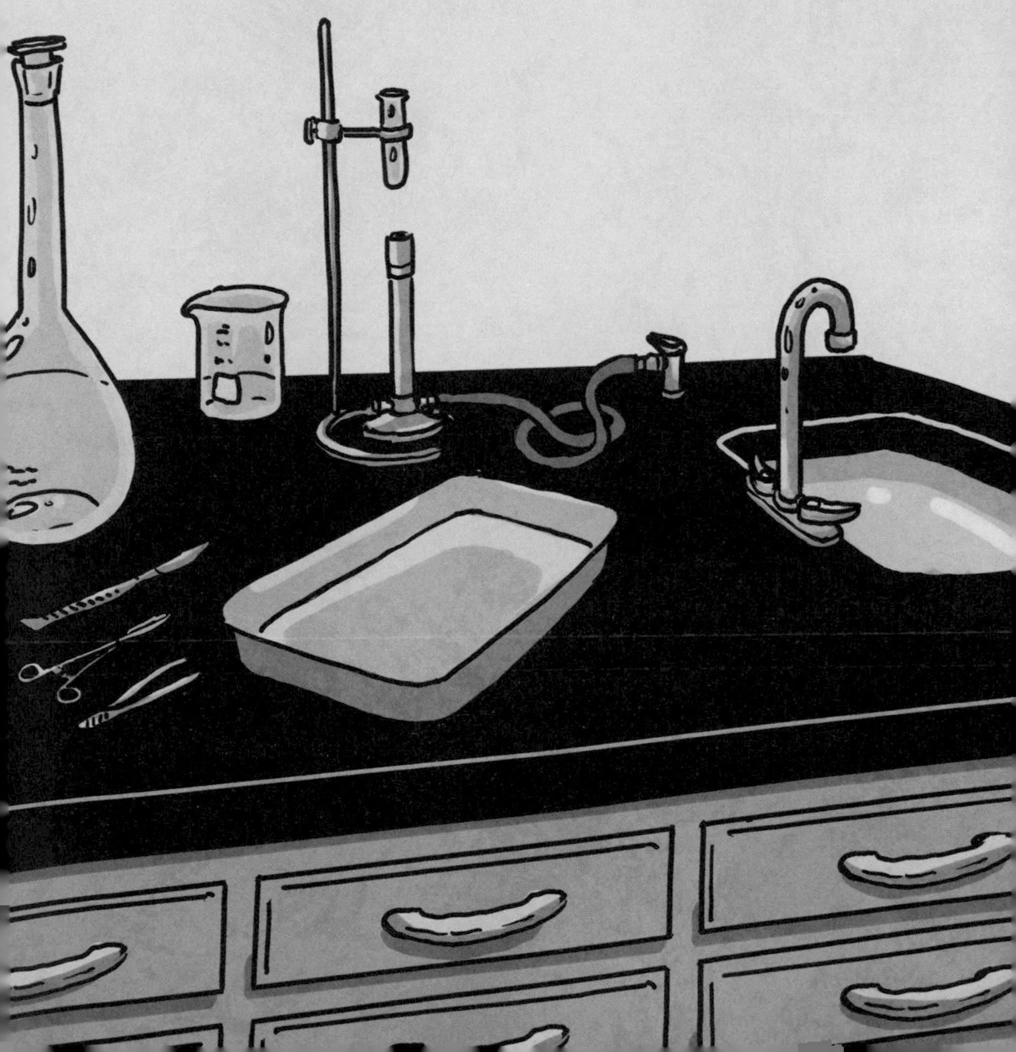

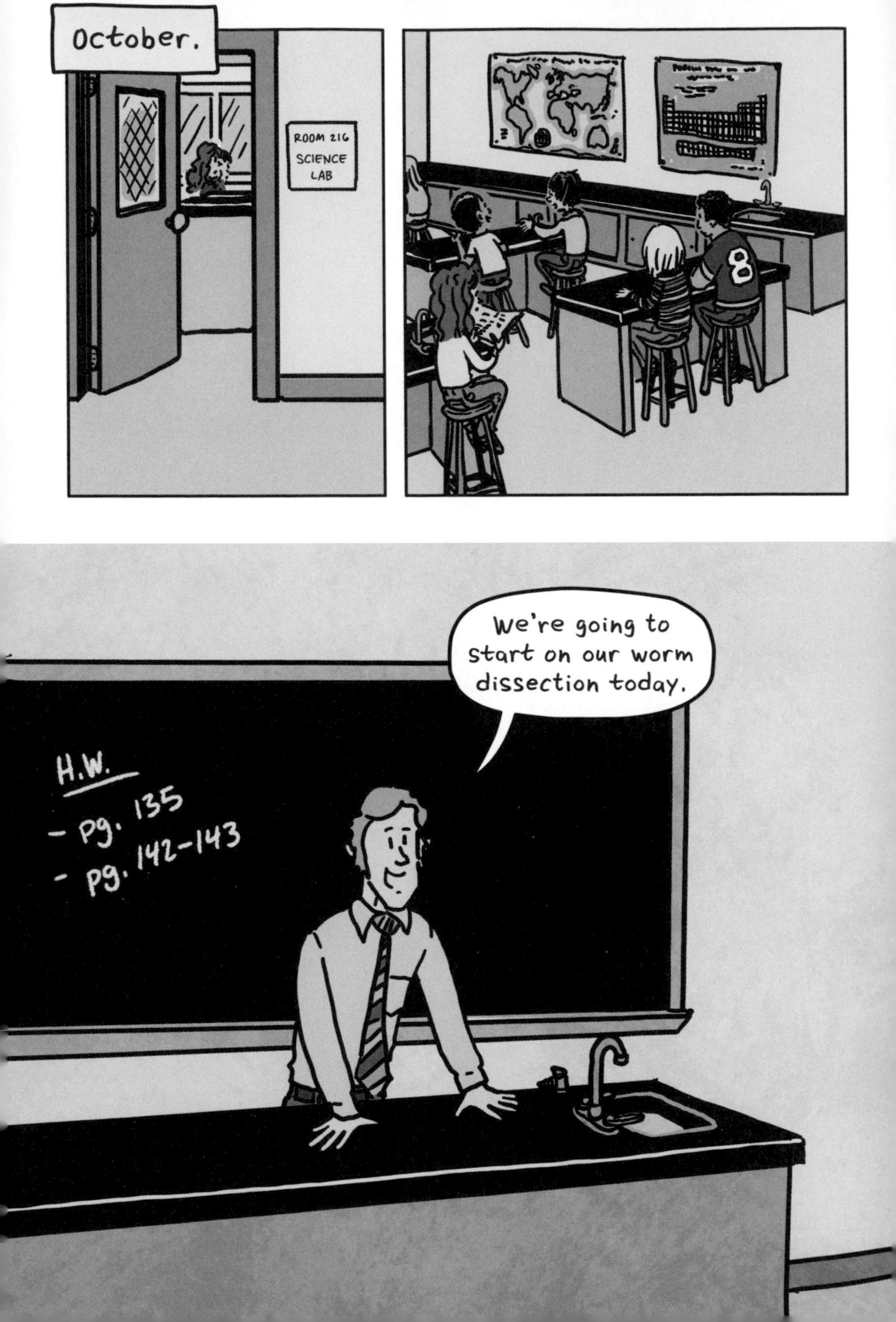
October.
ROOM 216
SCIENCE
LAB
8
We're going to start on our worm dissection today.
H.W.
- pg. 135
- pg. 142-143

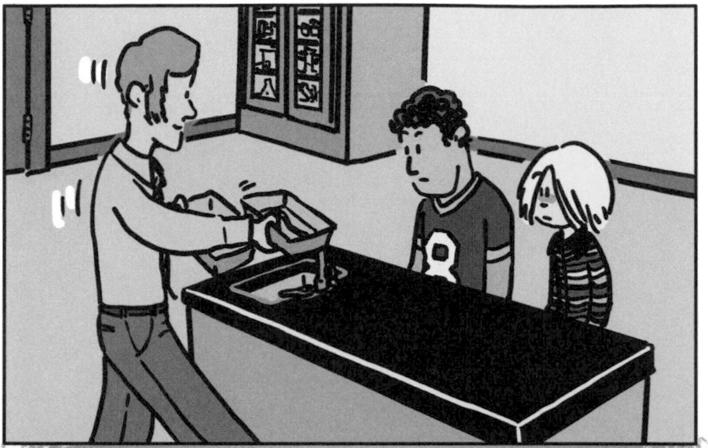

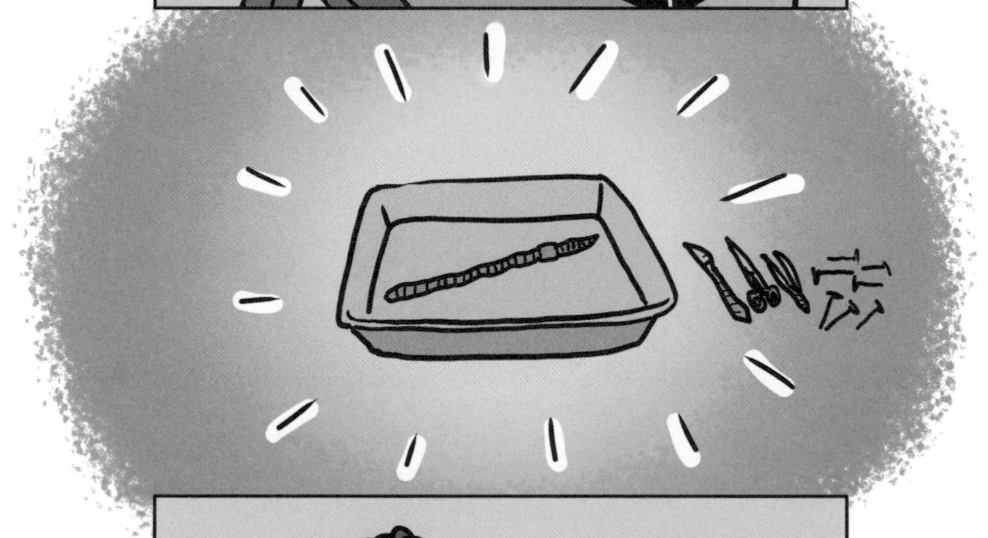

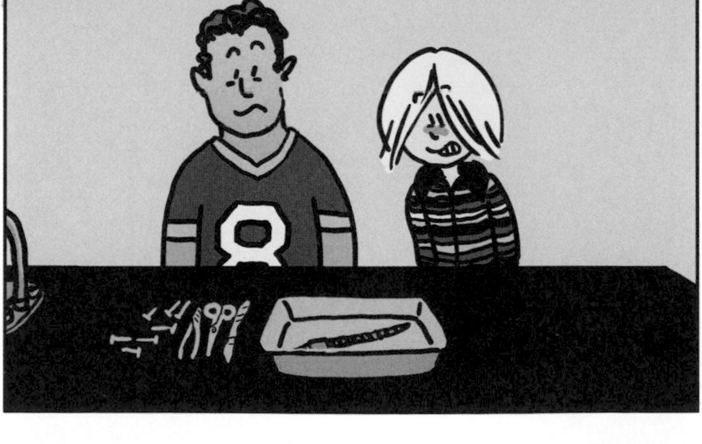

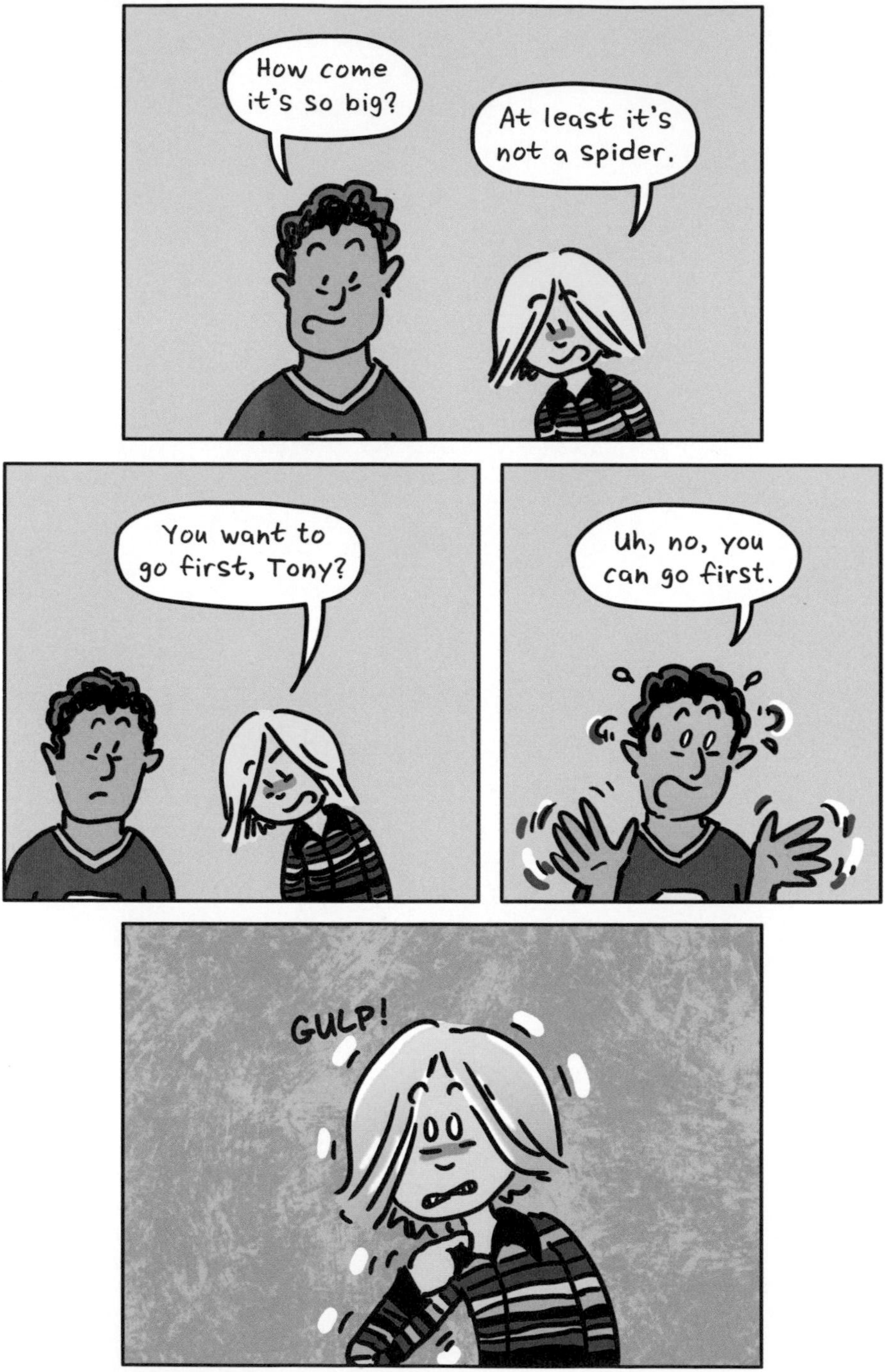
How come it's so big?
At least it's not a spider.
You want to go first, Tony?
Uh, no, you can go first.
GULP!

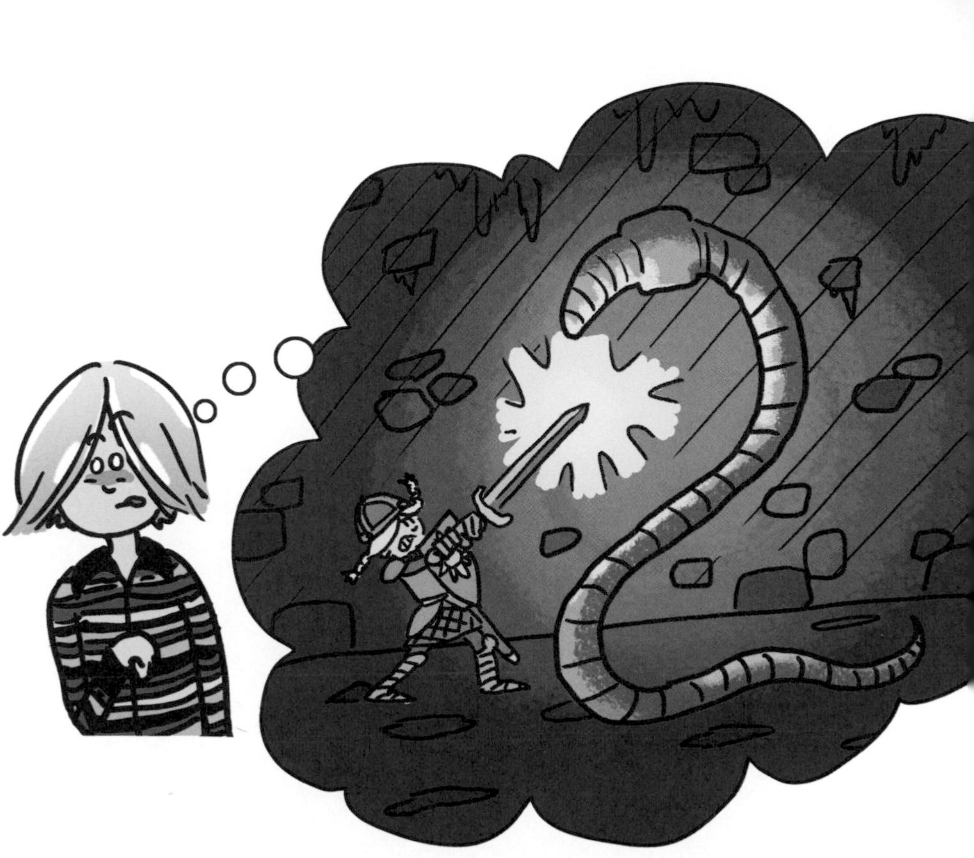

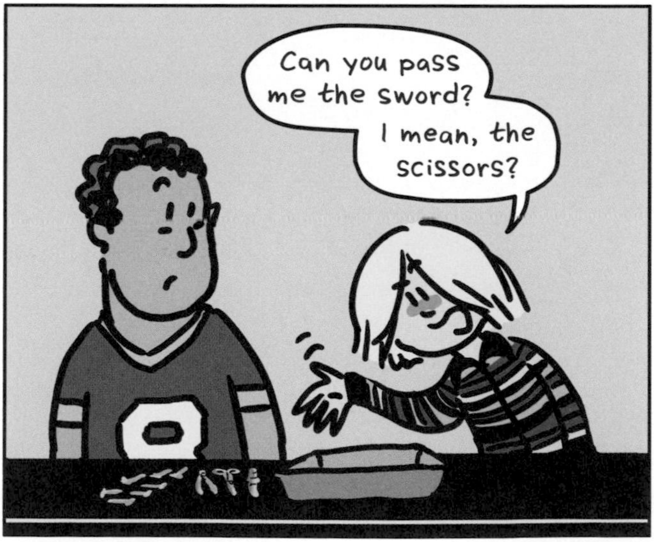

Can you pass me the sword?
I mean, the scissors?

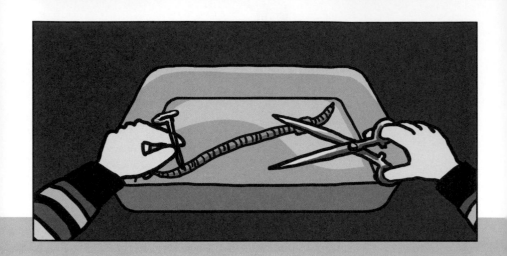

Ugh.

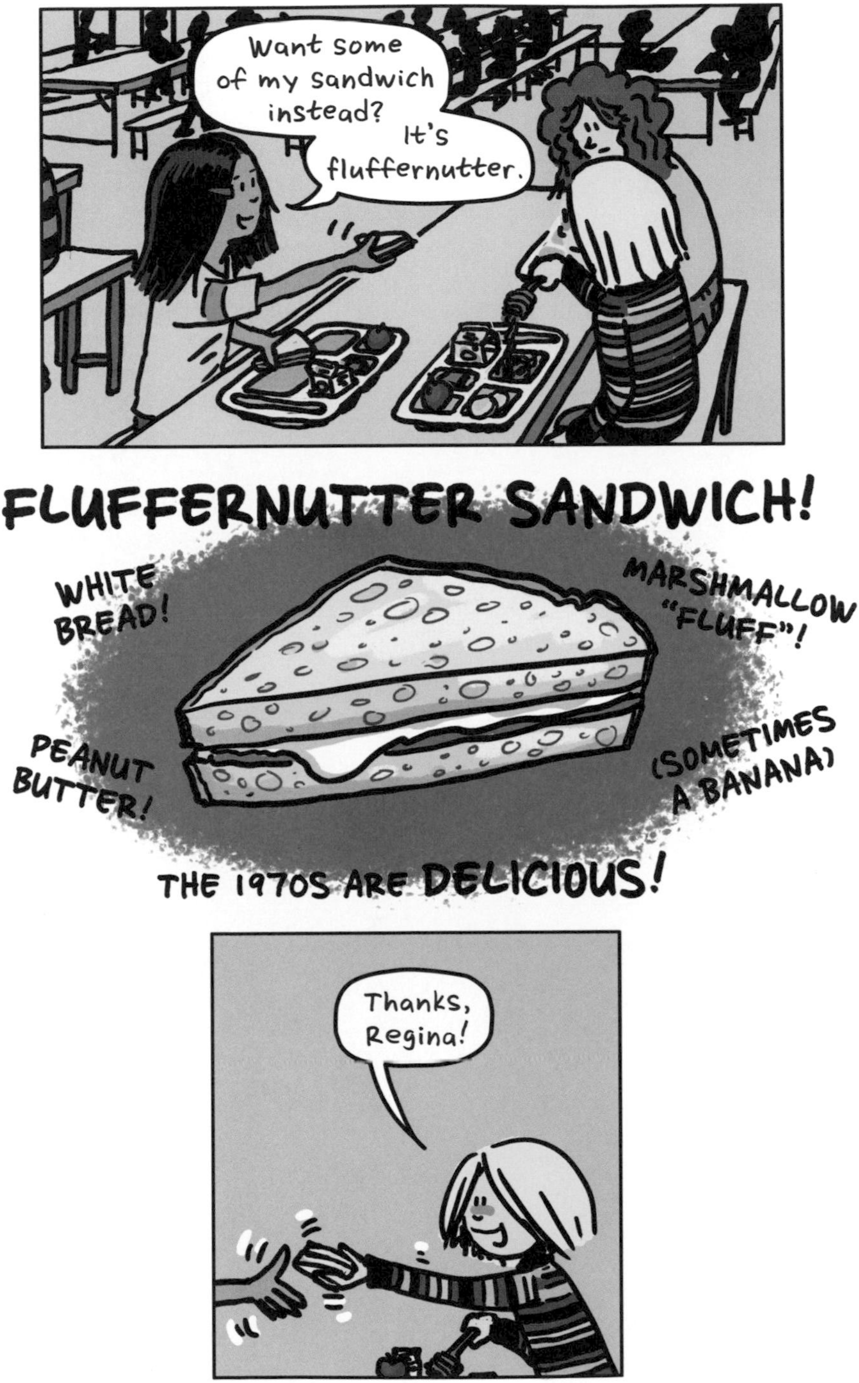
Want some of my sandwich instead? It's fluffernutter.
FLUFFERNUTTER SANDWICH!
WHITE BREAD!
MARSHMALLOW "FLUFF"!
PEANUT BUTTER!
(SOMETIMES A BANANA)
THE 1970S ARE DELICIOUS!
Thanks, Regina!

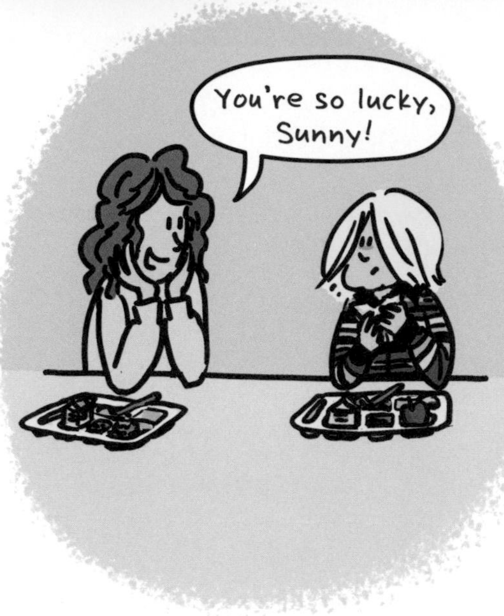
You're so lucky, Sunny!

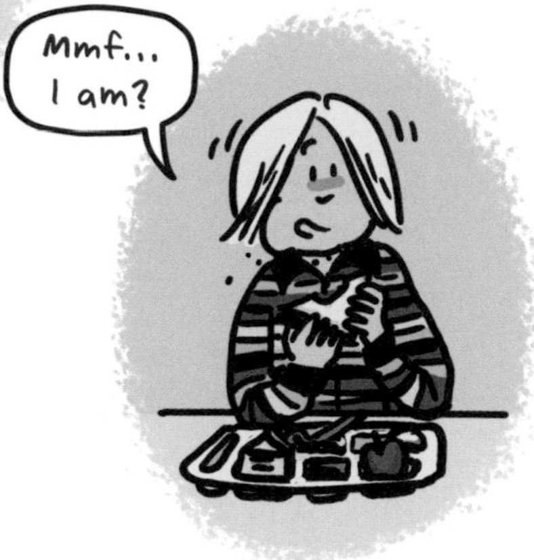
Mmf... I am?

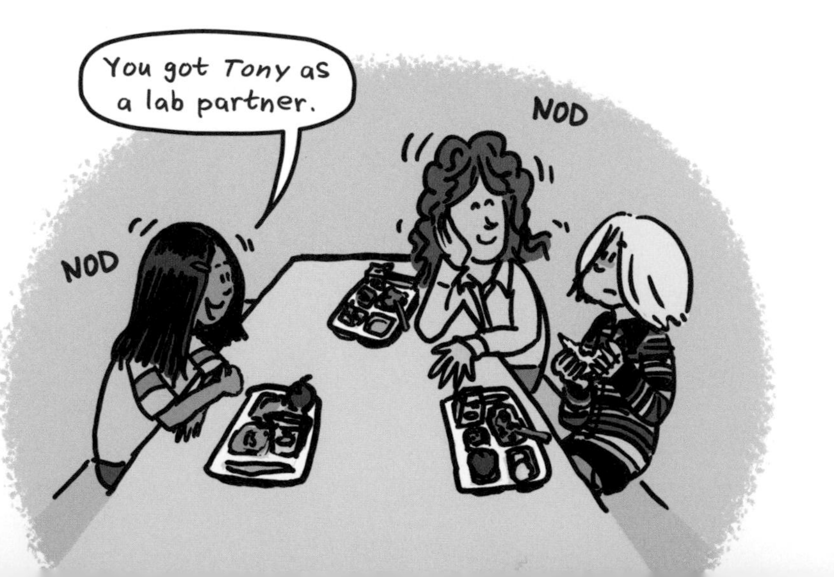
You got *Tony* as a lab partner.
NOD
NOD

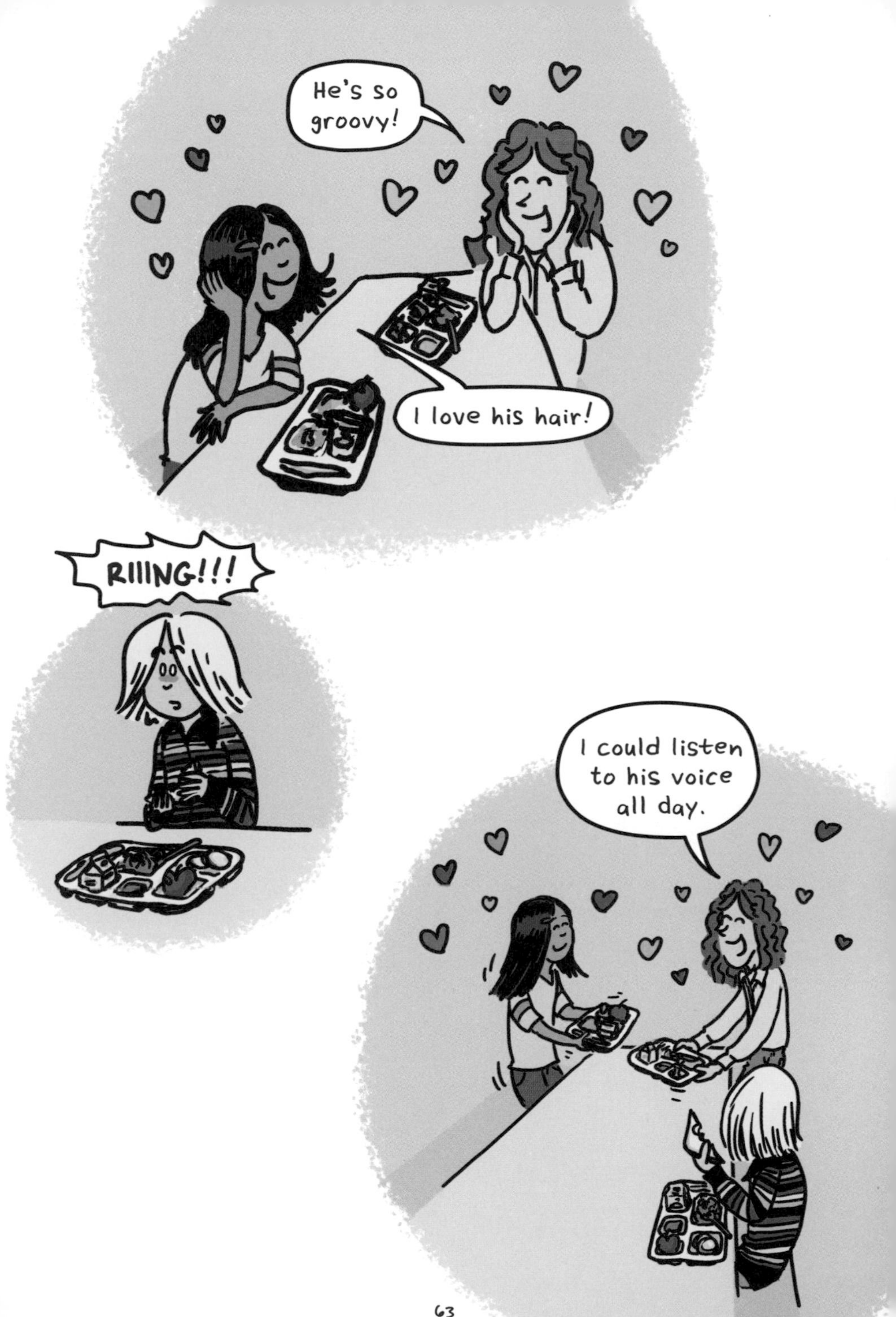
He's so groovy!
I love his hair!
RIIING!!!
I could listen to his voice all day.

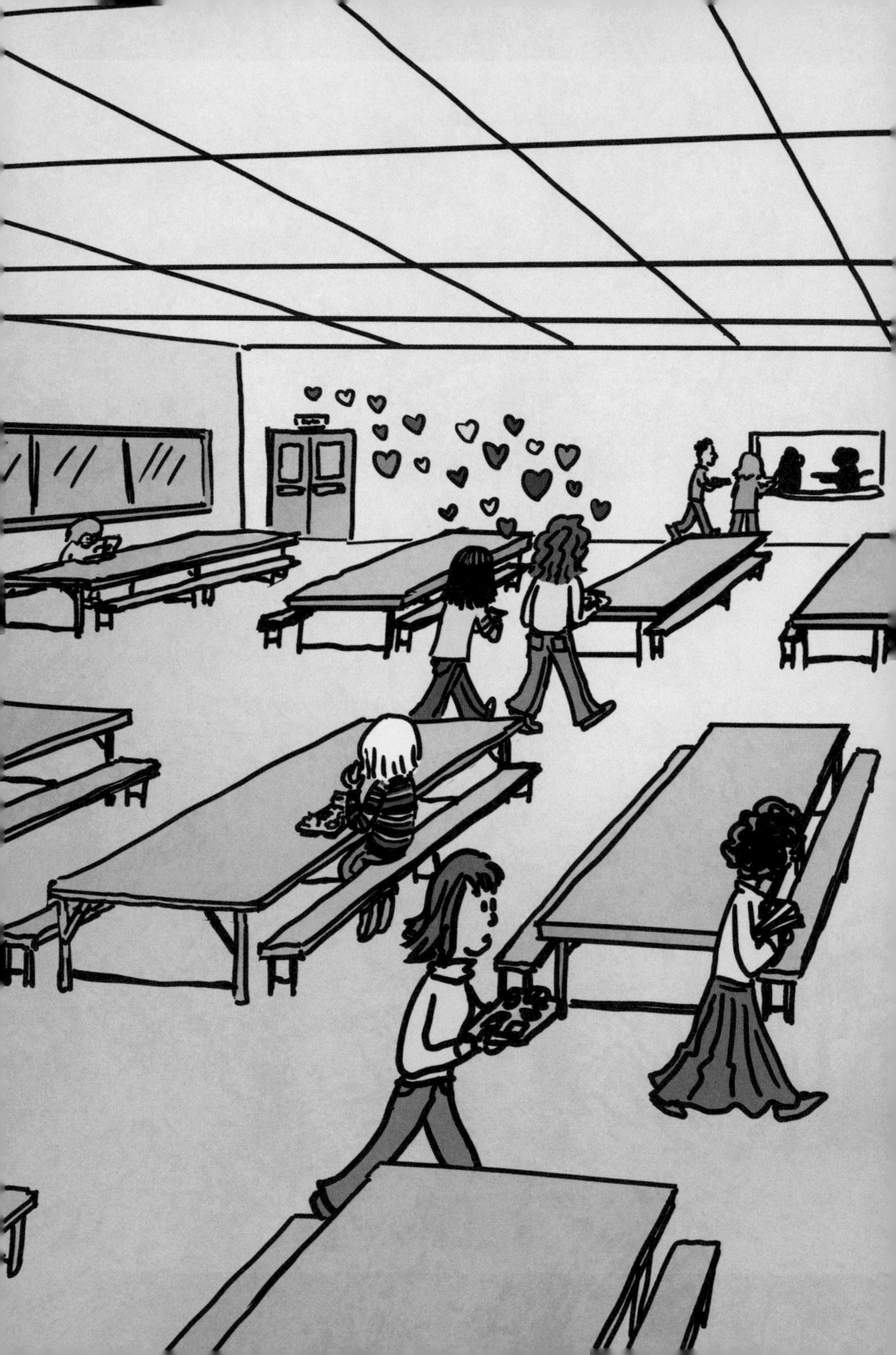

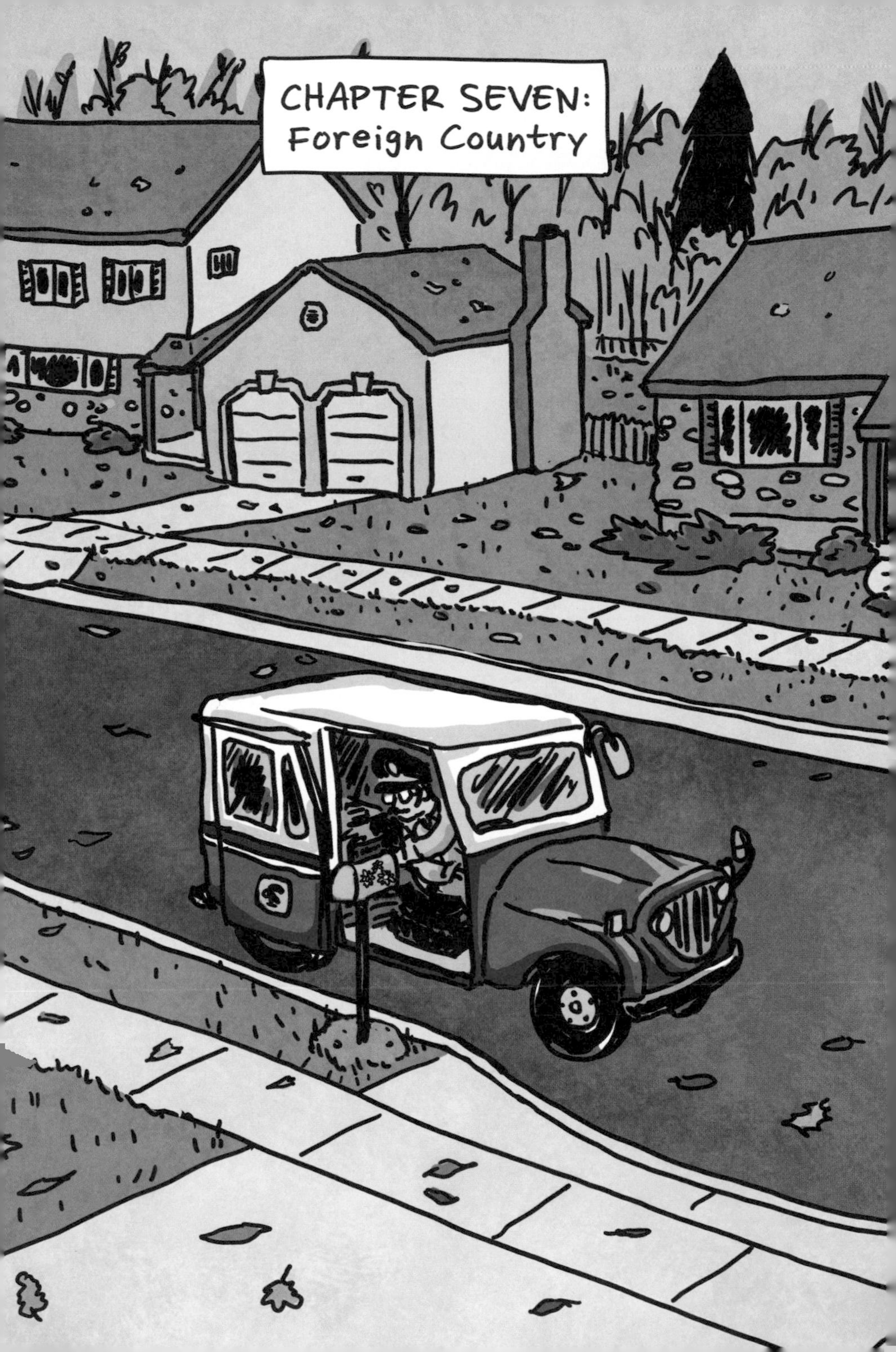
CHAPTER SEVEN:
Foreign Country

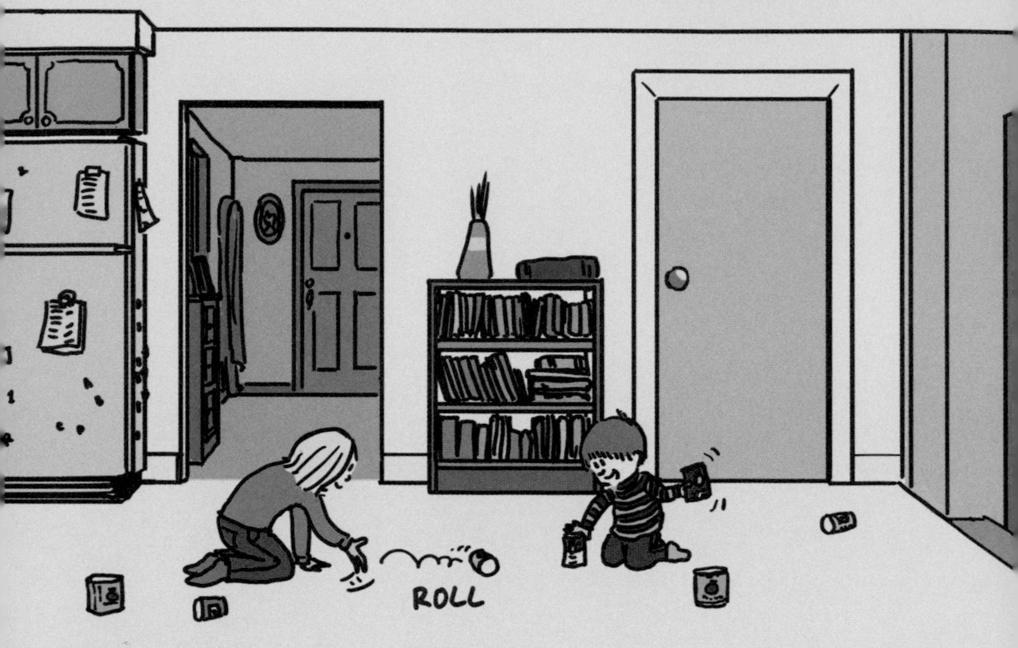
ROLL

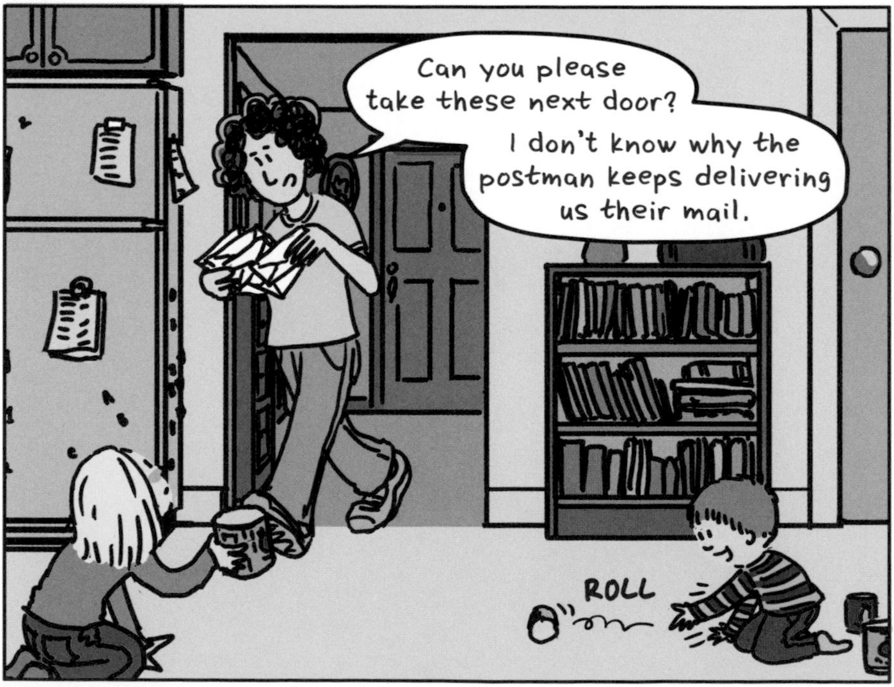
Can you please take these next door?
I don't know why the postman keeps delivering us their mail.
ROLL

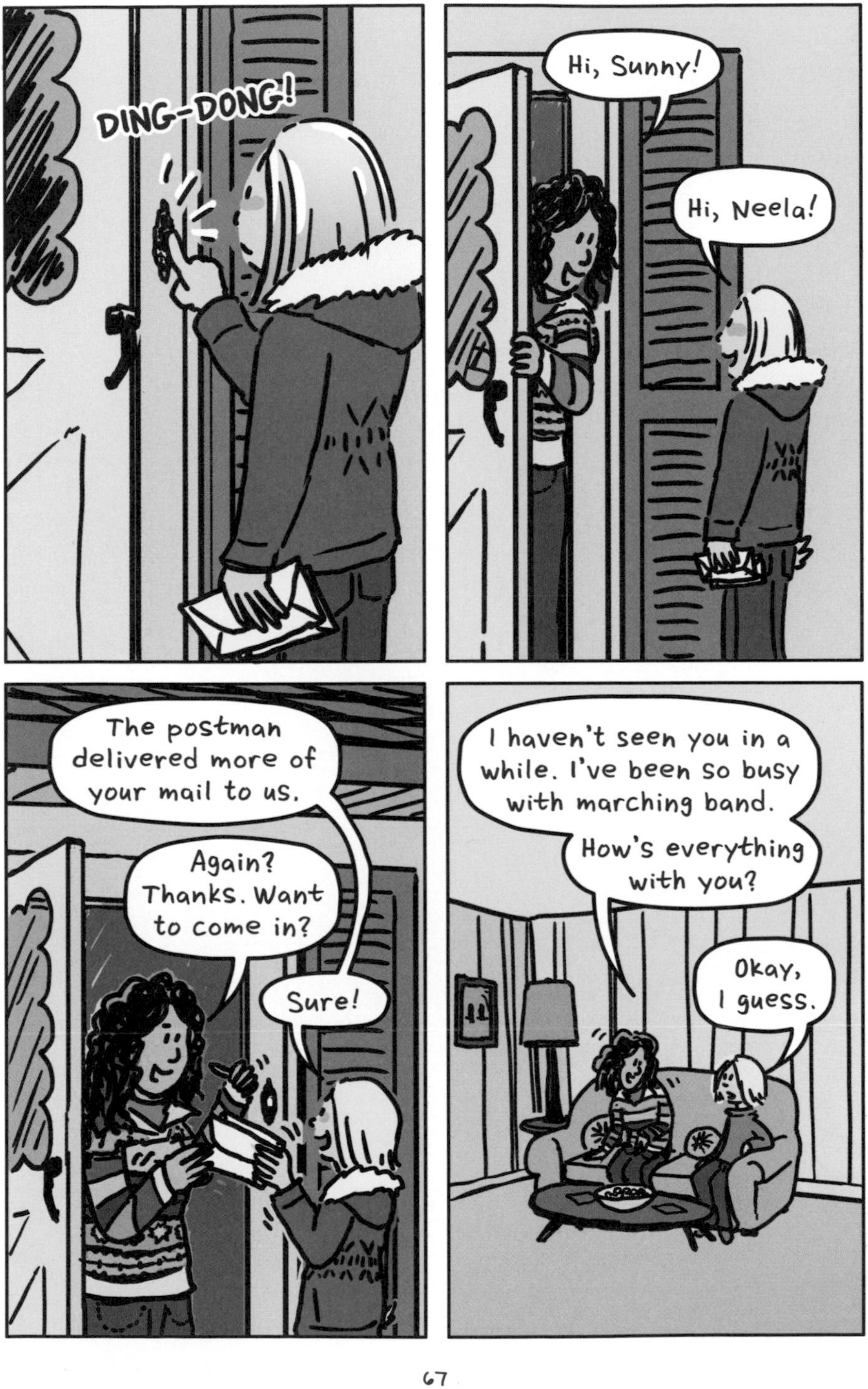
DING-DONG!
Hi, Sunny!
Hi, Neela!
The postman delivered more of your mail to us.
Again? Thanks. Want to come in?
Sure!
I haven't seen you in a while. I've been so busy with marching band.
How's everything with you?
Okay, I guess.

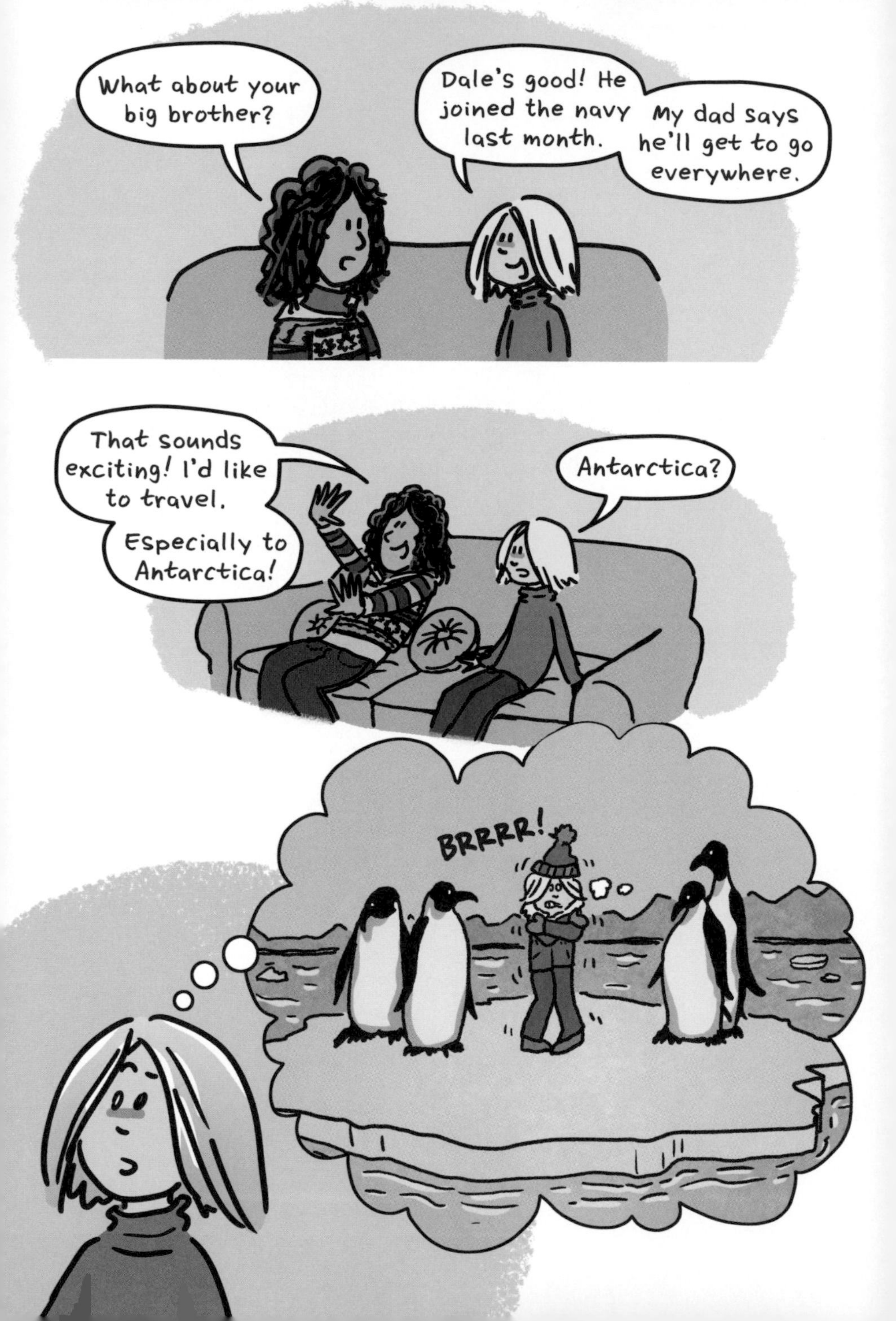
What about your big brother?
Dale's good! He joined the navy last month.
My dad says he'll get to go everywhere.
That sounds exciting! I'd like to travel.
Especially to Antarctica!
Antarctica?
BRRRR!

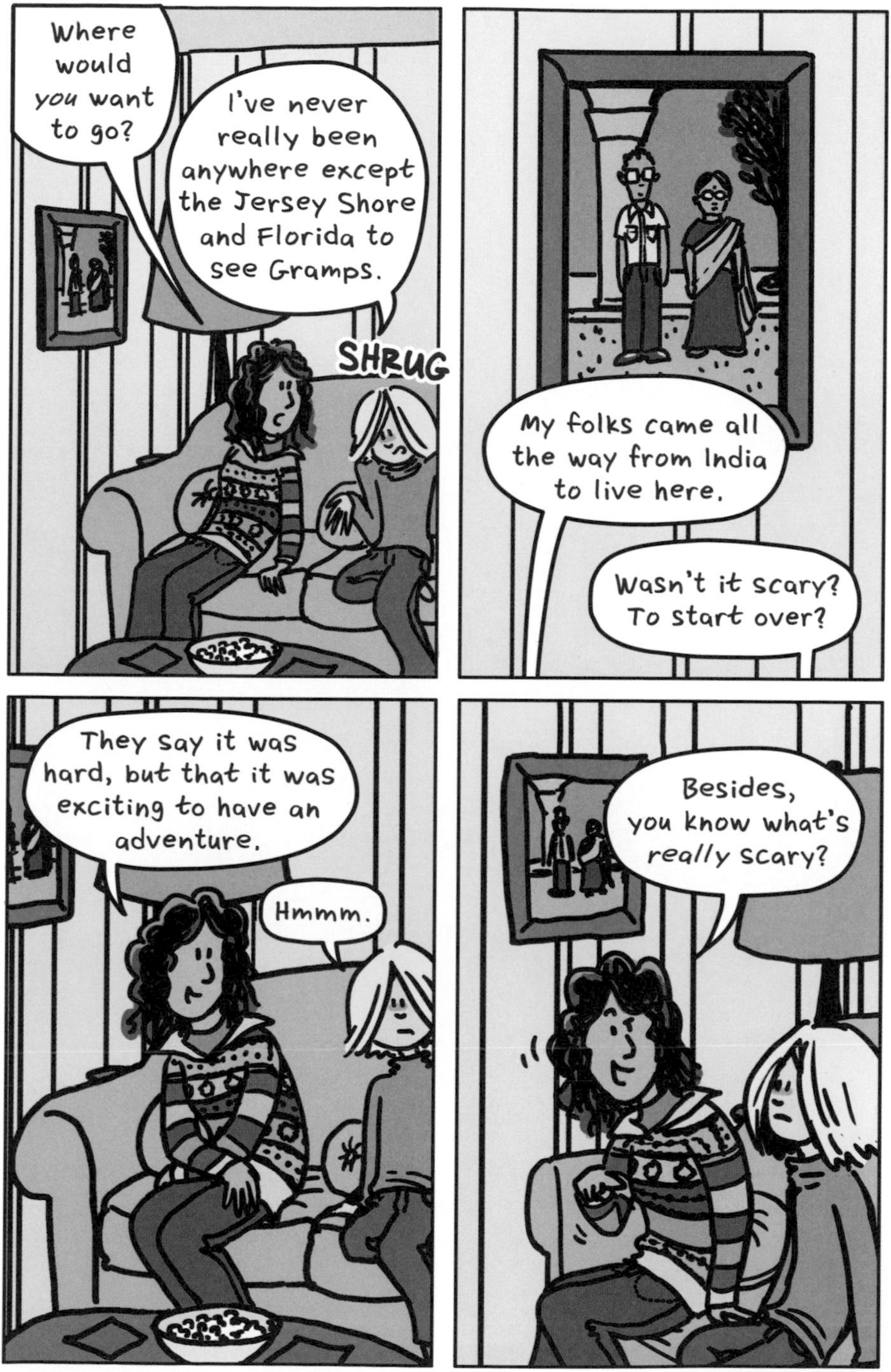
Where would *you* want to go?
I've never really been anywhere except the Jersey Shore and Florida to see Gramps.
SHRUG
My folks came all the way from India to live here.
Wasn't it scary? To start over?
They say it was hard, but that it was exciting to have an adventure.
Hmmm.
Besides, you know what's *really* scary?

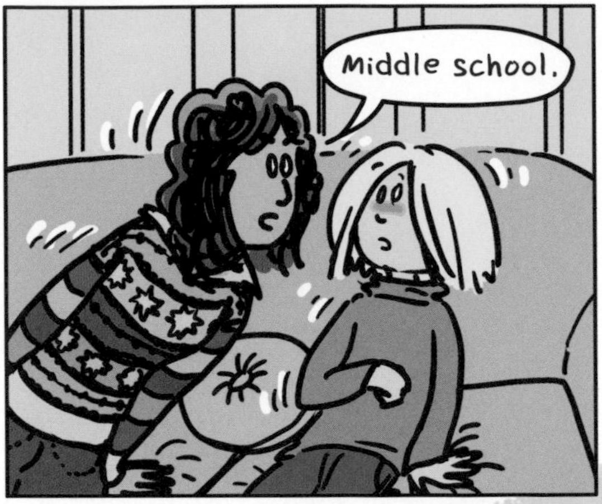
Middle school.

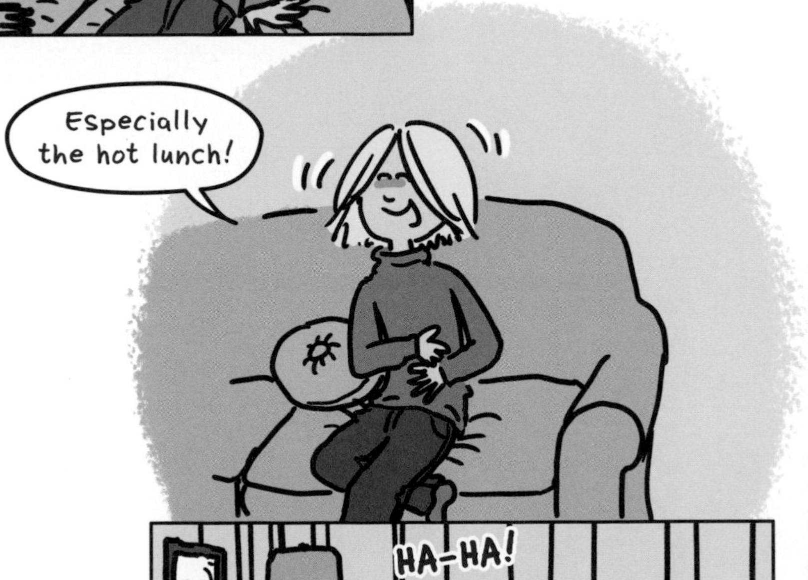
Especially the hot lunch!

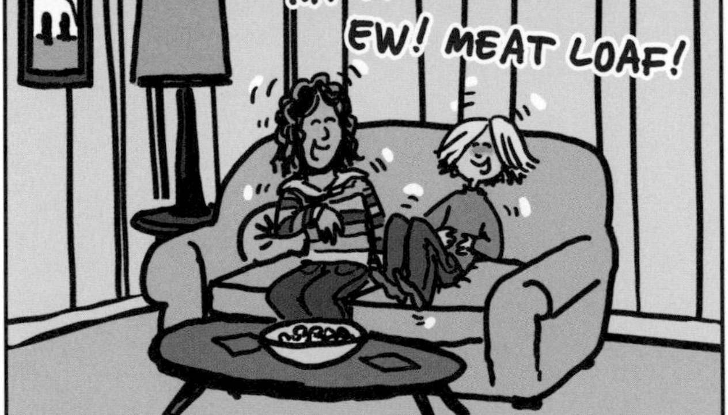
HA-HA!
EW! MEAT LOAF!

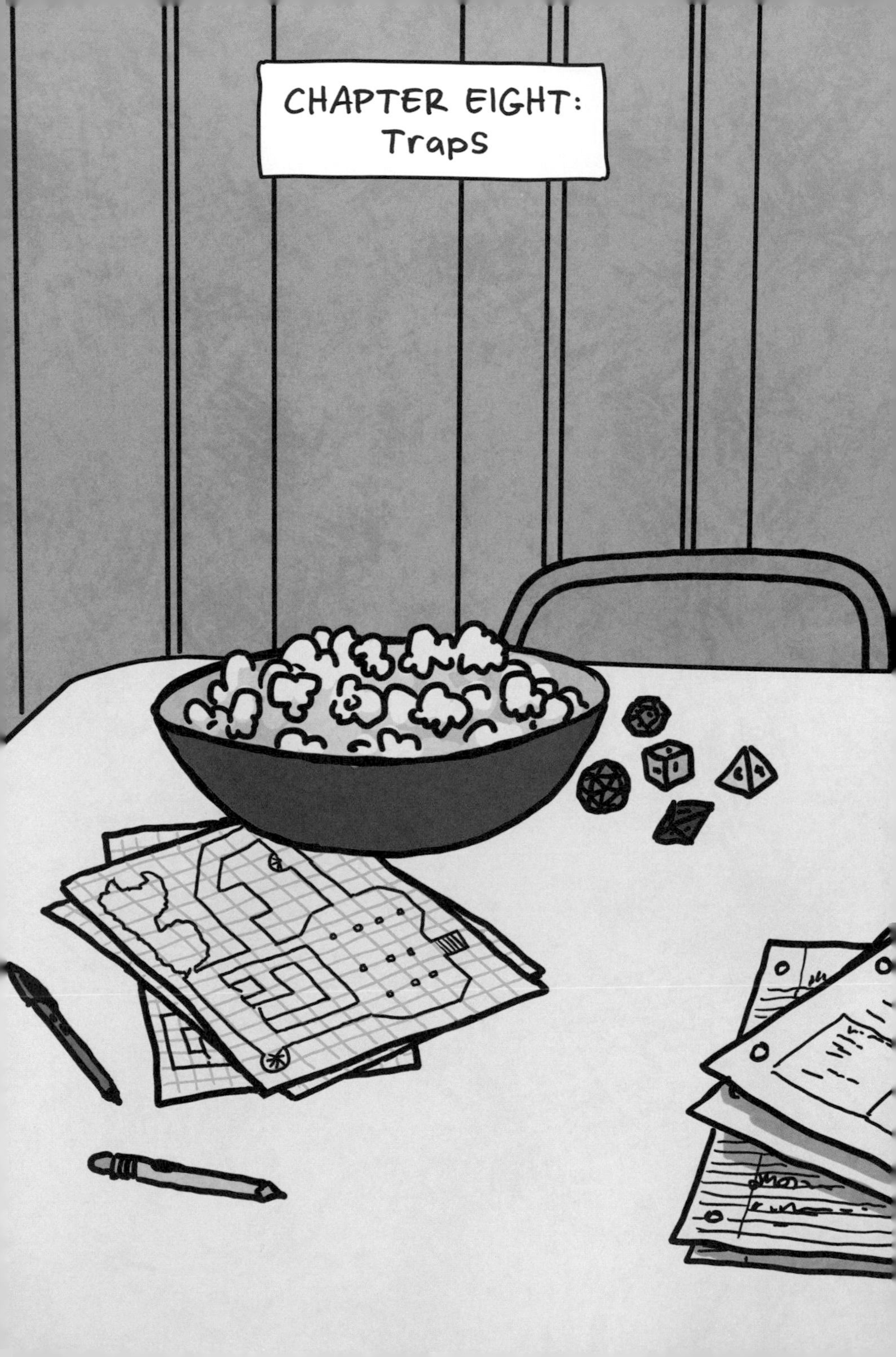
CHAPTER EIGHT:
Traps

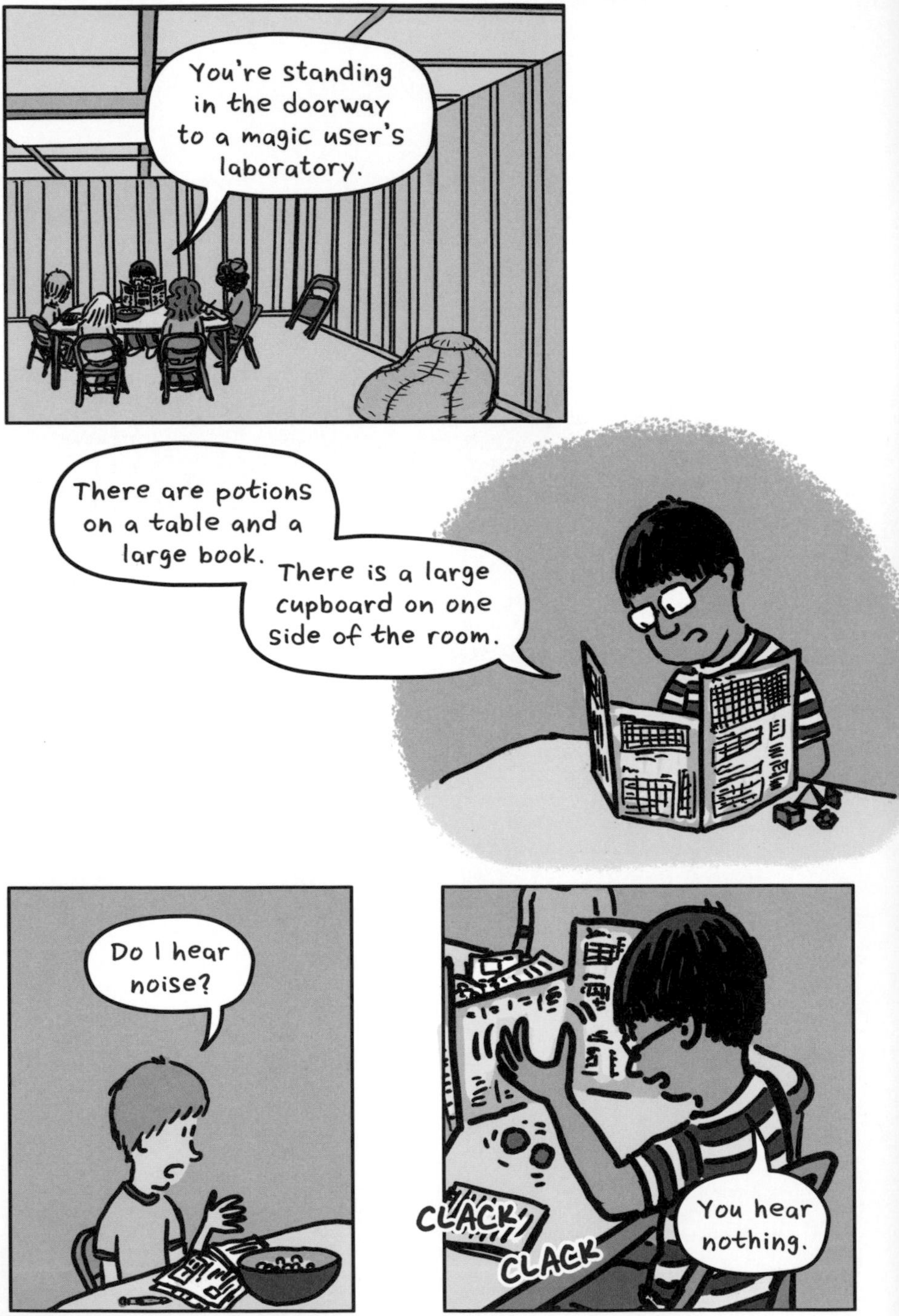
You're standing in the doorway to a magic user's laboratory.
There are potions on a table and a large book.
There is a large cupboard on one side of the room.
Do I hear noise?
CLACK
CLACK
You hear nothing.

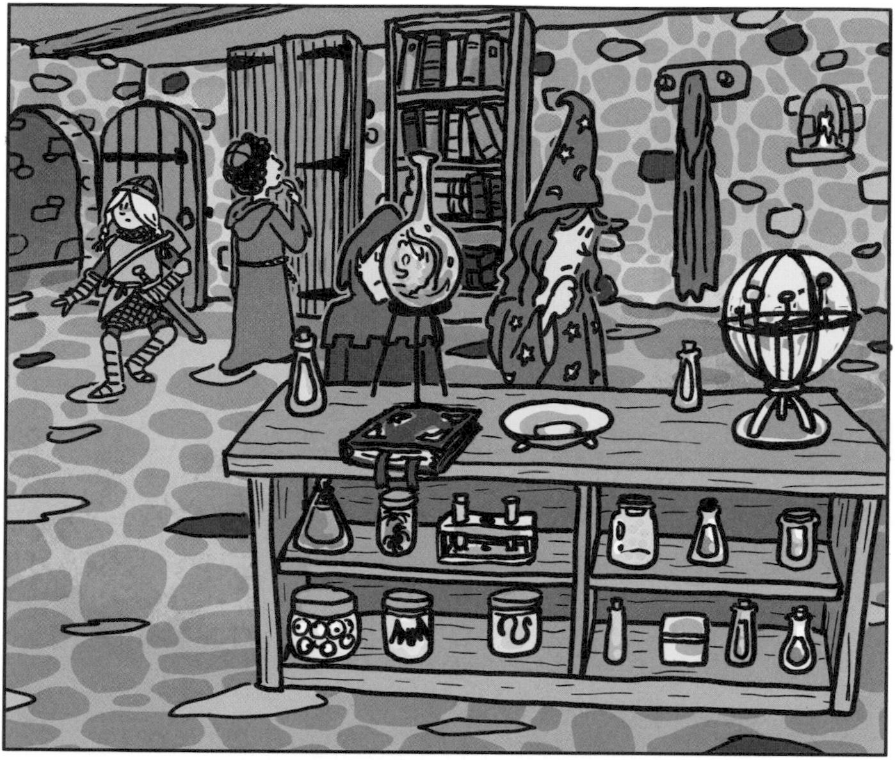

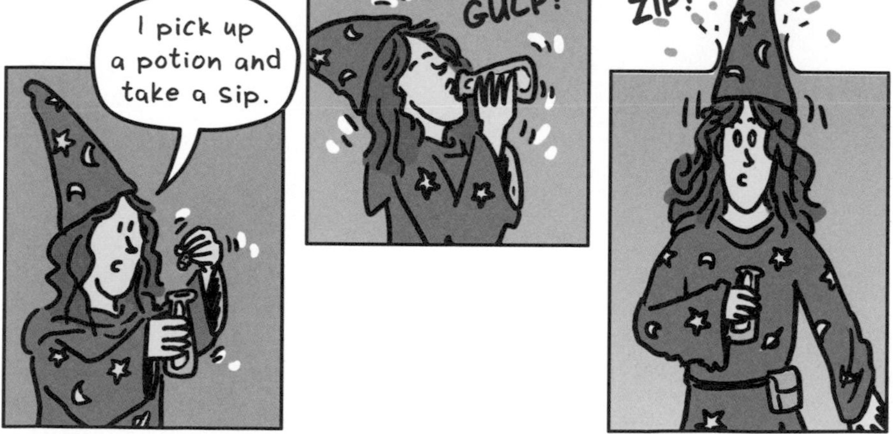
I pick up a potion and take a sip.
GULP!
ZIP!

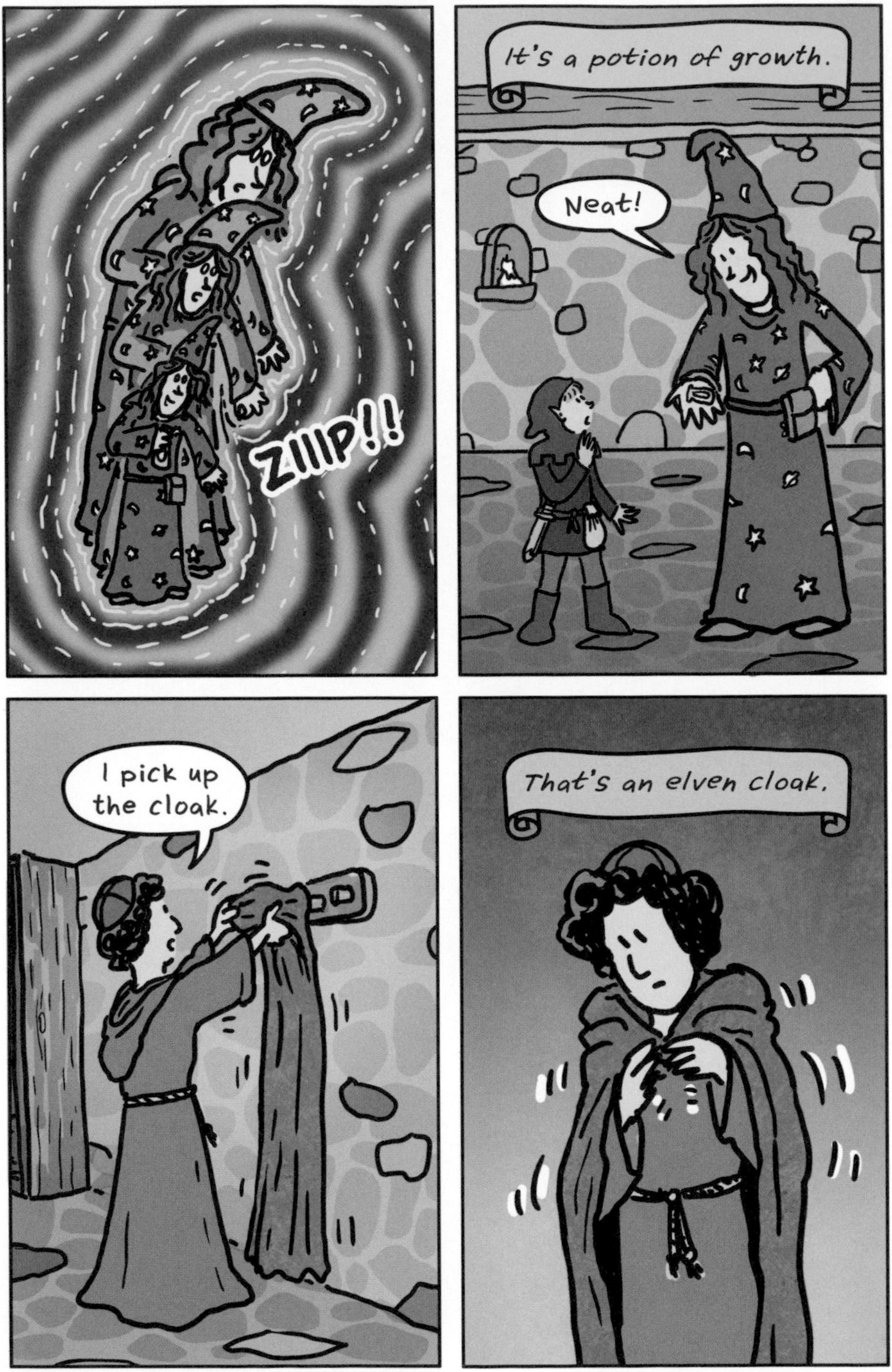
ZIIIP!!
It's a potion of growth.
Neat!
I pick up the cloak.
That's an elven cloak.

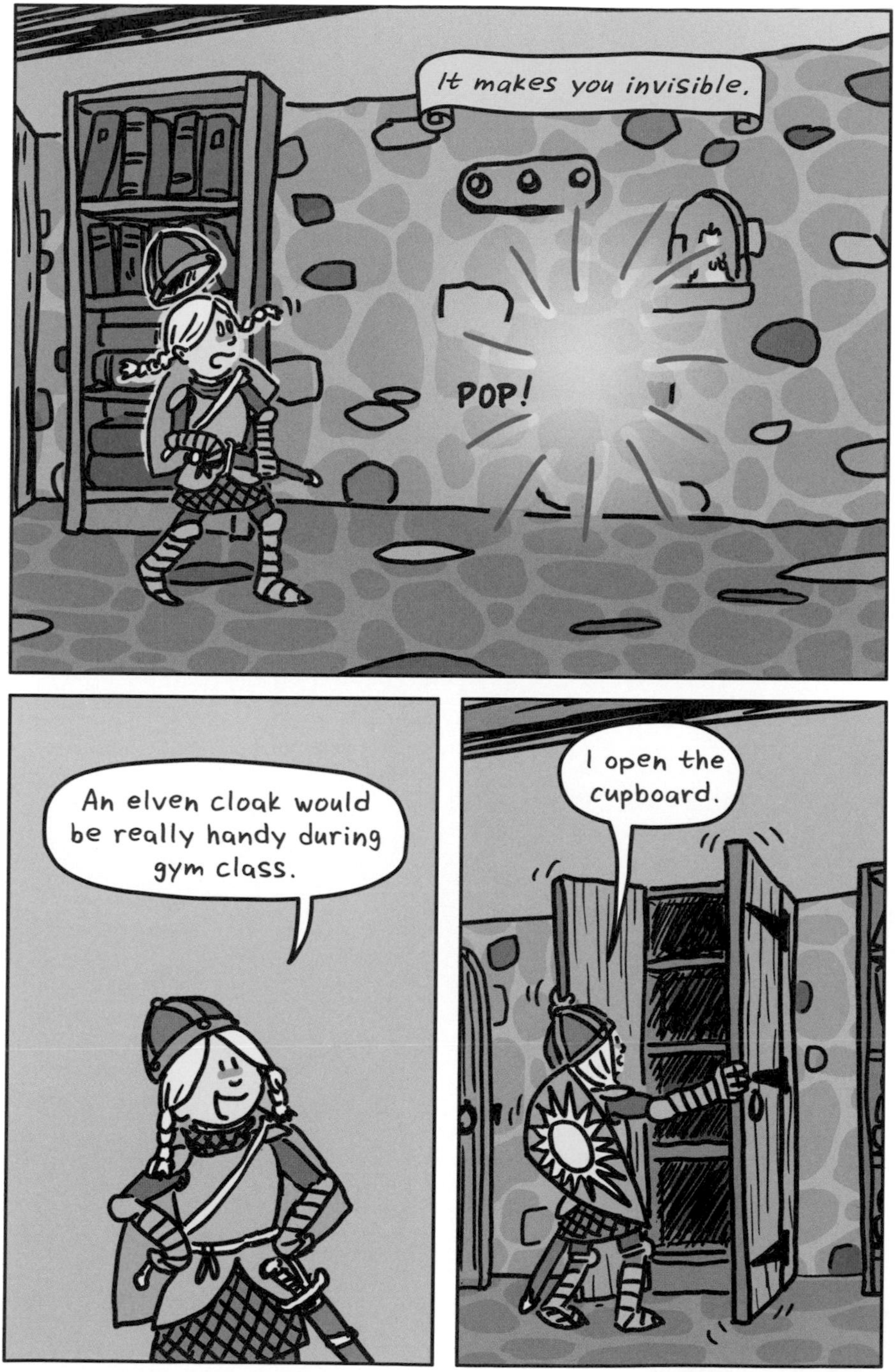
It makes you invisible.
POP!
An elven cloak would be really handy during gym class.
I open the cupboard.

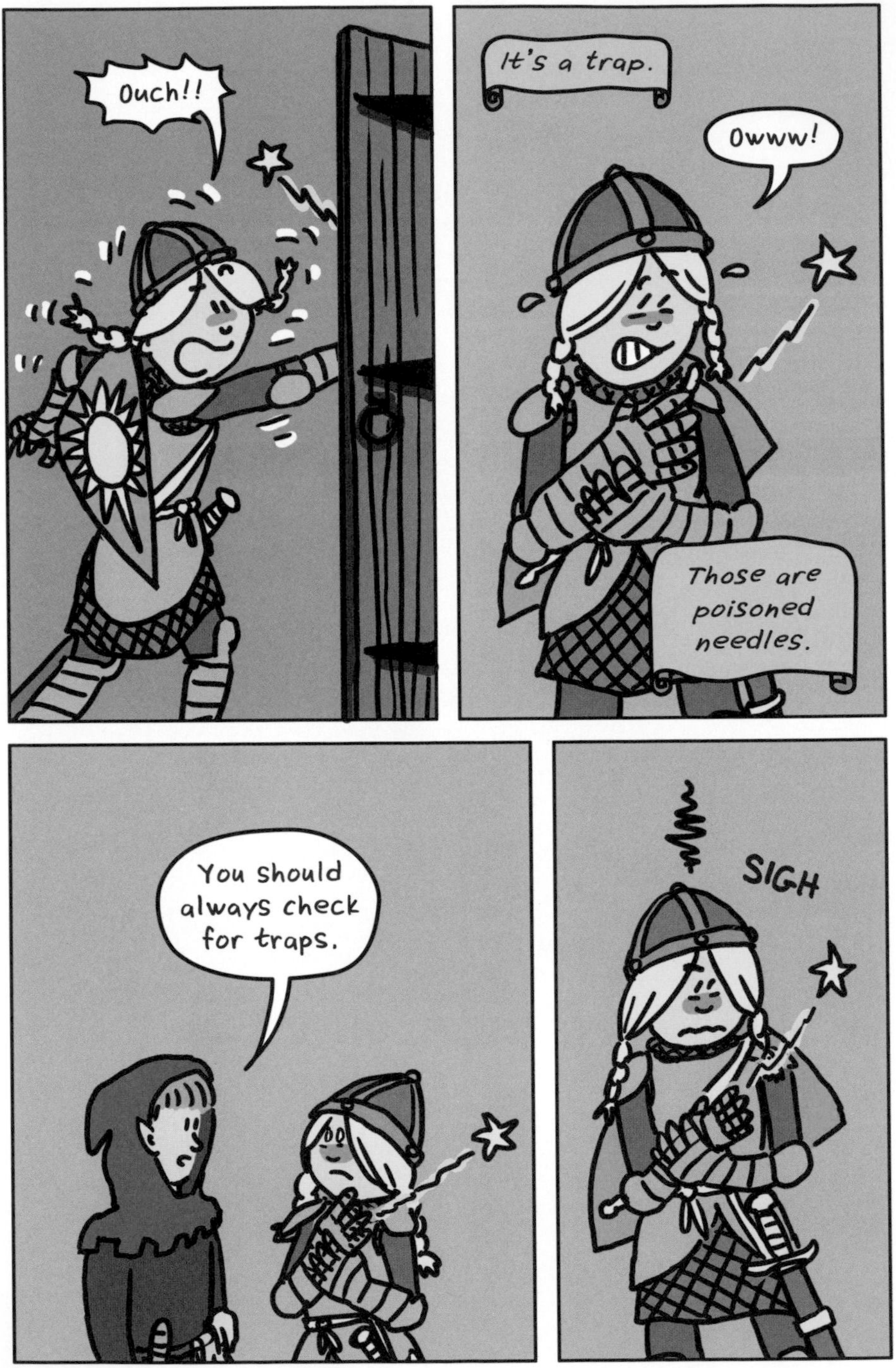
Ouch!!
It's a trap.
Owww!
Those are poisoned needles.
You should always check for traps.
SIGH

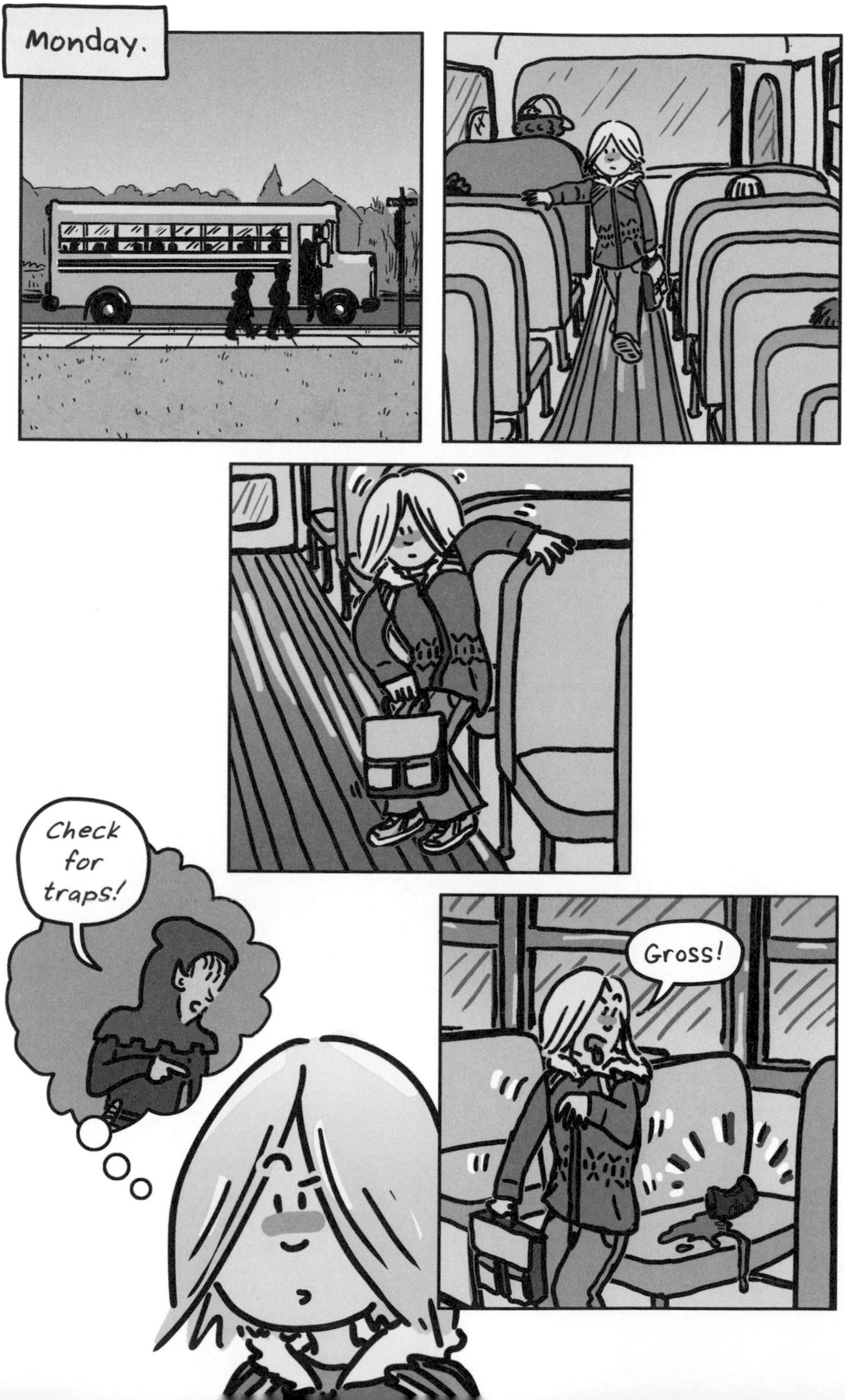
Monday.
Check for traps!
Gross!

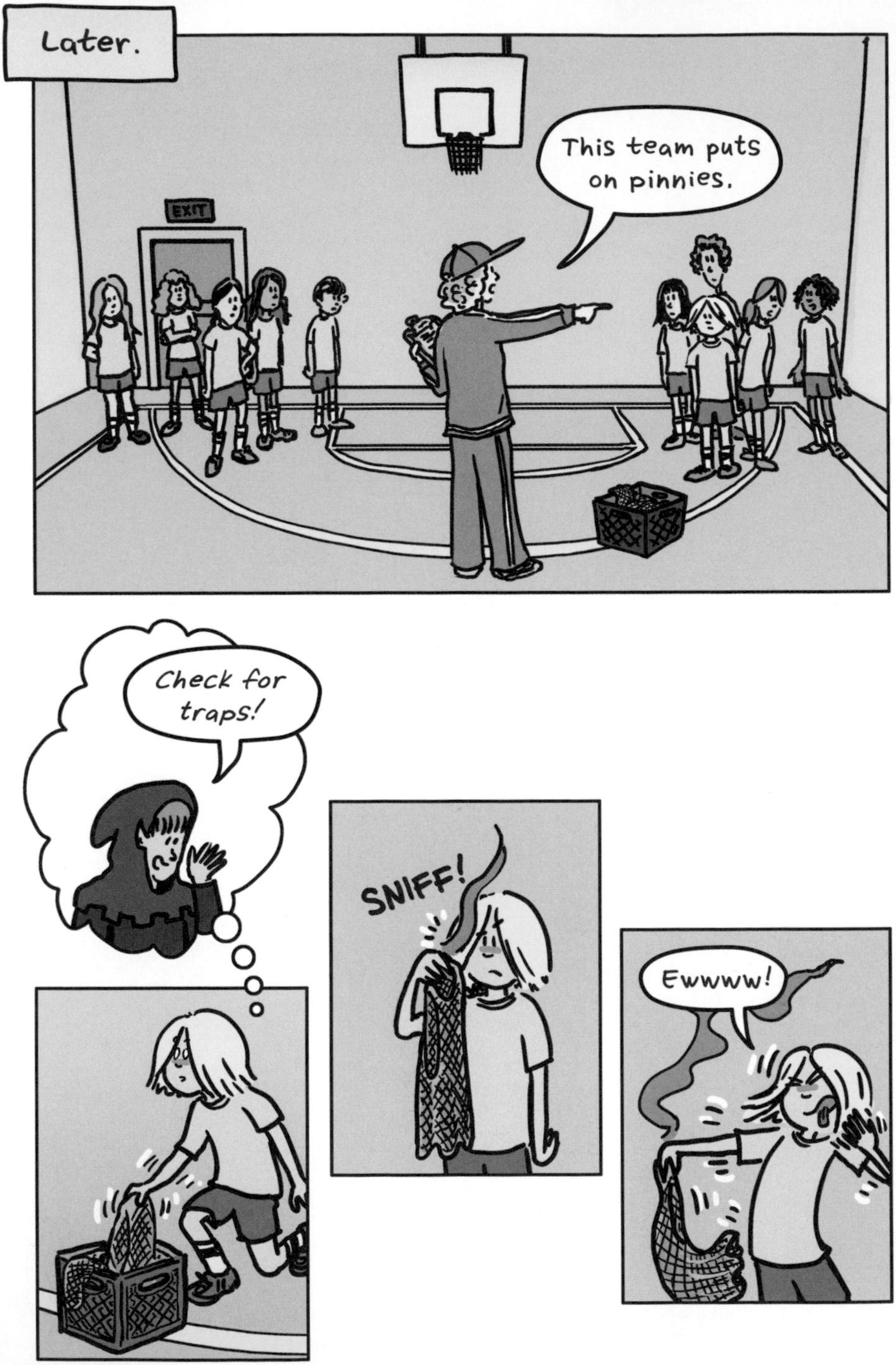
Later.
This team puts on pinnies.
Check for traps!
SNIFF!
Ewwww!

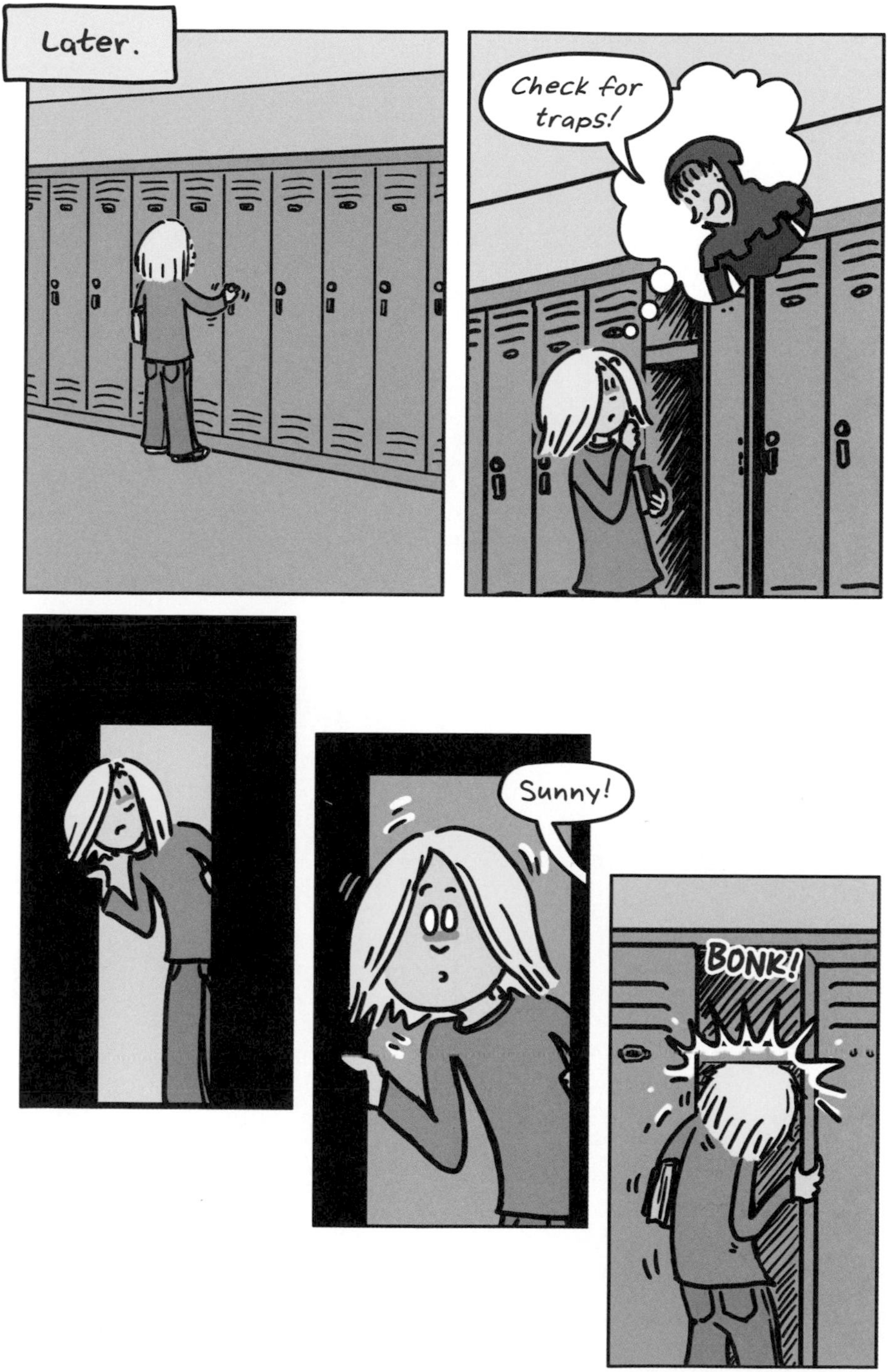
Later.
Check for traps!
Sunny!
BONK!

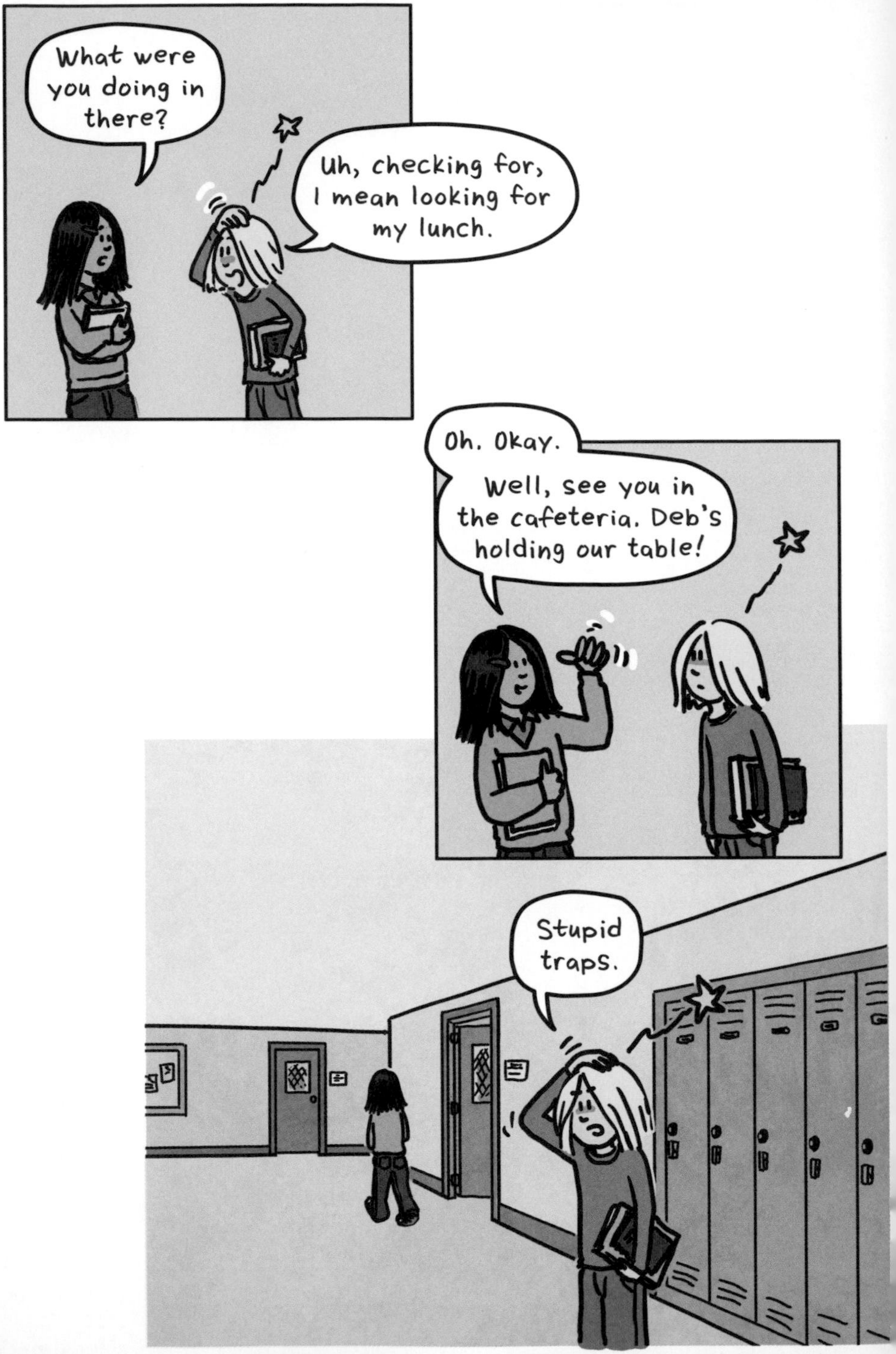
What were you doing in there?
Uh, checking for, I mean looking for my lunch.
Oh. Okay.
Well, see you in the cafeteria. Deb's holding our table!
Stupid traps.

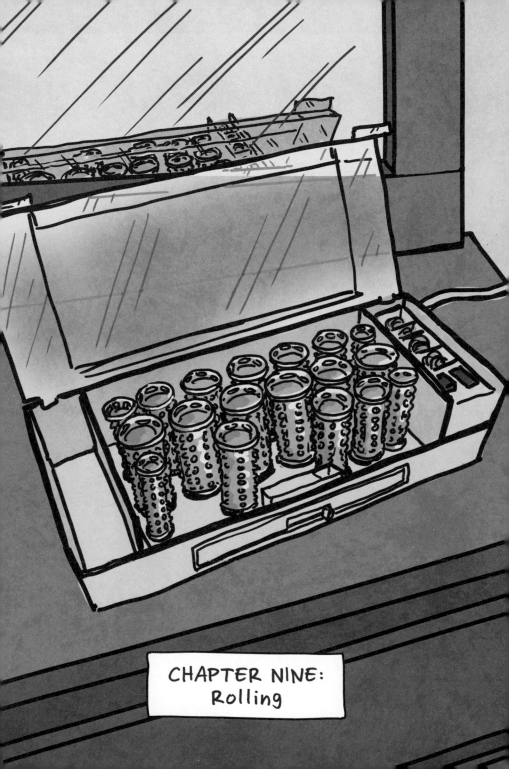

CHAPTER NINE:
Rolling

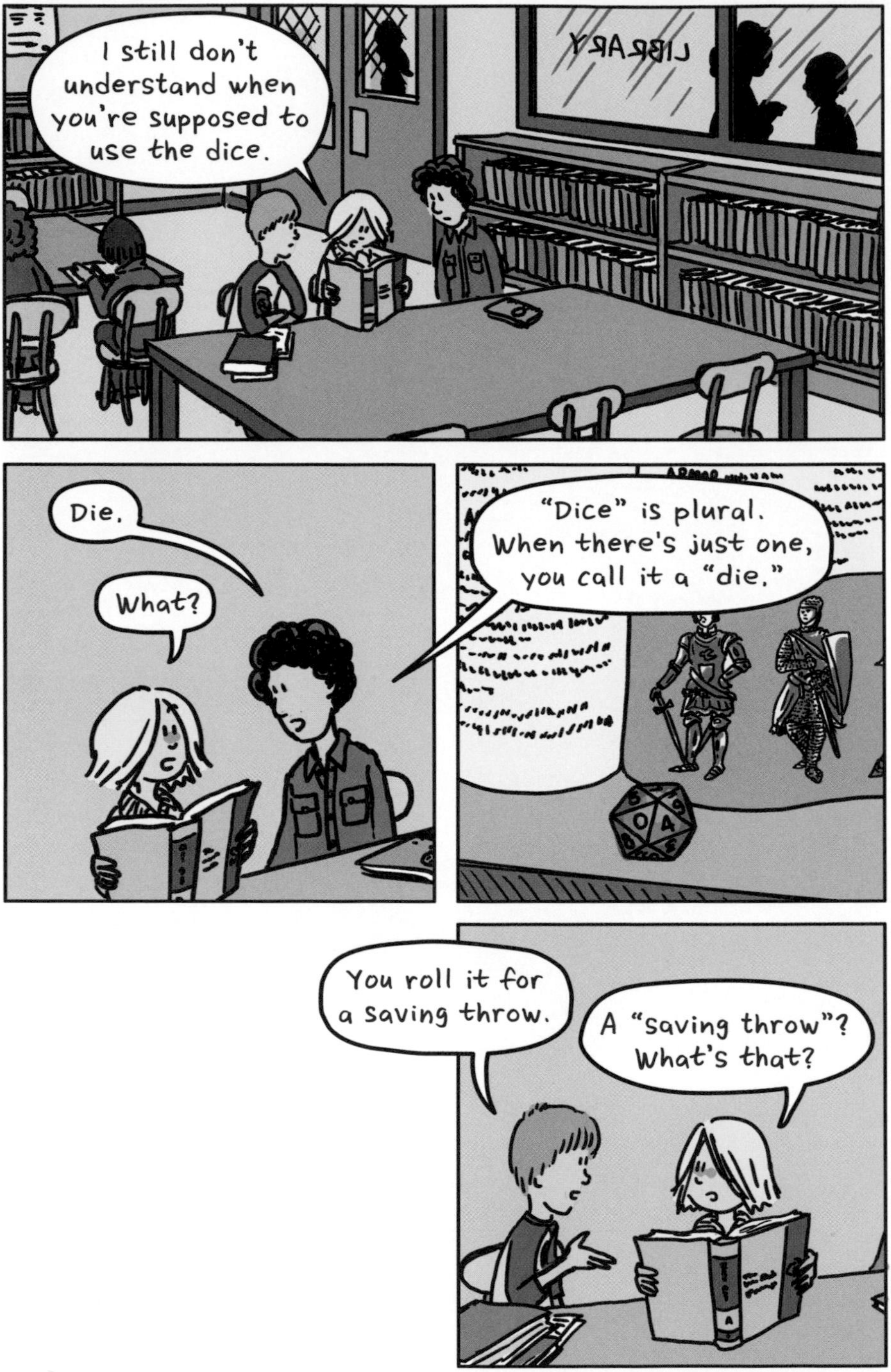
I still don't understand when you're supposed to use the dice.
LIBRARY
Die.
What?
"Dice" is plural. When there's just one, you call it a "die."
You roll it for a saving throw.
A "saving throw"? What's that?

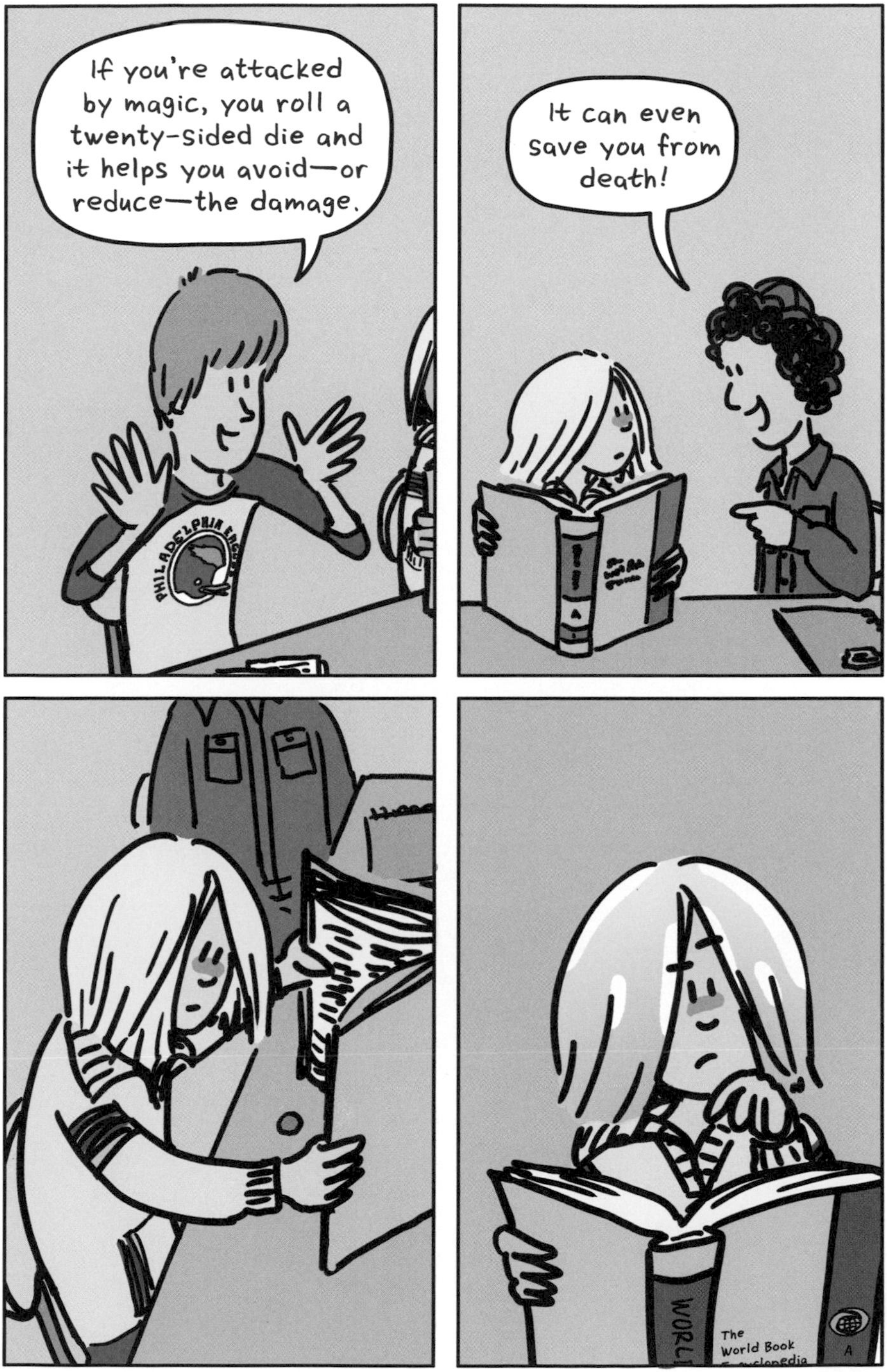
If you're attacked by magic, you roll a twenty-sided die and it helps you avoid—or reduce—the damage.
It can even save you from death!
The World Book

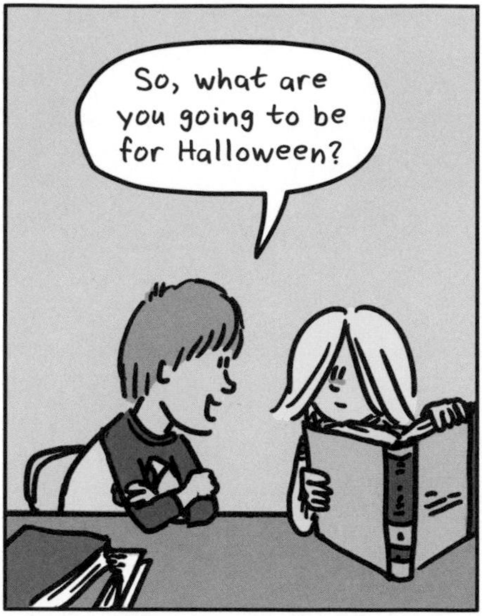
So, what are you going to be for Halloween?

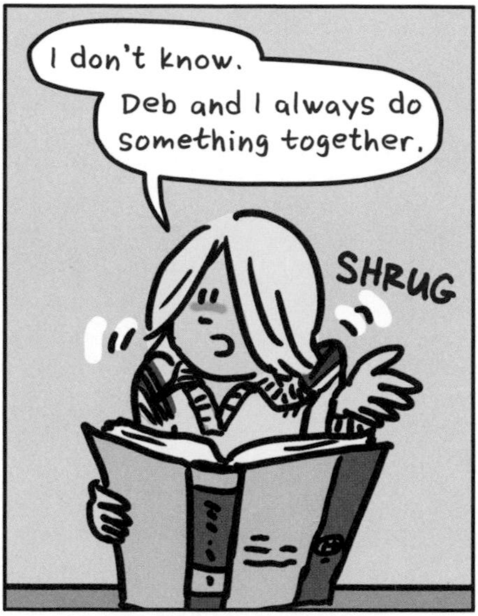
I don't know.
Deb and I always do something together.
SHRUG

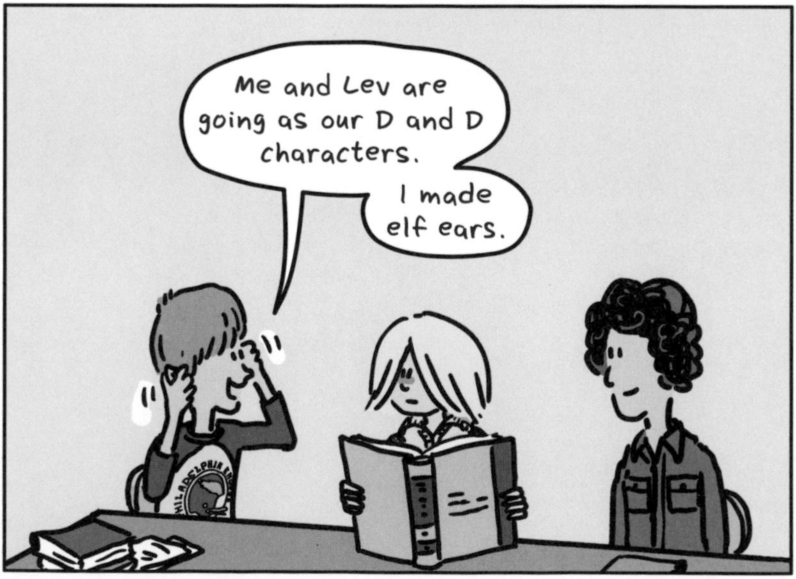
Me and Lev are going as our D and D characters.
I made elf ears.

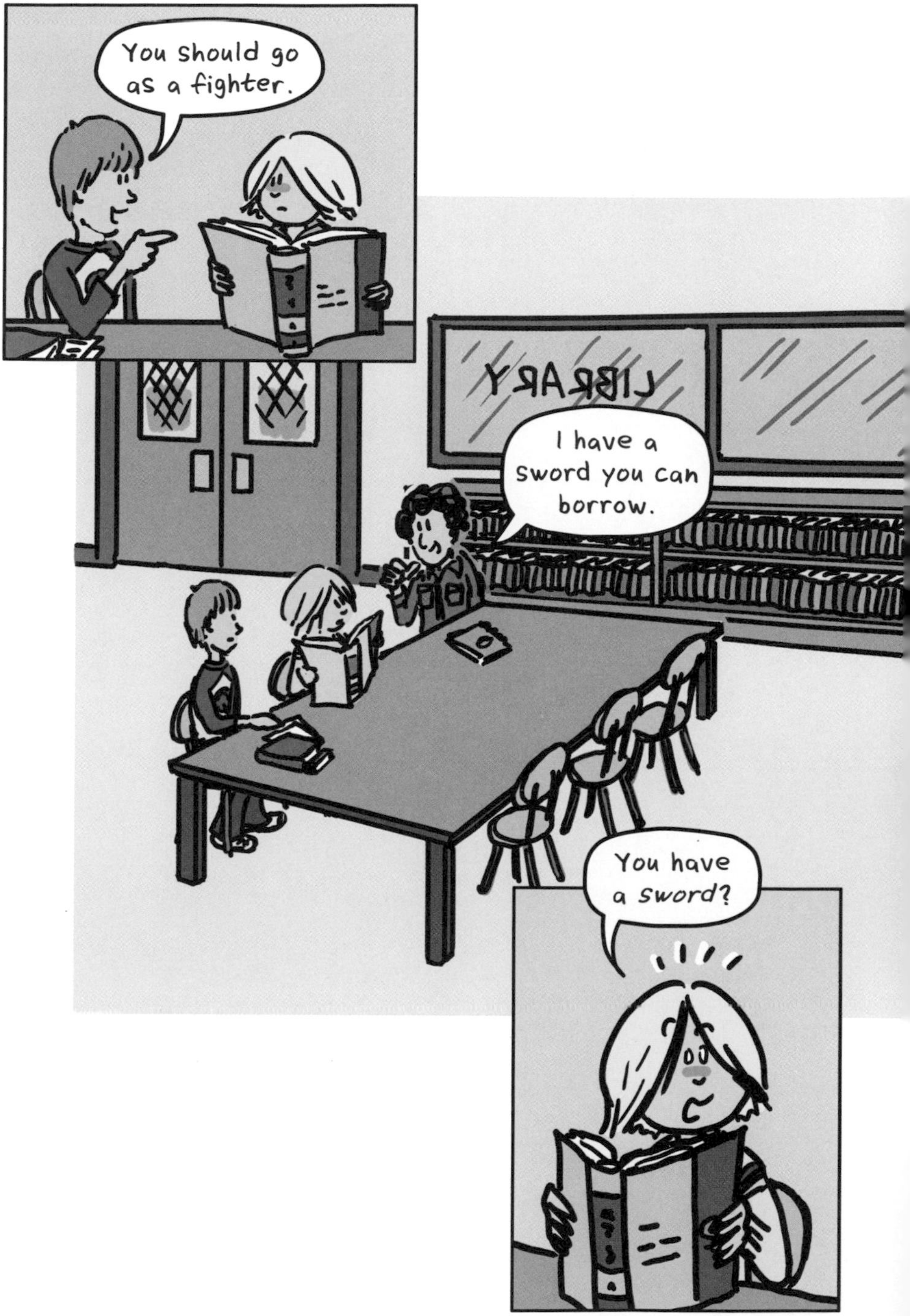
You should go as a fighter.
LIBRARY
I have a sword you can borrow.
You have a *sword*?

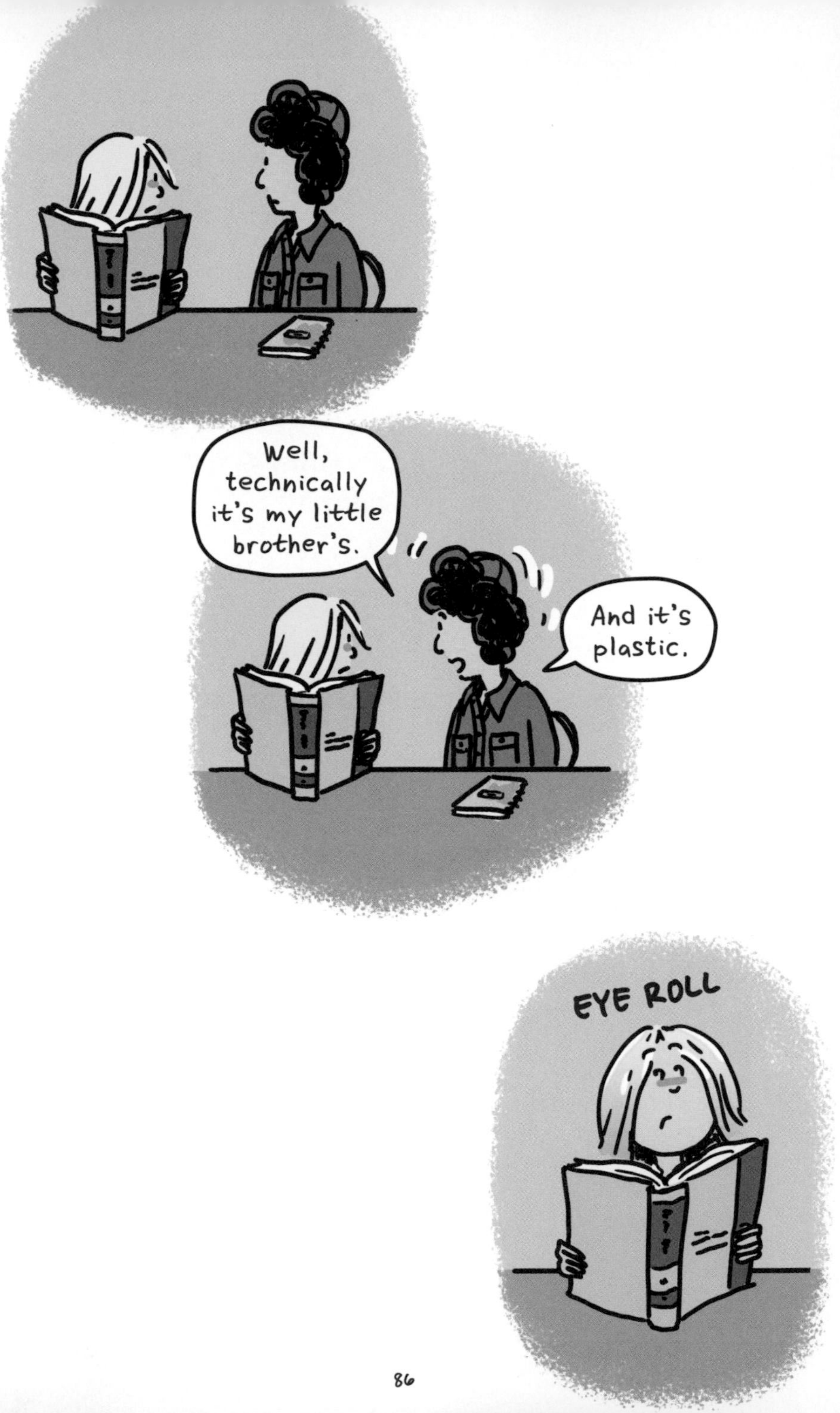
Well, technically it's my little brother's.
And it's plastic.
EYE ROLL

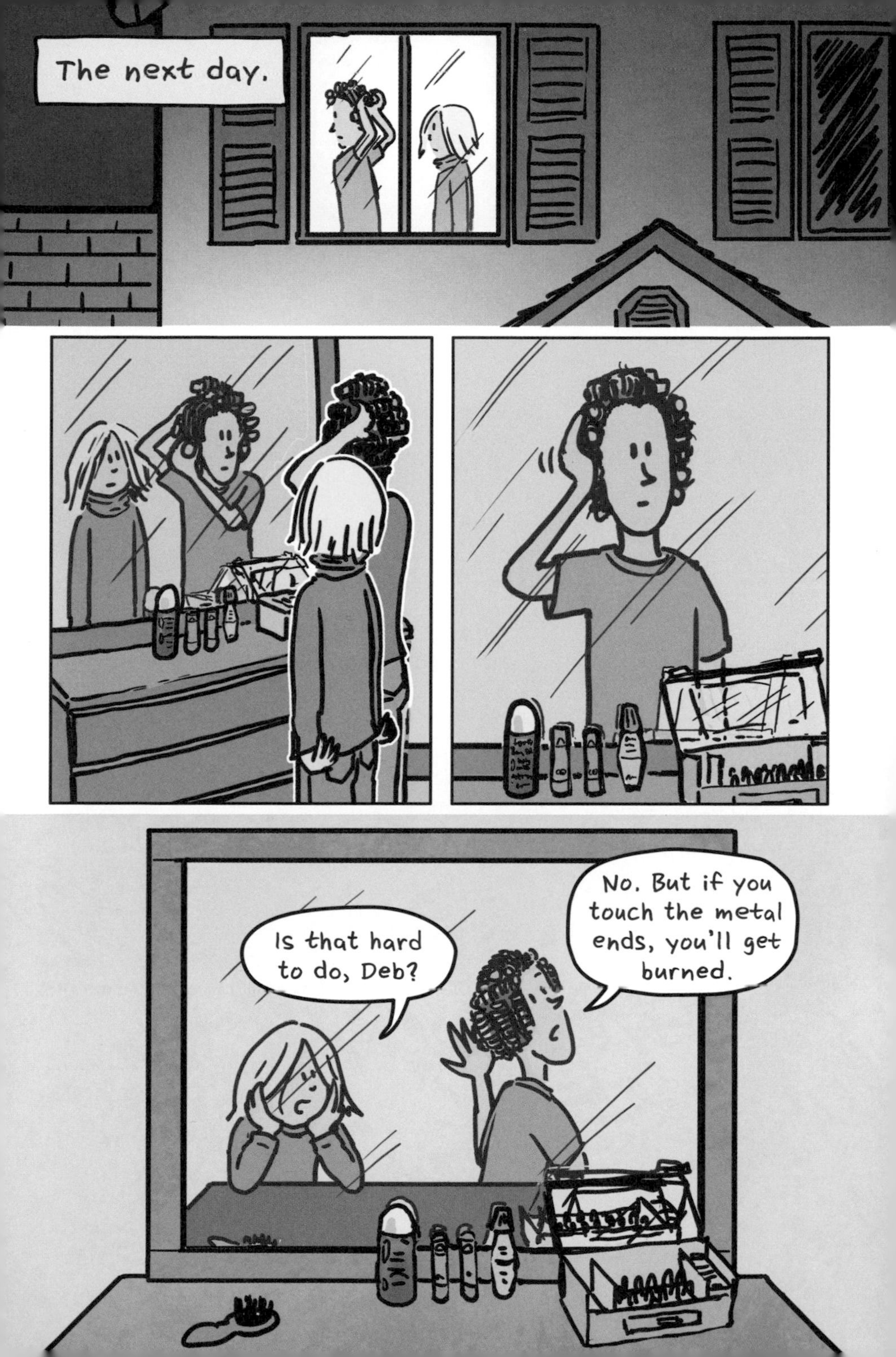
The next day.
Is that hard to do, Deb?
No. But if you touch the metal ends, you'll get burned.

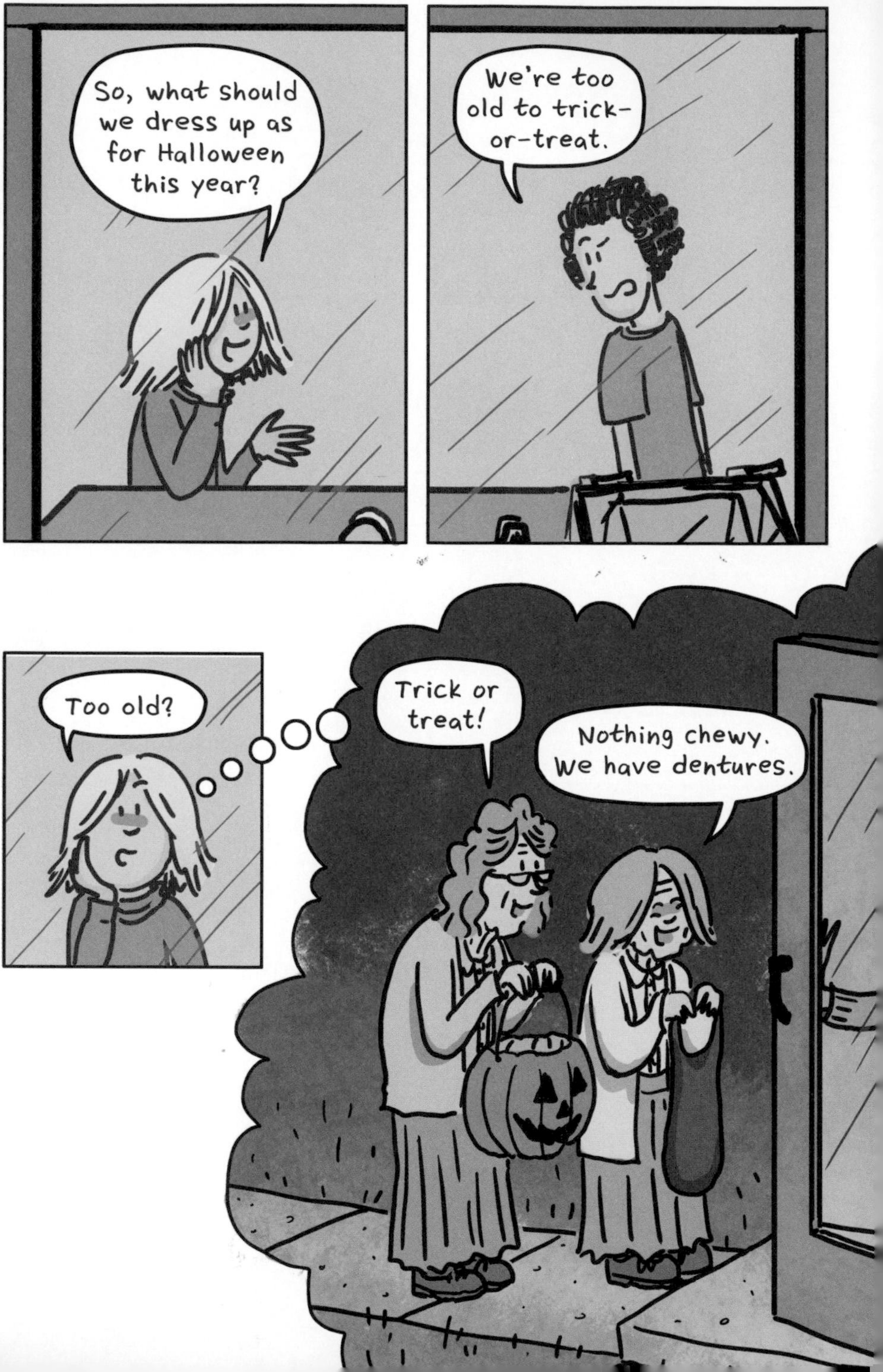
So, what should we dress up as for Halloween this year?
We're too old to trick-or-treat.
Too old?
Trick or treat!
Nothing chewy. We have dentures.

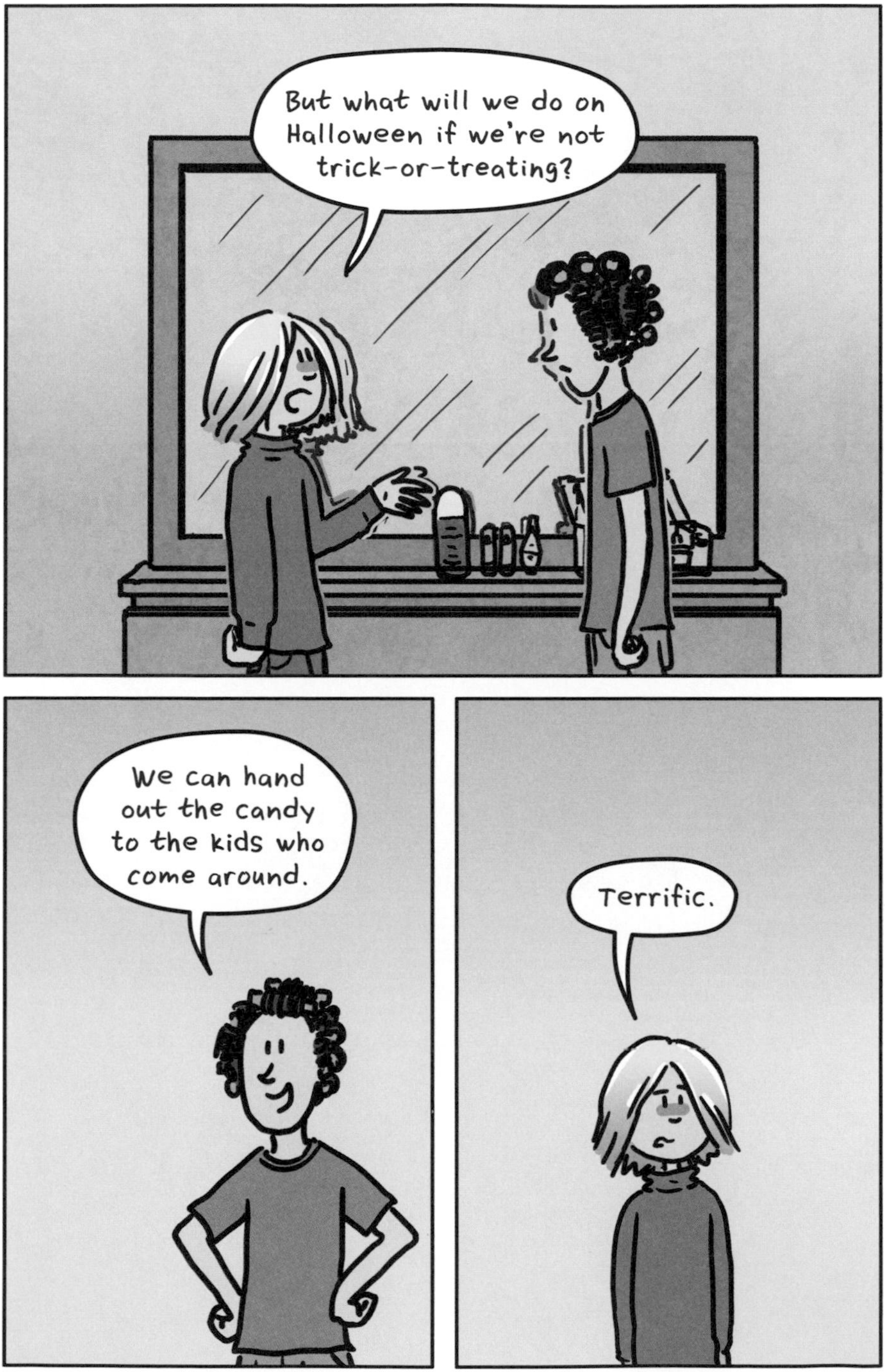
But what will we do on Halloween if we're not trick-or-treating?
We can hand out the candy to the kids who come around.
Terrific.

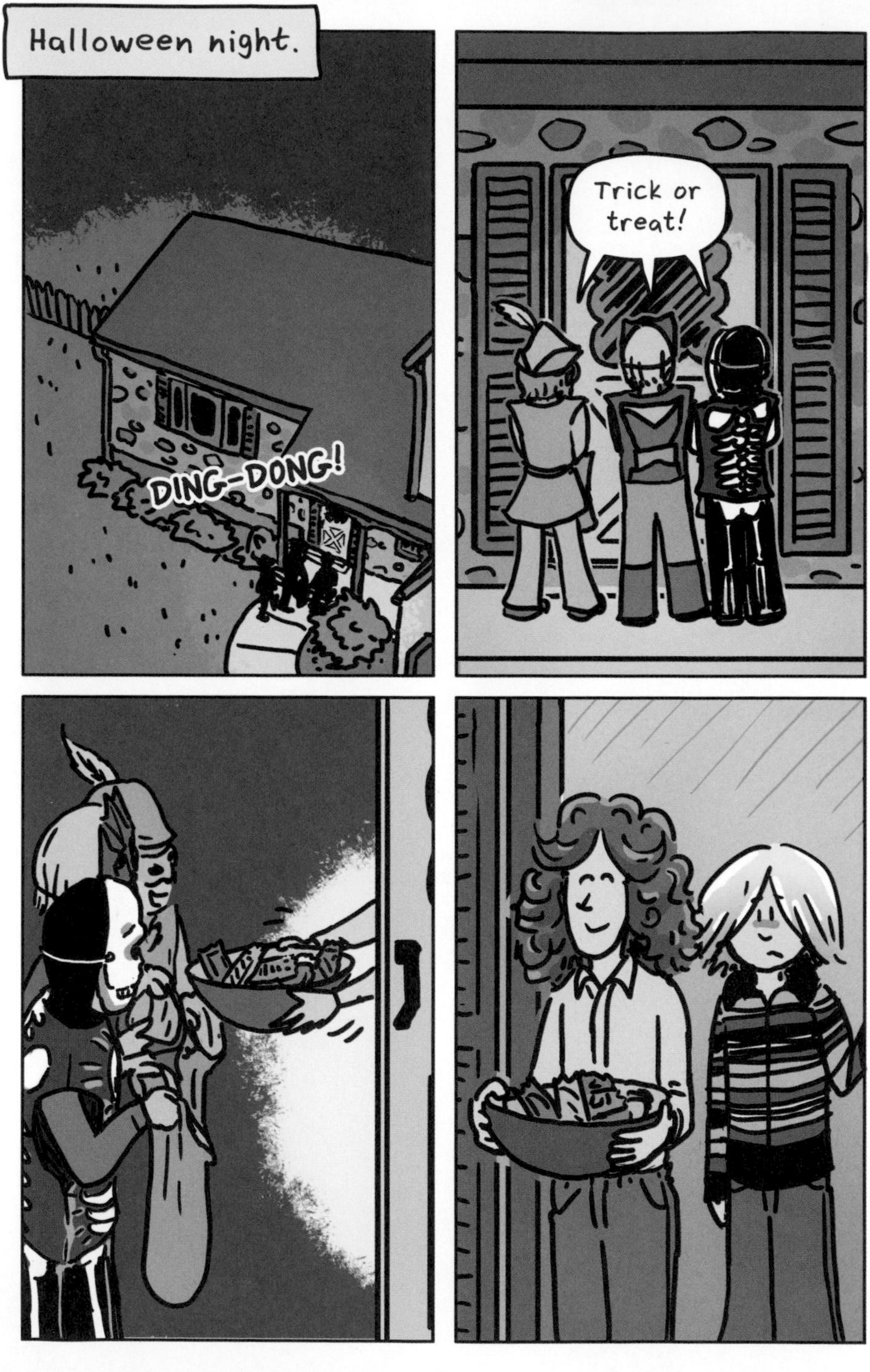
Halloween night.
DING-DONG!
Trick or treat!

CHAPTER TEN:
Bump

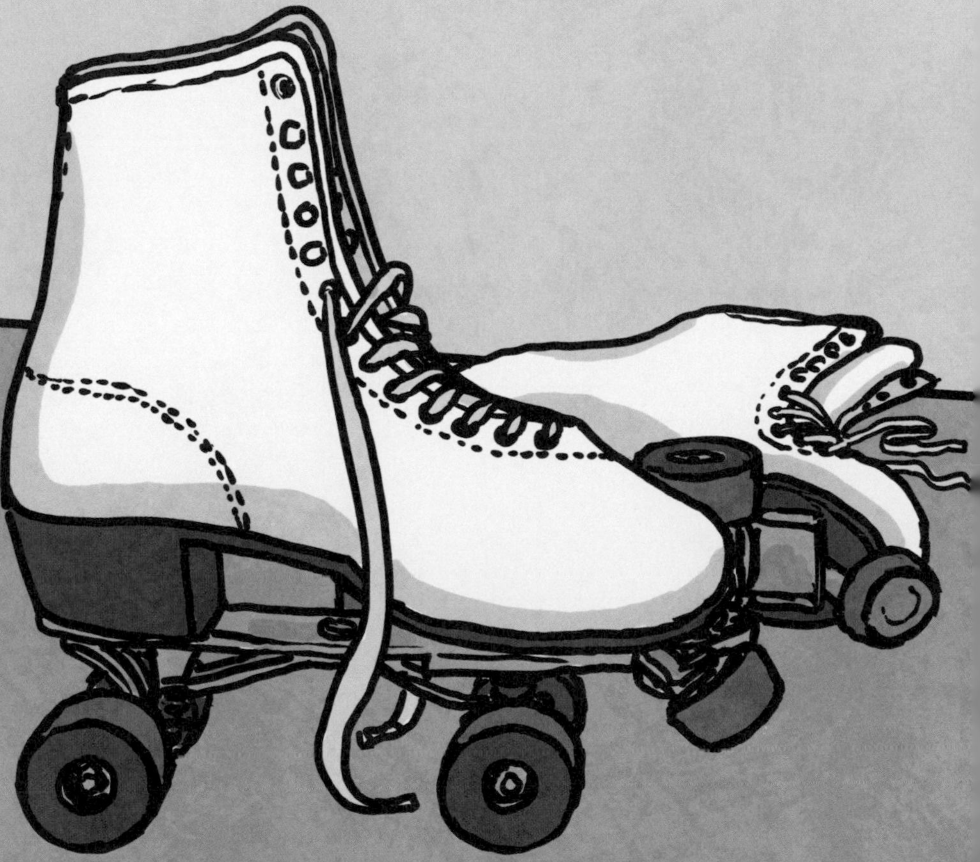

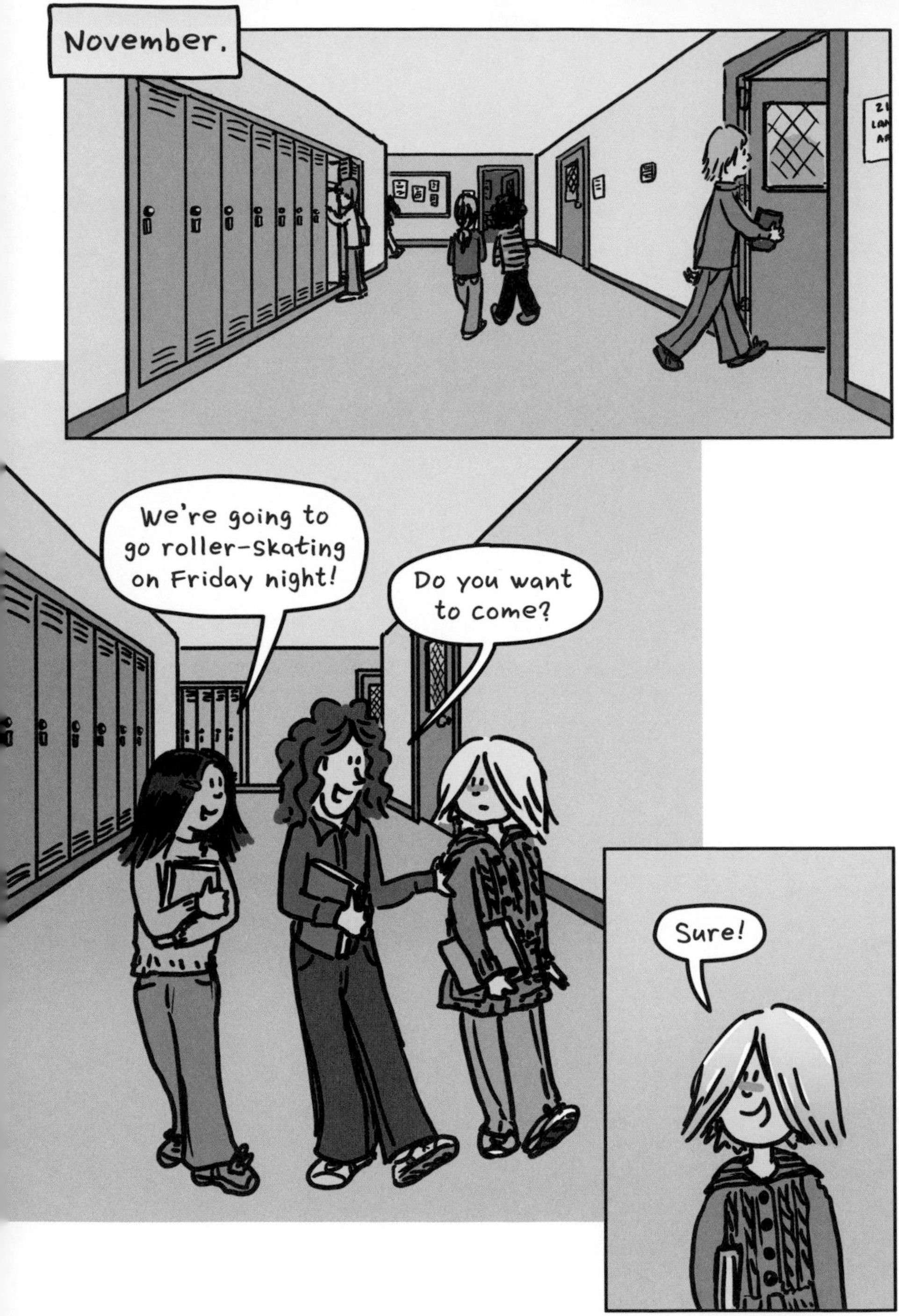
November.
We're going to go roller-skating on Friday night!
Do you want to come?
Sure!

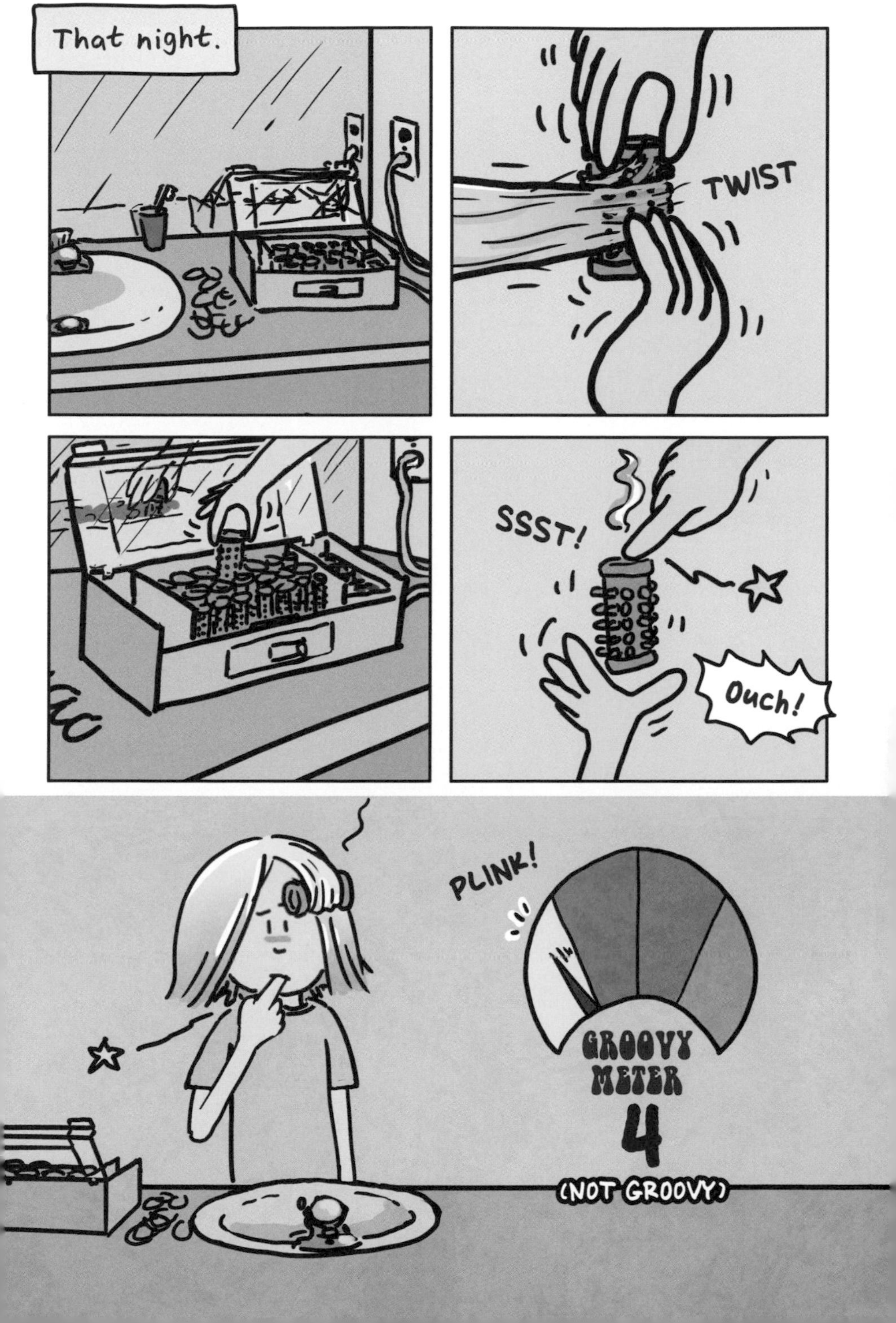
That night.
TWIST
SSST!
Ouch!
PLINK!
GROOVY METER
4
(NOT GROOVY)

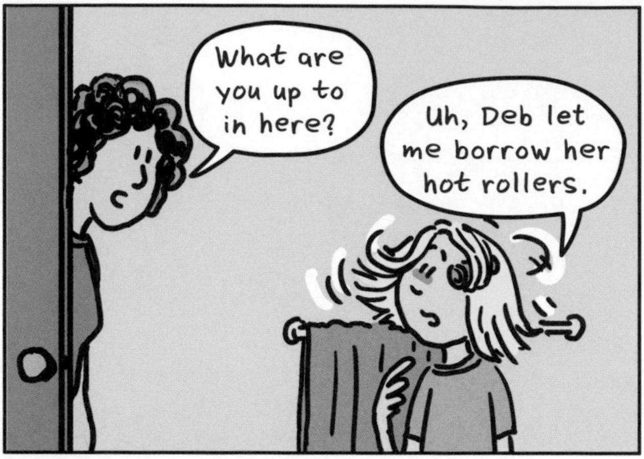
What are you up to in here?
Uh, Deb let me borrow her hot rollers.

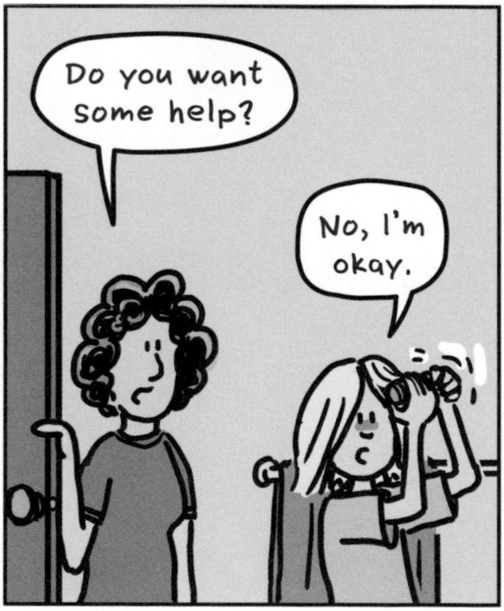
Do you want some help?
No, I'm okay.

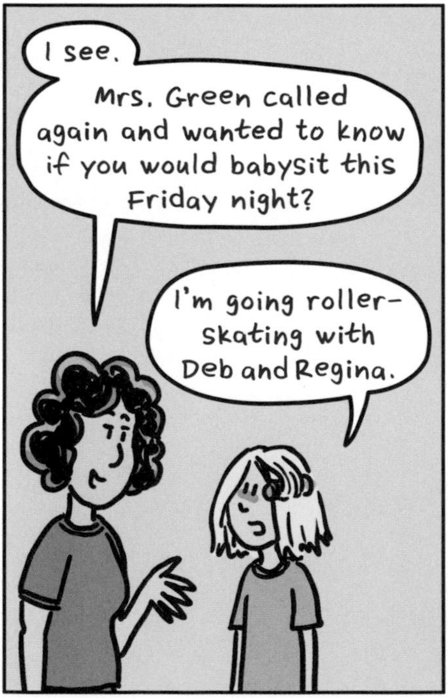
I see.
Mrs. Green called again and wanted to know if you would babysit this Friday night?
I'm going roller-skating with Deb and Regina.

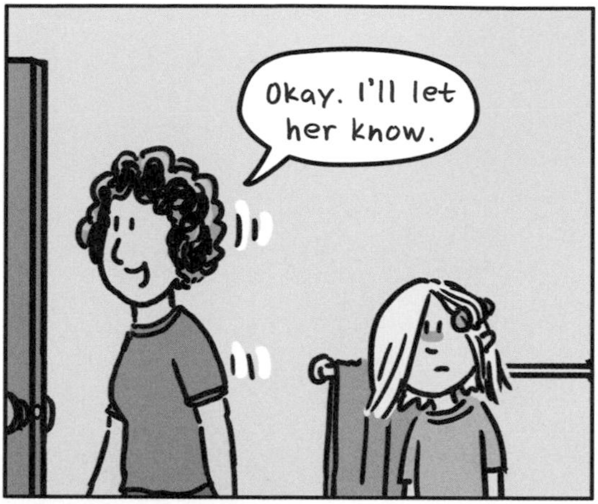
Okay. I'll let her know.

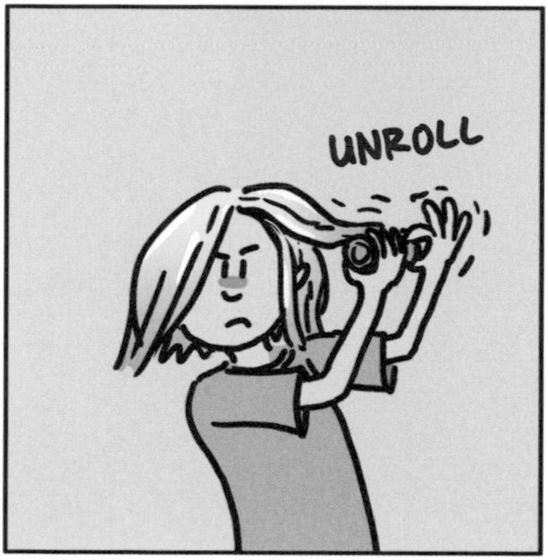
UNROLL

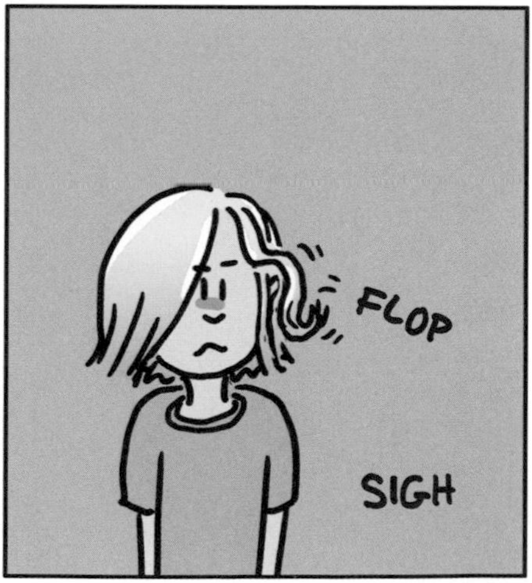
FLOP
SIGH

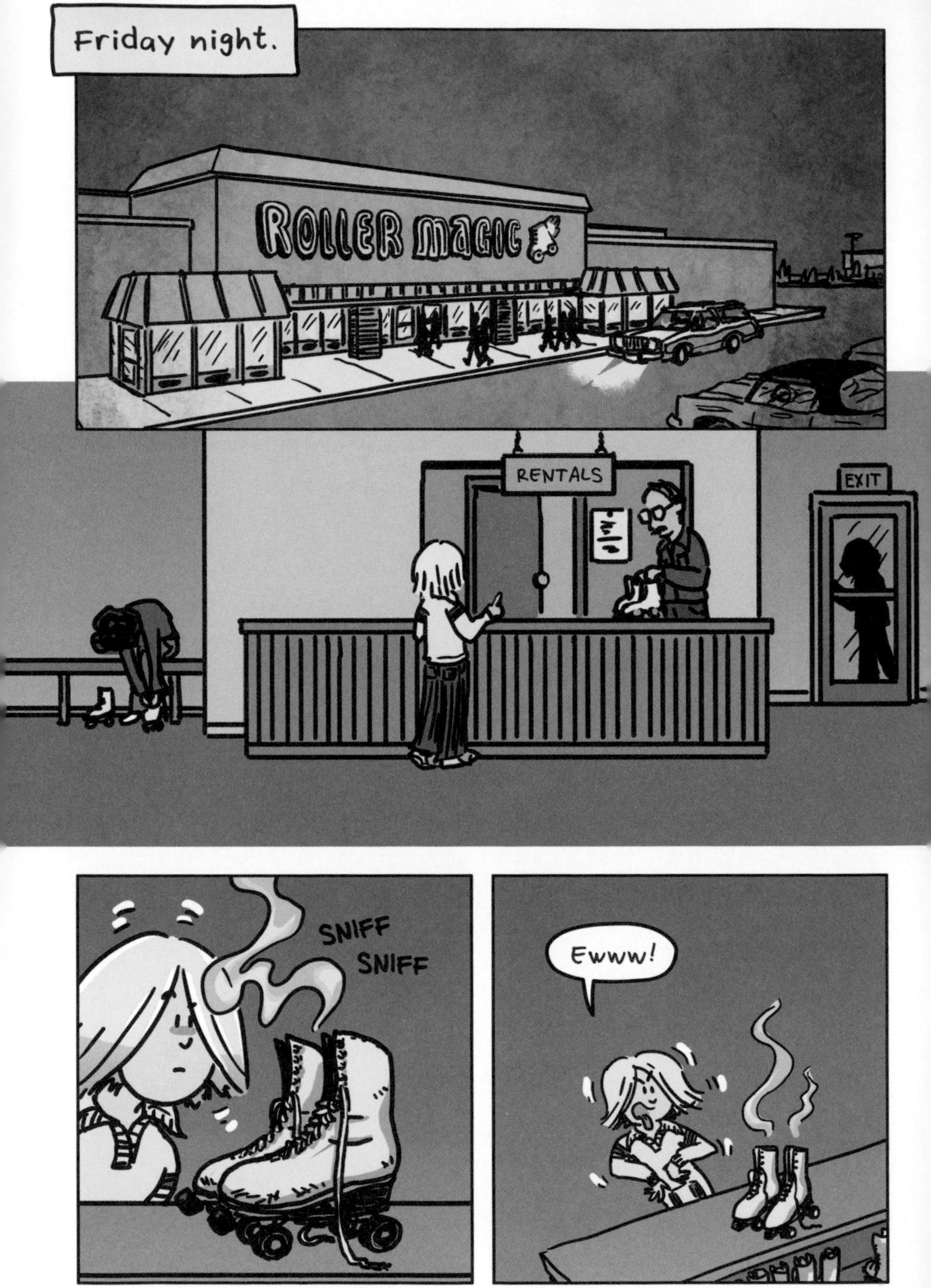
Friday night.
ROLLER MAGIC
RENTALS
EXIT
SNIFF
SNIFF
Ewww!

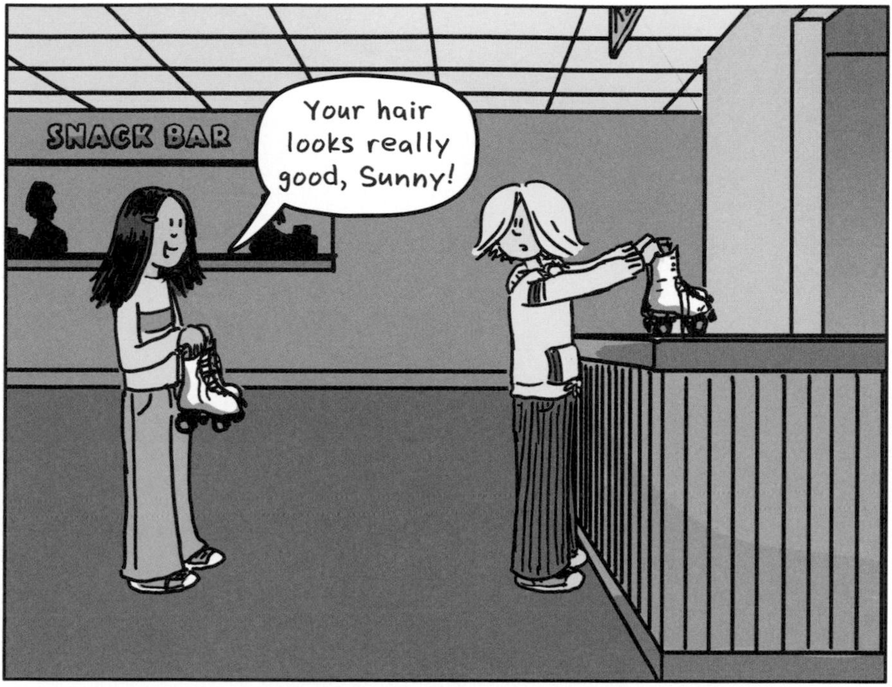
SNACK BAR
Your hair looks really good, Sunny!

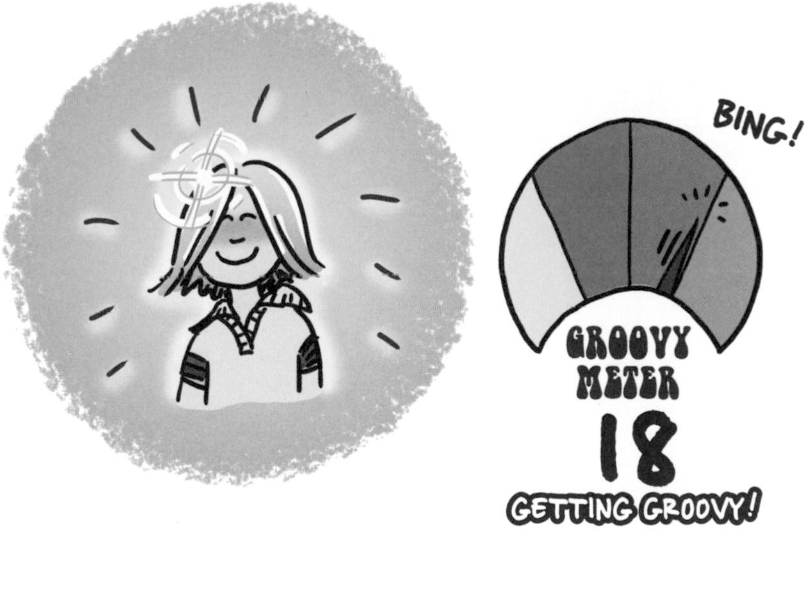
BING!
GROOVY METER
18
GETTING GROOVY!

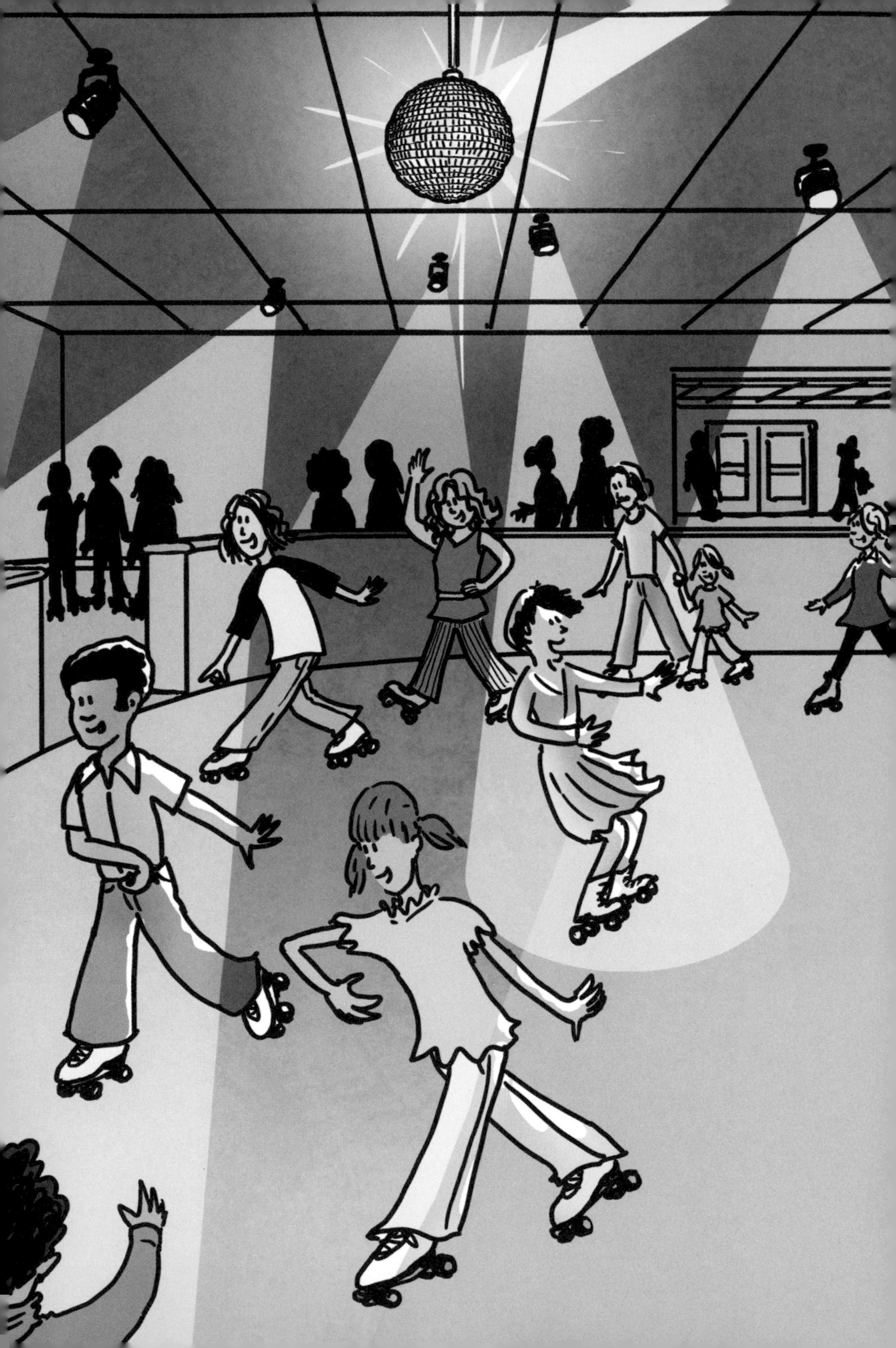

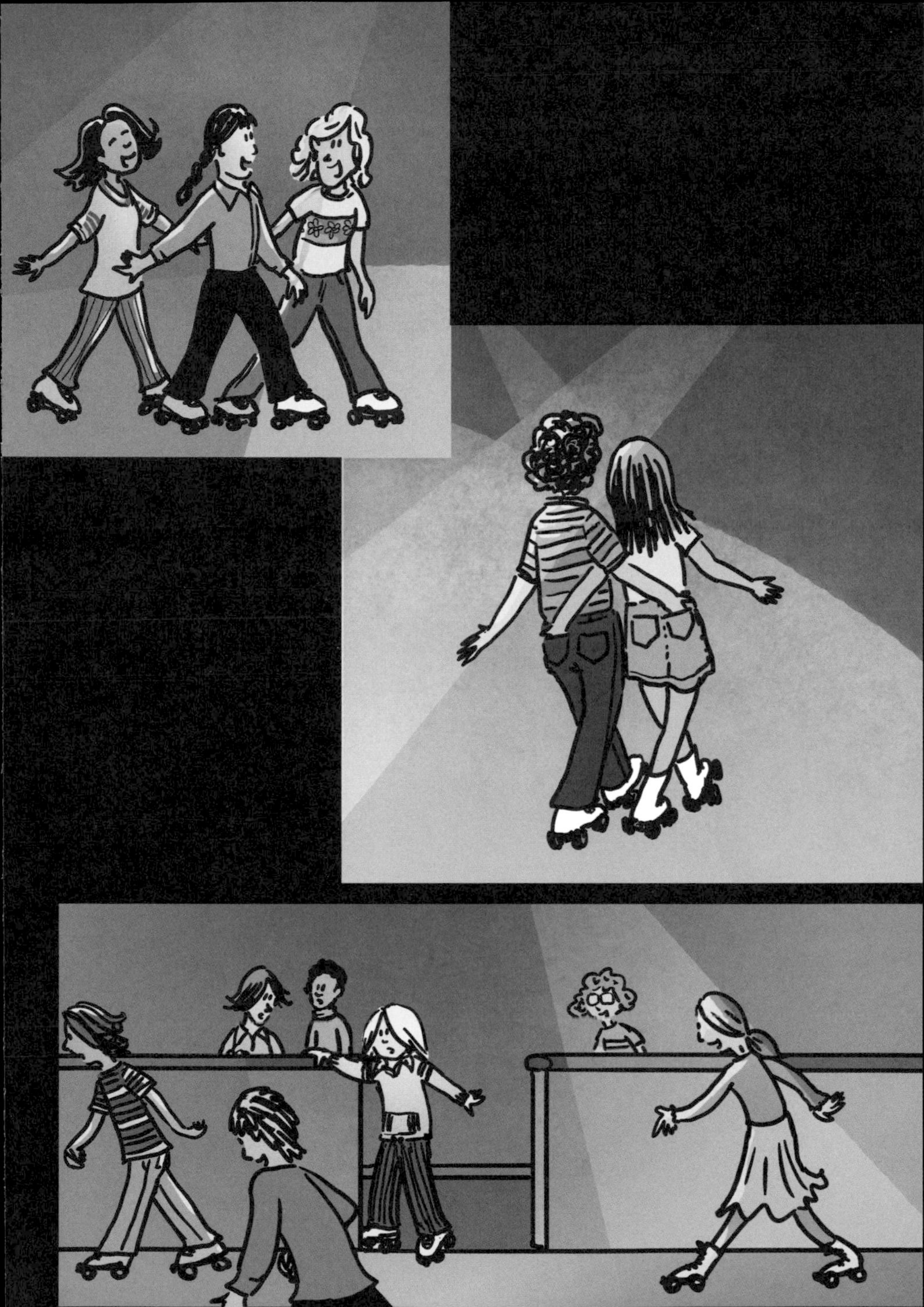

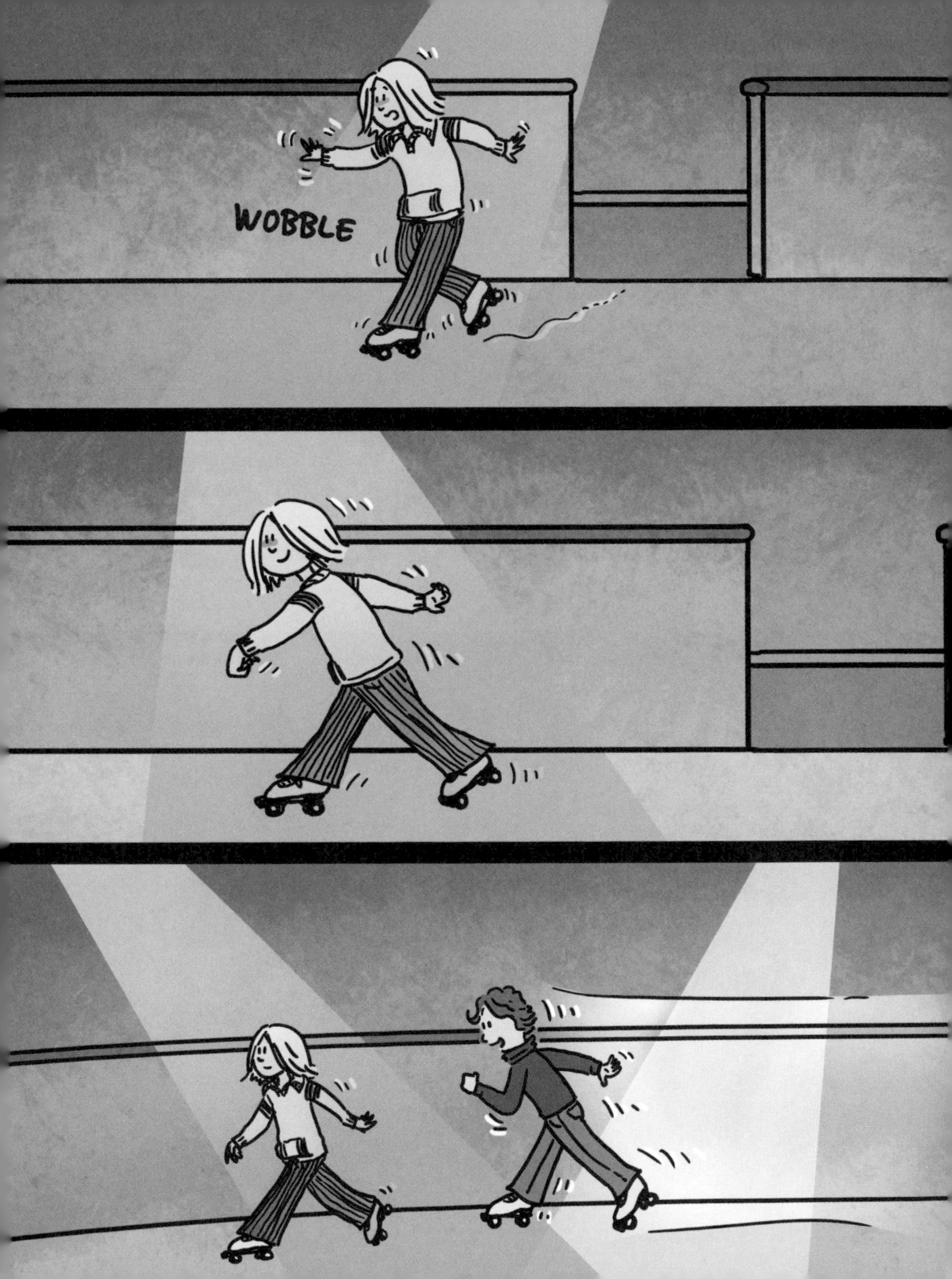
WOBBLE

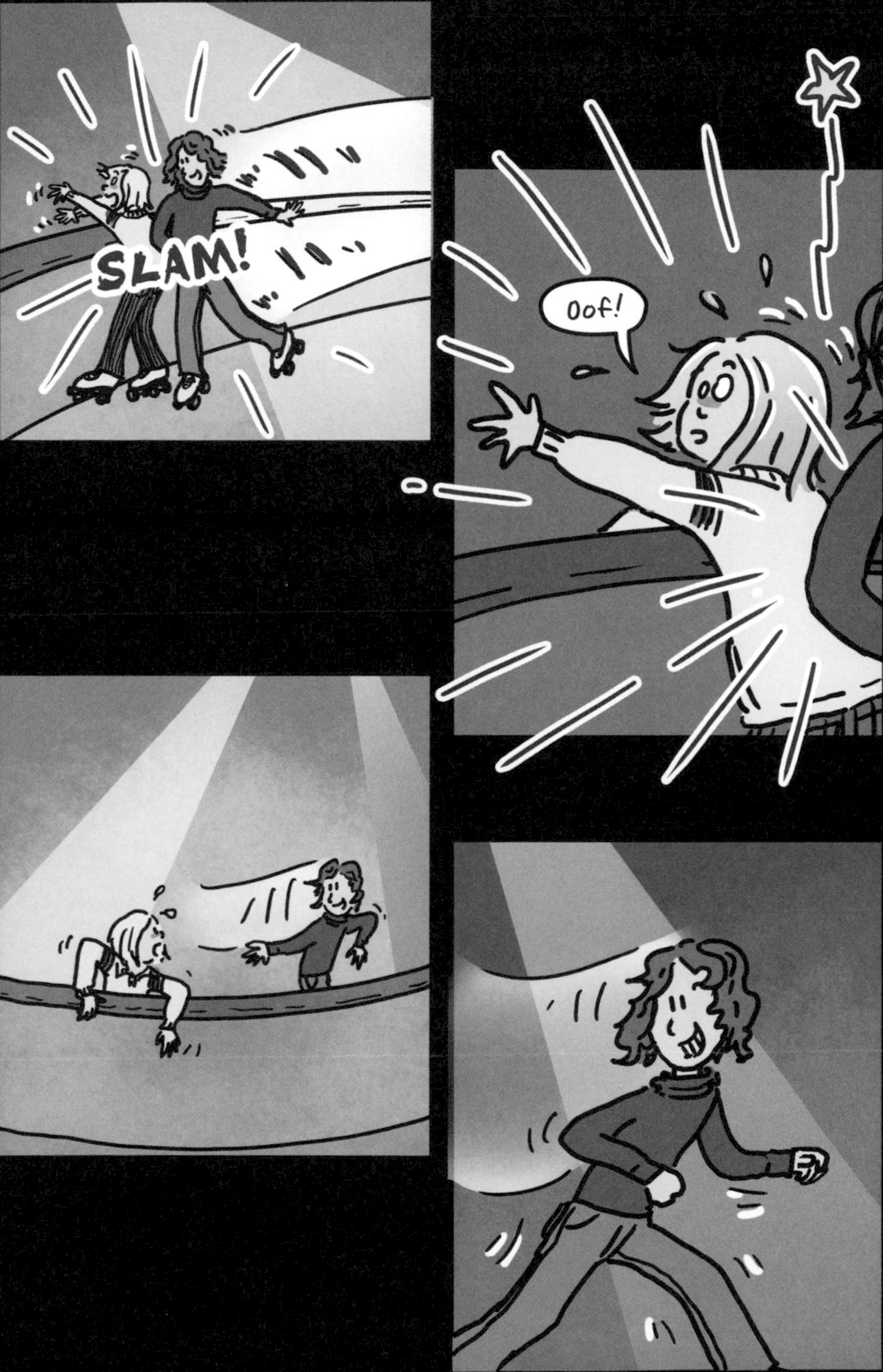
SLAM!
Oof!

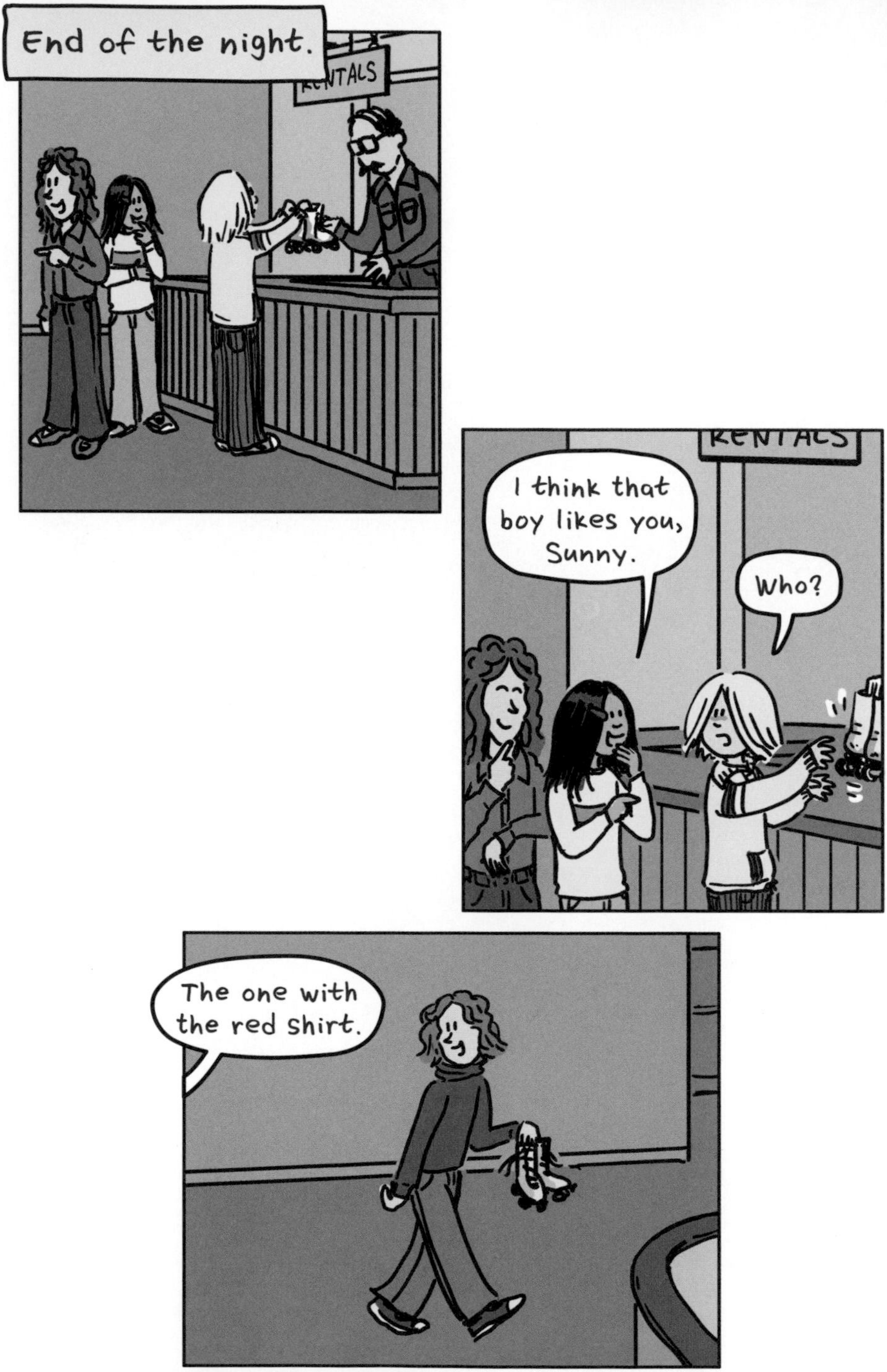
End of the night.
RENTALS
RENTALS
I think that boy likes you, Sunny.
Who?
The one with the red shirt.

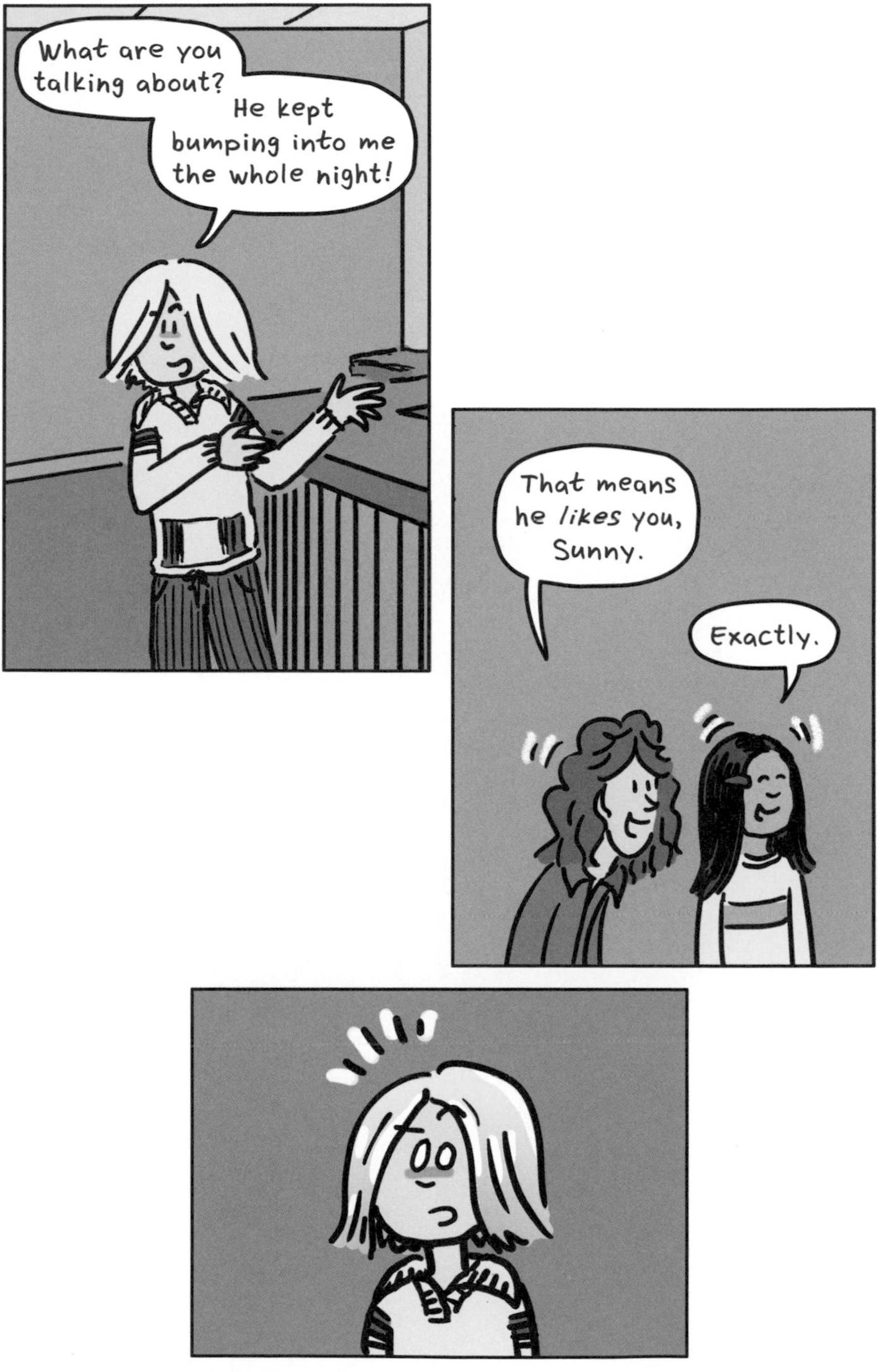
What are you talking about?
He kept bumping into me the whole night!
That means he *likes* you, Sunny.
Exactly.

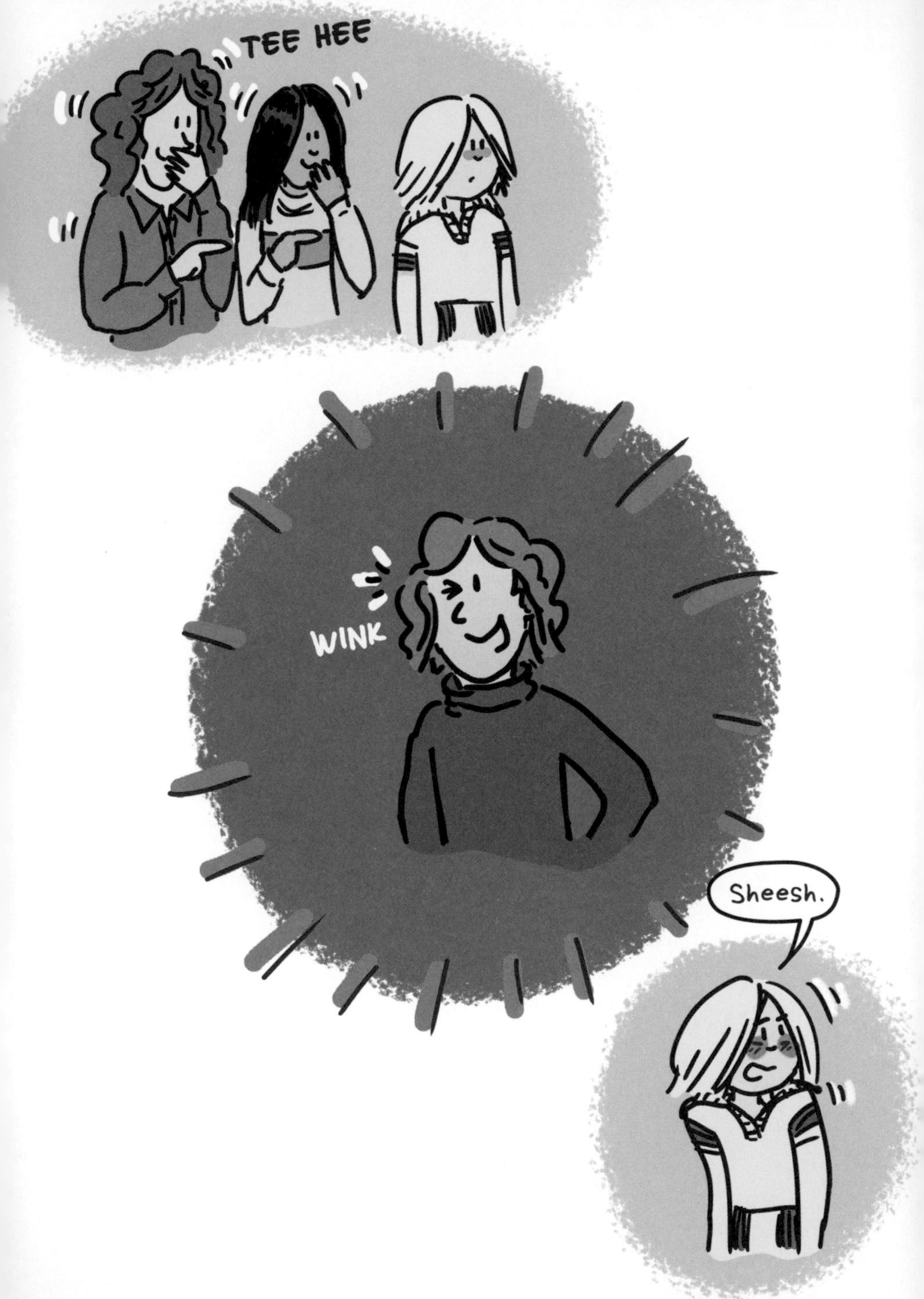
TEE HEE
WINK
Sheesh.

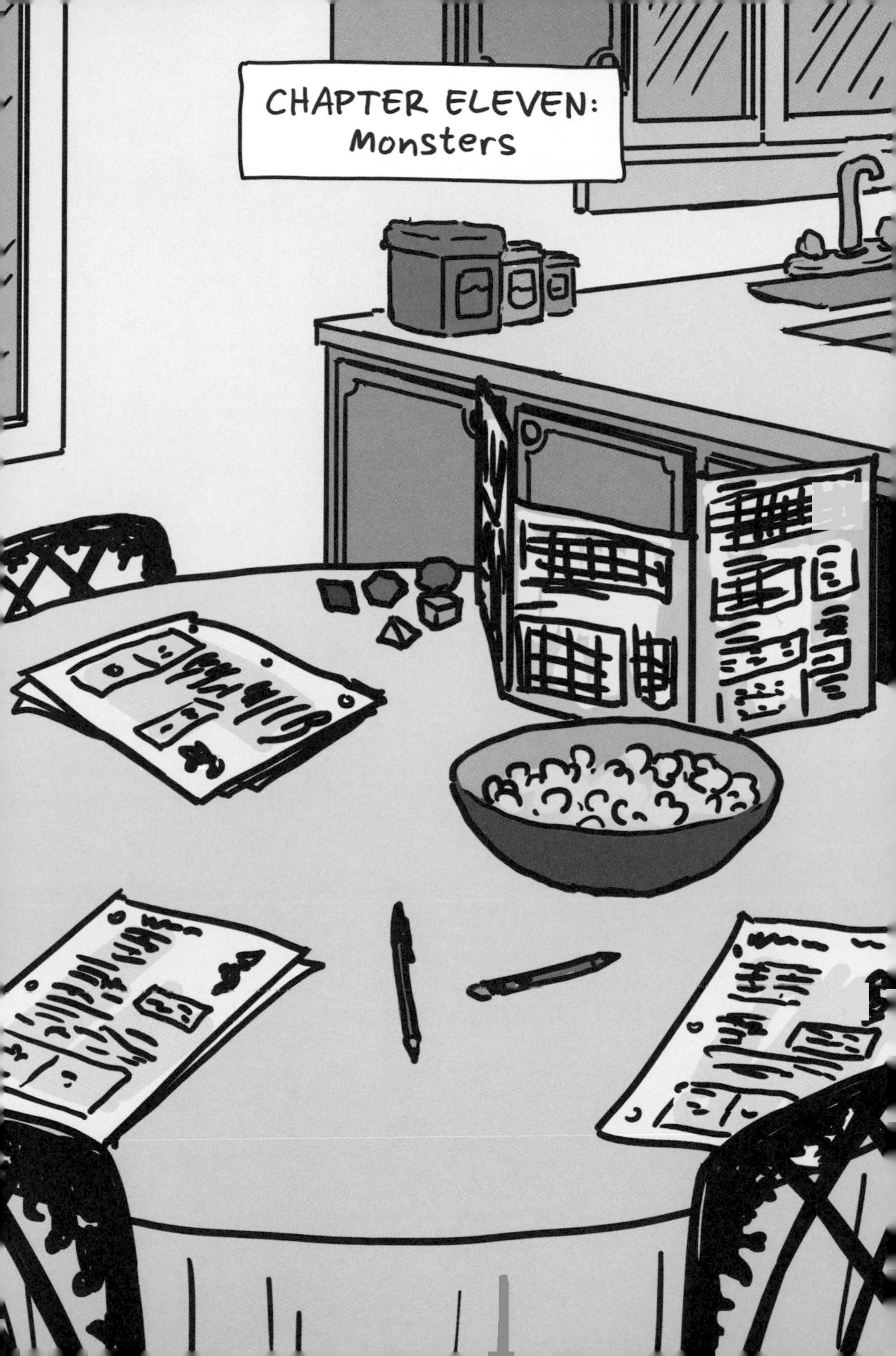
CHAPTER ELEVEN:
Monsters

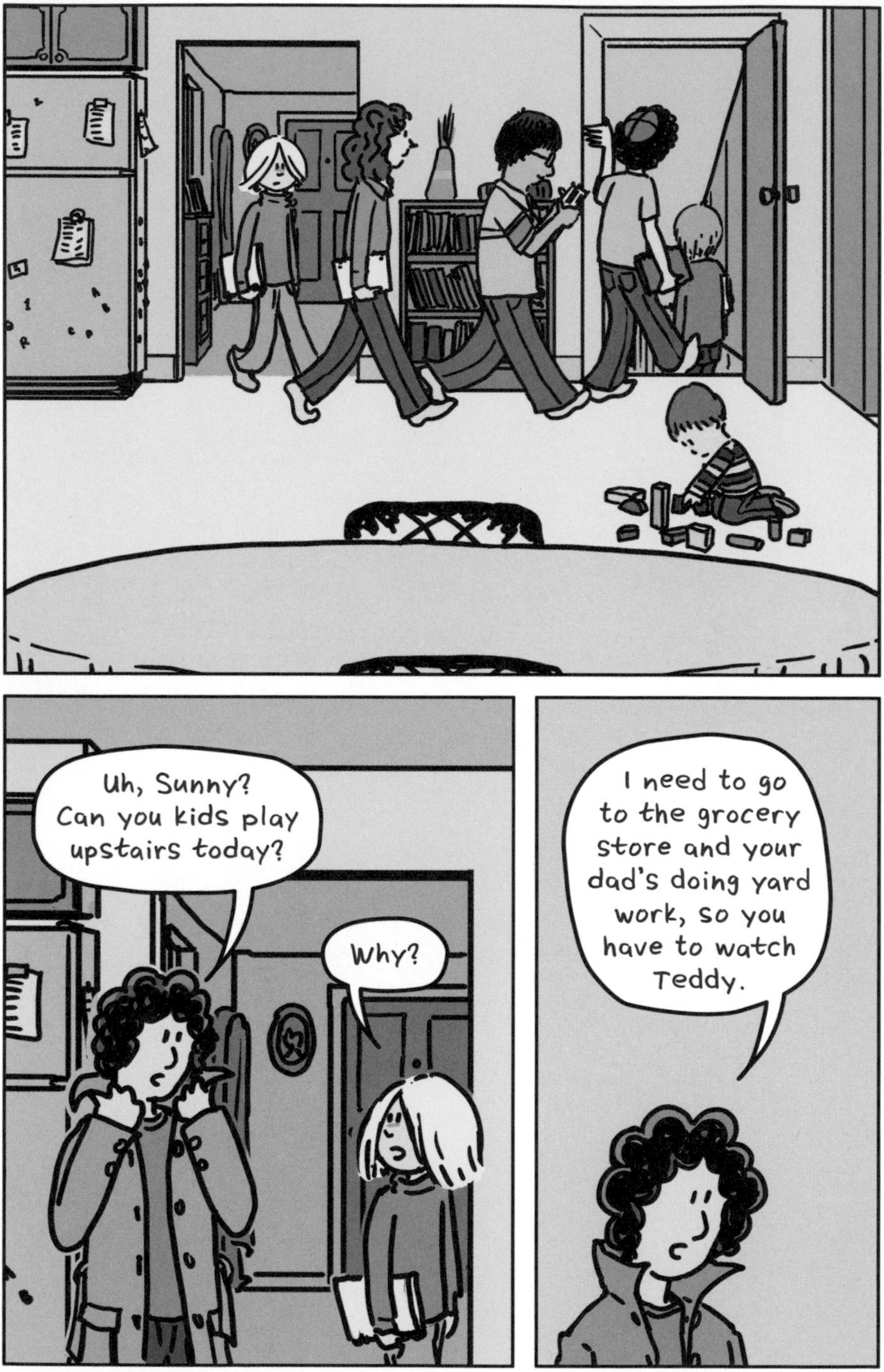
Uh, Sunny? Can you kids play upstairs today?
Why?
I need to go to the grocery store and your dad's doing yard work, so you have to watch Teddy.

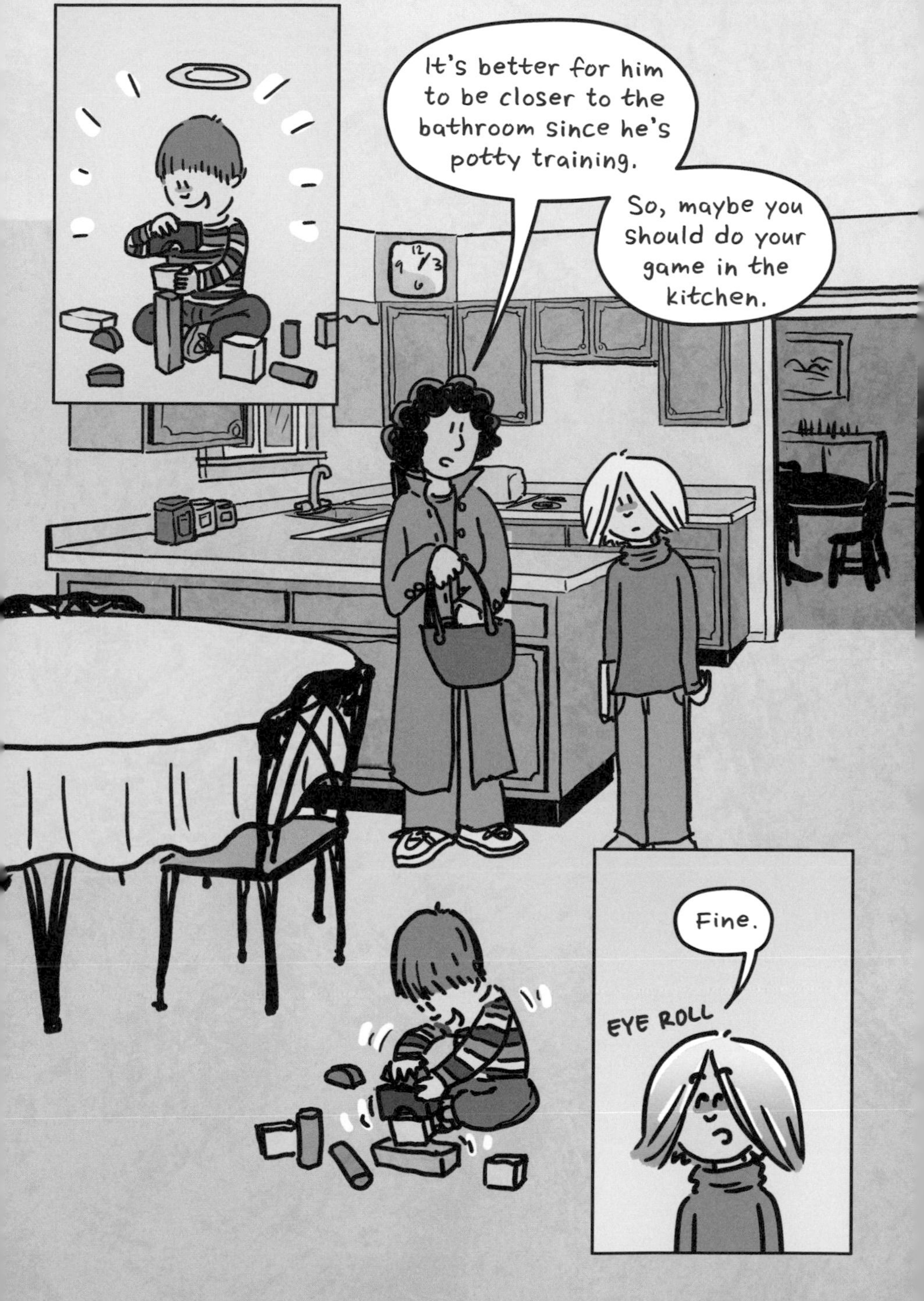

It's better for him to be closer to the bathroom since he's potty training.
So, maybe you should do your game in the kitchen.
Fine.
EYE ROLL

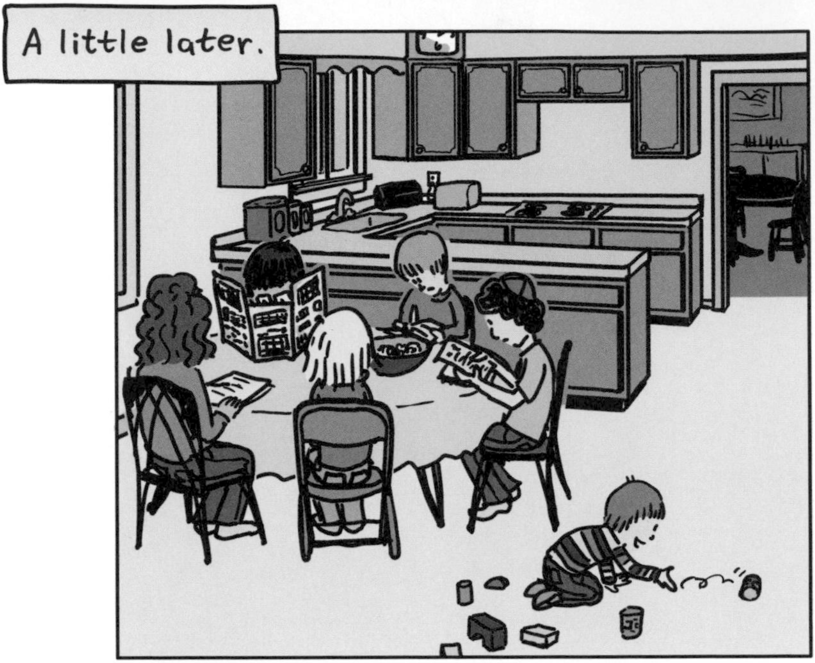
A little later.

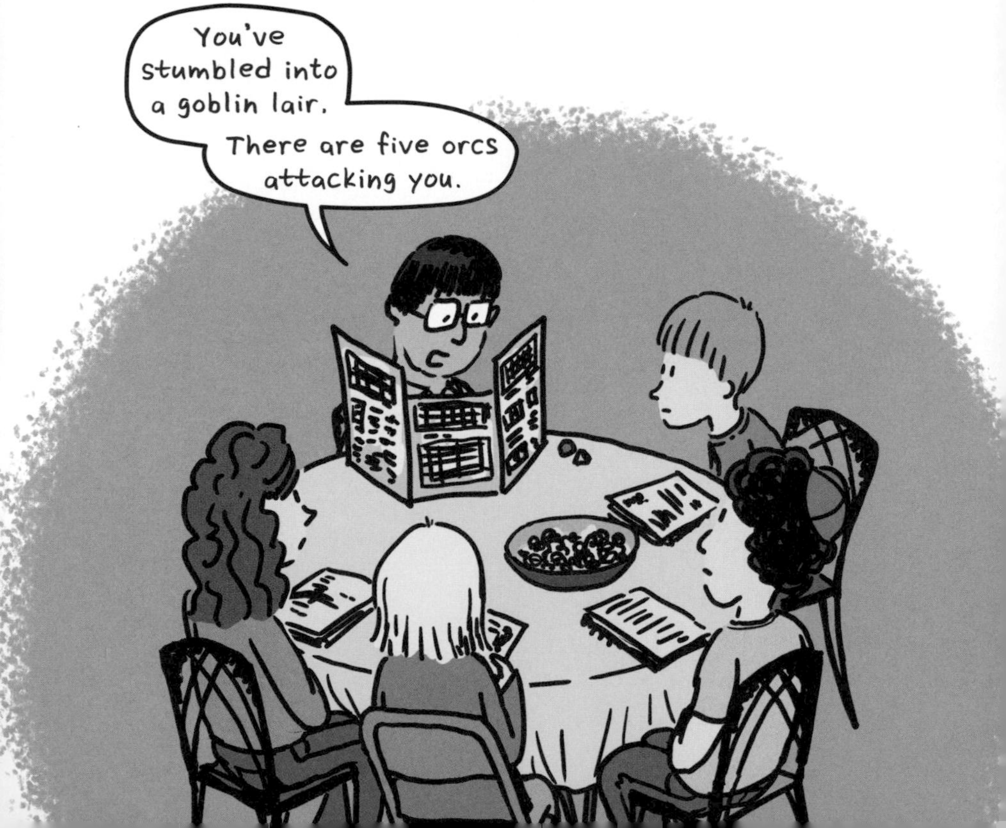
You've stumbled into a goblin lair.
There are five orcs attacking you.

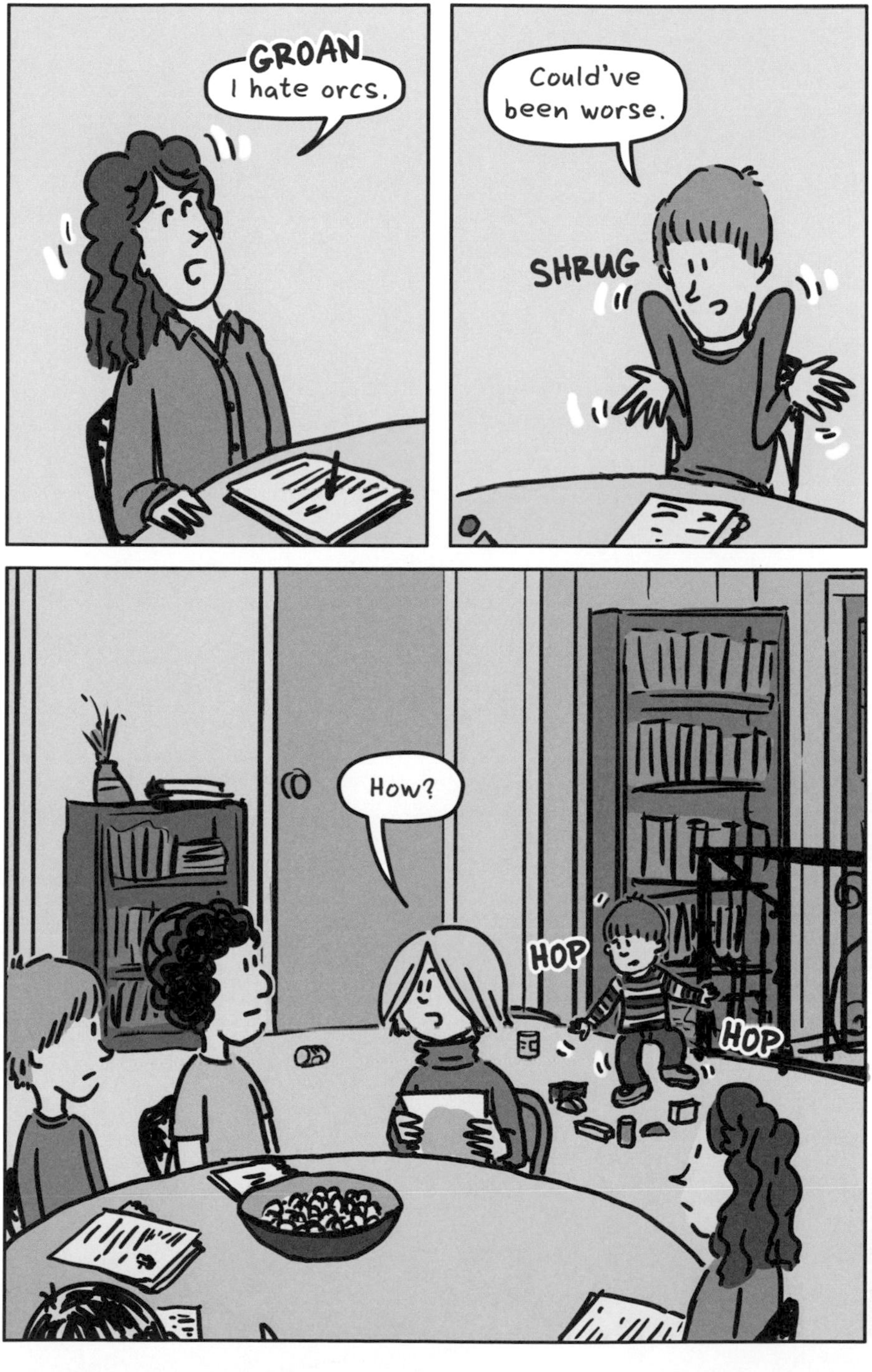
GROAN
I hate orcs.
Could've been worse.
SHRUG
How?
HOP
HOP

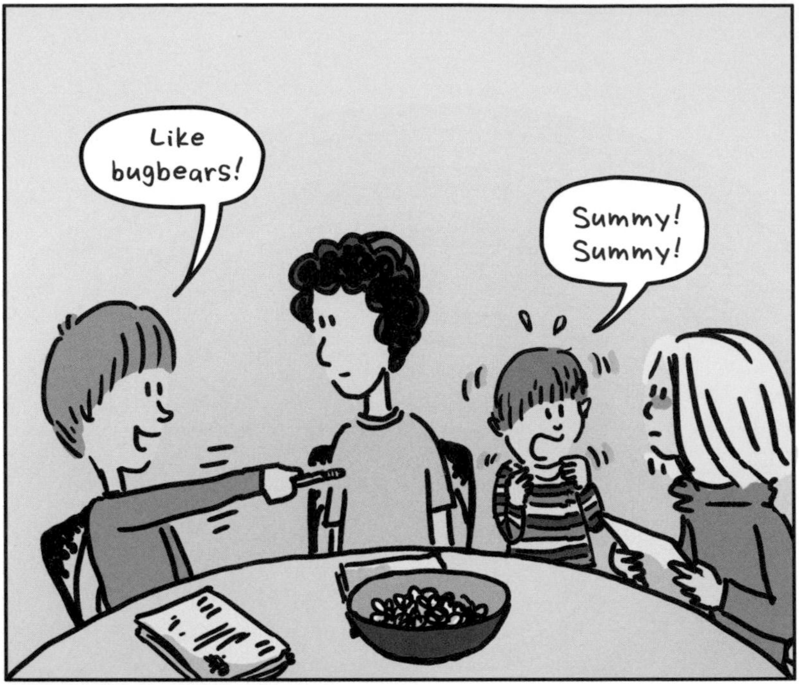
Like bugbears!
Summy! Summy!

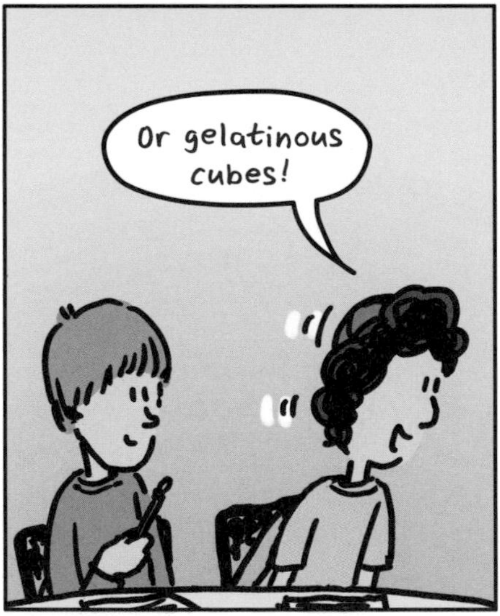
Or gelatinous cubes!

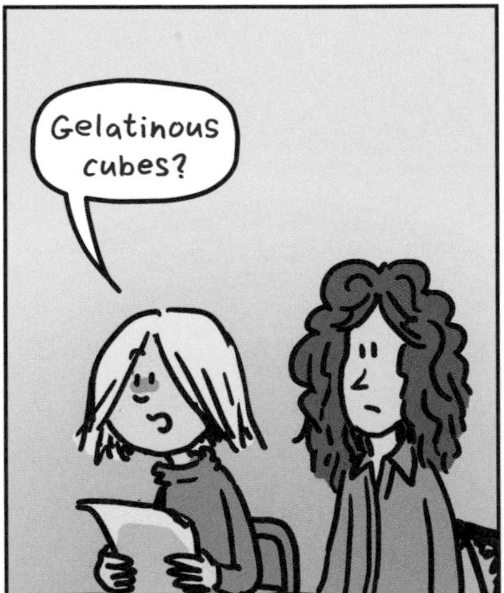
Gelatinous cubes?

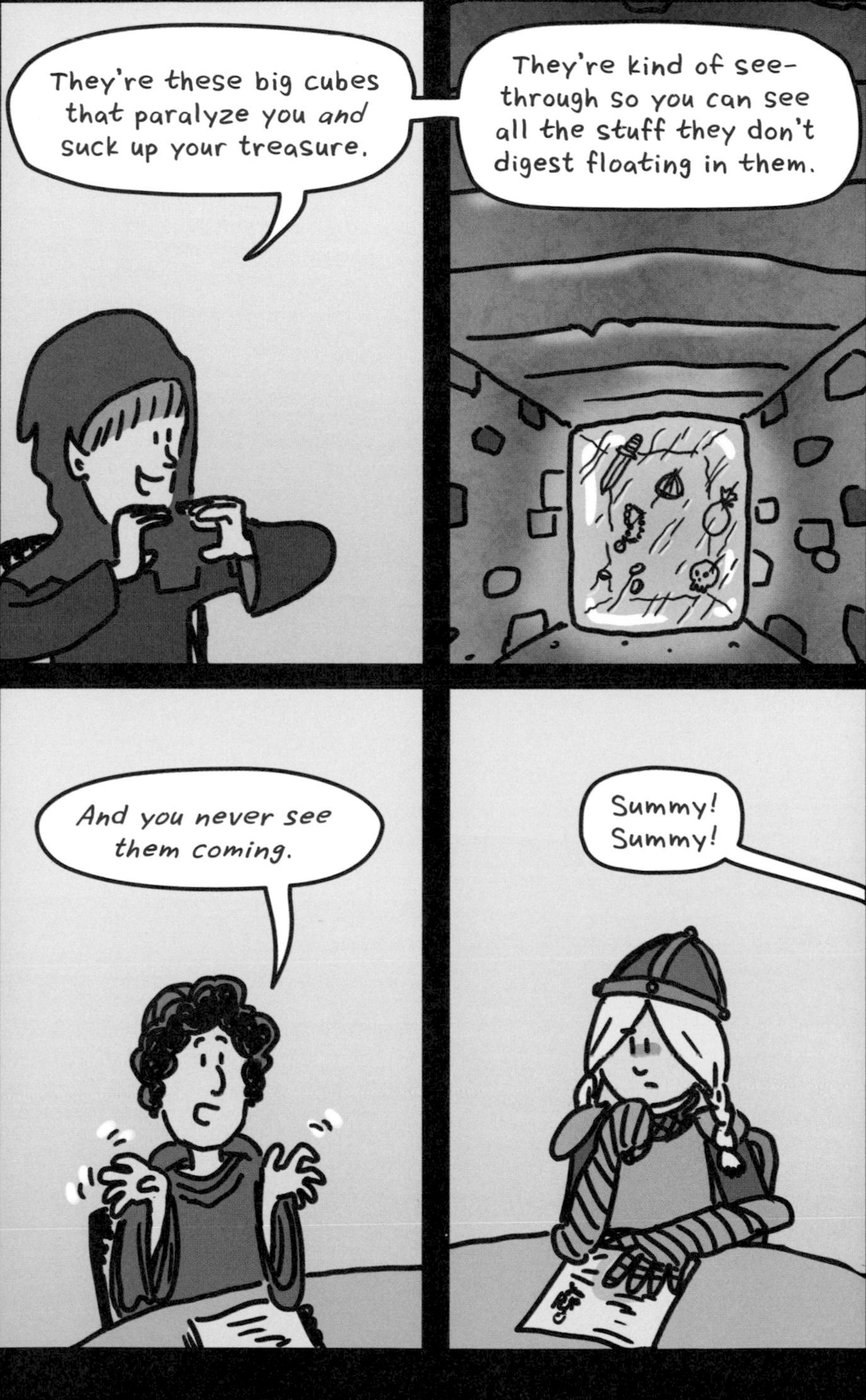
They're these big cubes that paralyze you *and* suck up your treasure.
They're kind of see-through so you can see all the stuff they don't digest floating in them.
And you never see them coming.
Summy! Summy!

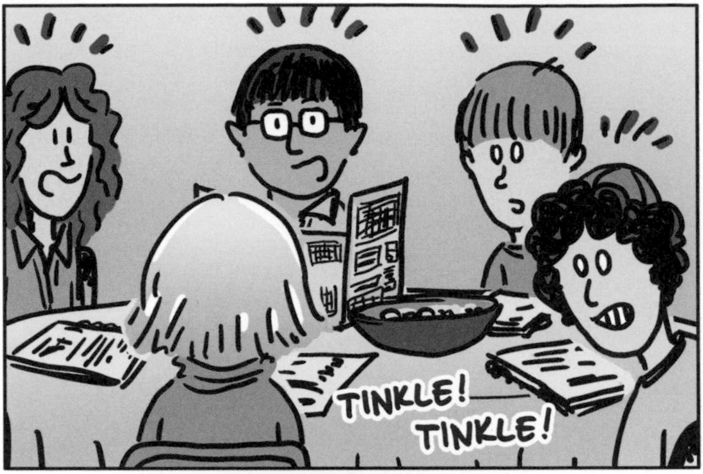
TINKLE!
TINKLE!

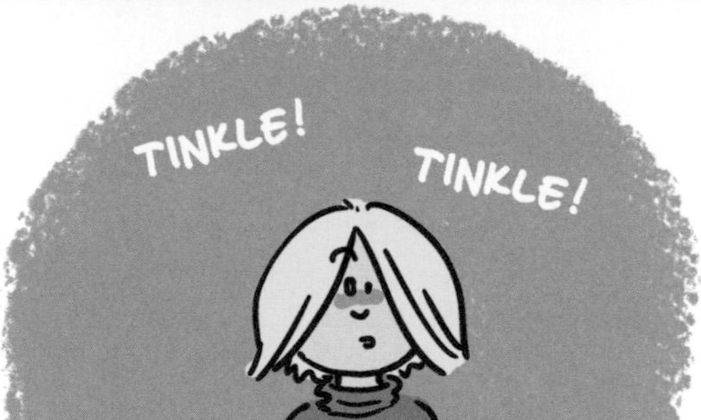
TINKLE!
TINKLE!

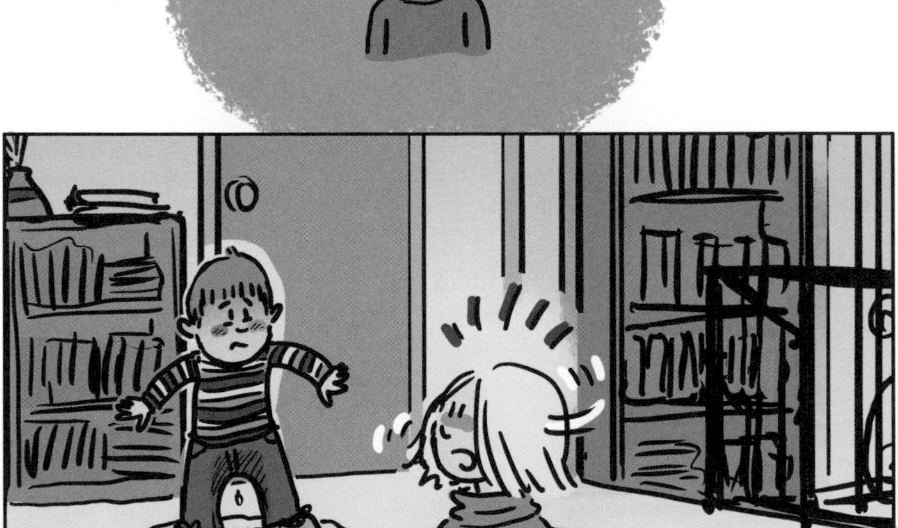

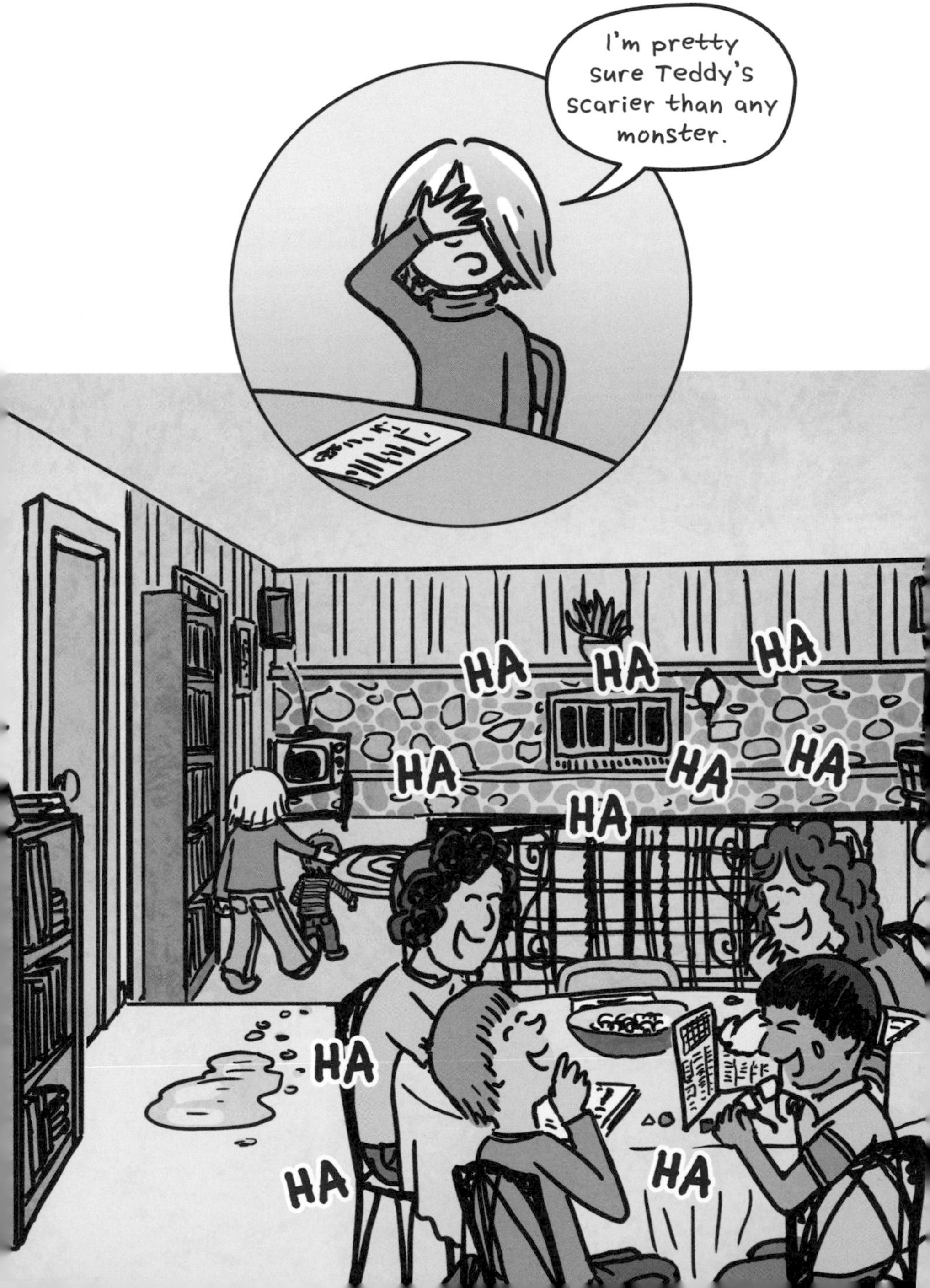
I'm pretty sure Teddy's scarier than any monster.
HA
HA
HA
HA
HA
HA
HA
HA
HA
HA

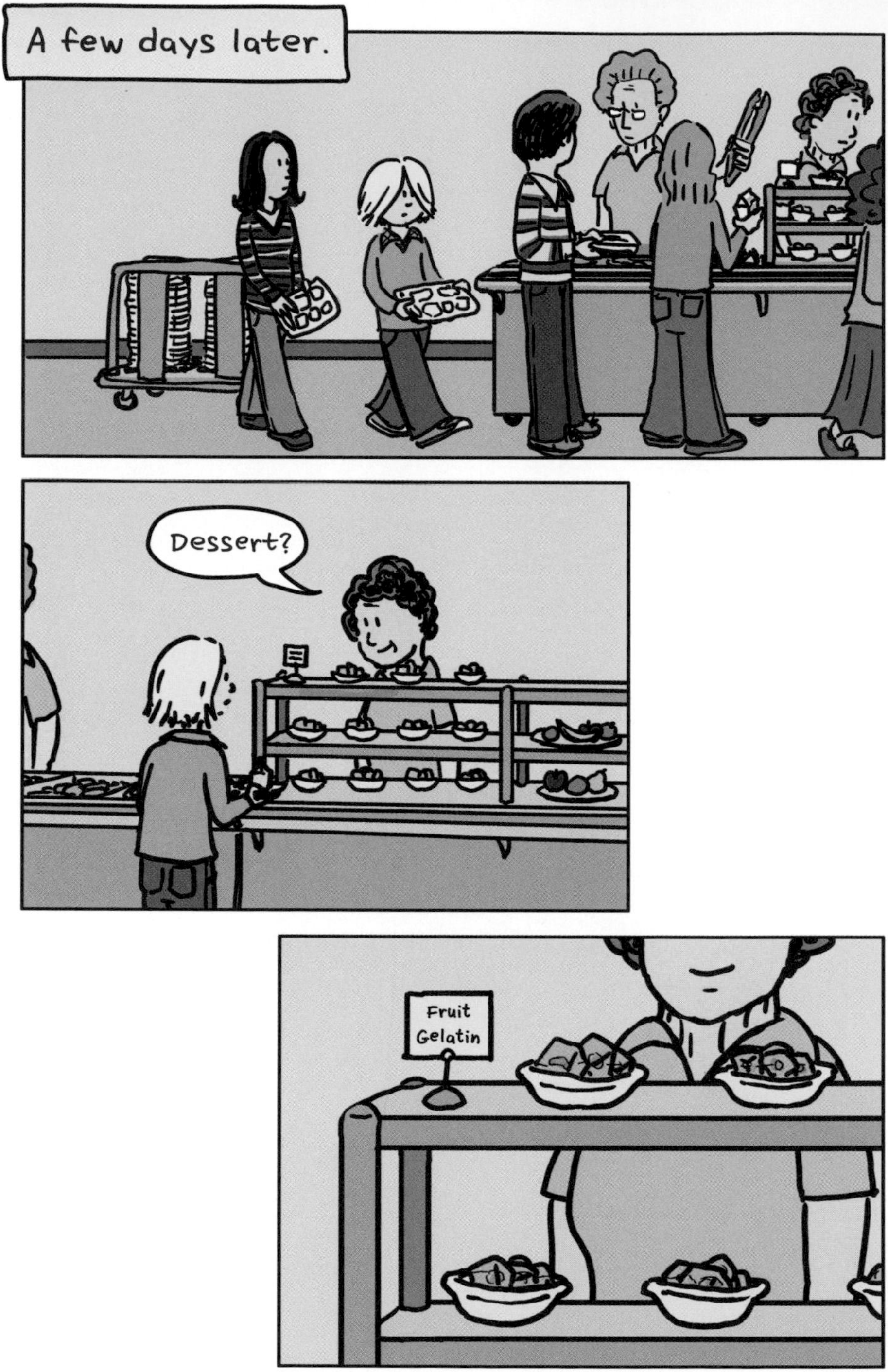
A few days later.
Dessert?
Fruit Gelatin

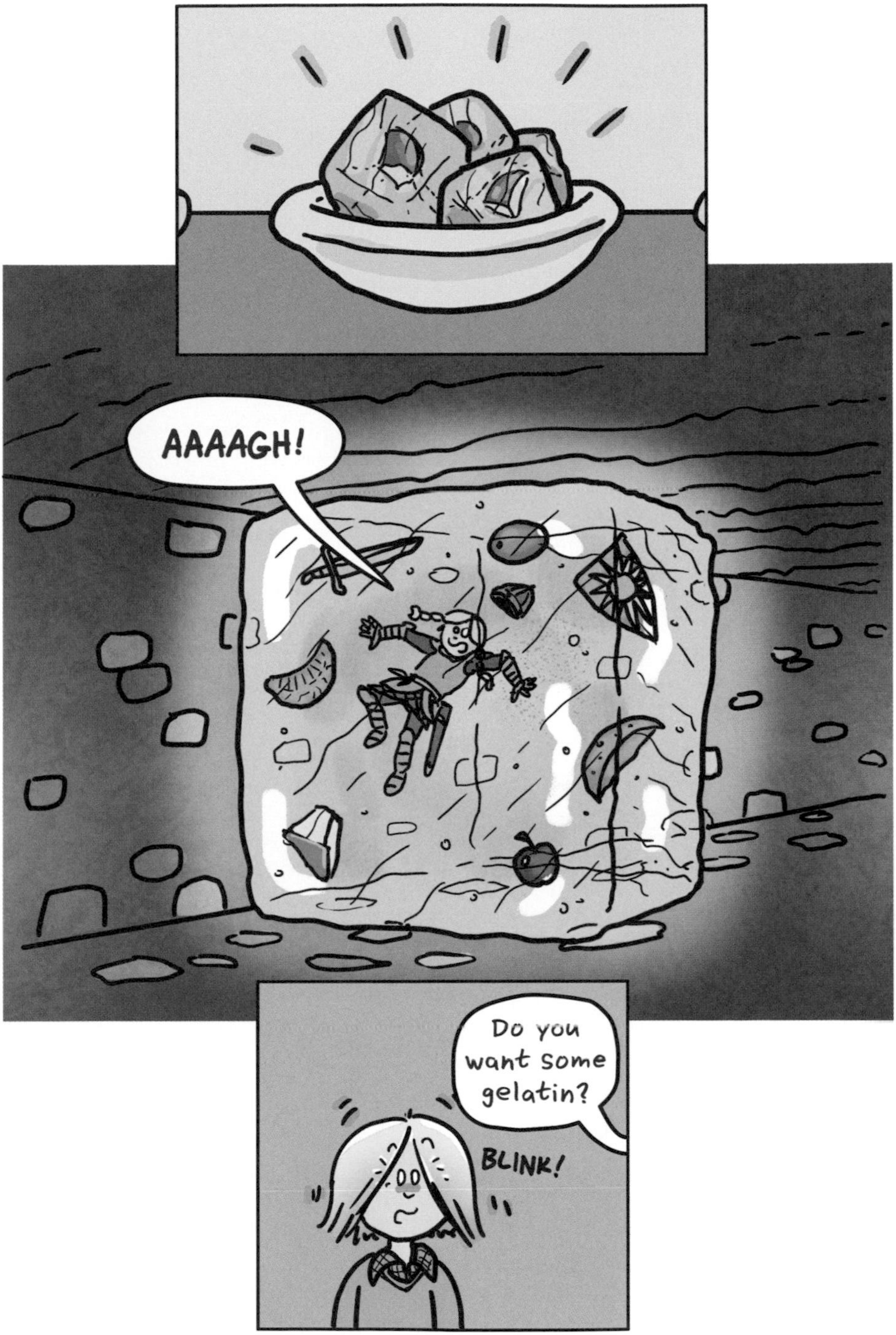
AAAAGH!
Do you want some gelatin?
BLINK!

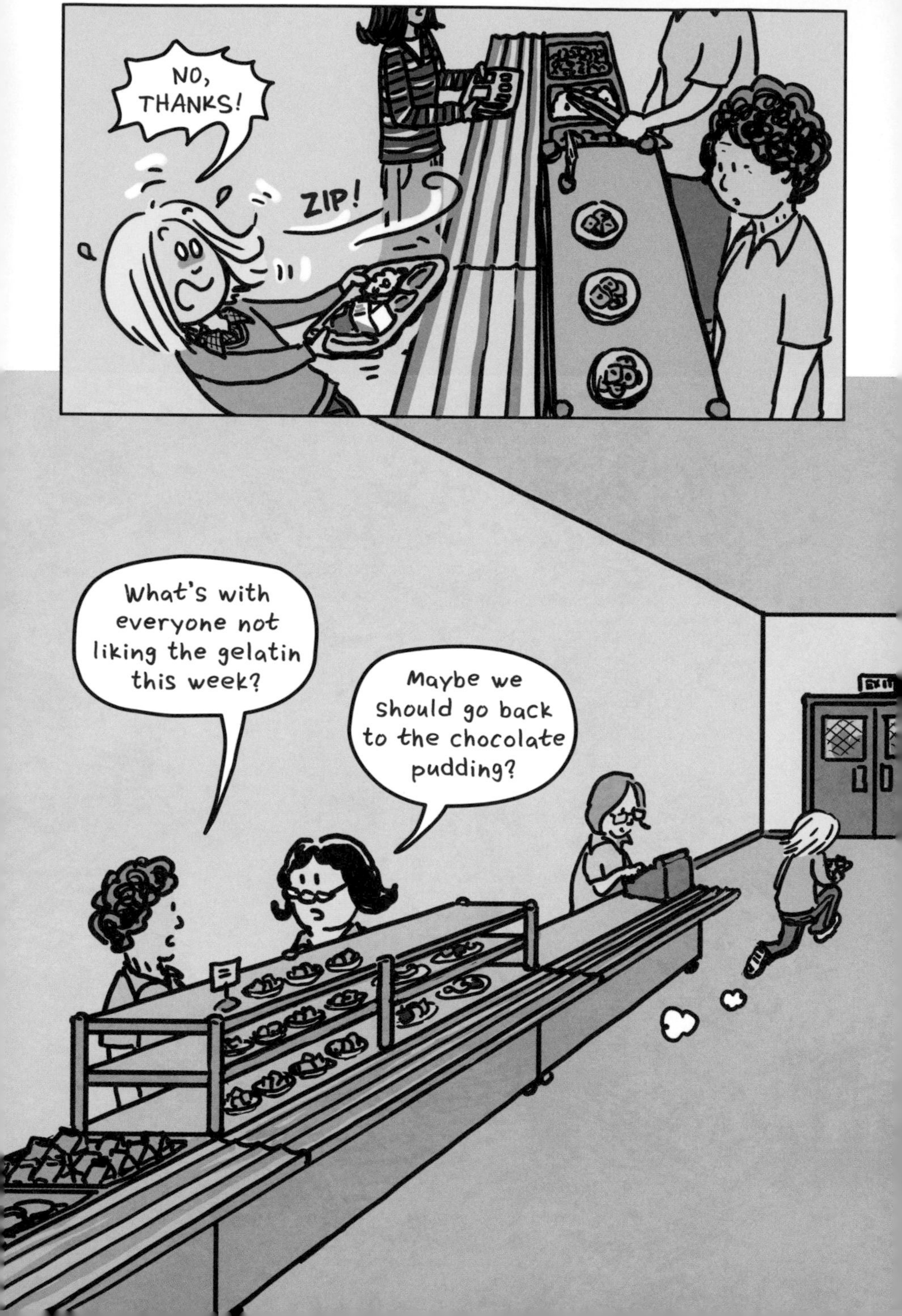
NO, THANKS!
ZIP!
What's with everyone not liking the gelatin this week?
Maybe we should go back to the chocolate pudding?
EXIT

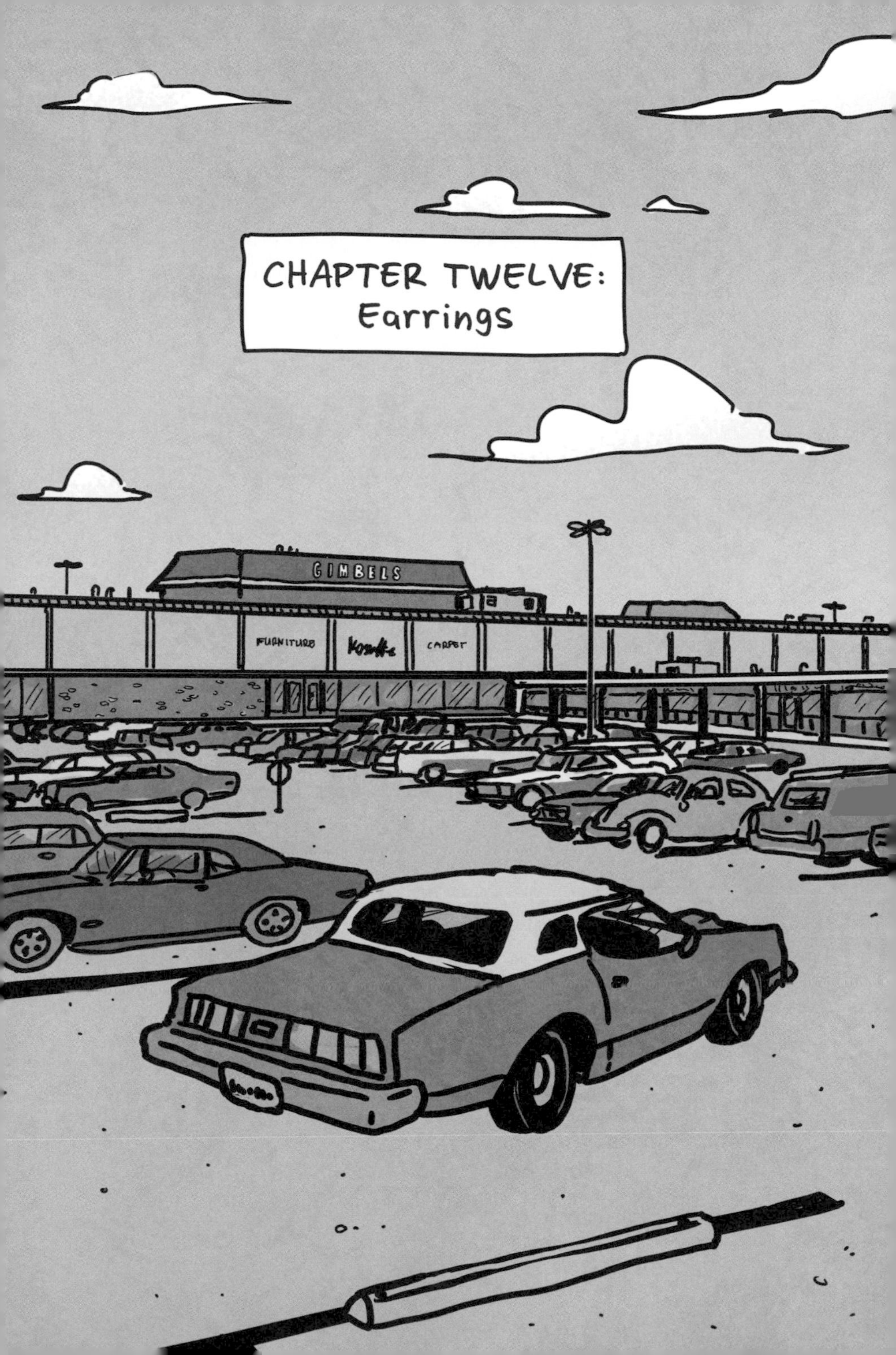
CHAPTER TWELVE:
Earrings
GIMBELS
FURNITURE
CARPET

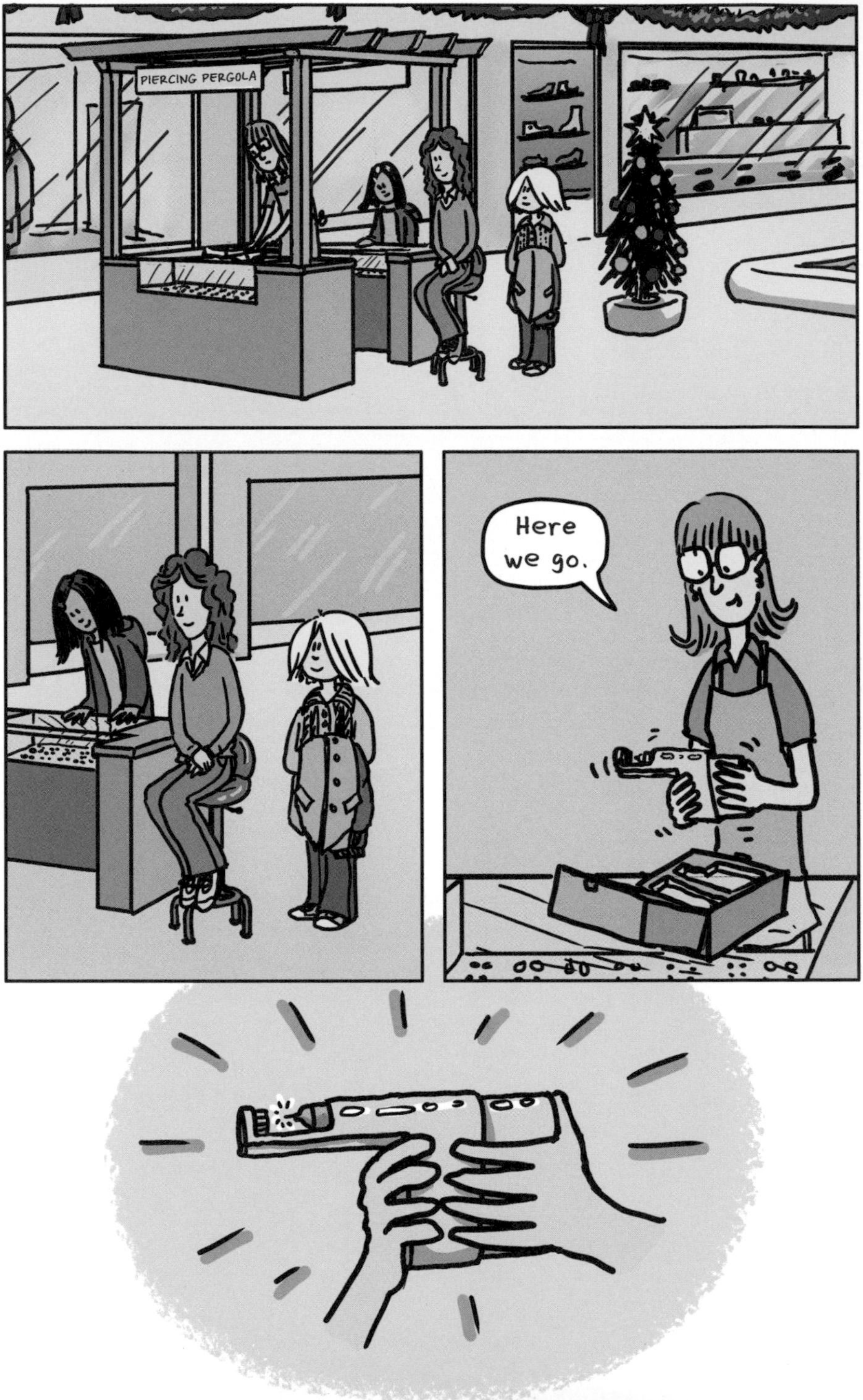
PIERCING PERGOLA
Here we go.

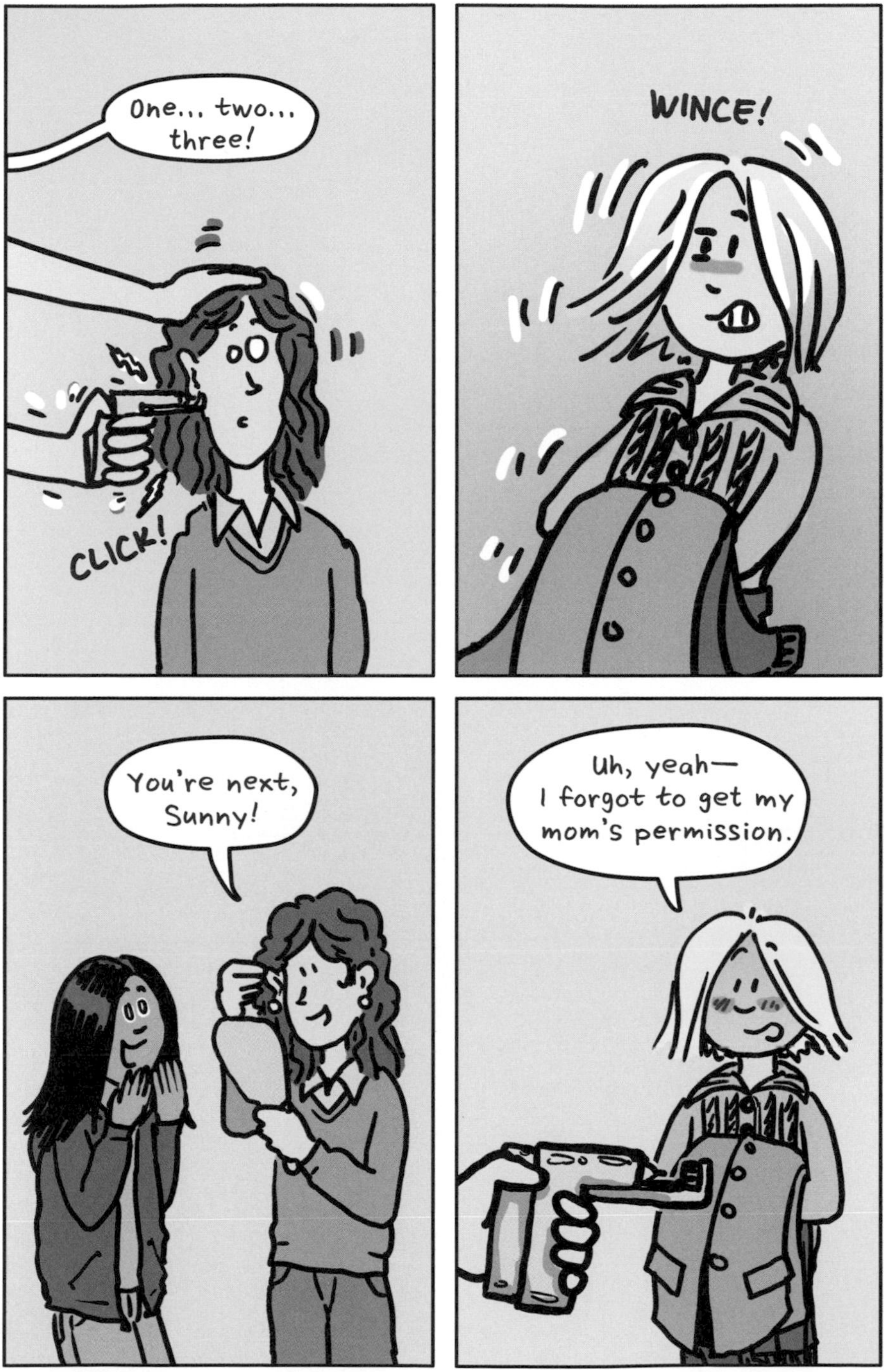
One... two... three!
CLICK!
WINCE!
You're next, Sunny!
Uh, yeah—
I forgot to get my mom's permission.

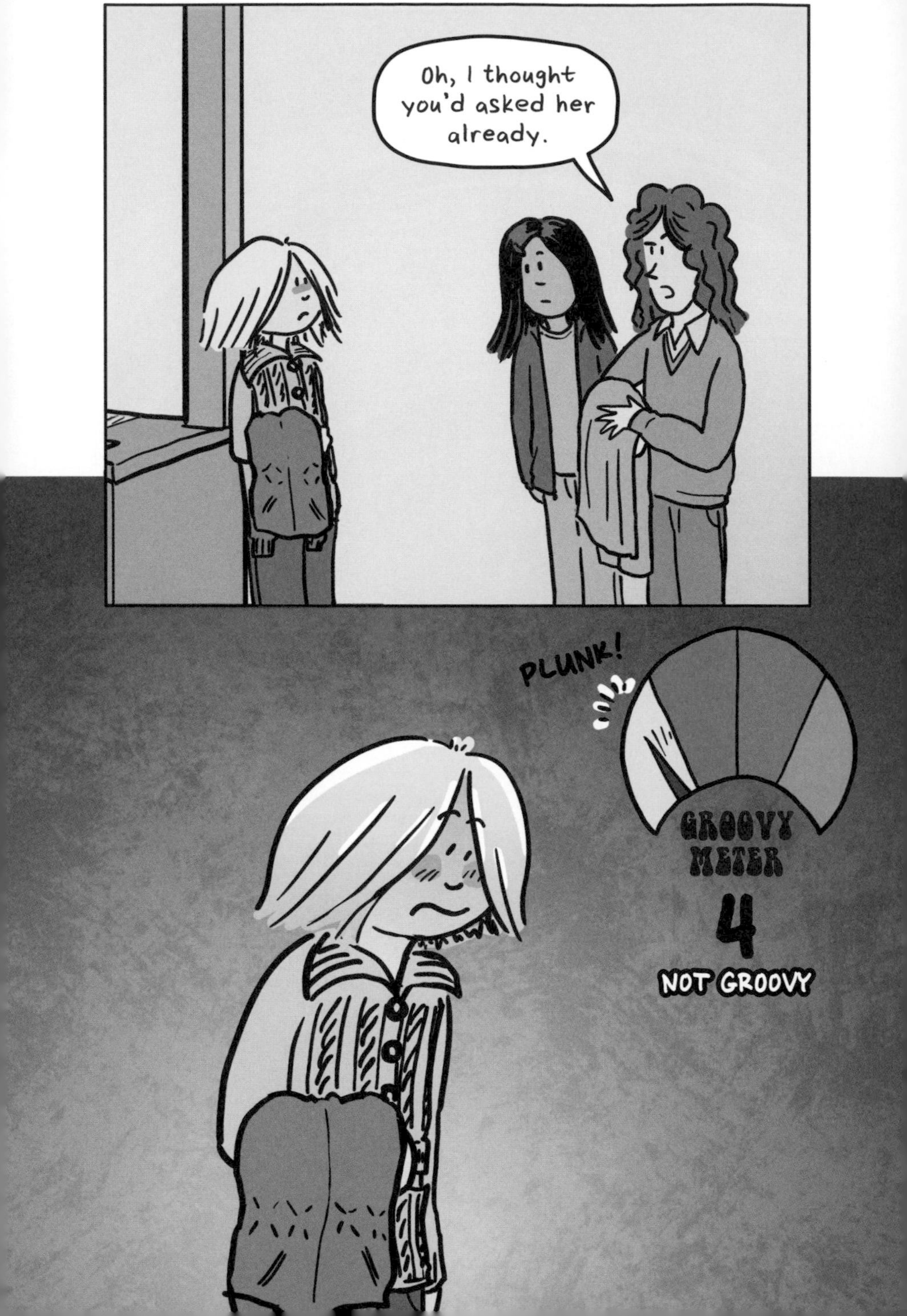
Oh, I thought you'd asked her already.
PLUNK!
GROOVY METER
4
NOT GROOVY

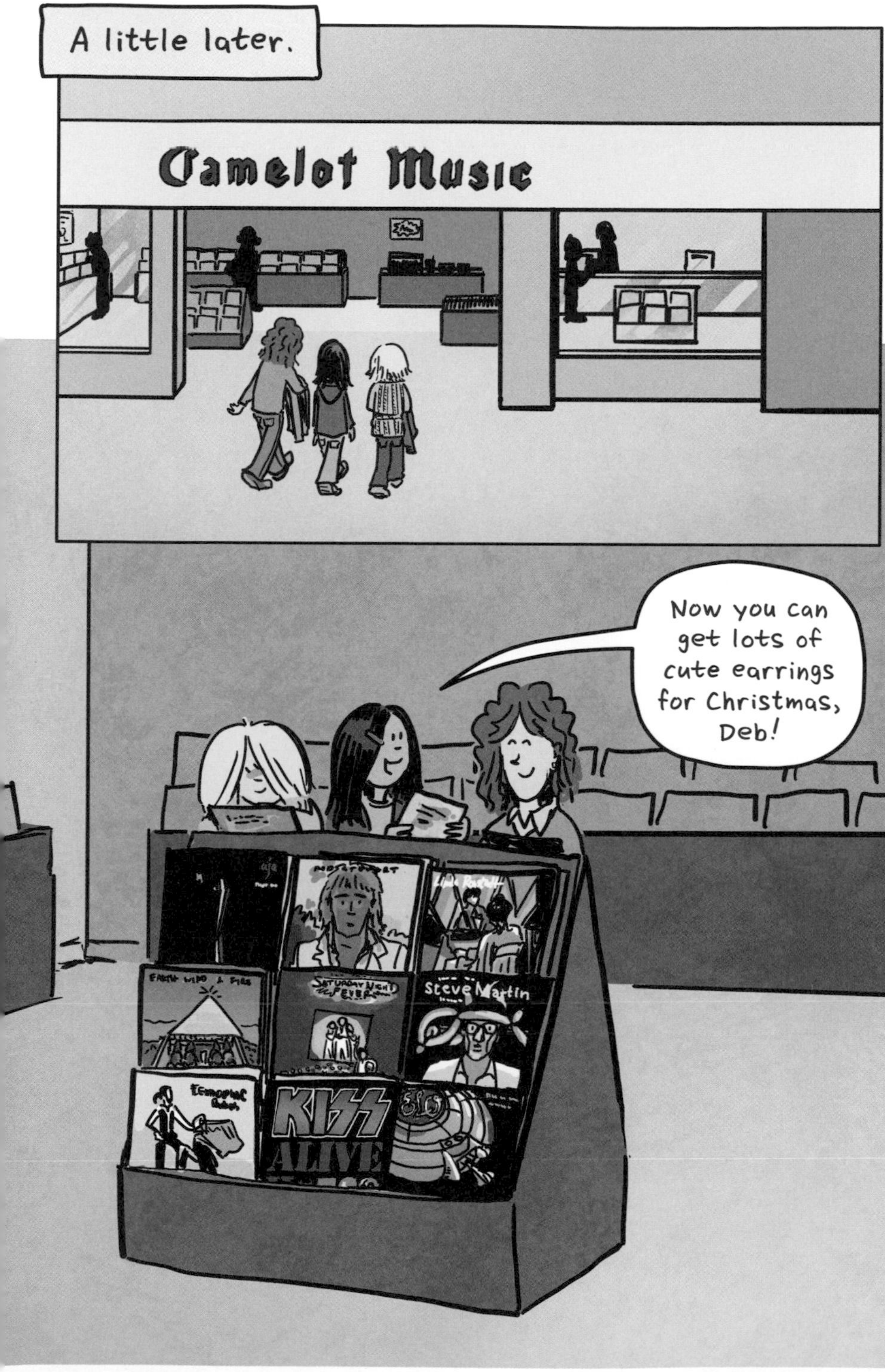
A little later.
Camelot Music
Now you can get lots of cute earrings for Christmas, Deb!
Steve Martin
KISS
ALIVE

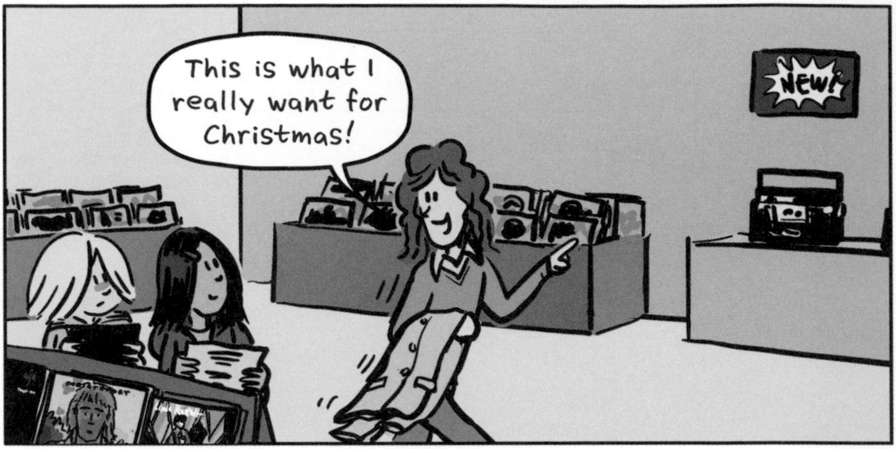
This is what I really want for Christmas!
NEW!

PORTABLE CASSETTE PLAYER!

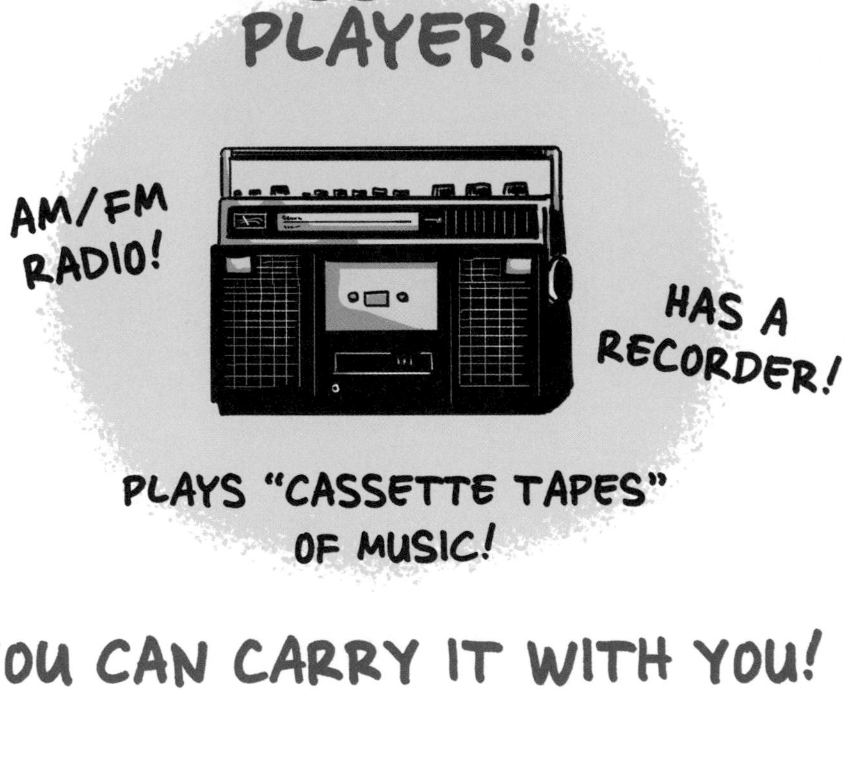
AM/FM RADIO!
HAS A RECORDER!
PLAYS "CASSETTE TAPES" OF MUSIC!

YOU CAN CARRY IT WITH YOU!

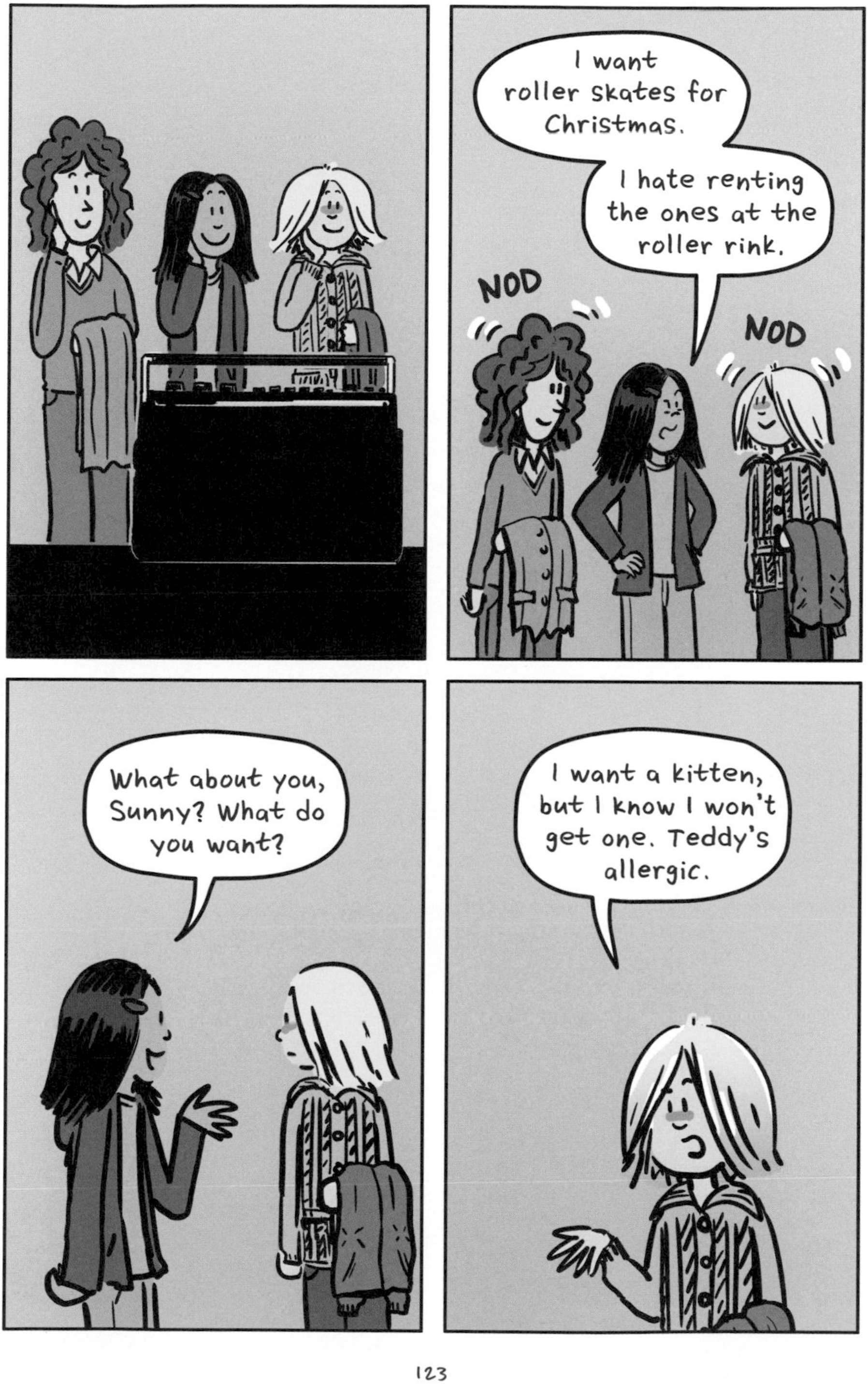
I want roller skates for Christmas.
I hate renting the ones at the roller rink.
NOD
NOD
What about you, Sunny? What do you want?
I want a kitten, but I know I won't get one. Teddy's allergic.

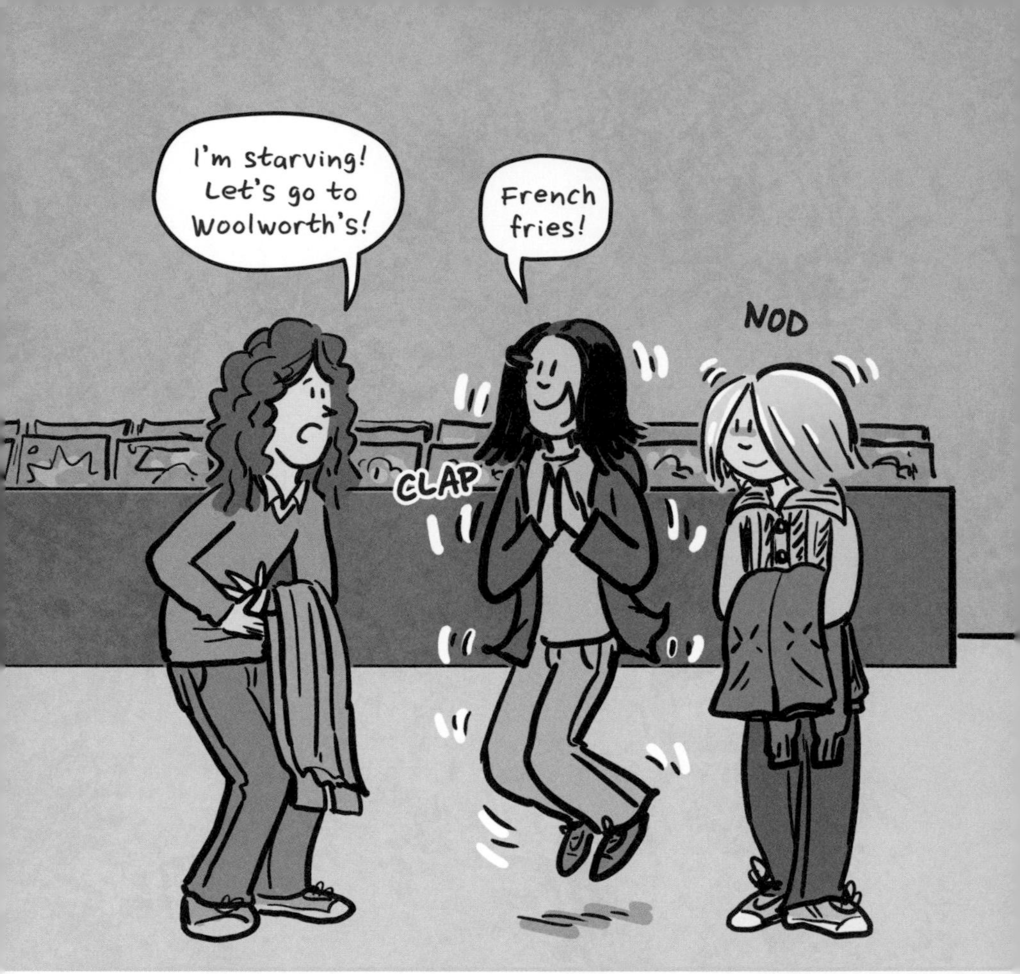
I'm starving! Let's go to Woolworth's!
French fries!
CLAP
NOD

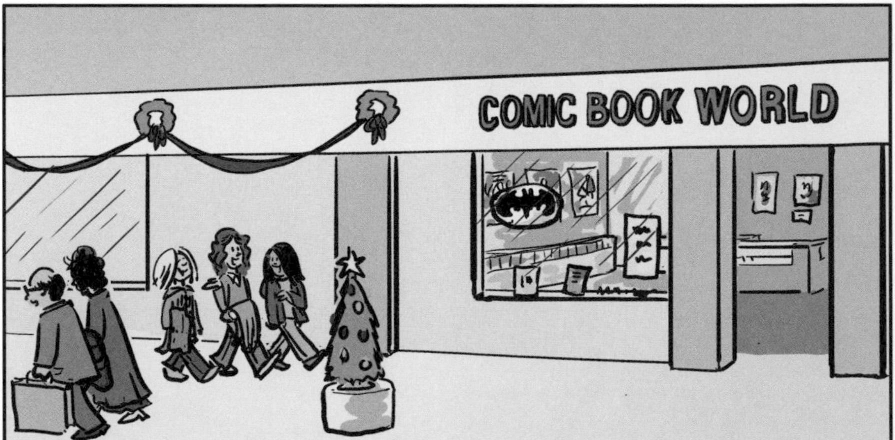
COMIC BOOK WORLD

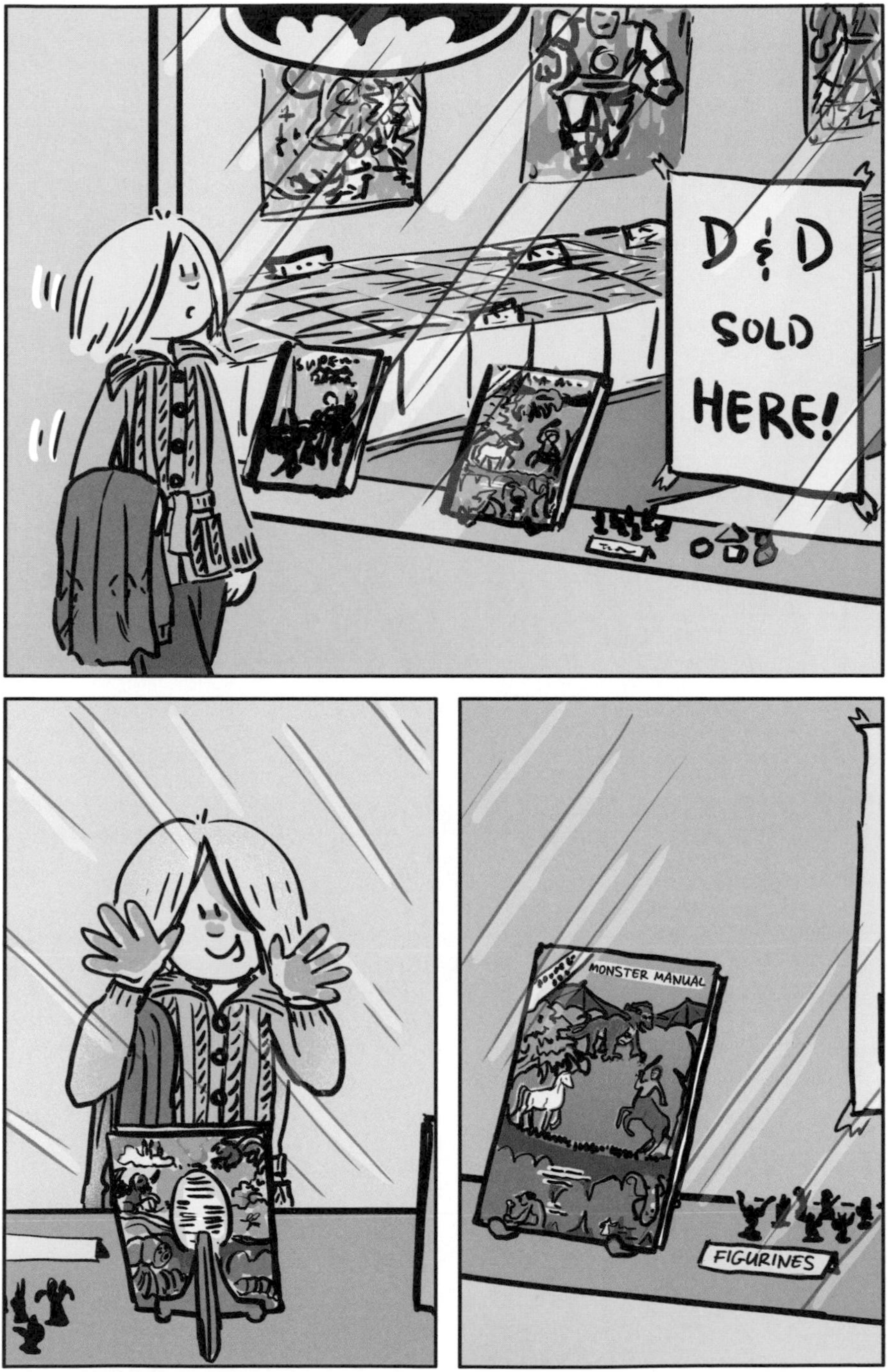
D & D
SOLD
HERE!
MONSTER MANUAL
FIGURINES

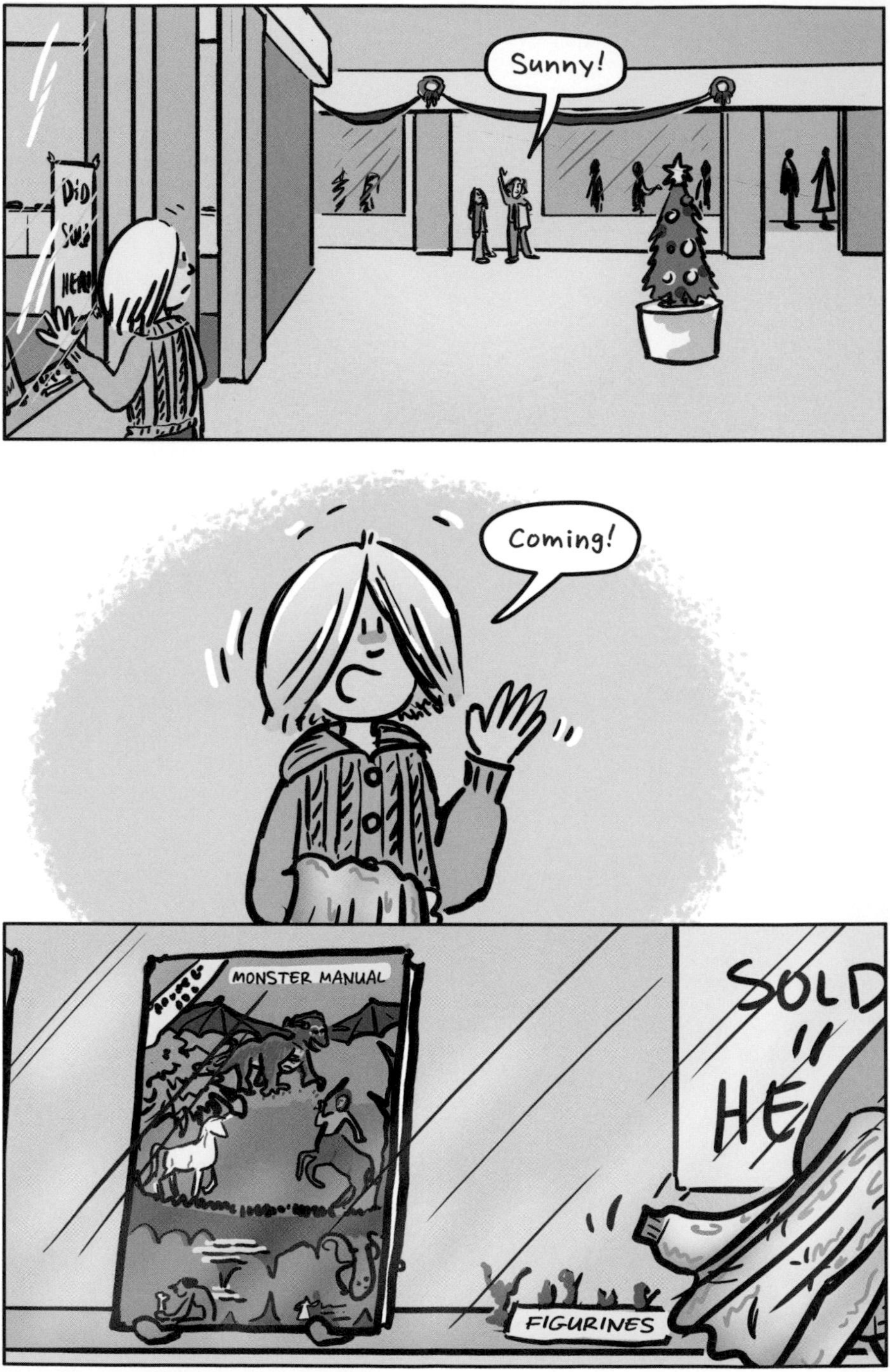
Sunny!
Coming!
MONSTER MANUAL
SOLD
FIGURINES

CHAPTER THIRTEEN: Reindeer Games

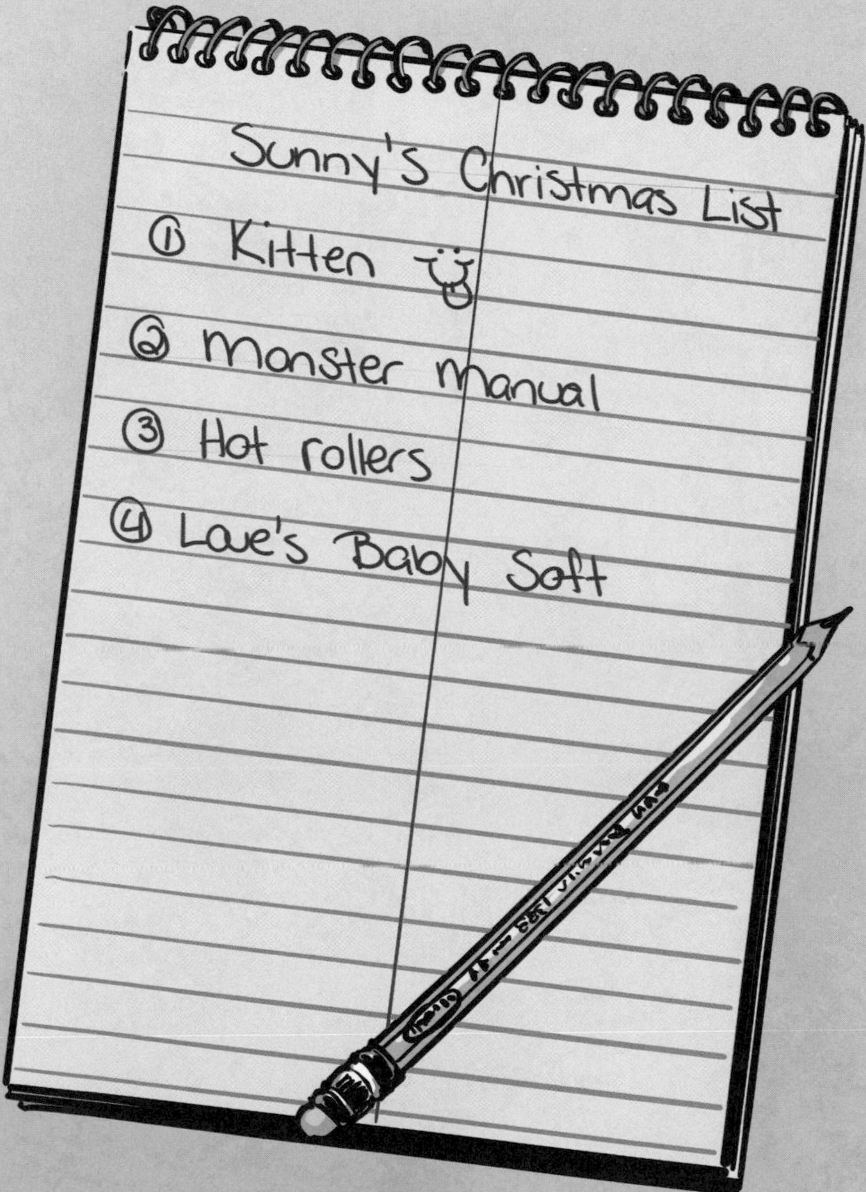
Sunny's Christmas List
① Kitten
② Monster manual
③ Hot rollers
④ Love's Baby Soft

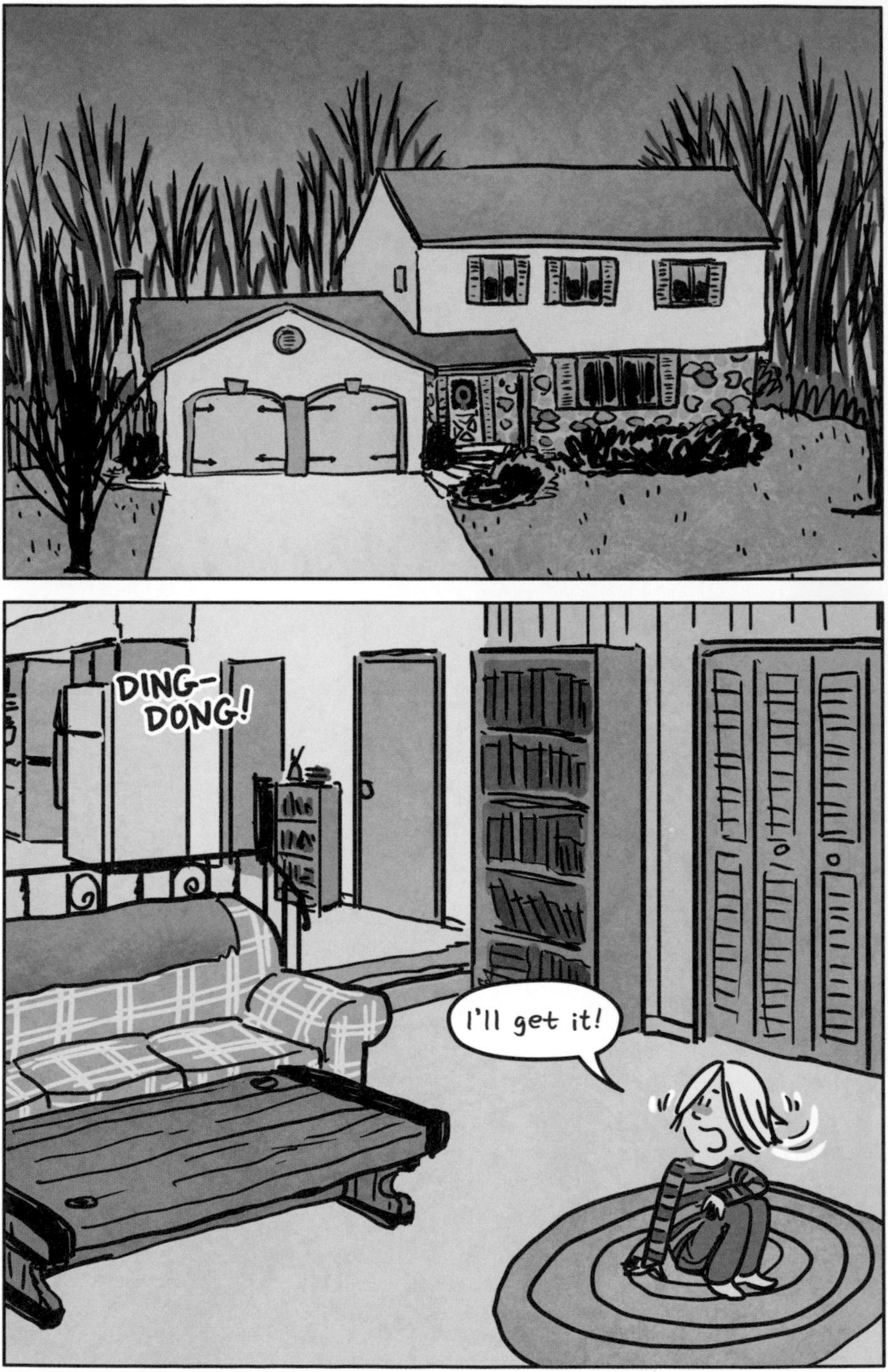
DING-DONG!
I'll get it!

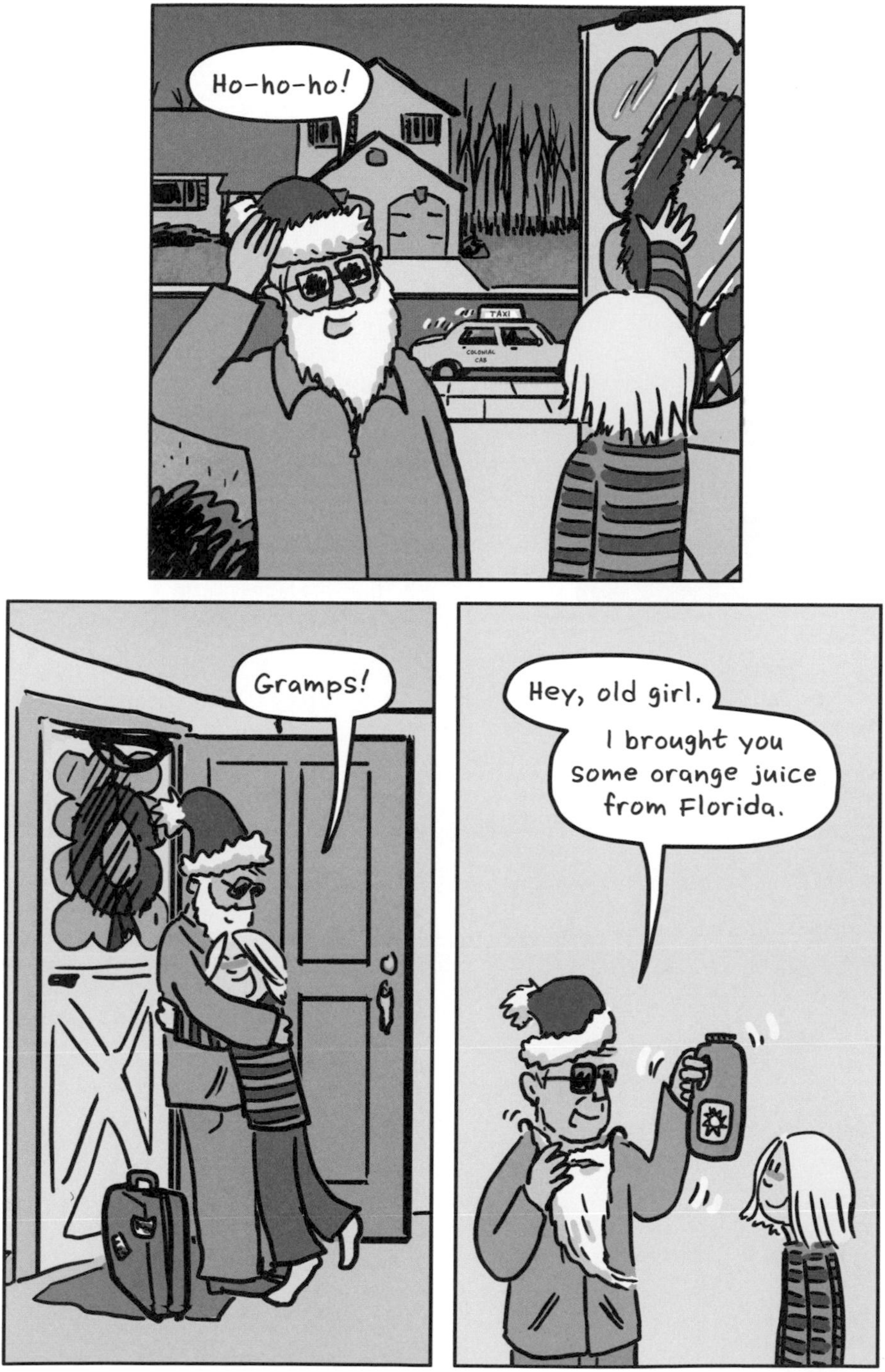
Ho-ho-ho!
TAXI
Gramps!
Hey, old girl.
I brought you some orange juice from Florida.

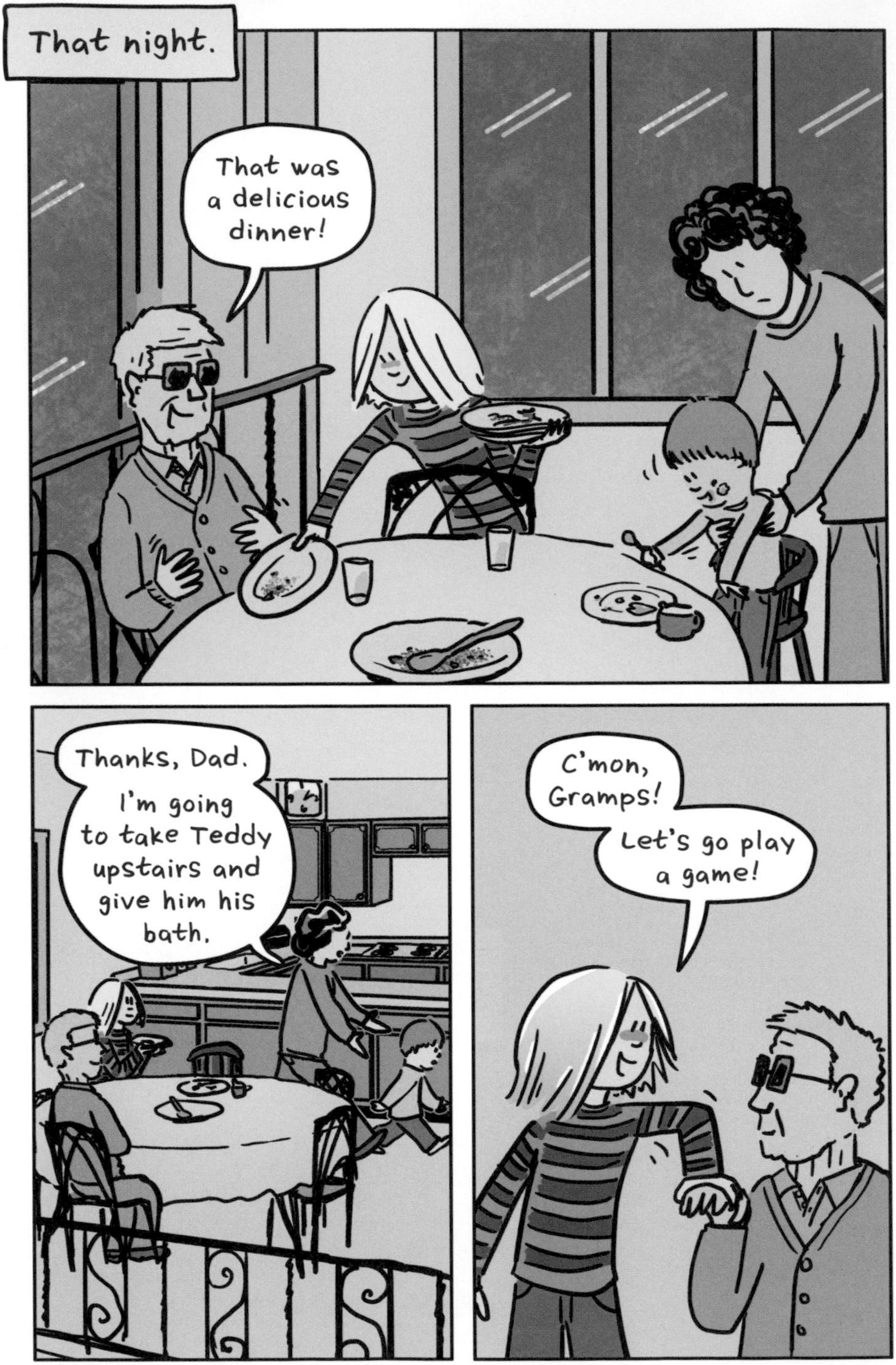

That night.
That was a delicious dinner!
Thanks, Dad.
I'm going to take Teddy upstairs and give him his bath.
C'mon, Gramps!
Let's go play a game!

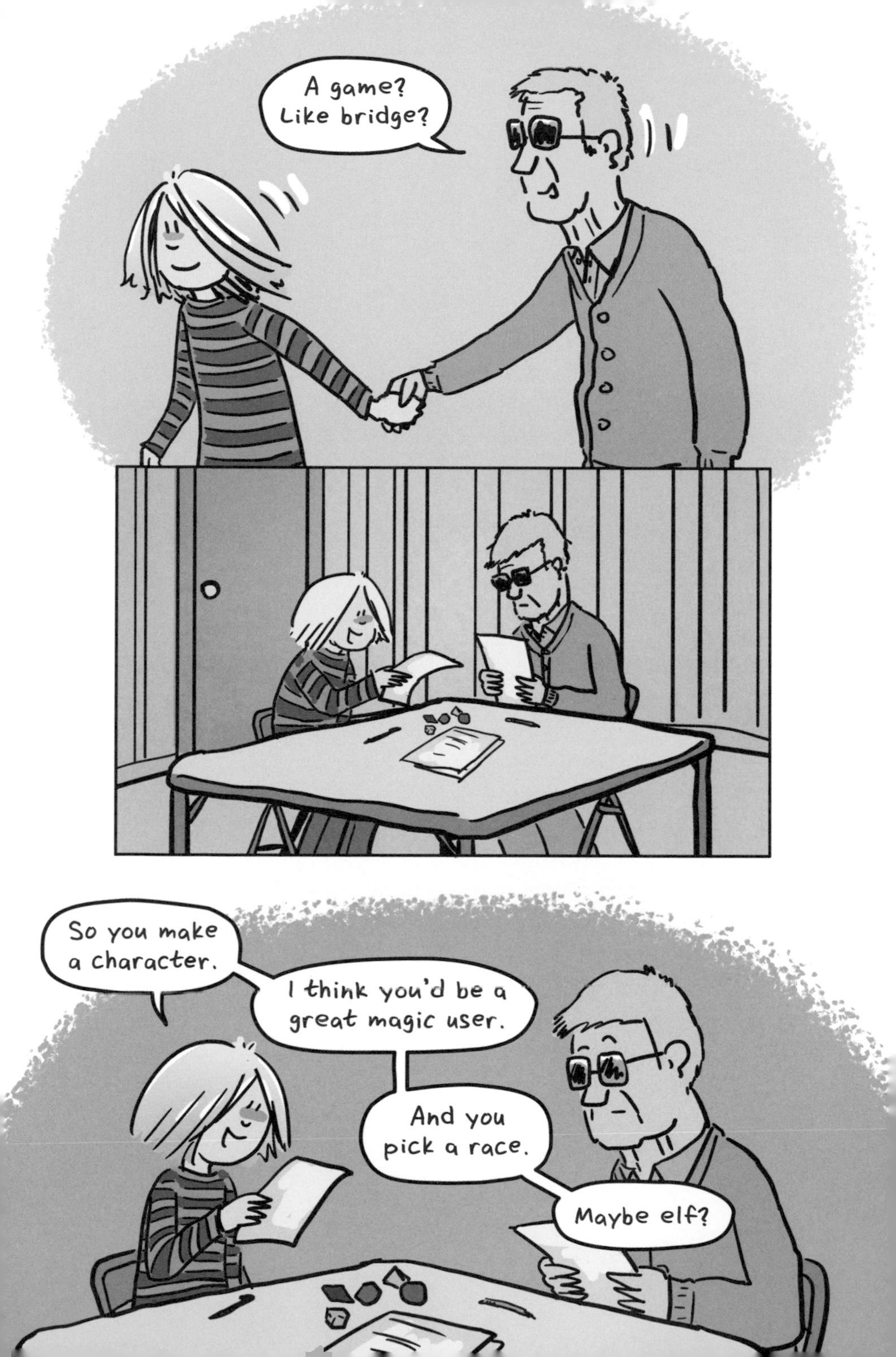
A game? Like bridge?
So you make a character.
I think you'd be a great magic user.
And you pick a race.
Maybe elf?

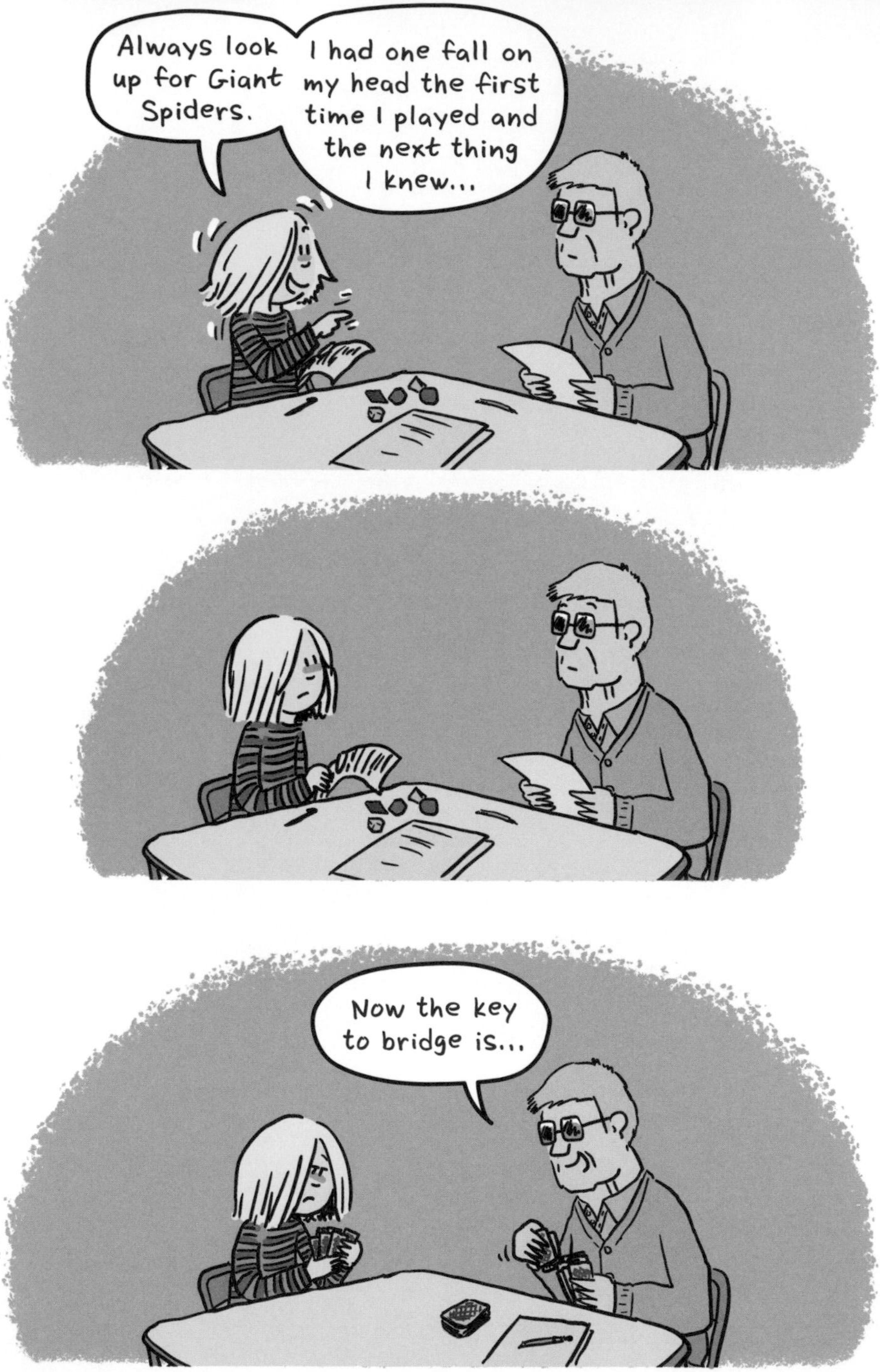
Always look up for Giant Spiders.
I had one fall on my head the first time I played and the next thing I knew...
Now the key to bridge is...

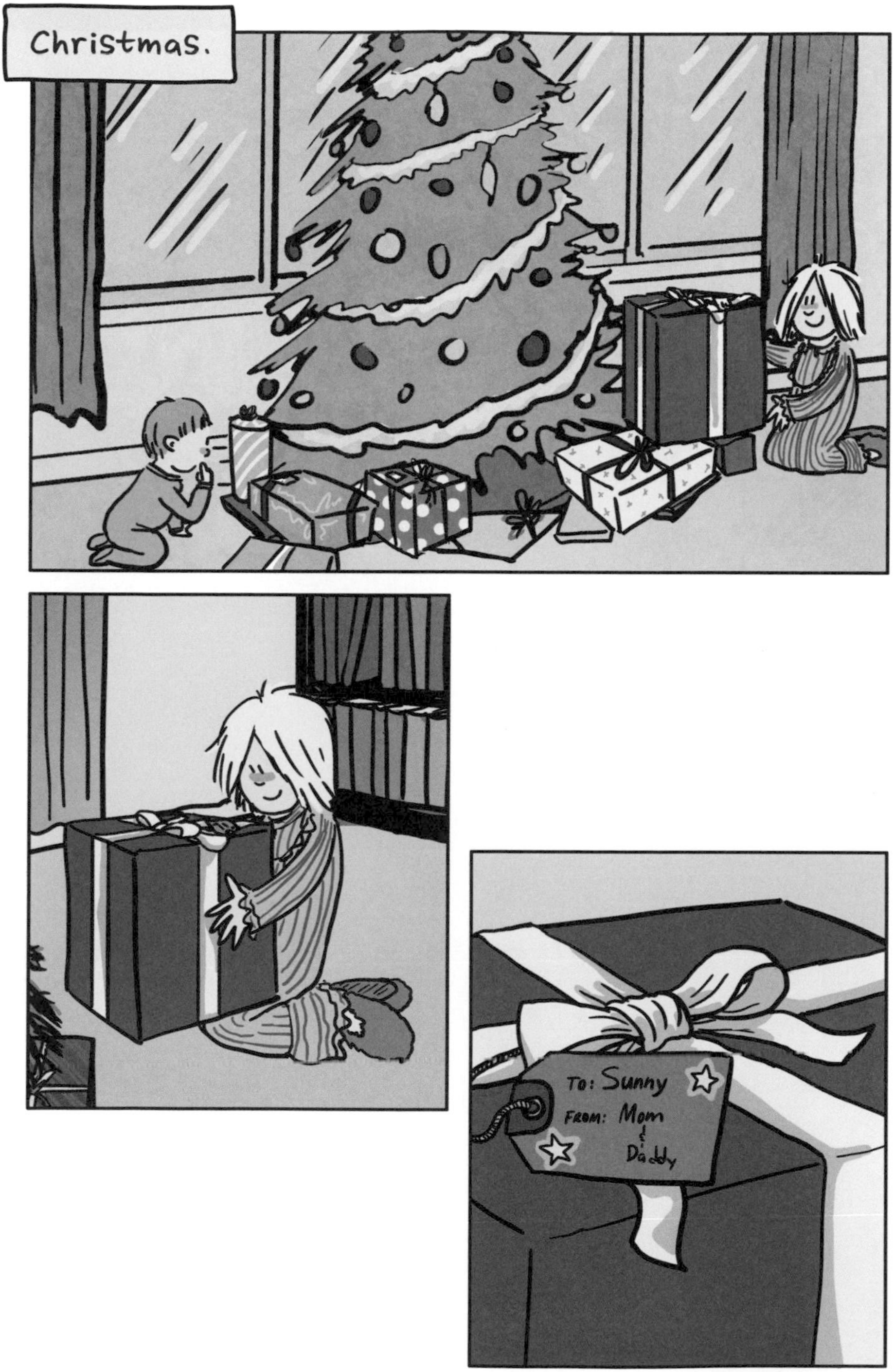
Christmas.
To: Sunny
From: Mom & Daddy

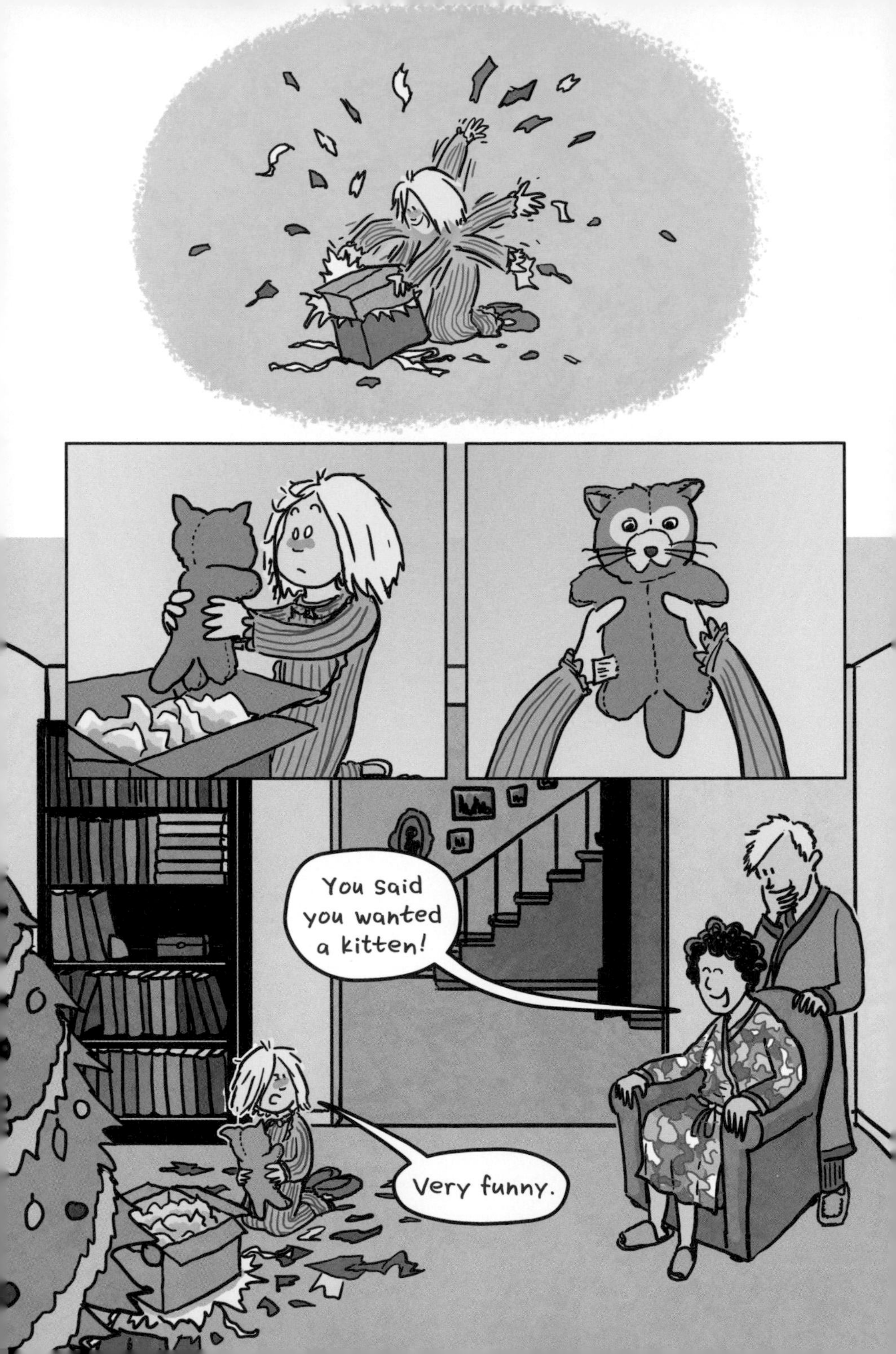
You said you wanted a kitten!
Very funny.

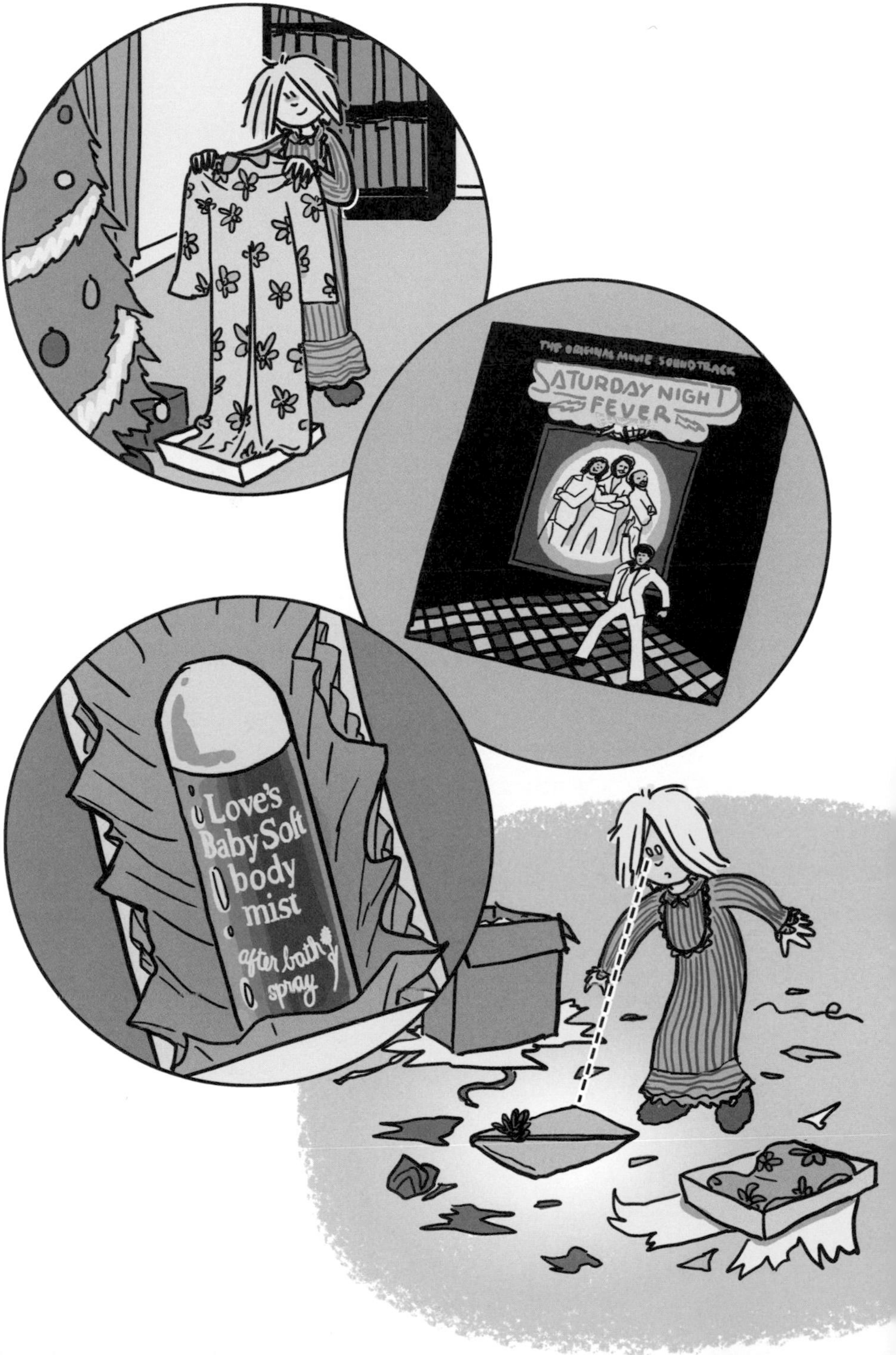
THE ORIGINAL MOVIE SOUNDTRACK
SATURDAY NIGHT FEVER
Love's Baby Soft body mist
after bath spray

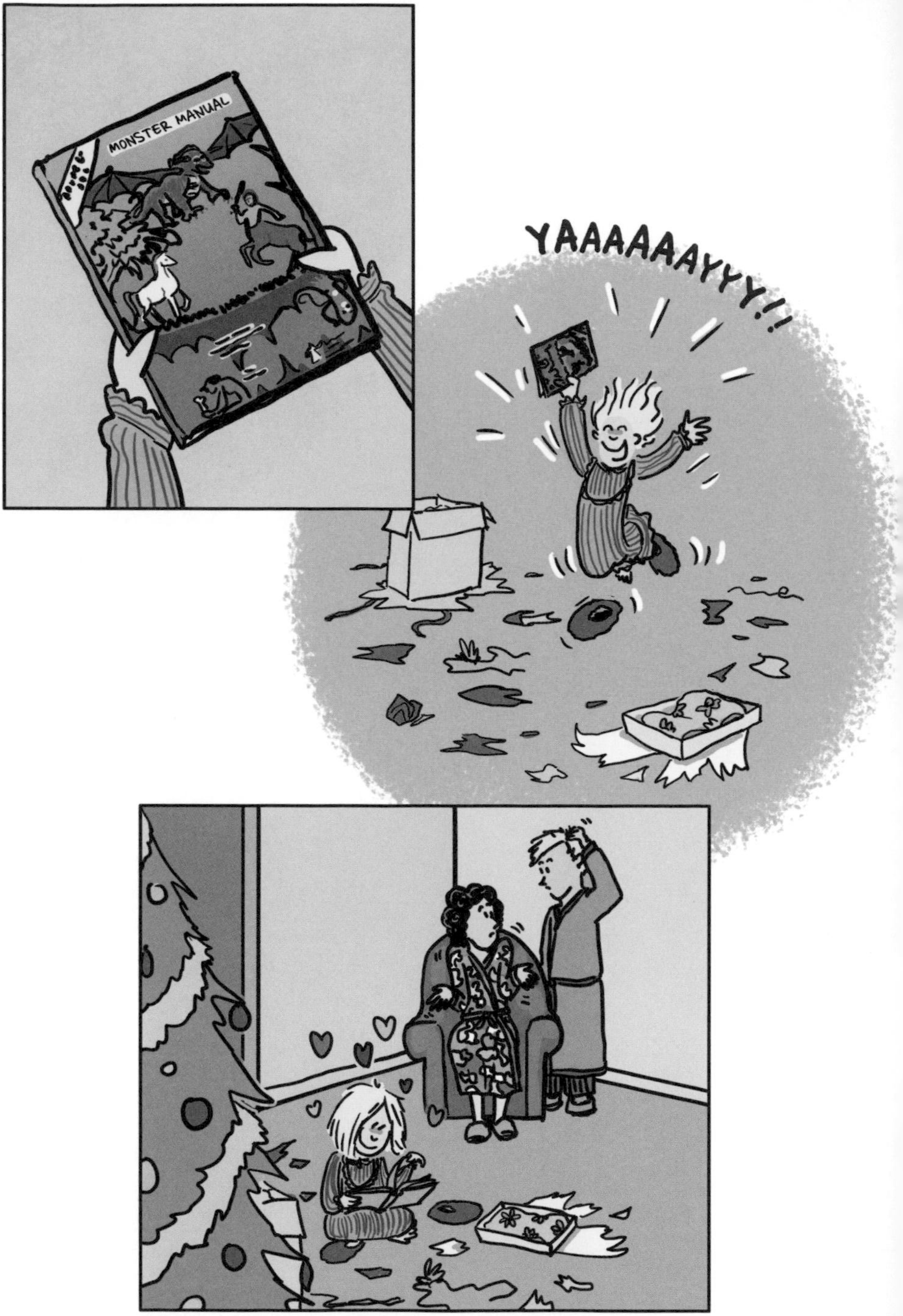
MONSTER MANUAL
YAAAAAAYYY!!

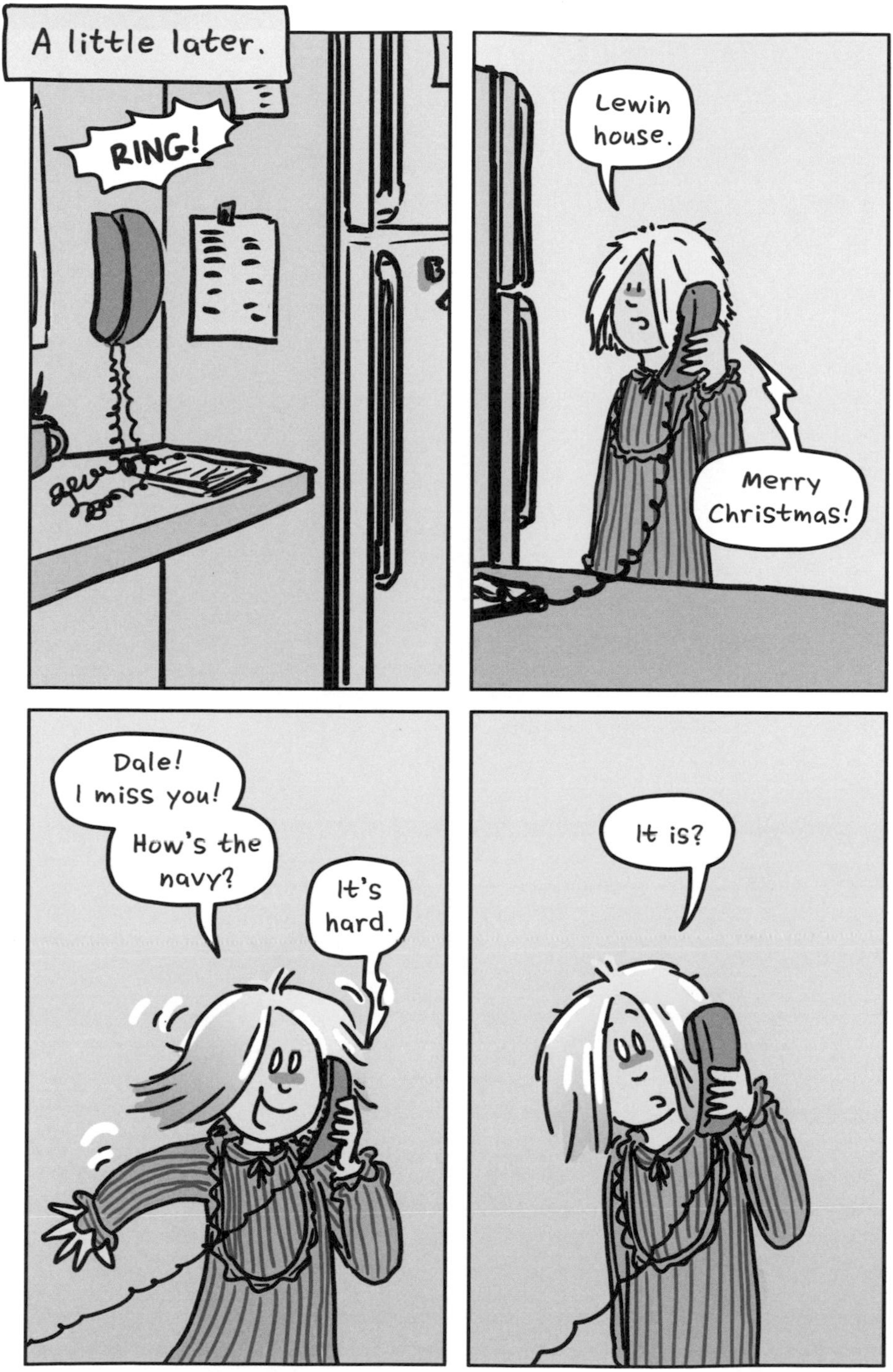
A little later.
RING!
Lewin house.
Merry Christmas!
Dale! I miss you!
How's the navy?
It's hard.
It is?

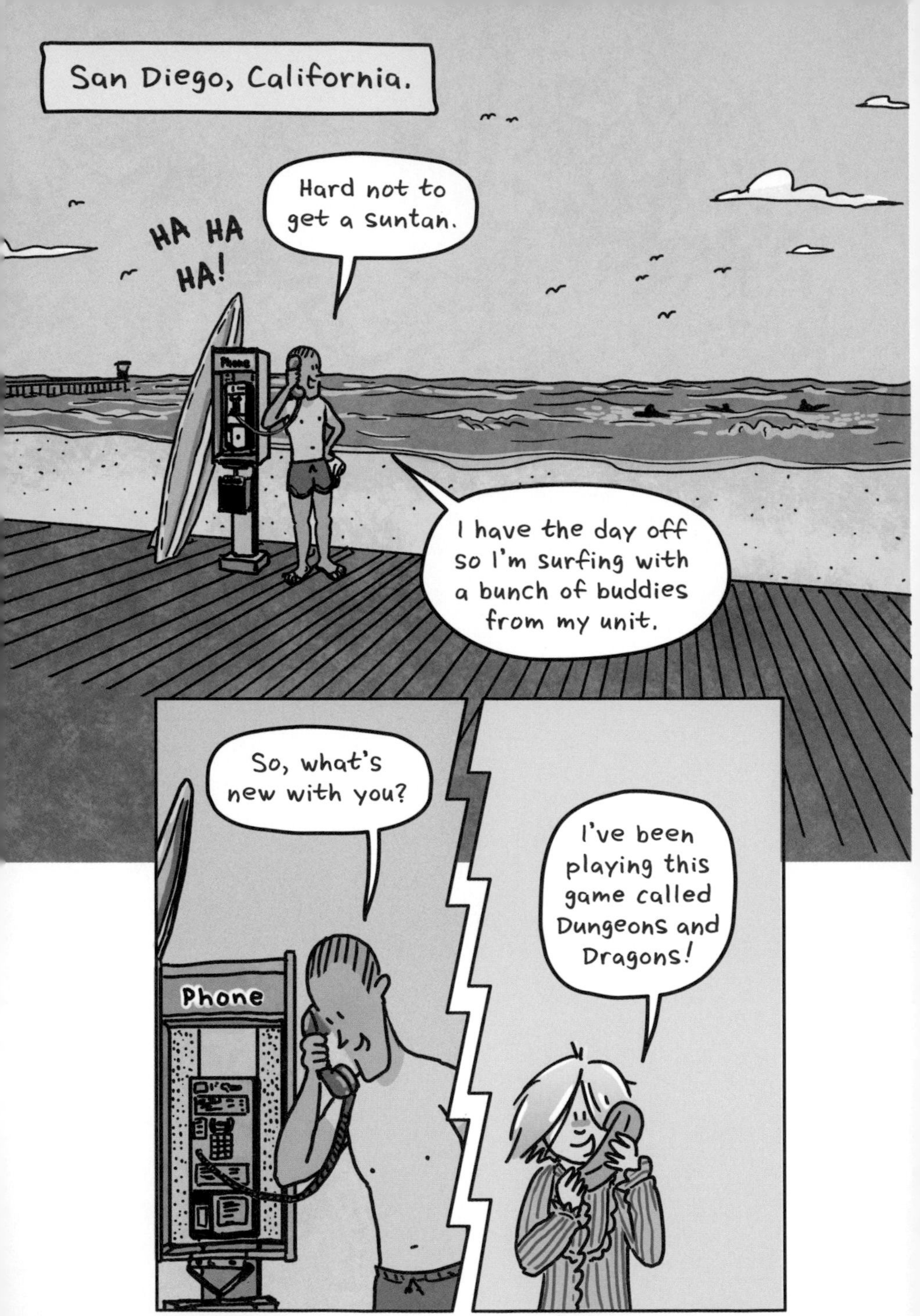
San Diego, California.
HA HA HA!
Hard not to get a suntan.
Phone
I have the day off so I'm surfing with a bunch of buddies from my unit.
So, what's new with you?
Phone
I've been playing this game called Dungeons and Dragons!

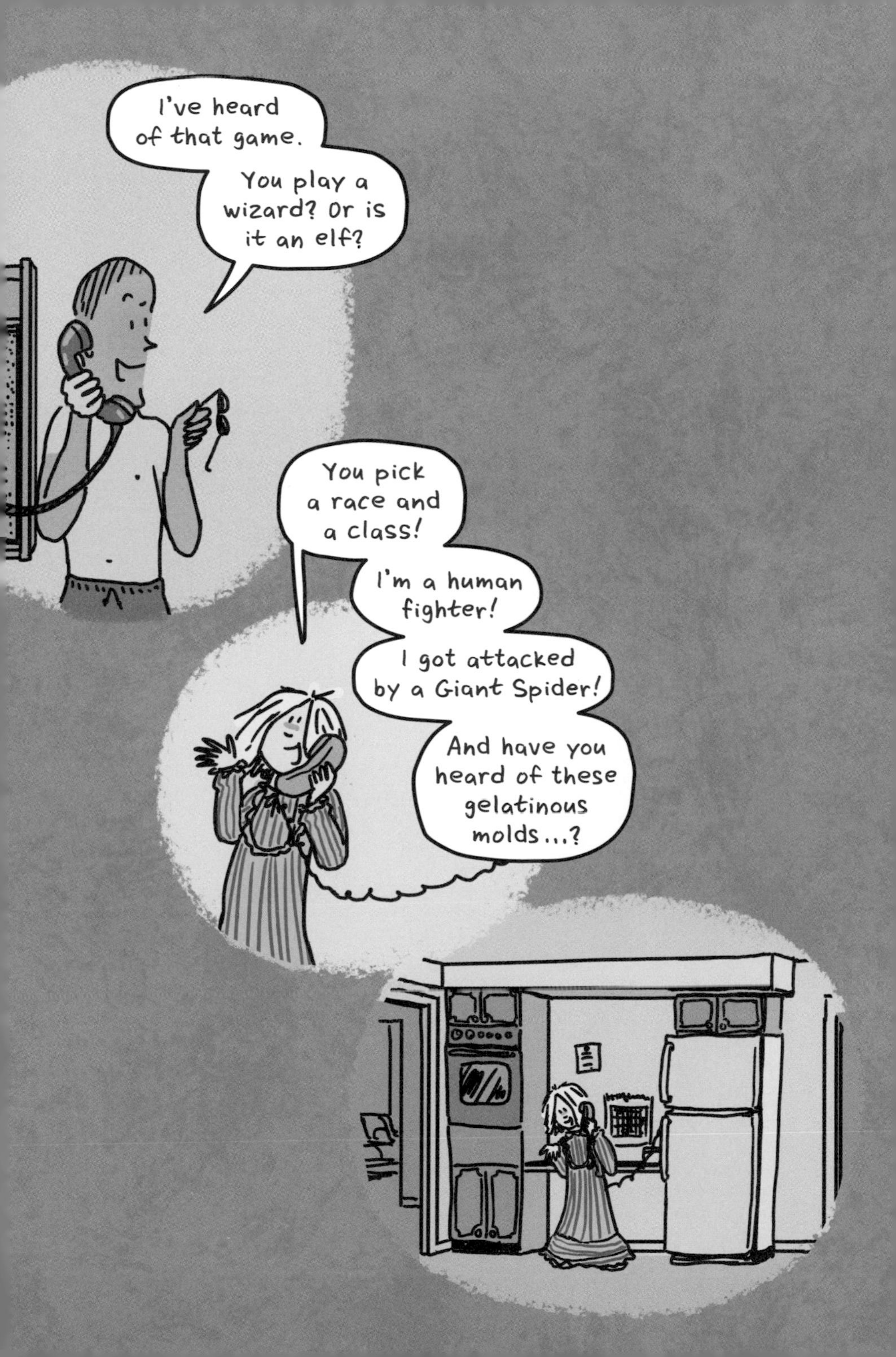
I've heard of that game.
You play a wizard? Or is it an elf?
You pick a race and a class!
I'm a human fighter!
I got attacked by a Giant Spider!
And have you heard of these gelatinous molds...?

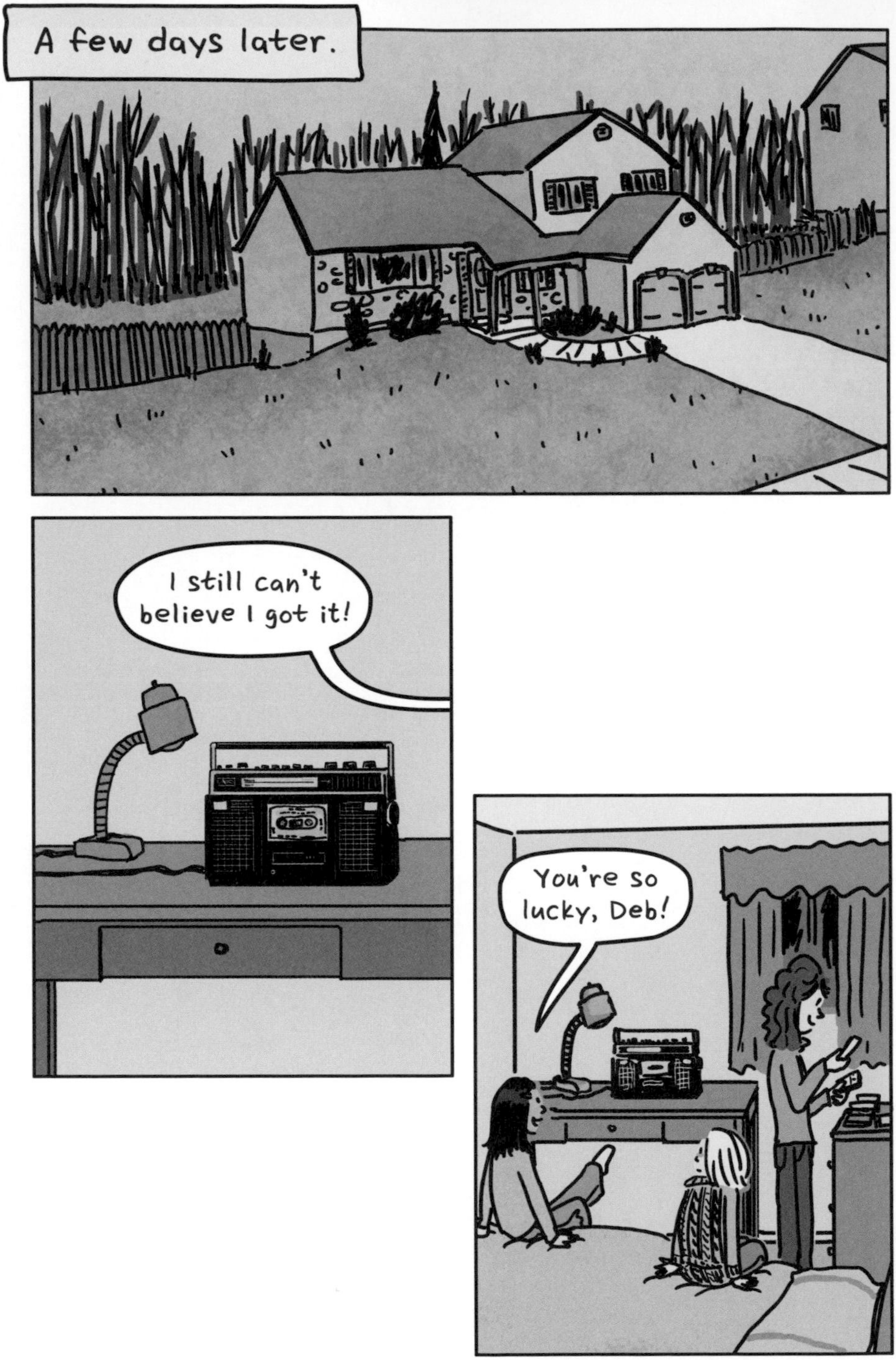
A few days later.
I still can't believe I got it!
You're so lucky, Deb!

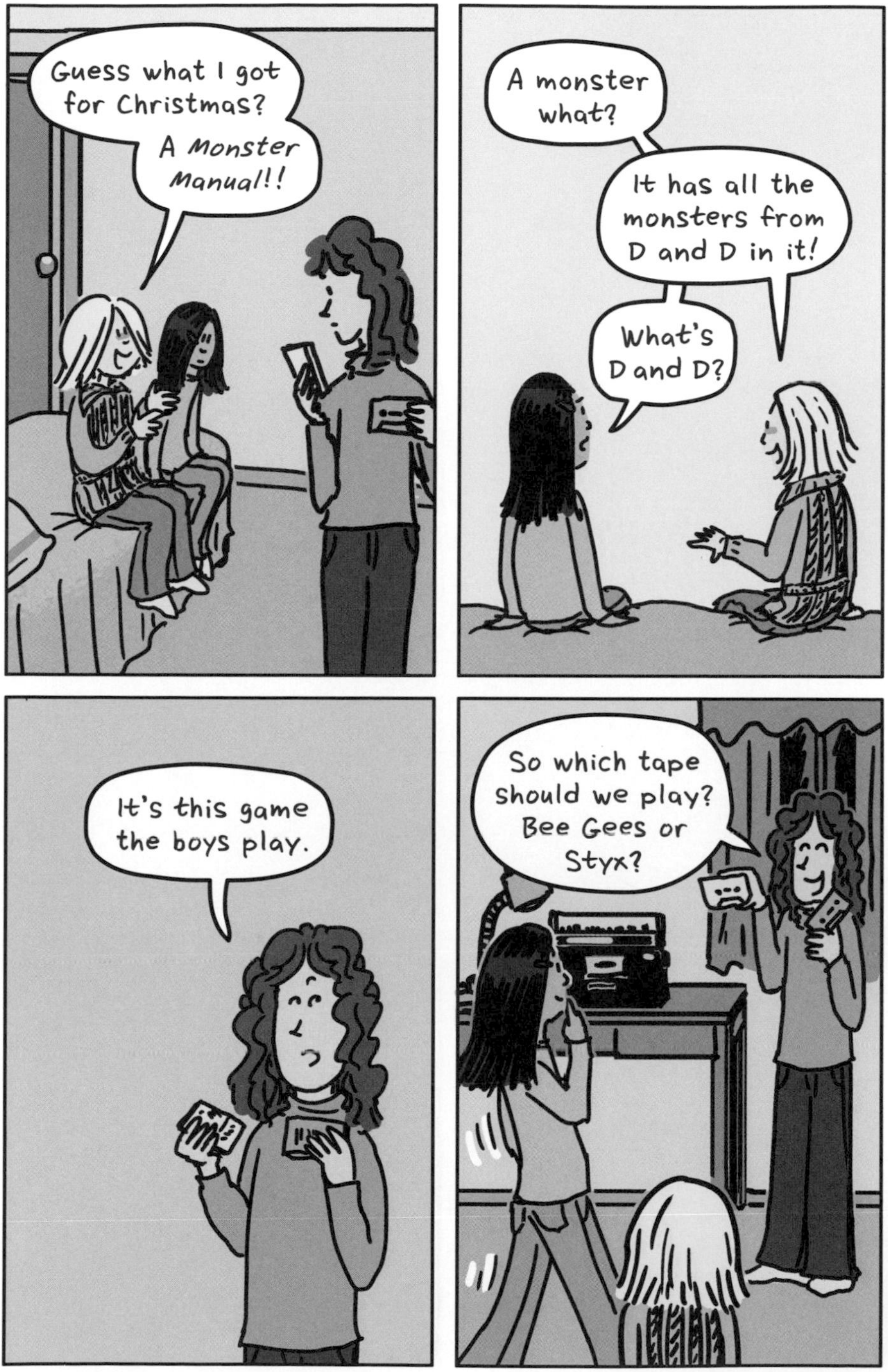
Guess what I got for Christmas?
A Monster Manual!!
A monster what?
It has all the monsters from D and D in it!
What's D and D?
It's this game the boys play.
So which tape should we play? Bee Gees or Styx?

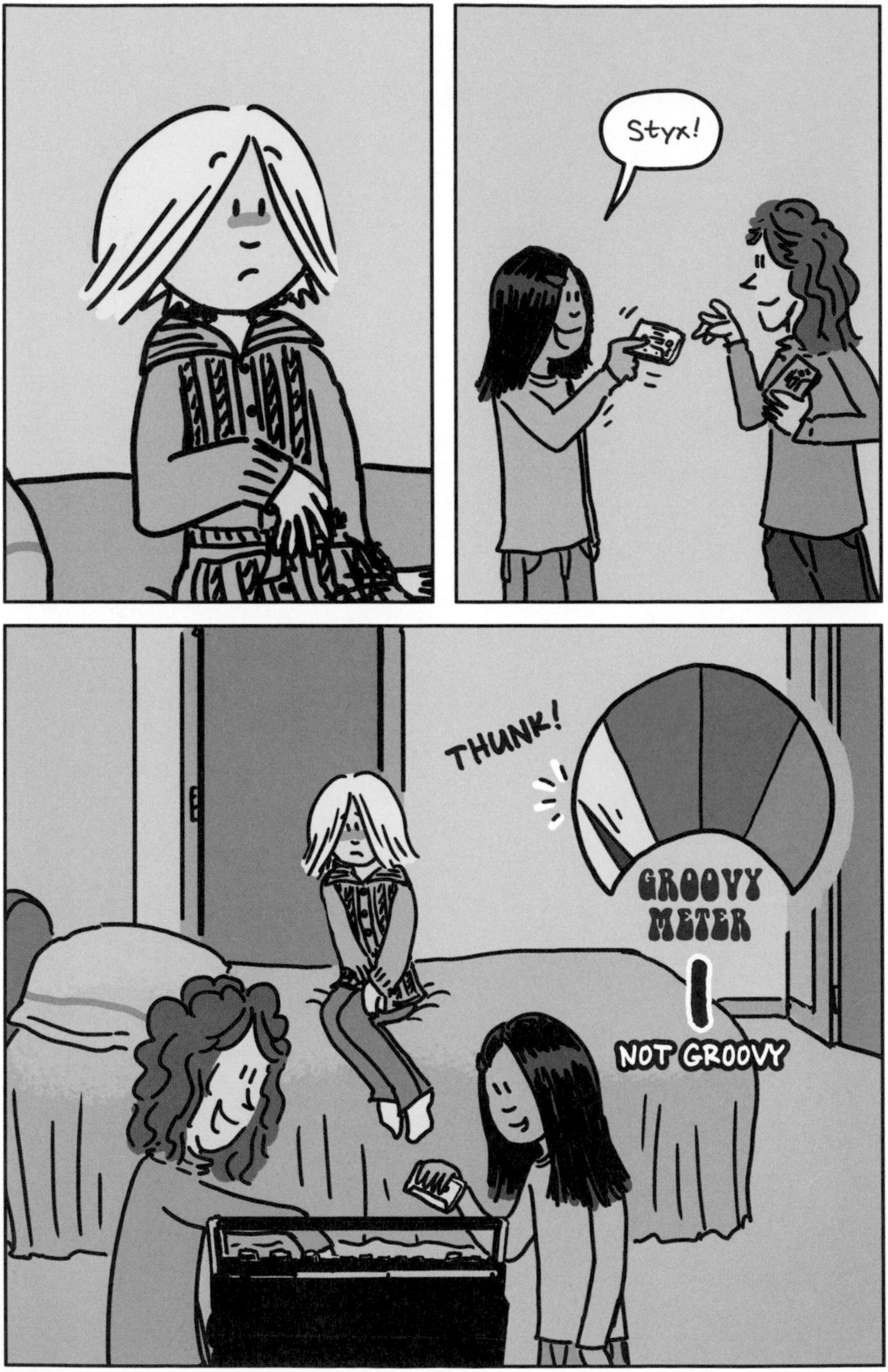
Styx!
THUNK!
GROOVY METER
NOT GROOVY

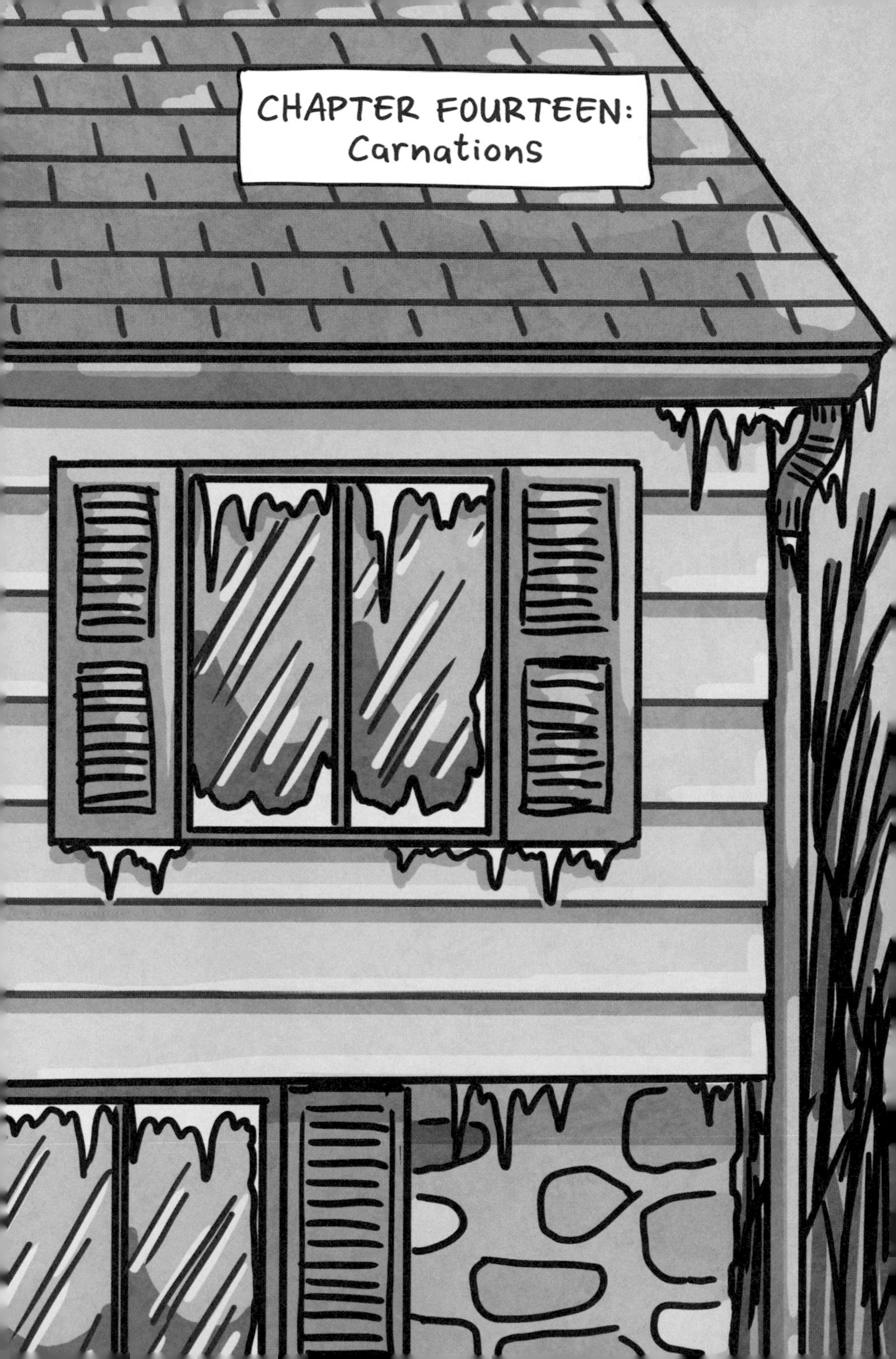
CHAPTER FOURTEEN:
Carnations

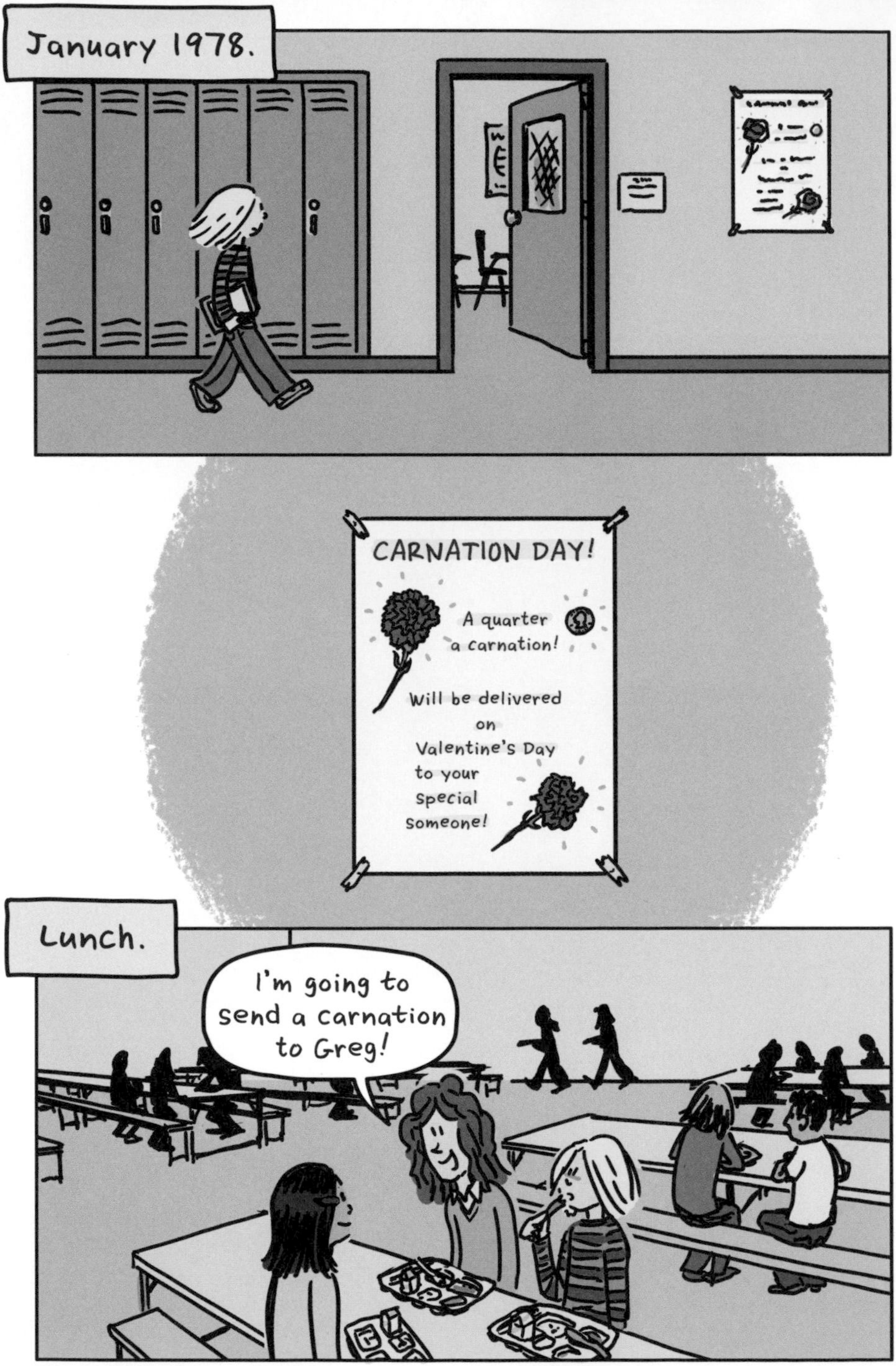

January 1978.
CARNATION DAY!
A quarter a carnation!
Will be delivered on Valentine's Day to your special someone!
Lunch.
I'm going to send a carnation to Greg!

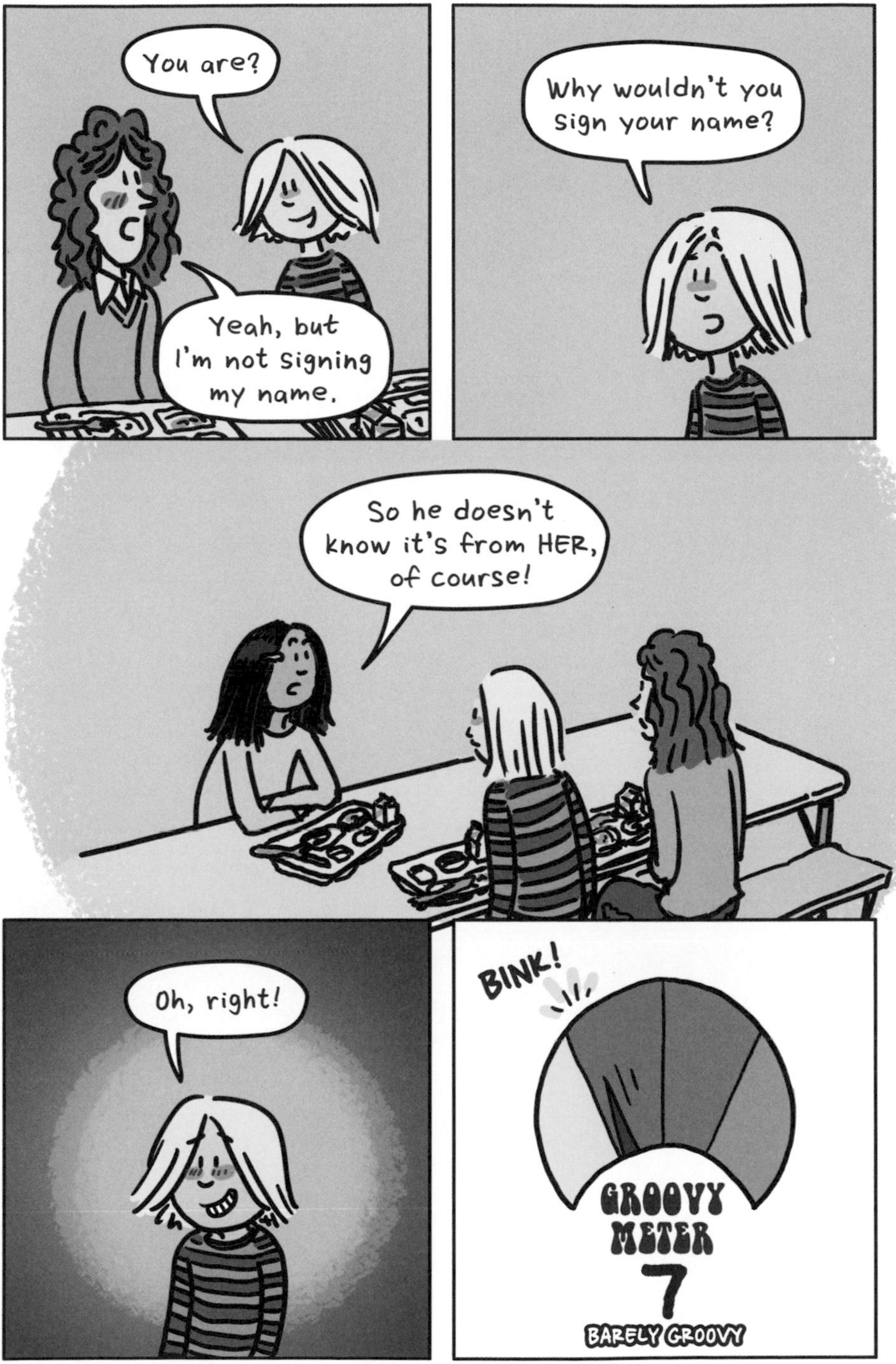
You are?
Yeah, but I'm not signing my name.
Why wouldn't you sign your name?
So he doesn't know it's from HER, of course!
Oh, right!
BINK!
GROOVY METER
7
BARELY GROOVY

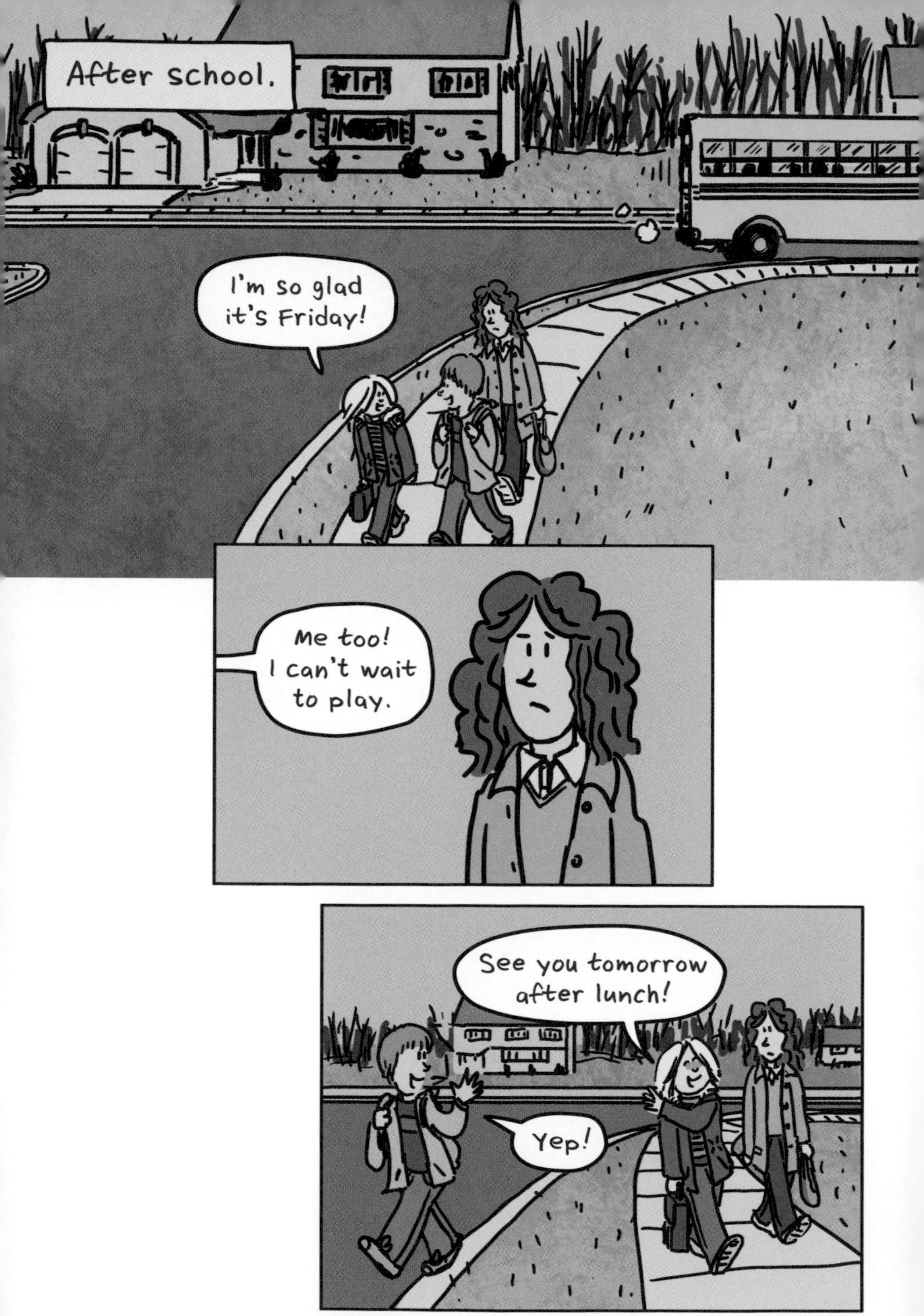
After school.
I'm so glad it's Friday!
Me too! I can't wait to play.
See you tomorrow after lunch!
Yep!

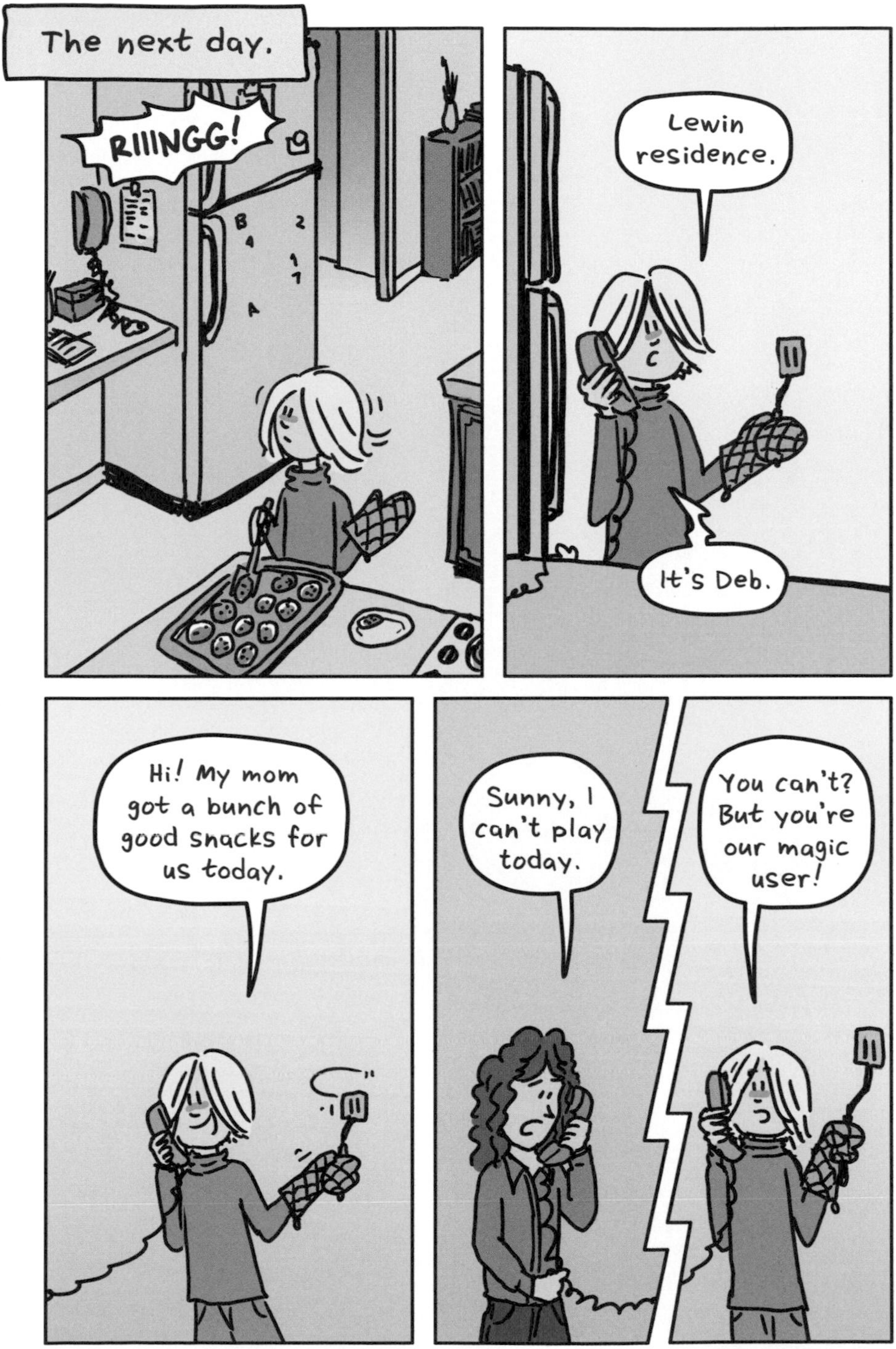
The next day.
RIIINGG!
Lewin residence.
It's Deb.
Hi! My mom got a bunch of good snacks for us today.
Sunny, I can't play today.
You can't? But you're our magic user!

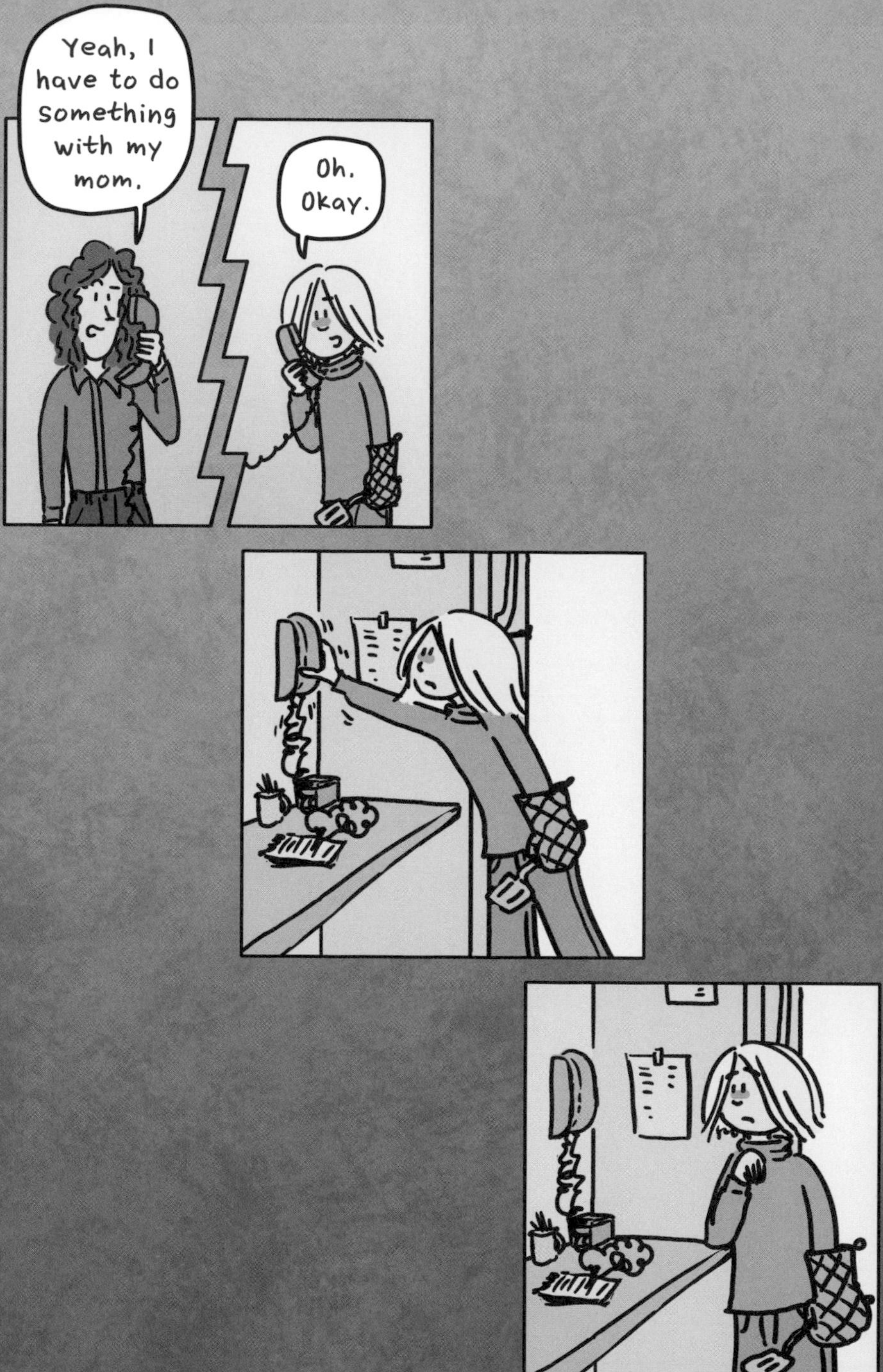
Yeah, I have to do something with my mom.
Oh. Okay.

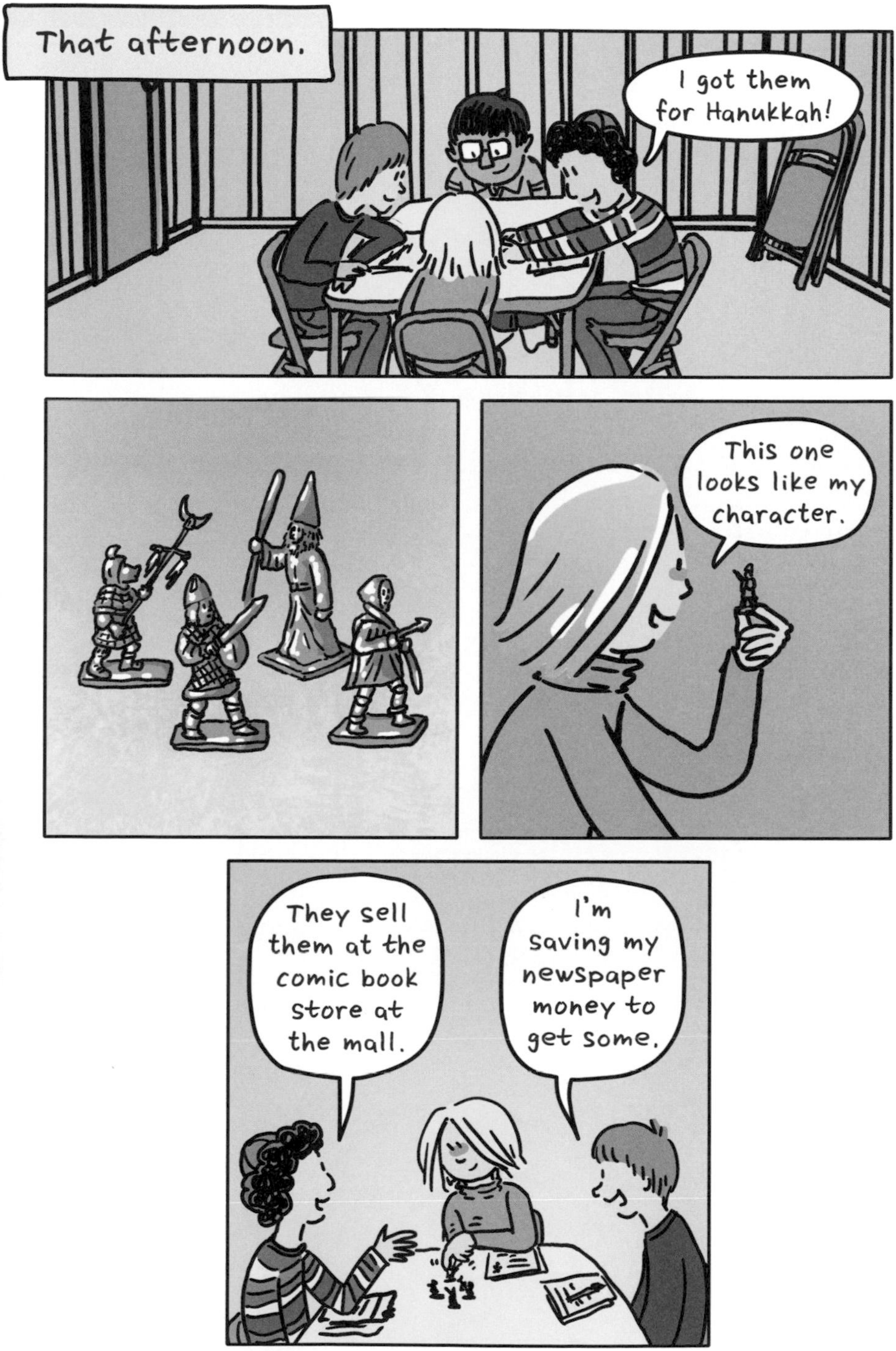
That afternoon.
I got them for Hanukkah!
This one looks like my character.
They sell them at the comic book store at the mall.
I'm saving my newspaper money to get some.

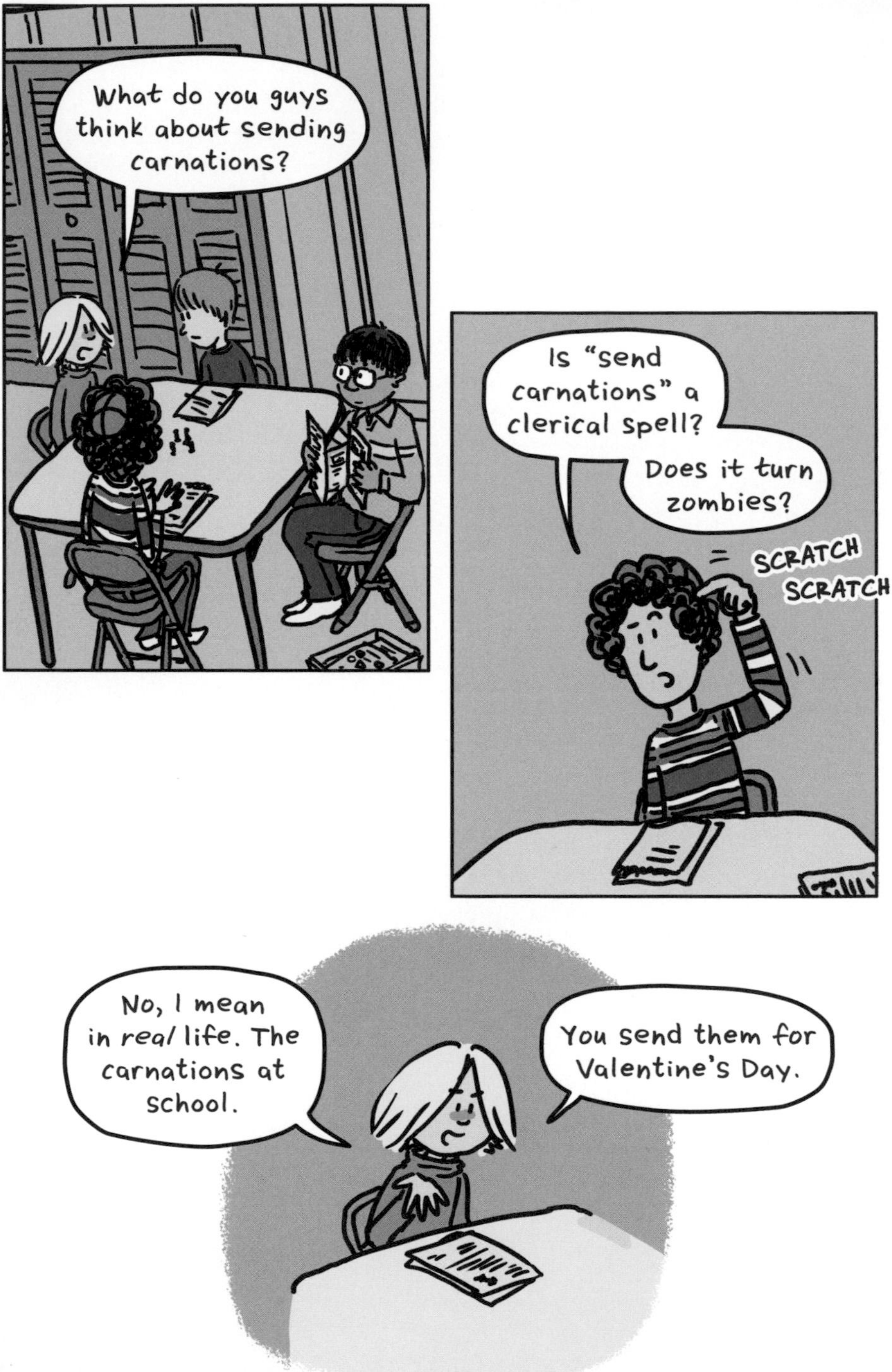
What do you guys think about sending carnations?
Is "send carnations" a clerical spell?
Does it turn zombies?
SCRATCH SCRATCH
No, I mean in *real* life. The carnations at school.
You send them for Valentine's Day.

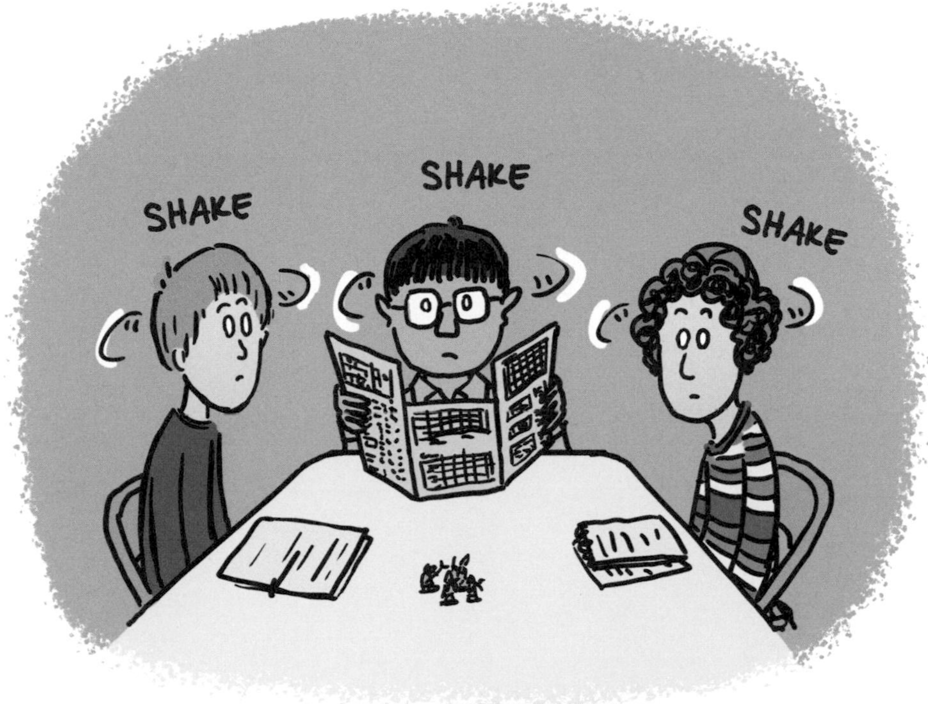
SHAKE
SHAKE
SHAKE

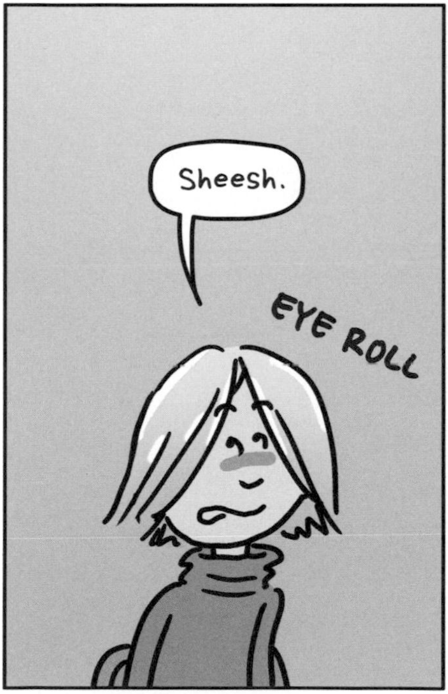
Sheesh.
EYE ROLL

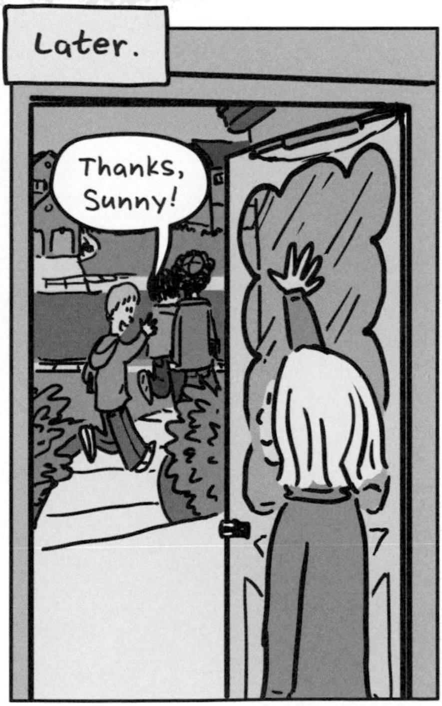
Later.
Thanks, Sunny!

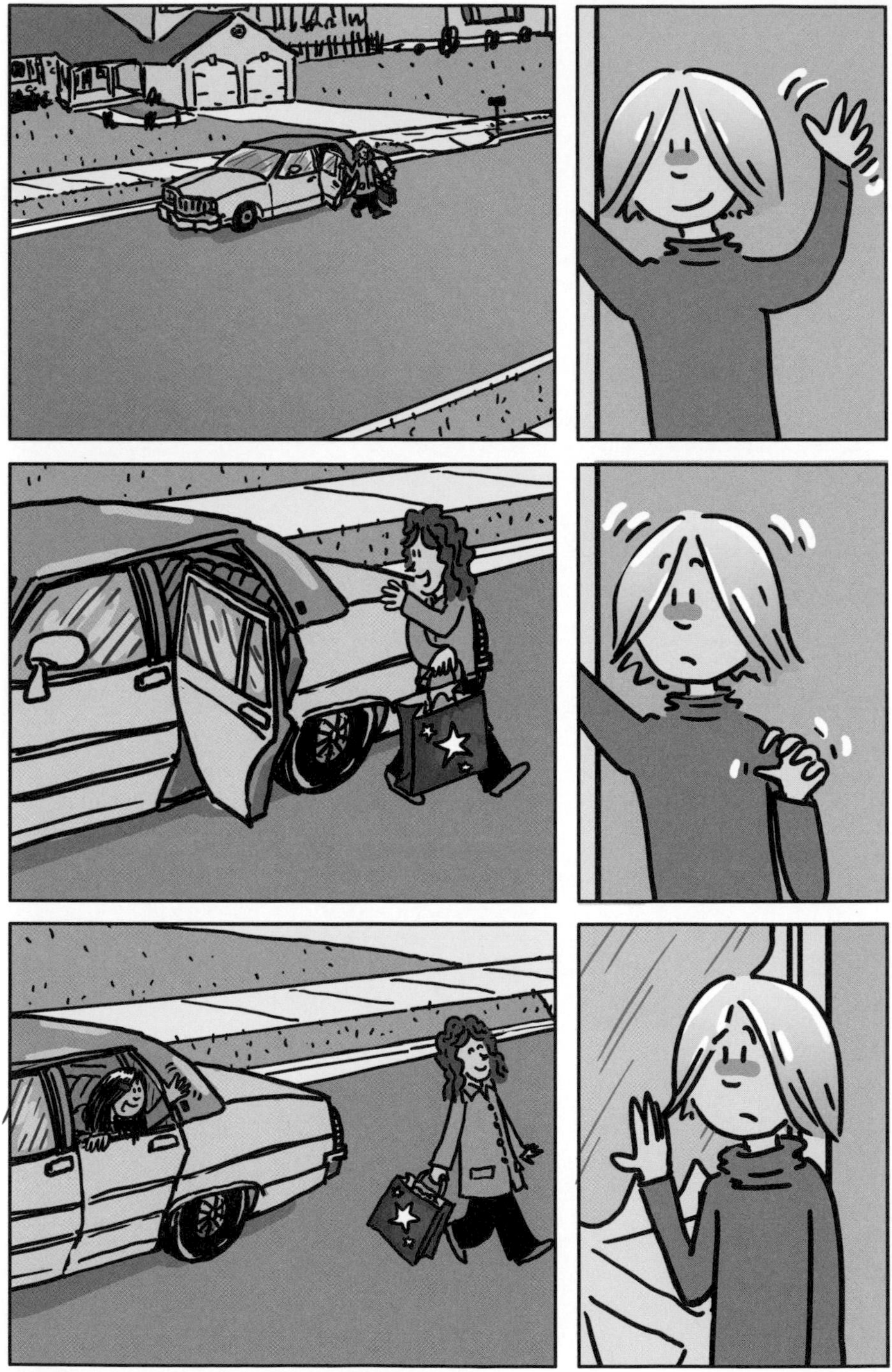

CHAPTER FIFTEEN: Secret Pal

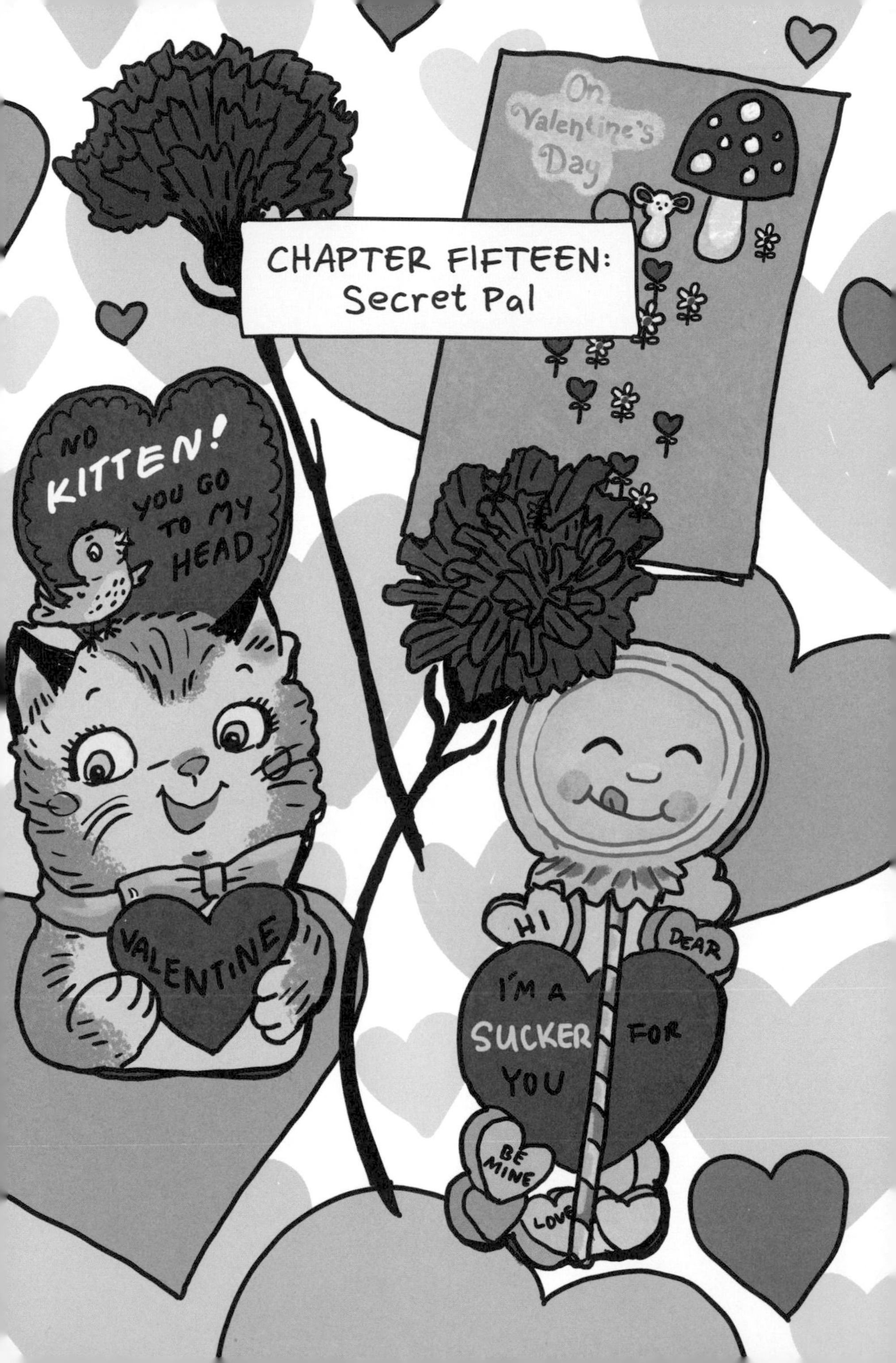
On Valentine's Day
NO KITTEN! YOU GO TO MY HEAD
VALENTINE
HI
DEAR
I'M A SUCKER FOR YOU
BE MINE
LOVE

Valentine's Day.

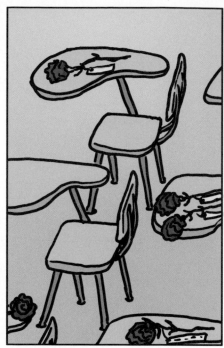

154

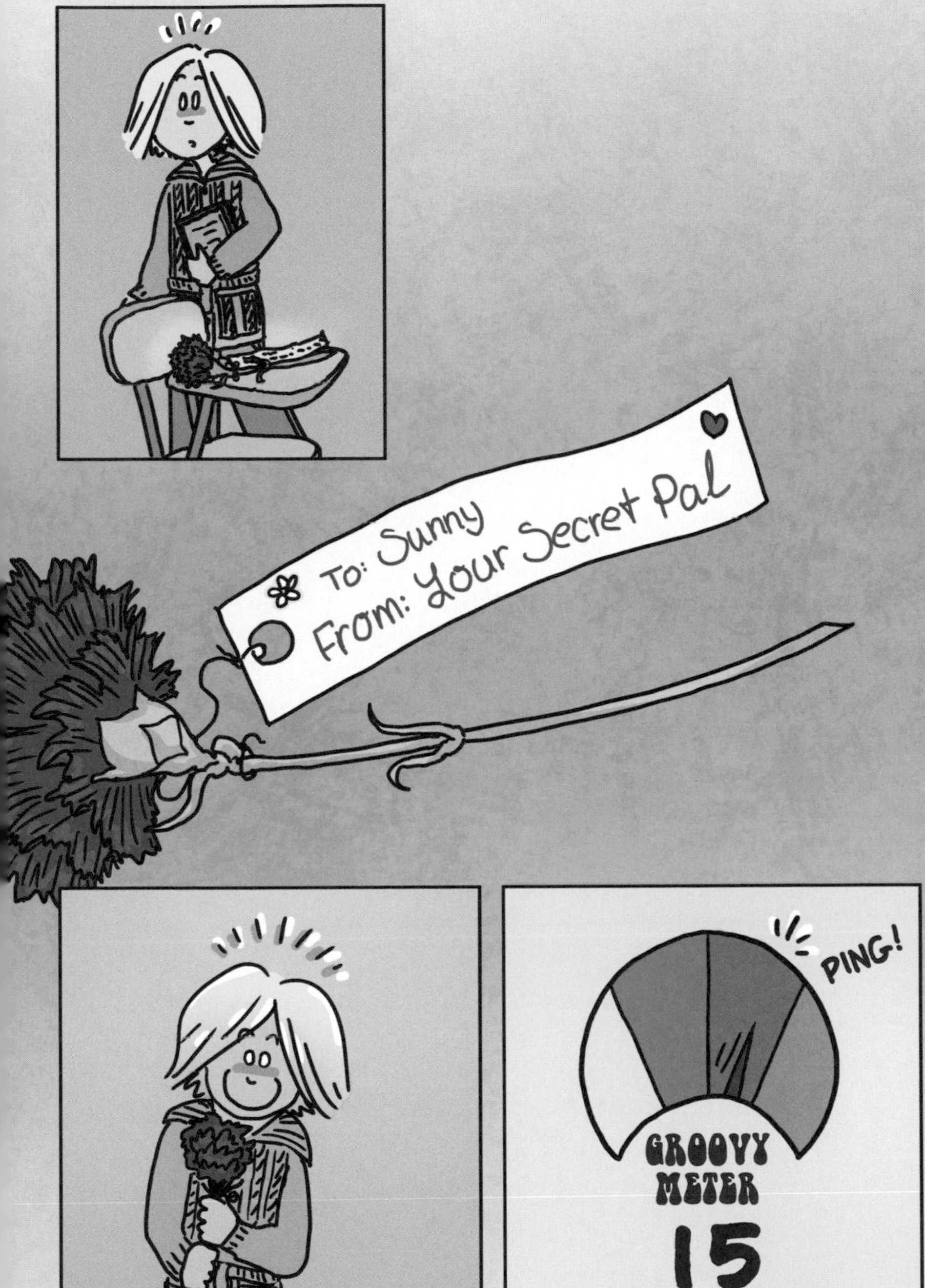
To: Sunny
From: Your Secret Pal
PING!
GROOVY METER
15
GETTING GROOVY!

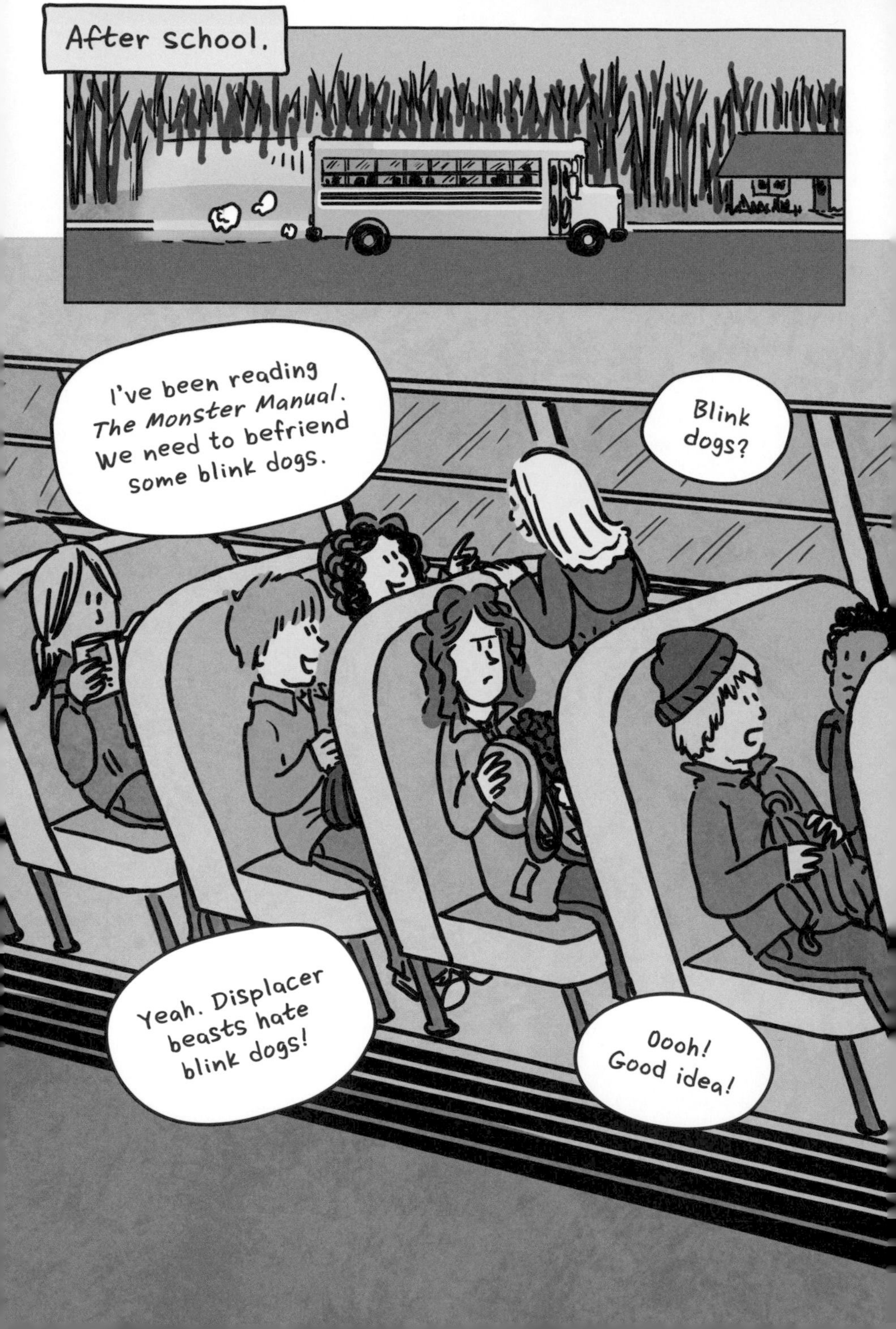
After school.
I've been reading *The Monster Manual*. We need to befriend some blink dogs.
Blink dogs?
Yeah. Displacer beasts hate blink dogs!
Oooh! Good idea!

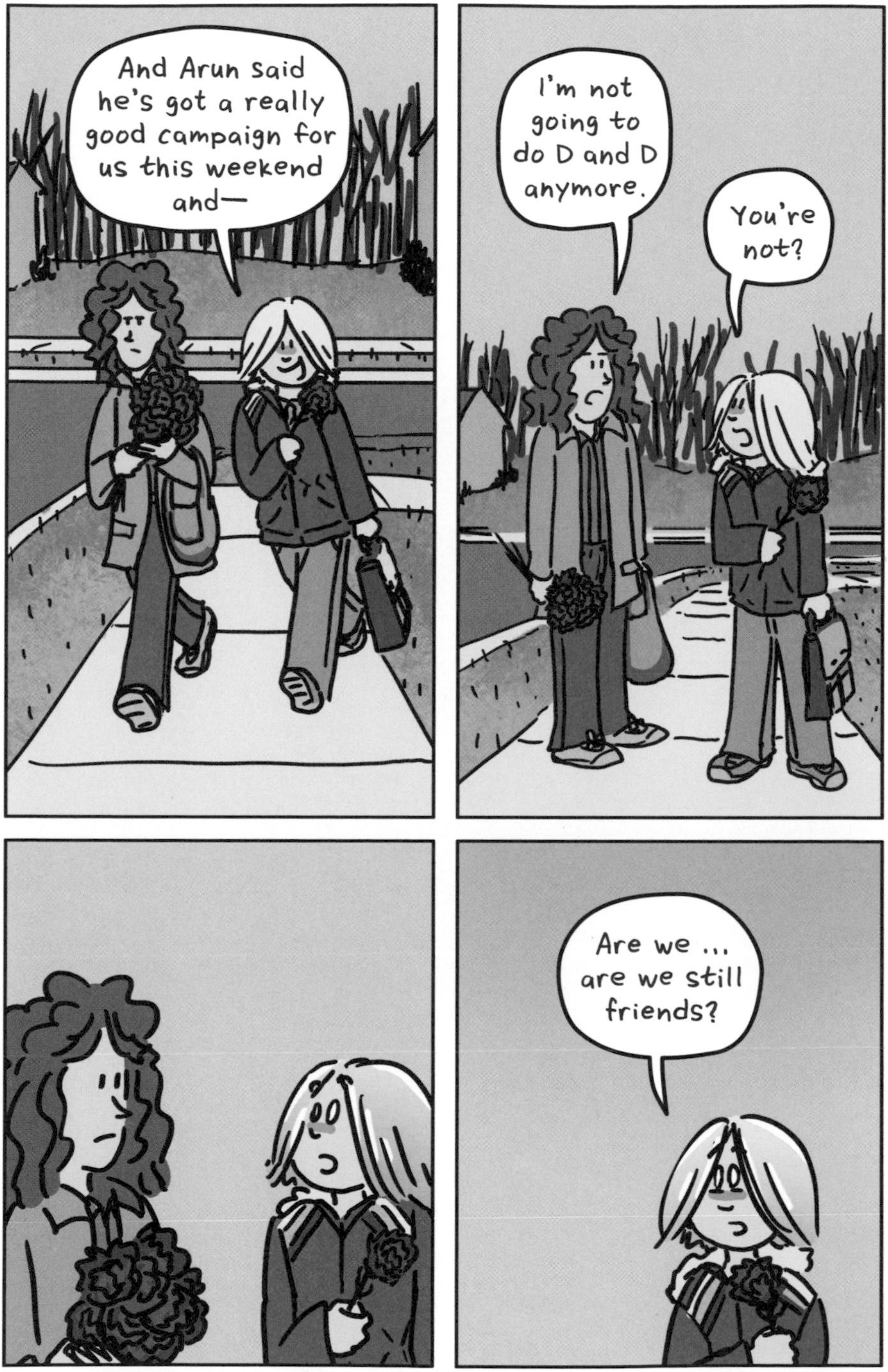
And Arun said he's got a really good campaign for us this weekend and—
I'm not going to do D and D anymore.
You're not?
Are we ... are we still friends?

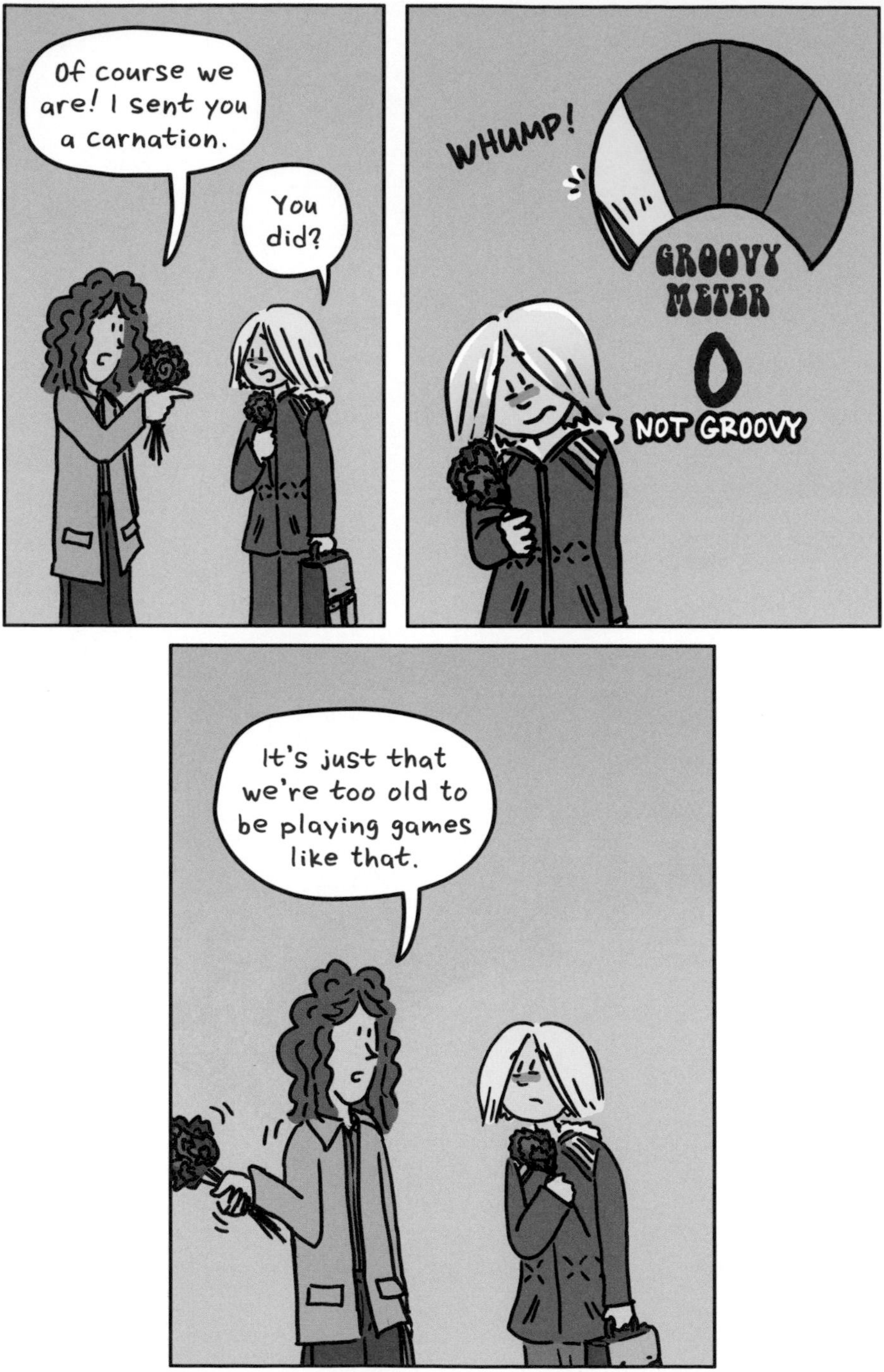
Of course we are! I sent you a carnation.
You did?
WHUMP!
GROOVY METER
0
NOT GROOVY
It's just that we're too old to be playing games like that.

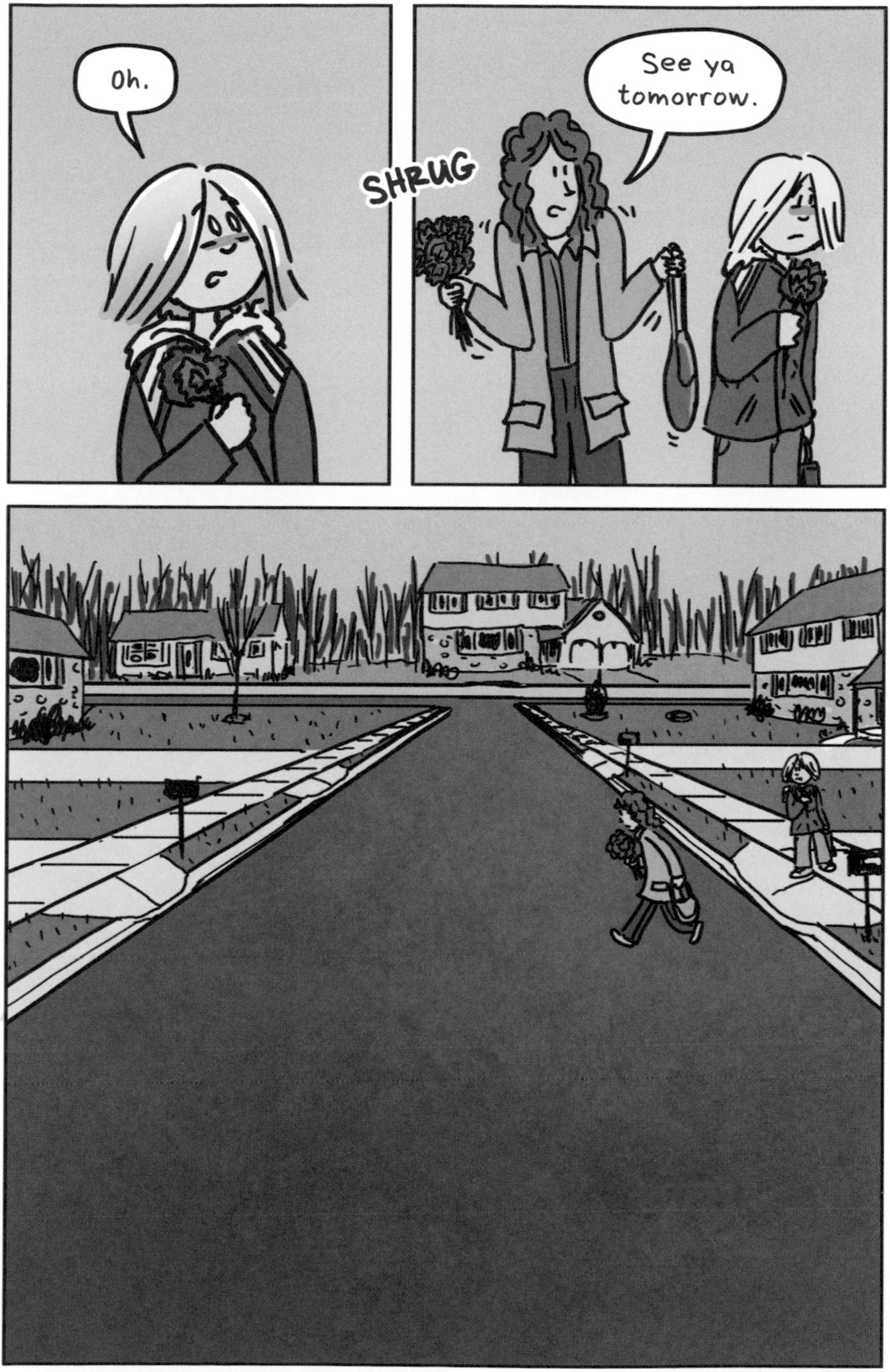
Oh.
SHRUG
See ya tomorrow.

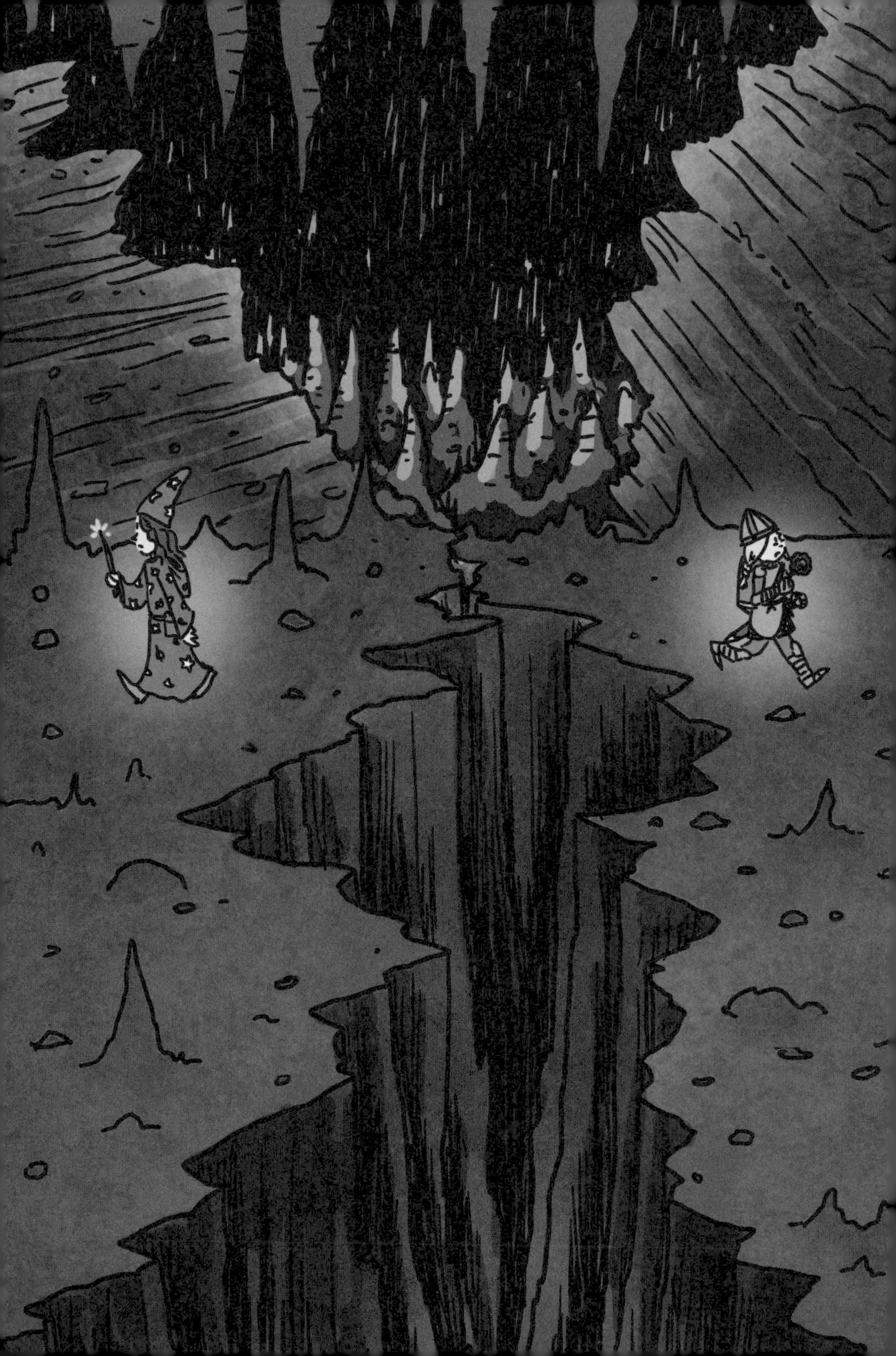

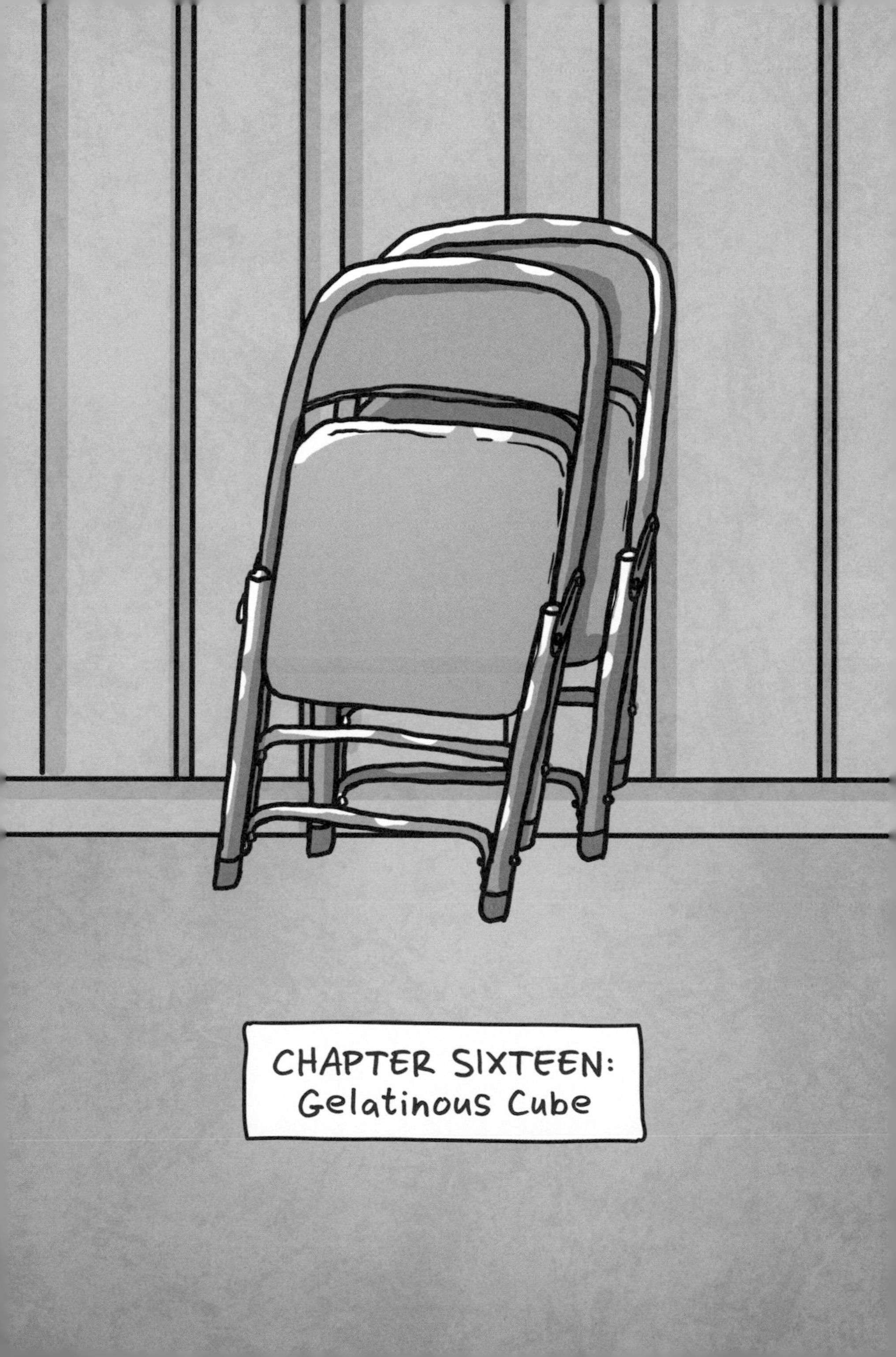

CHAPTER SIXTEEN: Gelatinous Cube

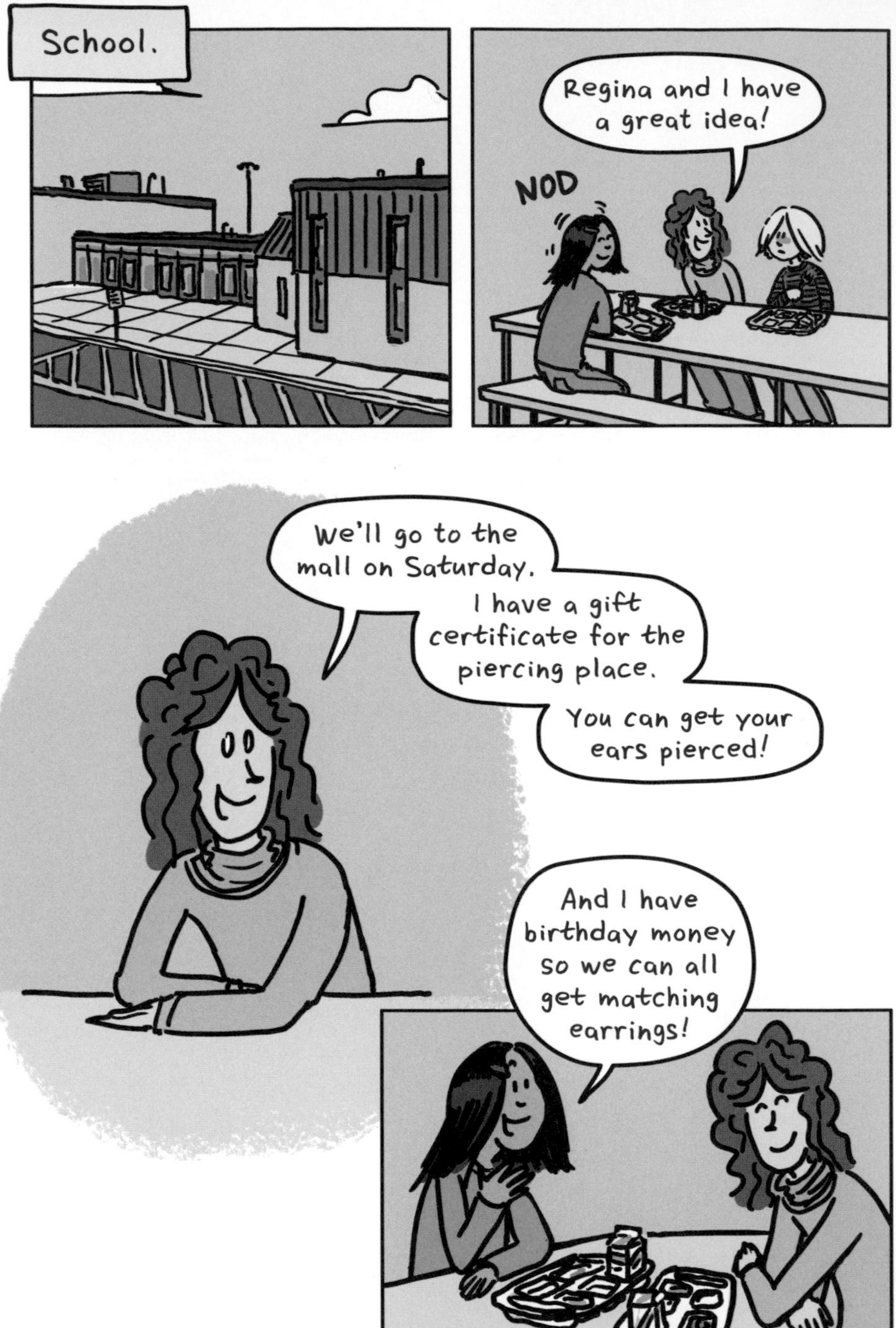
School.
Regina and I have a great idea!
NOD
We'll go to the mall on Saturday.
I have a gift certificate for the piercing place.
You can get your ears pierced!
And I have birthday money so we can all get matching earrings!

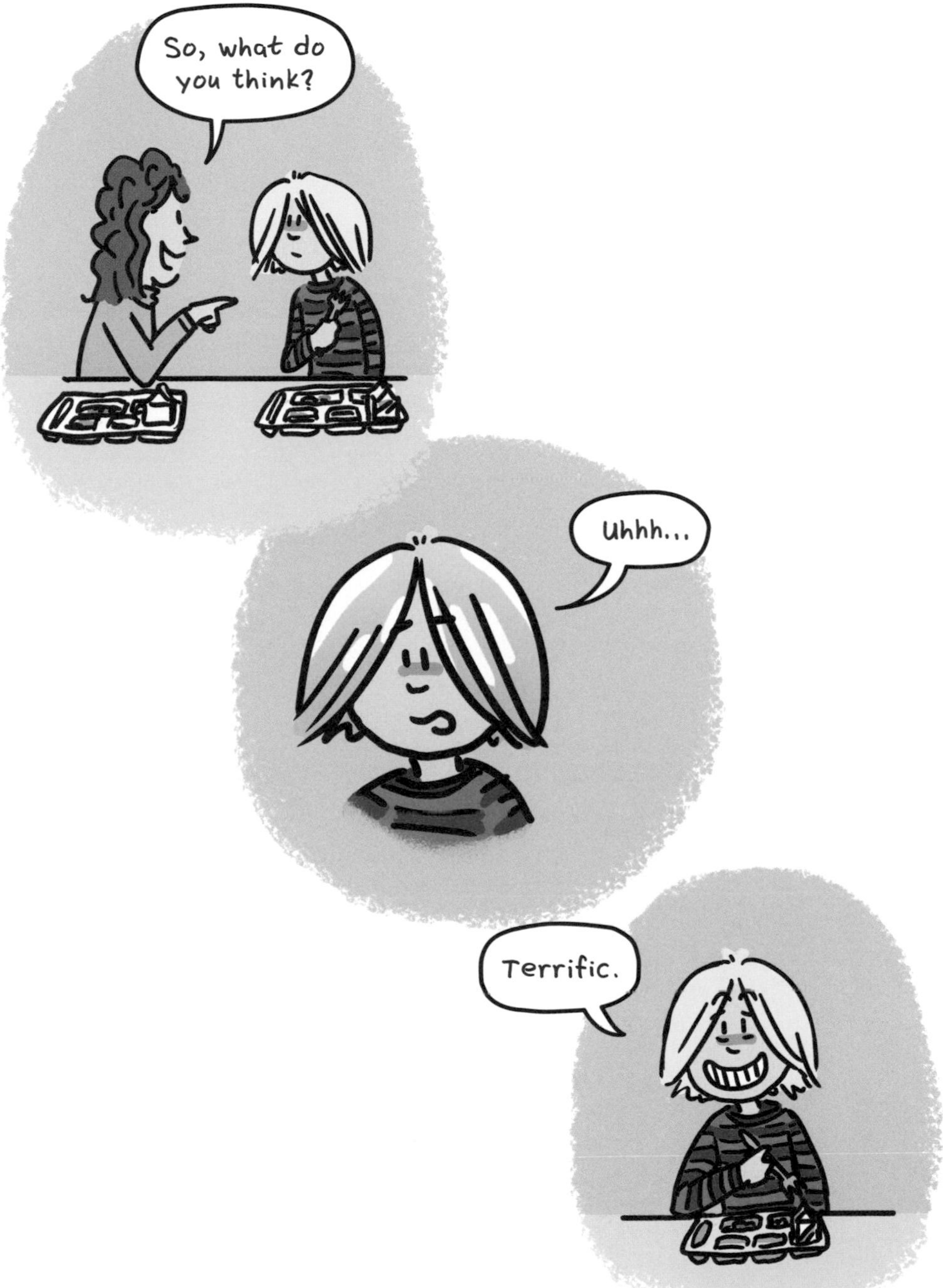
So, what do you think?
Uhhh...
Terrific.

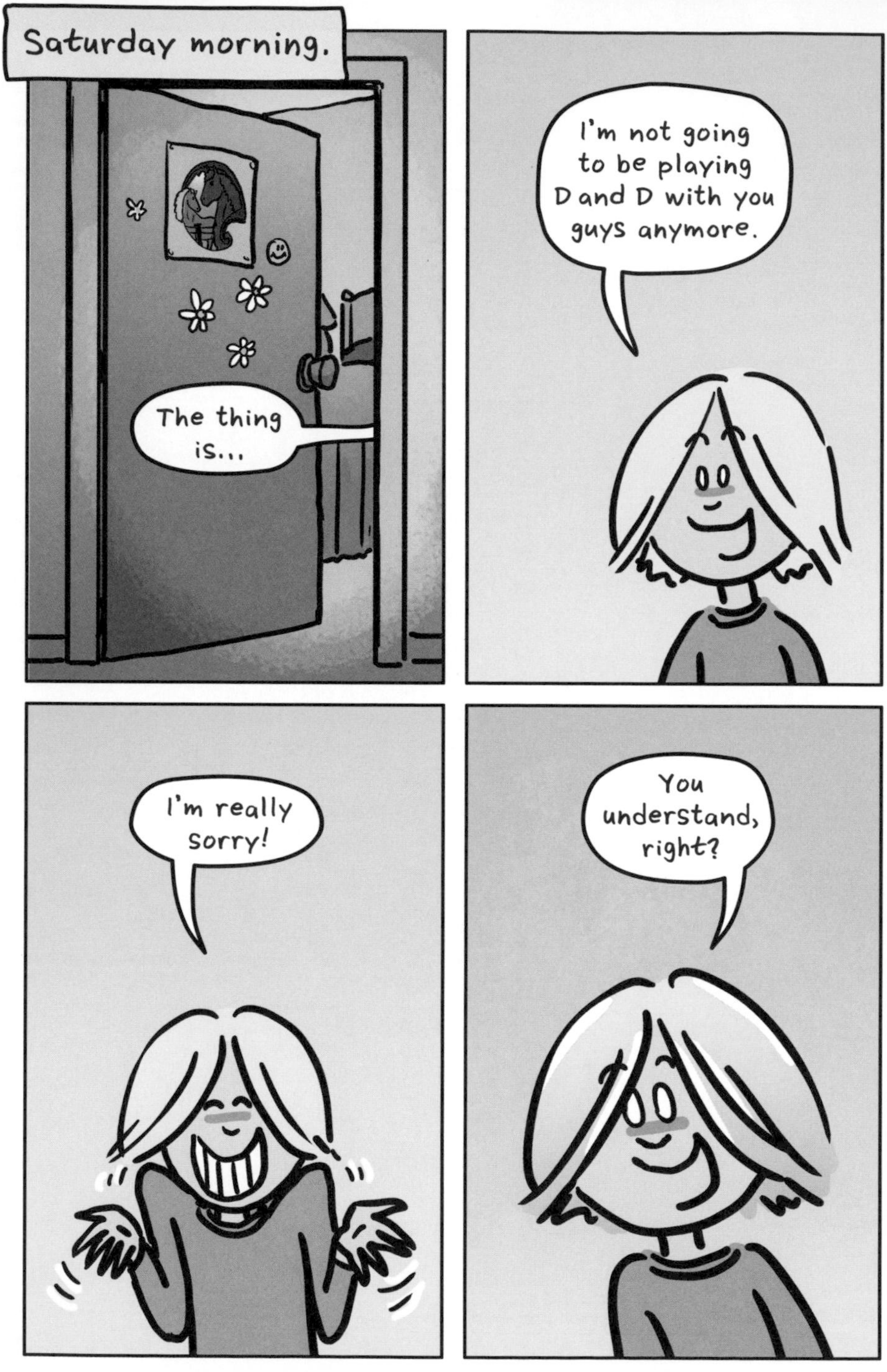

Saturday morning.
The thing is...
I'm not going to be playing D and D with you guys anymore.
I'm really sorry!
You understand, right?

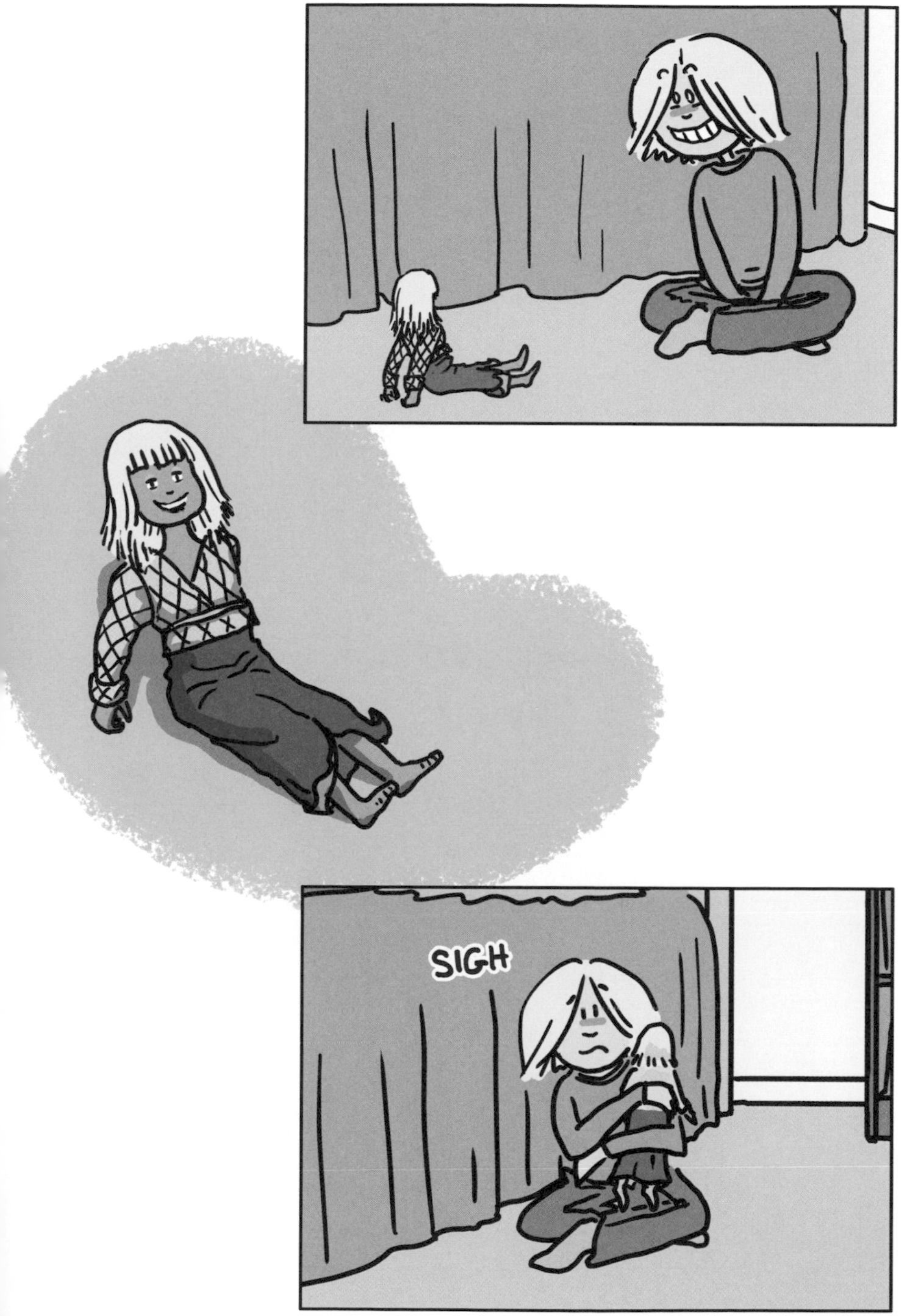
SIGH

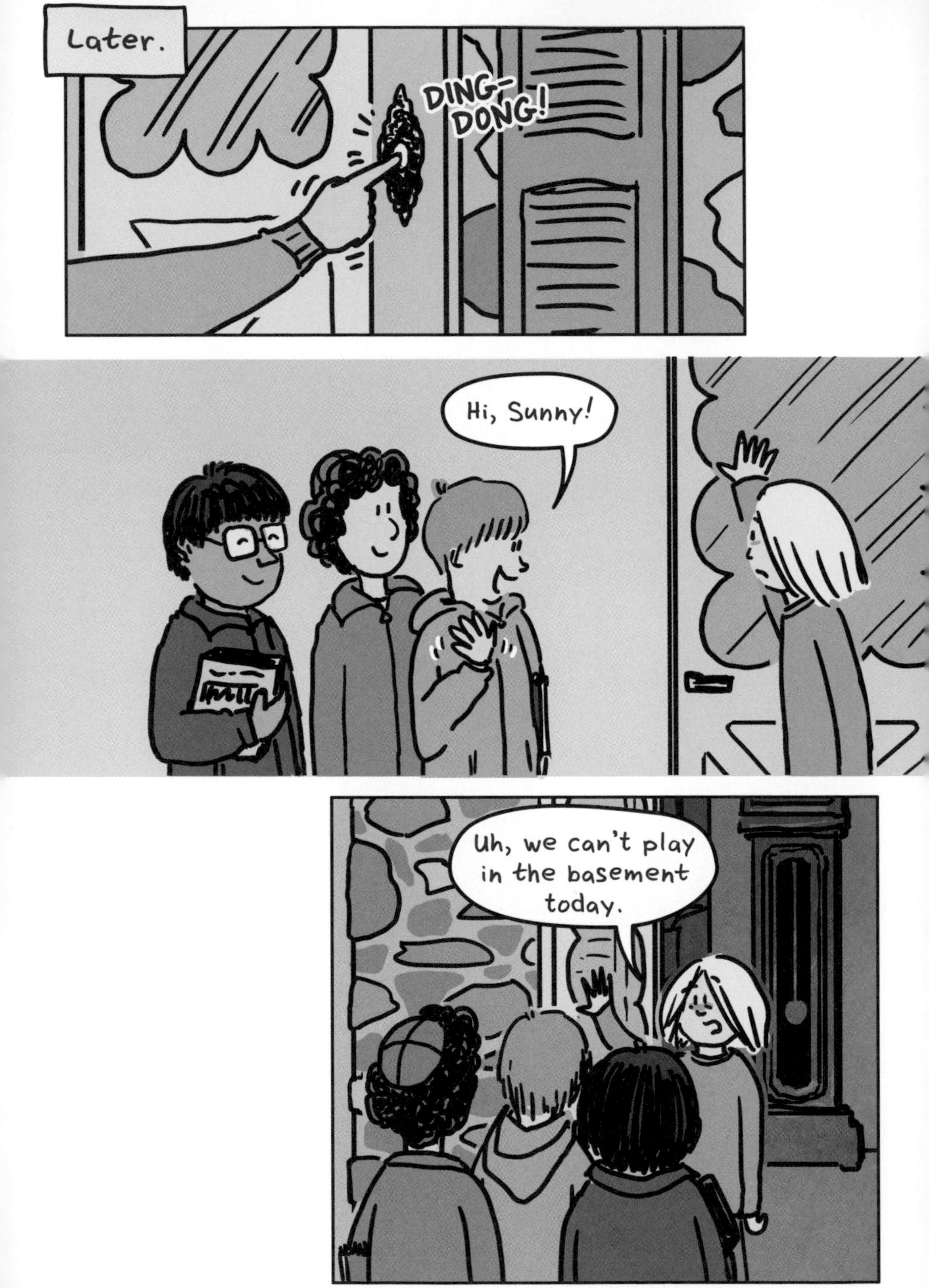
Later.
DING-DONG!
Hi, Sunny!
Uh, we can't play in the basement today.

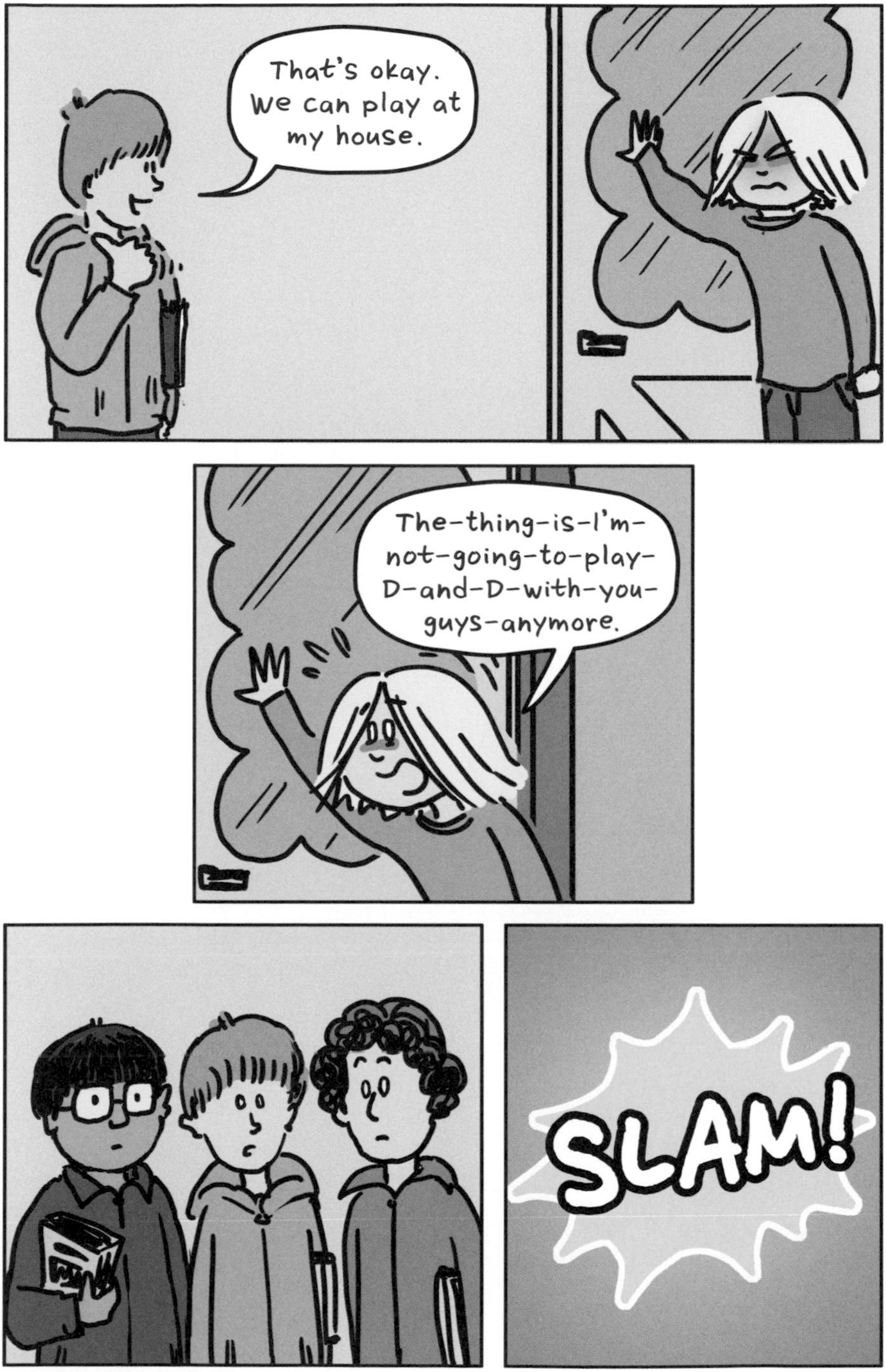
That's okay. We can play at my house.
The-thing-is-I'm-not-going-to-play-D-and-D-with-you-guys-anymore.
SLAM!

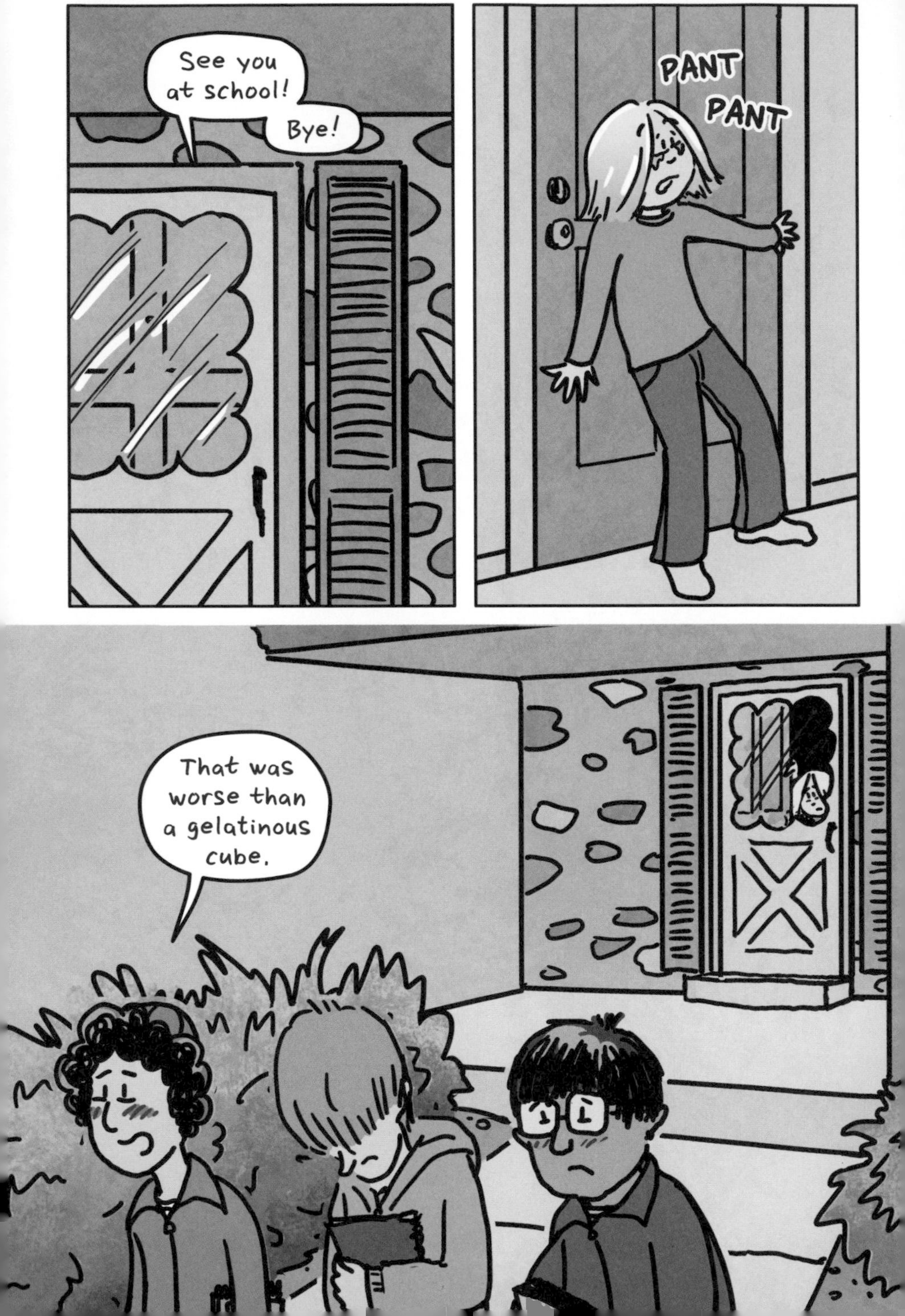
See you at school!
Bye!
PANT
PANT
That was worse than a gelatinous cube.

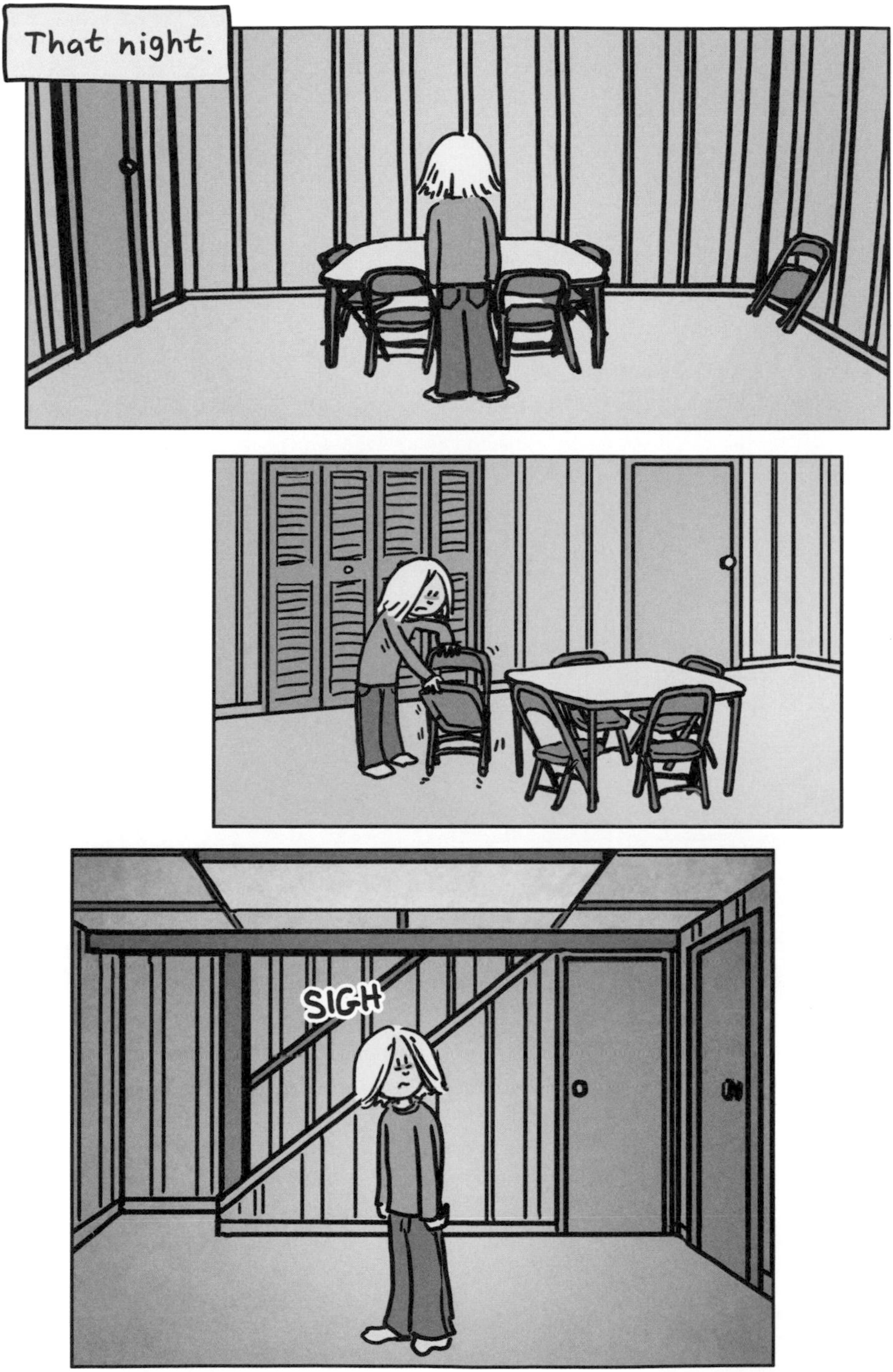
That night.
SIGH

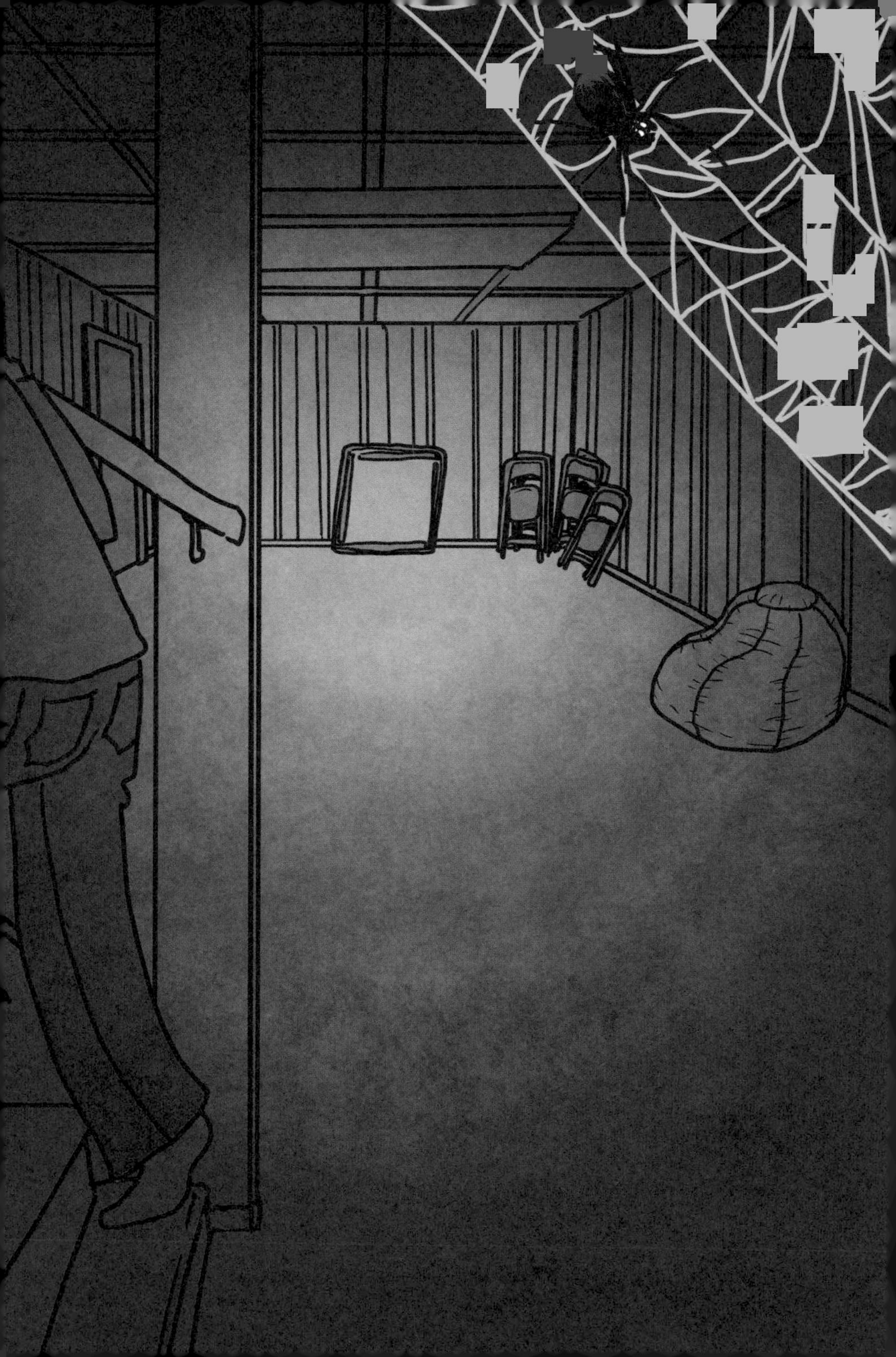

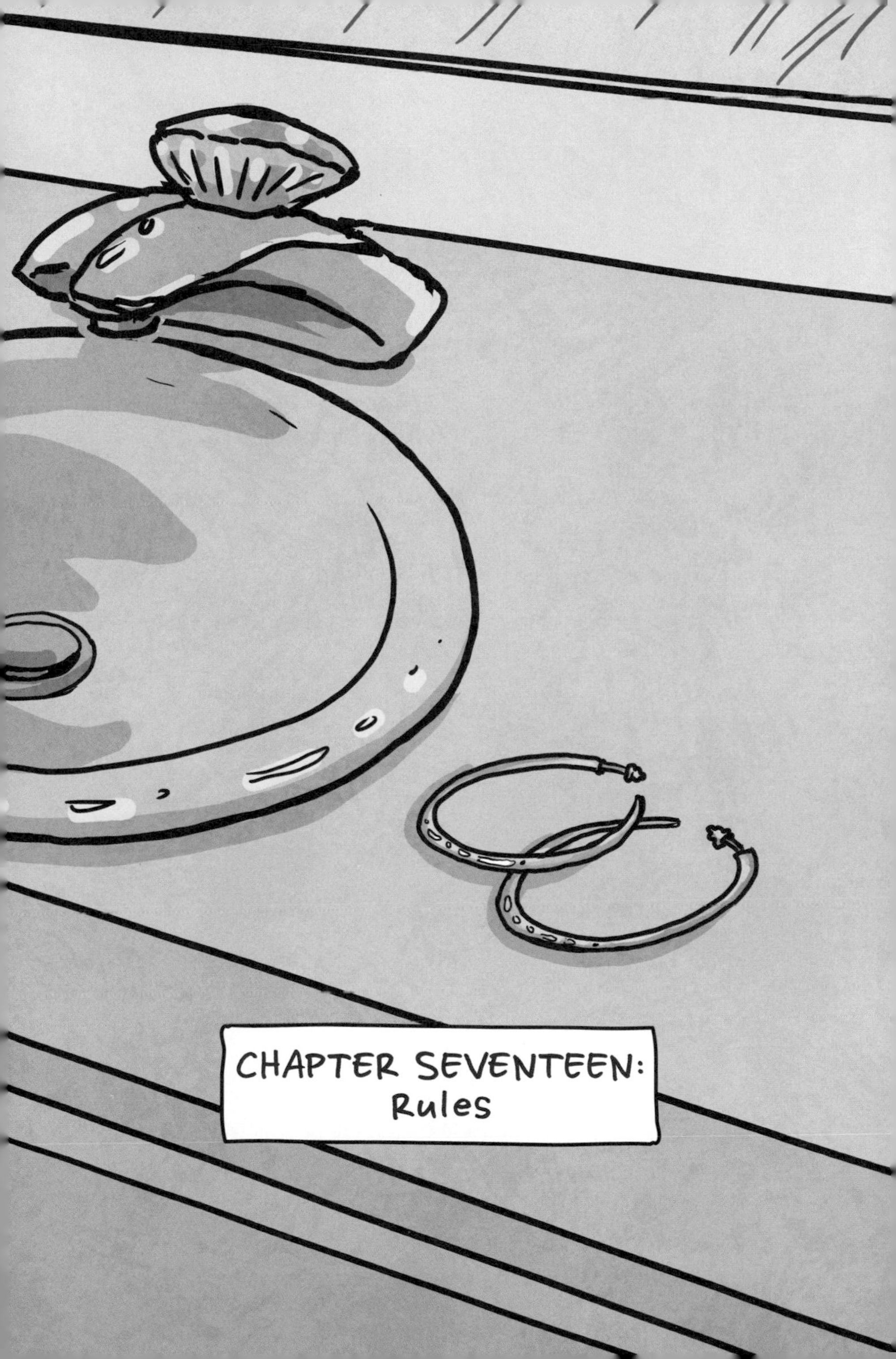
CHAPTER SEVENTEEN:
Rules

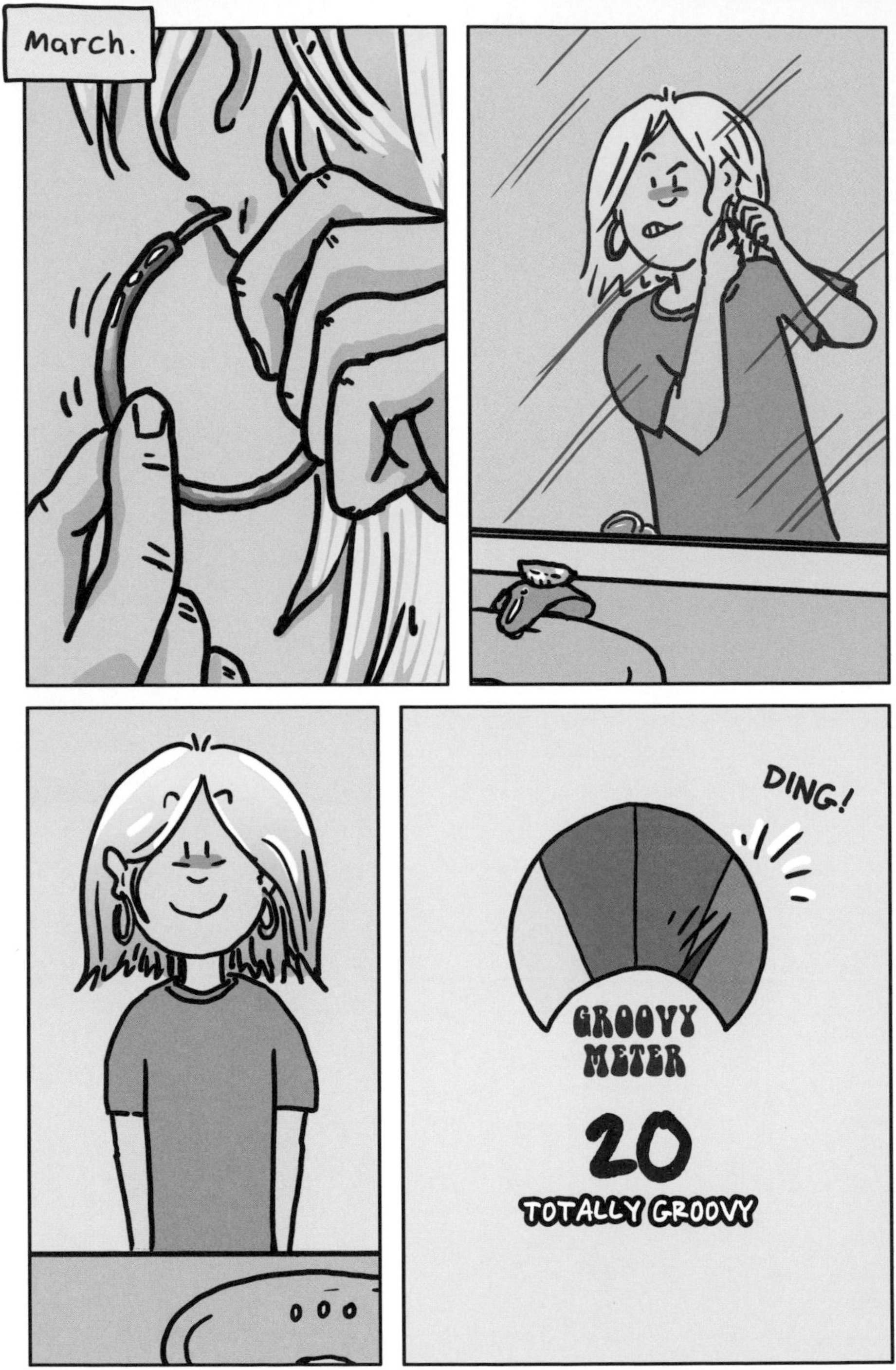
March.
DING!
GROOVY METER
20
TOTALLY GROOVY

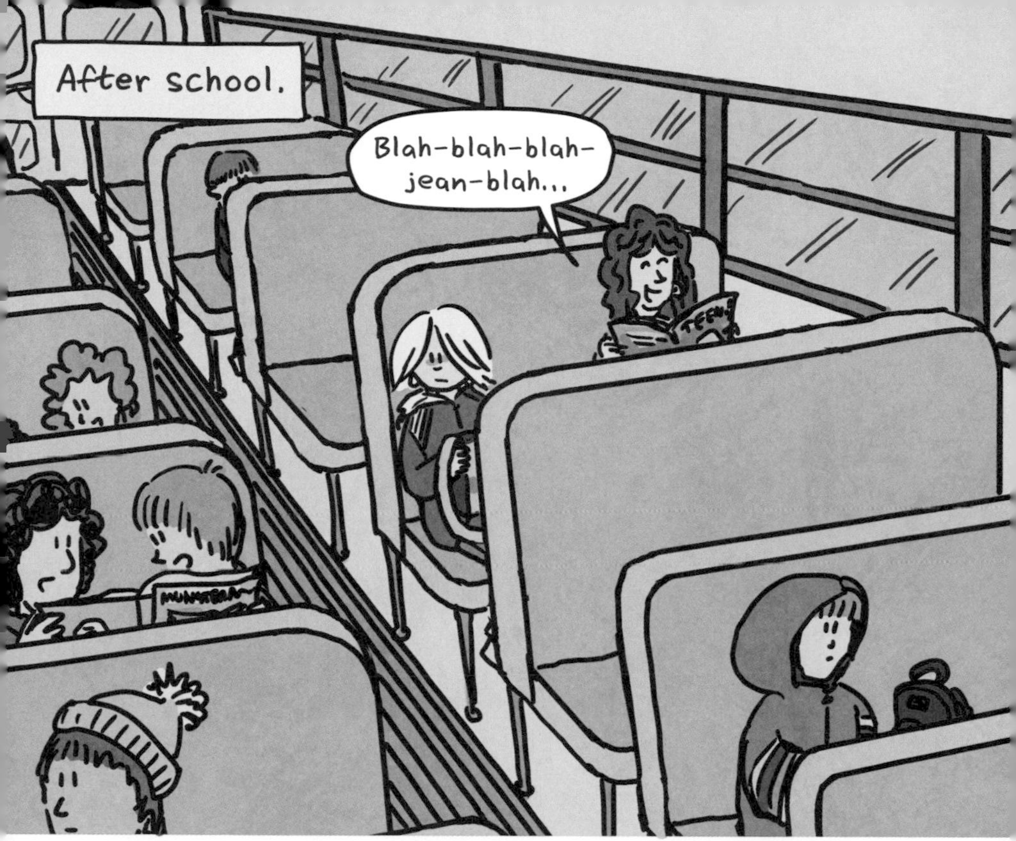
After school.
Blah-blah-blah-jean-blah...

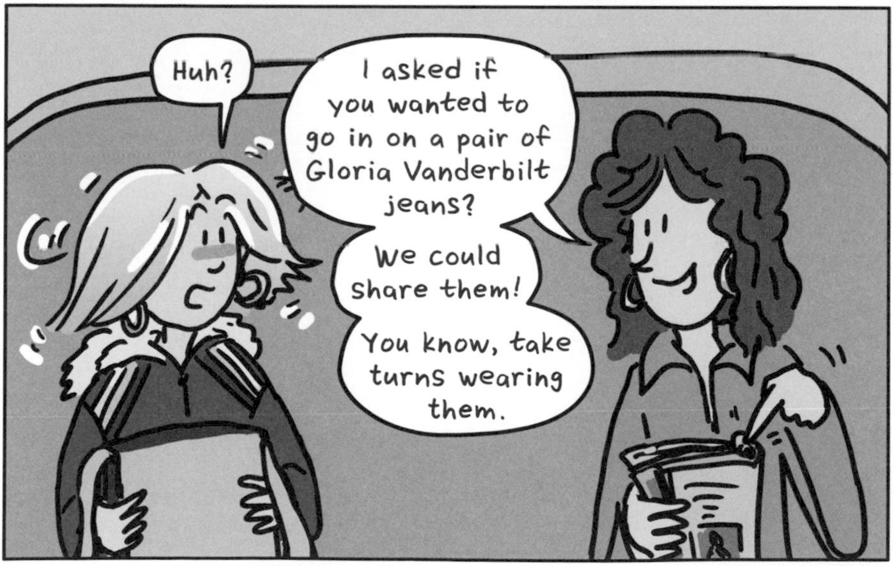
Huh?
I asked if you wanted to go in on a pair of Gloria Vanderbilt jeans?
We could share them!
You know, take turns wearing them.

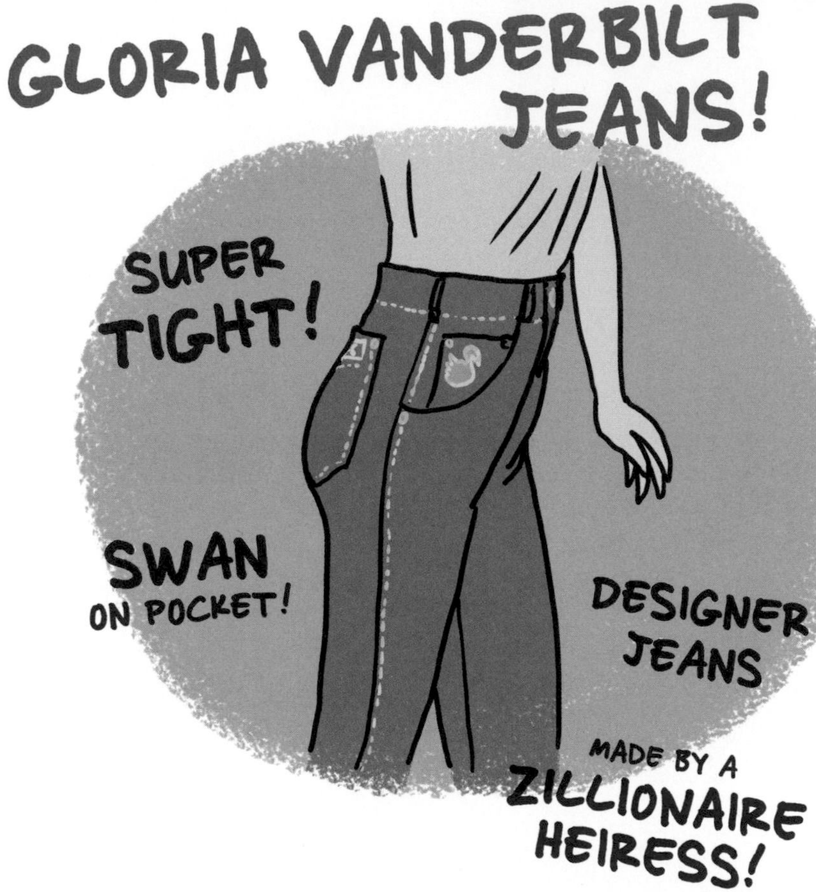
GLORIA VANDERBILT JEANS!
SUPER TIGHT!
SWAN ON POCKET!
DESIGNER JEANS
MADE BY A ZILLIONAIRE HEIRESS!

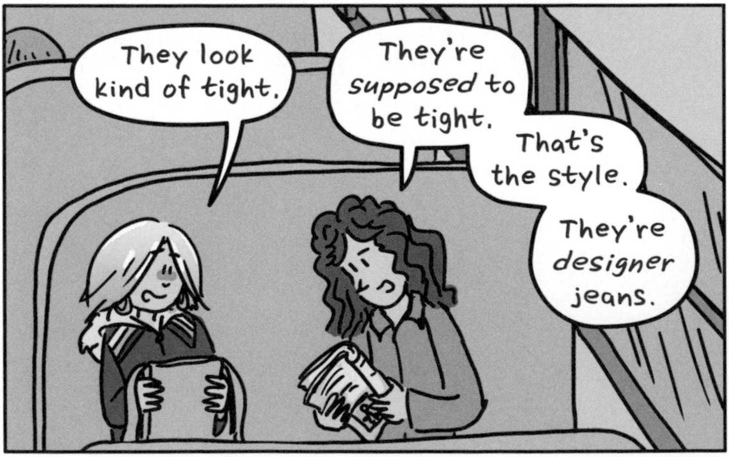
They look kind of tight.
They're *supposed* to be tight.
That's the style.
They're *designer* jeans.

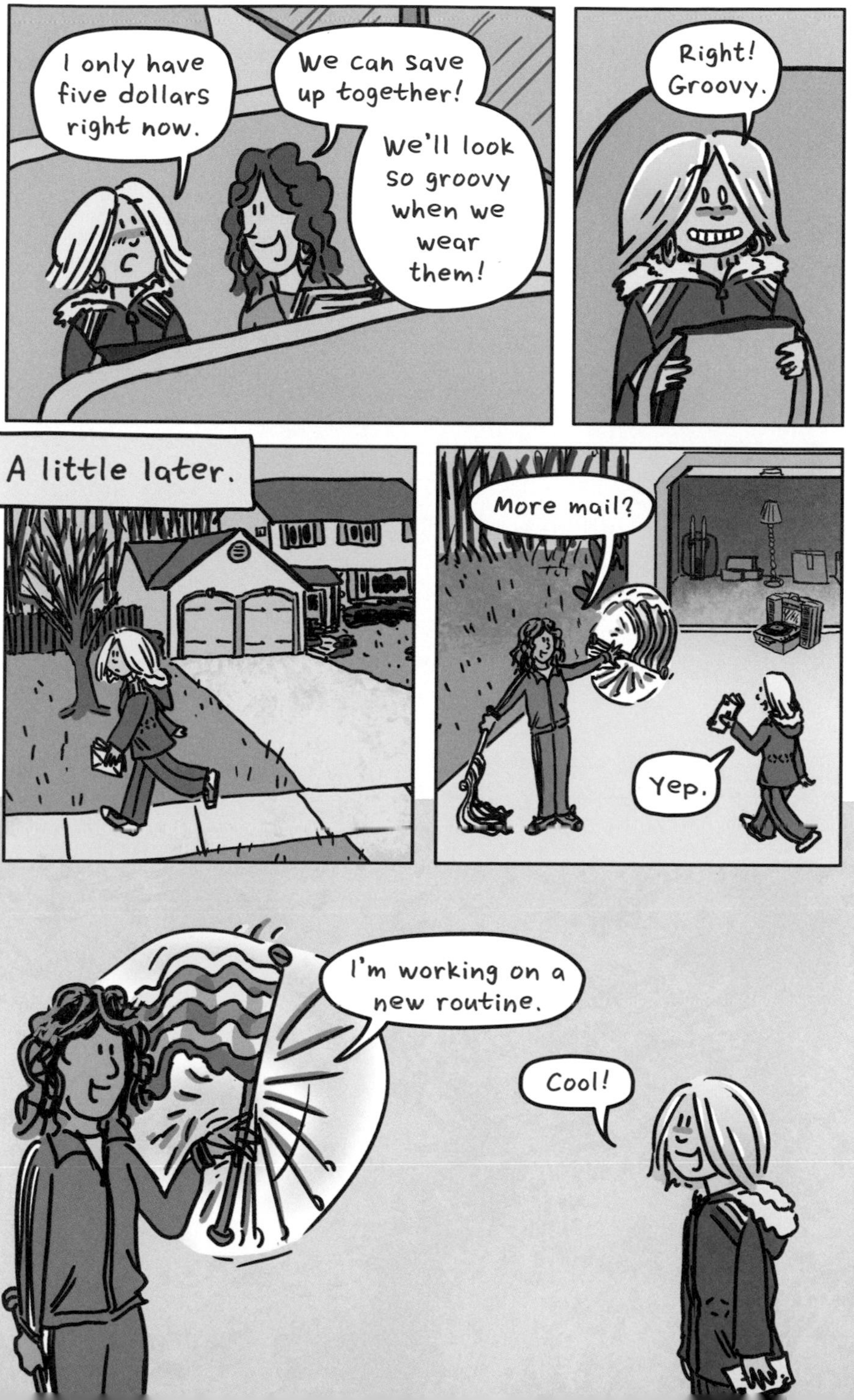
I only have five dollars right now.
We can save up together!
We'll look so groovy when we wear them!
Right! Groovy.
A little later.
More mail?
Yep.
I'm working on a new routine.
Cool!

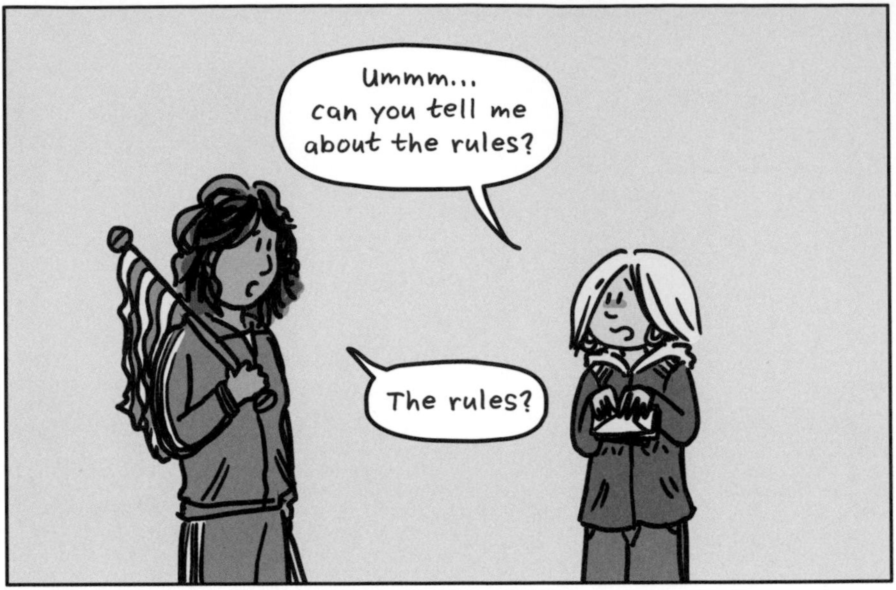
Ummm...
can you tell me
about the rules?
The rules?

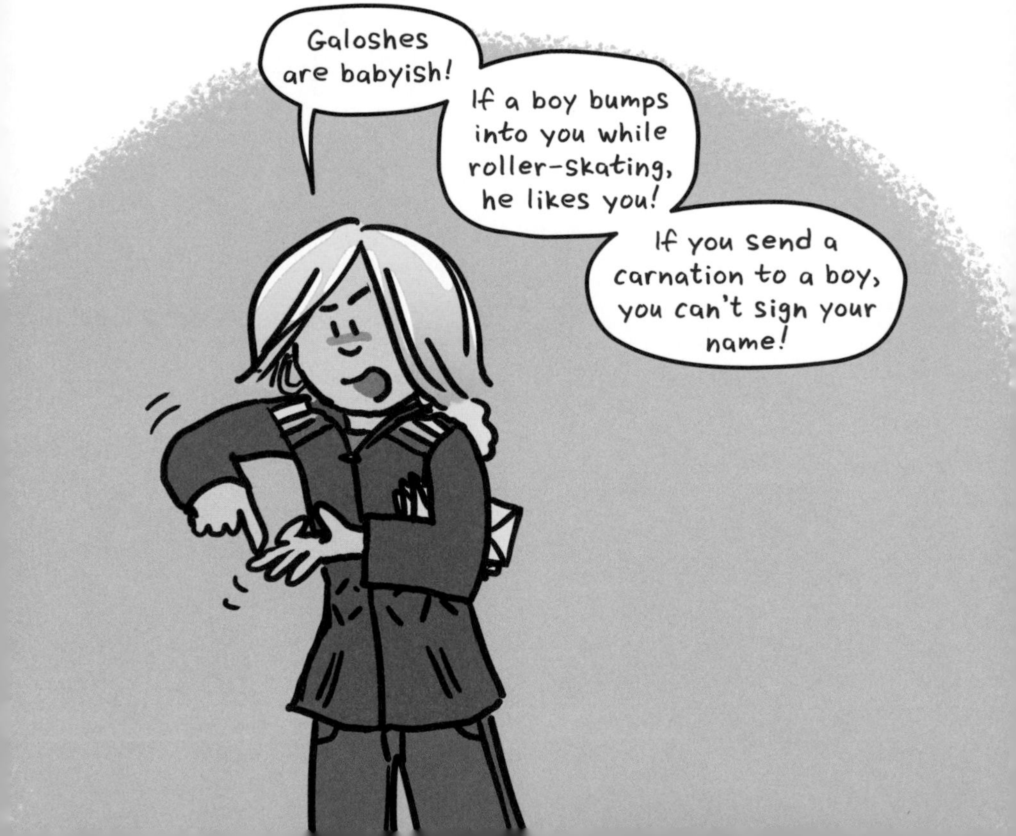
Galoshes
are babyish!
If a boy bumps
into you while
roller-skating,
he likes you!
If you send a
carnation to a boy,
you can't sign your
name!

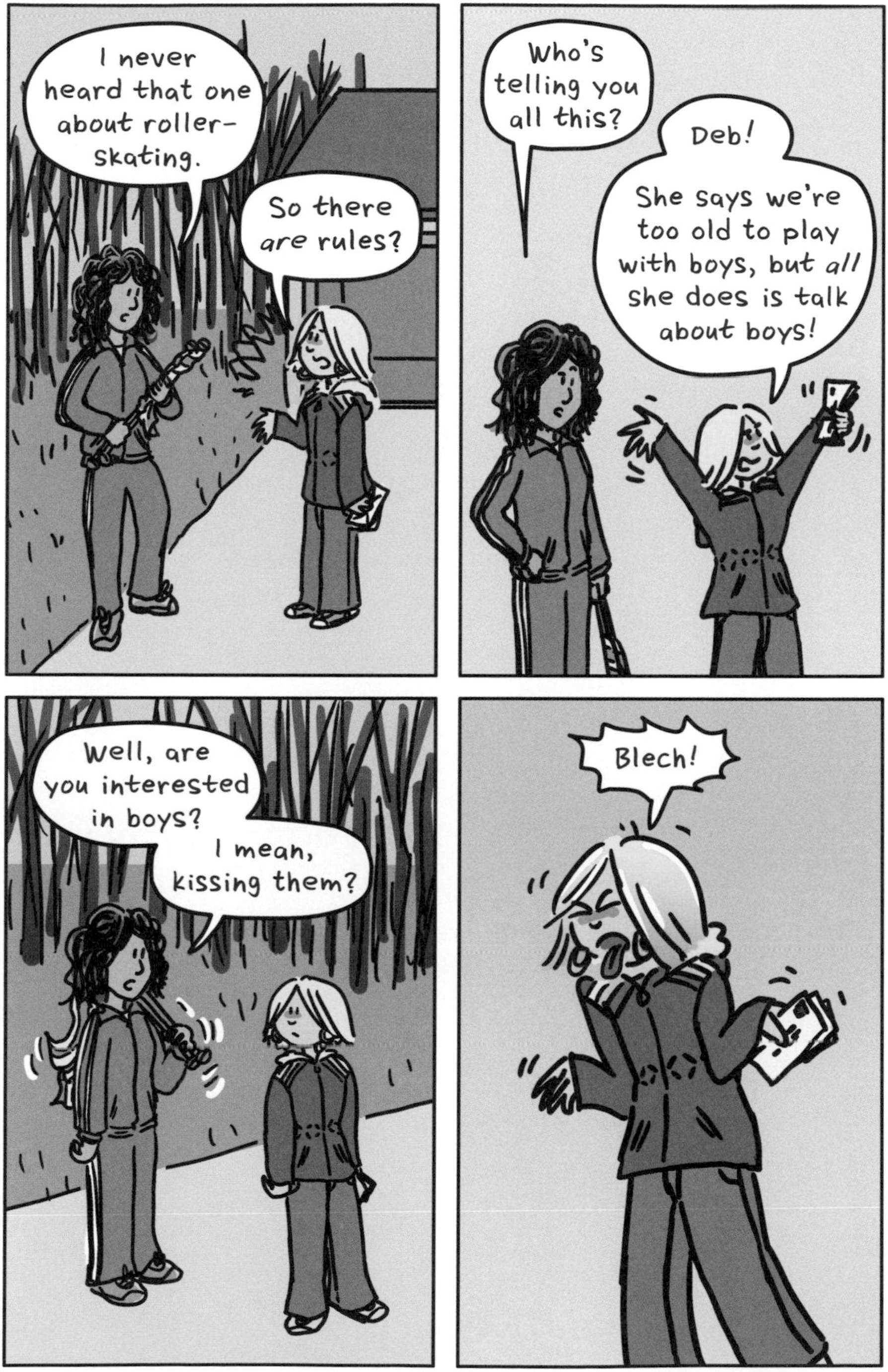
I never heard that one about roller-skating.
So there *are* rules?
Who's telling you all this?
Deb!
She says we're too old to play with boys, but *all* she does is talk about boys!
Well, are you interested in boys?
I mean, kissing them?
Blech!

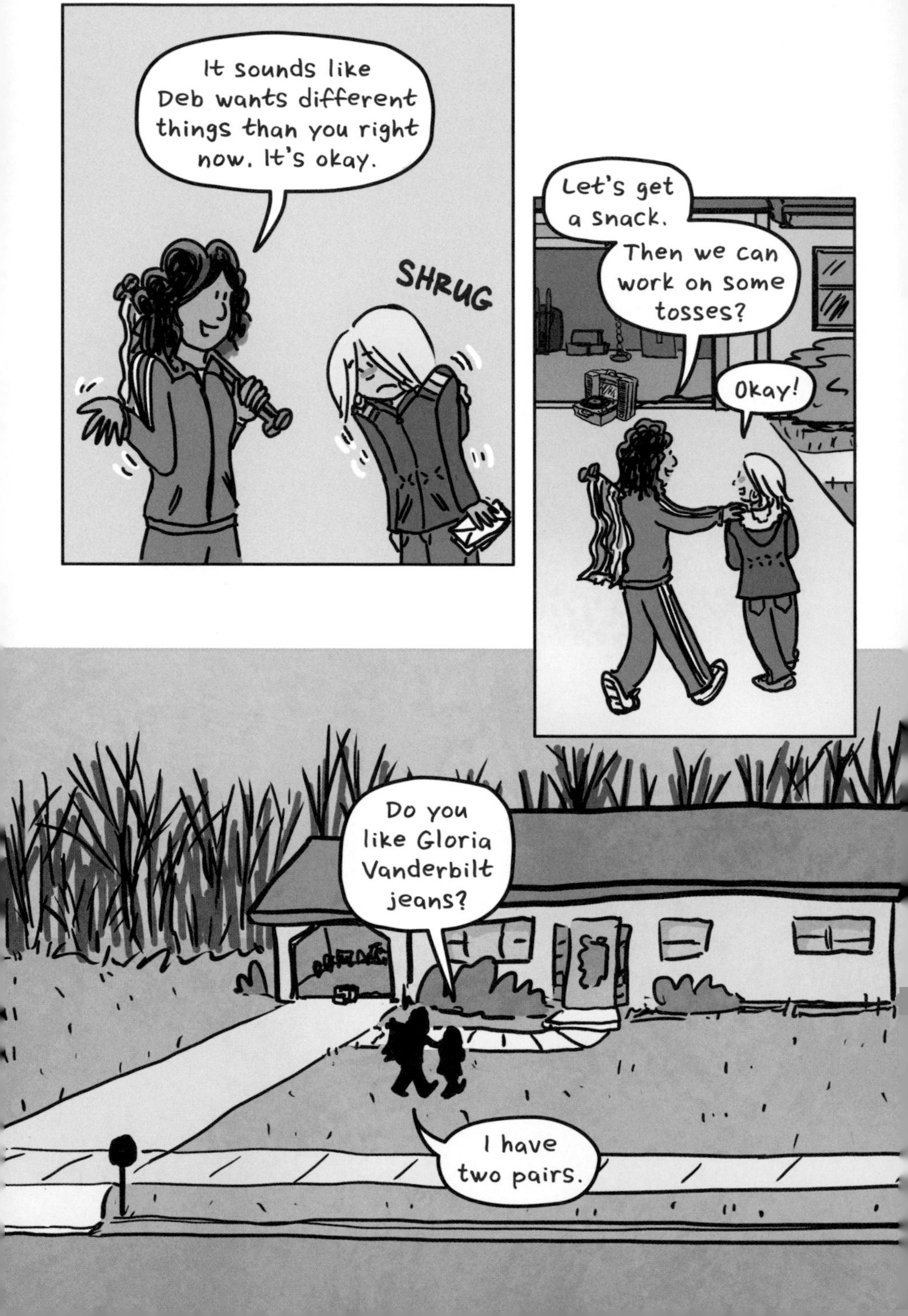
It sounds like Deb wants different things than you right now. It's okay.
SHRUG
Let's get a snack.
Then we can work on some tosses?
Okay!
Do you like Gloria Vanderbilt jeans?
I have two pairs.

CHAPTER EIGHTEEN:
Tissue-Paper Flowers

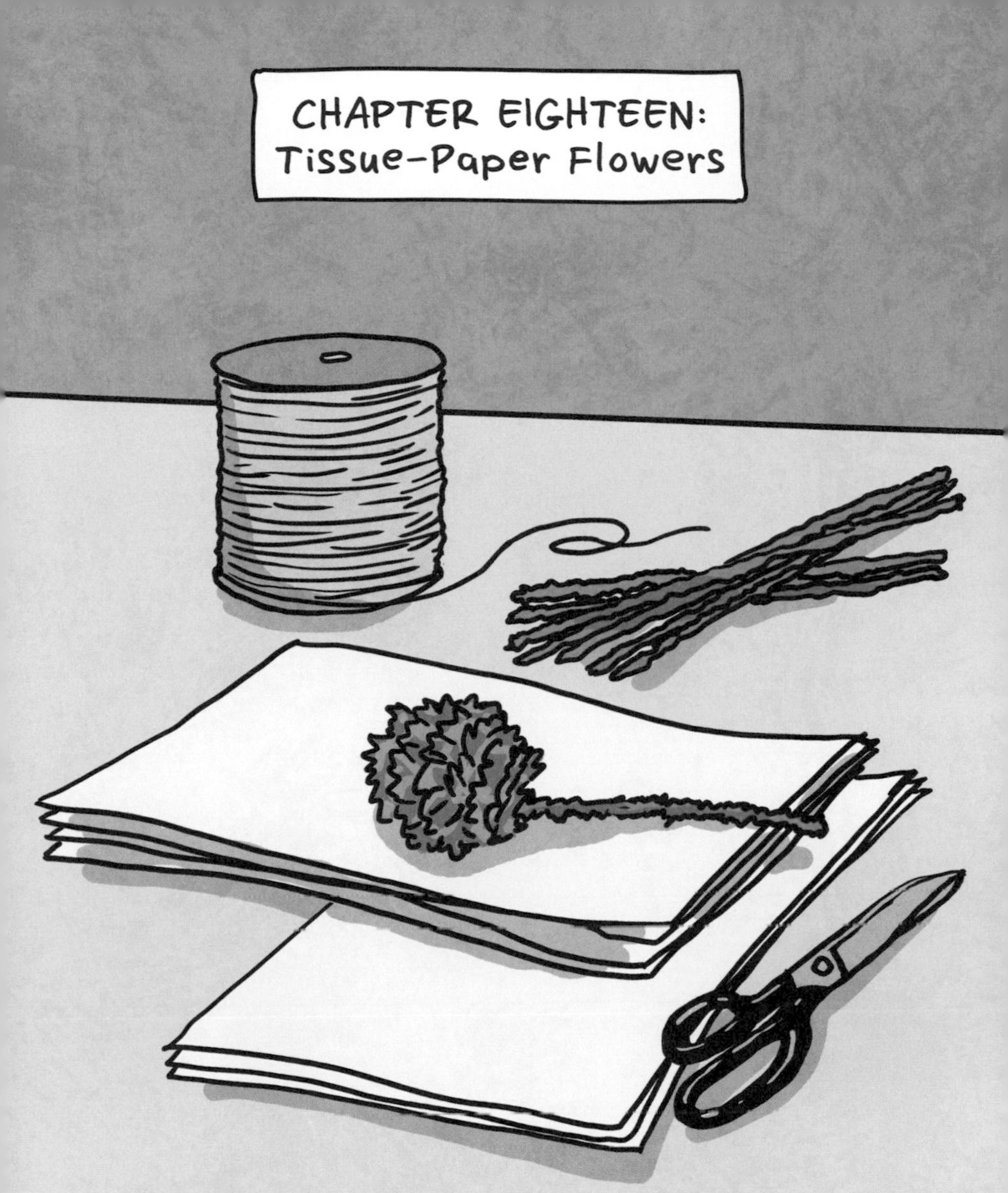

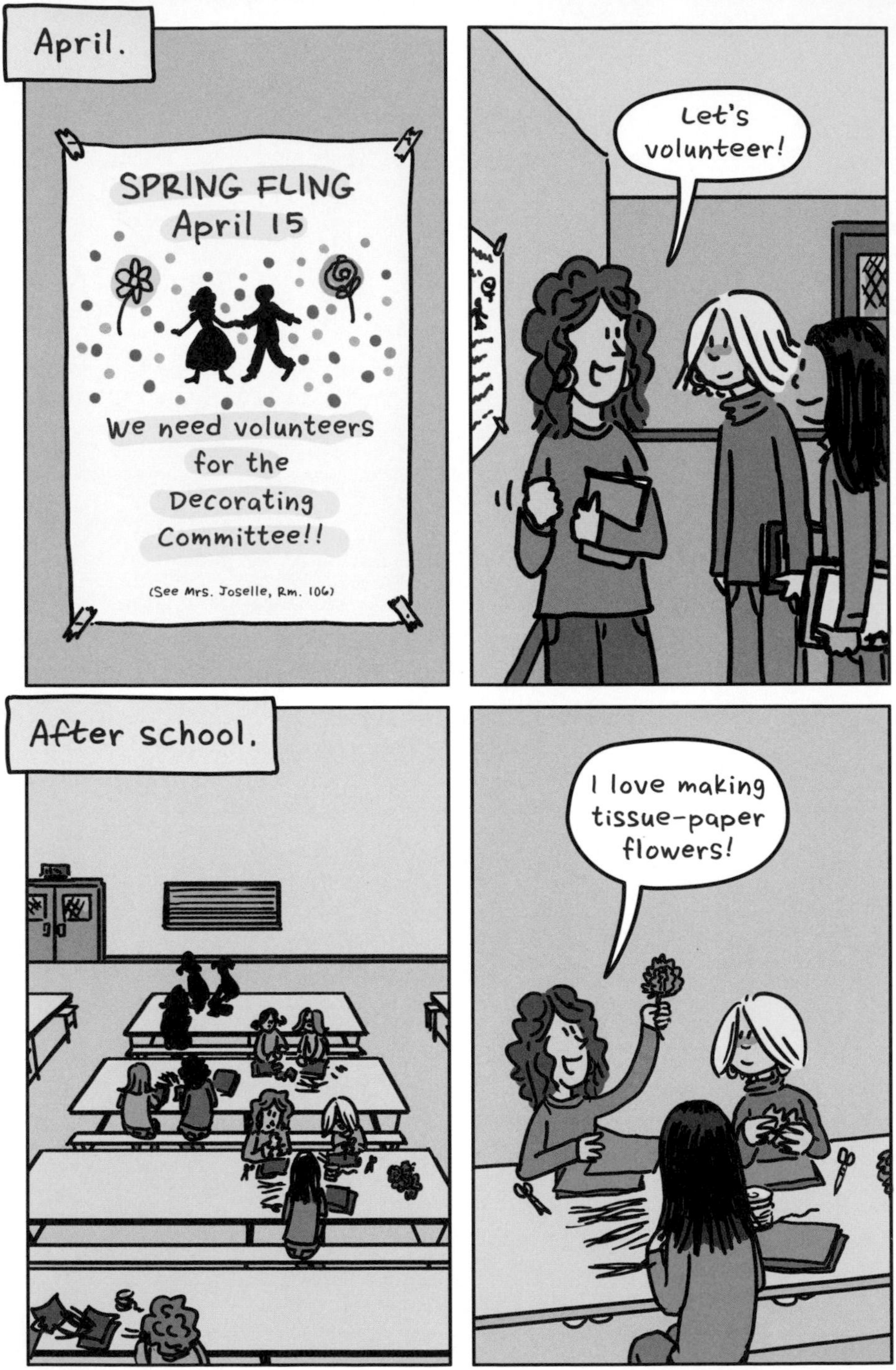
April.
SPRING FLING
April 15
We need volunteers for the Decorating Committee!!
(See Mrs. Joselle, Rm. 106)
Let's volunteer!
After school.
I love making tissue-paper flowers!

HOW TO MAKE A TISSUE-PAPER FLOWER!

1) Get tissue paper.

2) Fold like a fan.

3) Tie a string.

4) Pull the tissue into petals.

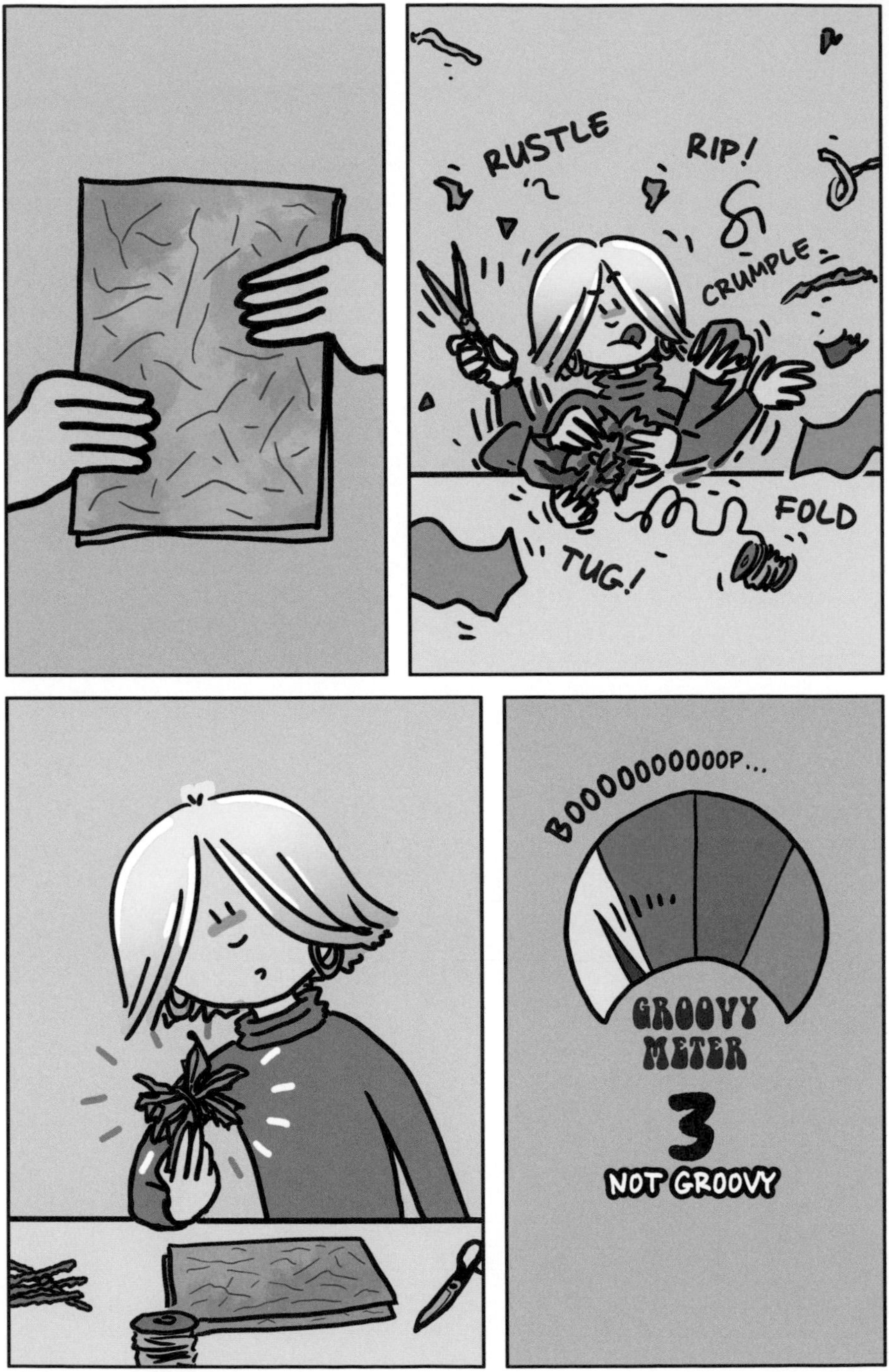
RUSTLE
RIP!
CRUMPLE
FOLD
TUG!
BOOOOOOOOOOP...
GROOVY METER
3
NOT GROOVY

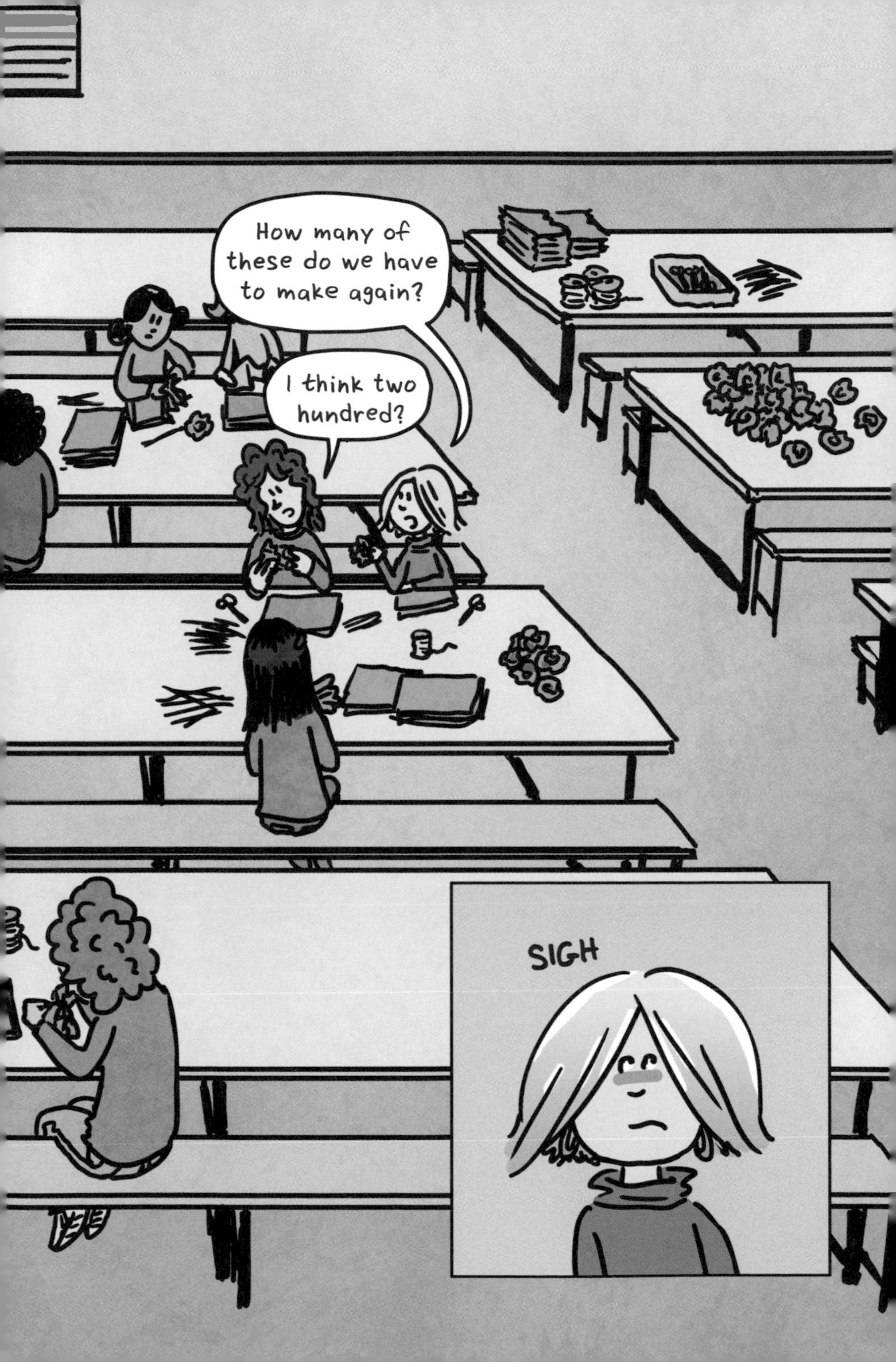
How many of these do we have to make again?
I think two hundred?
SIGH

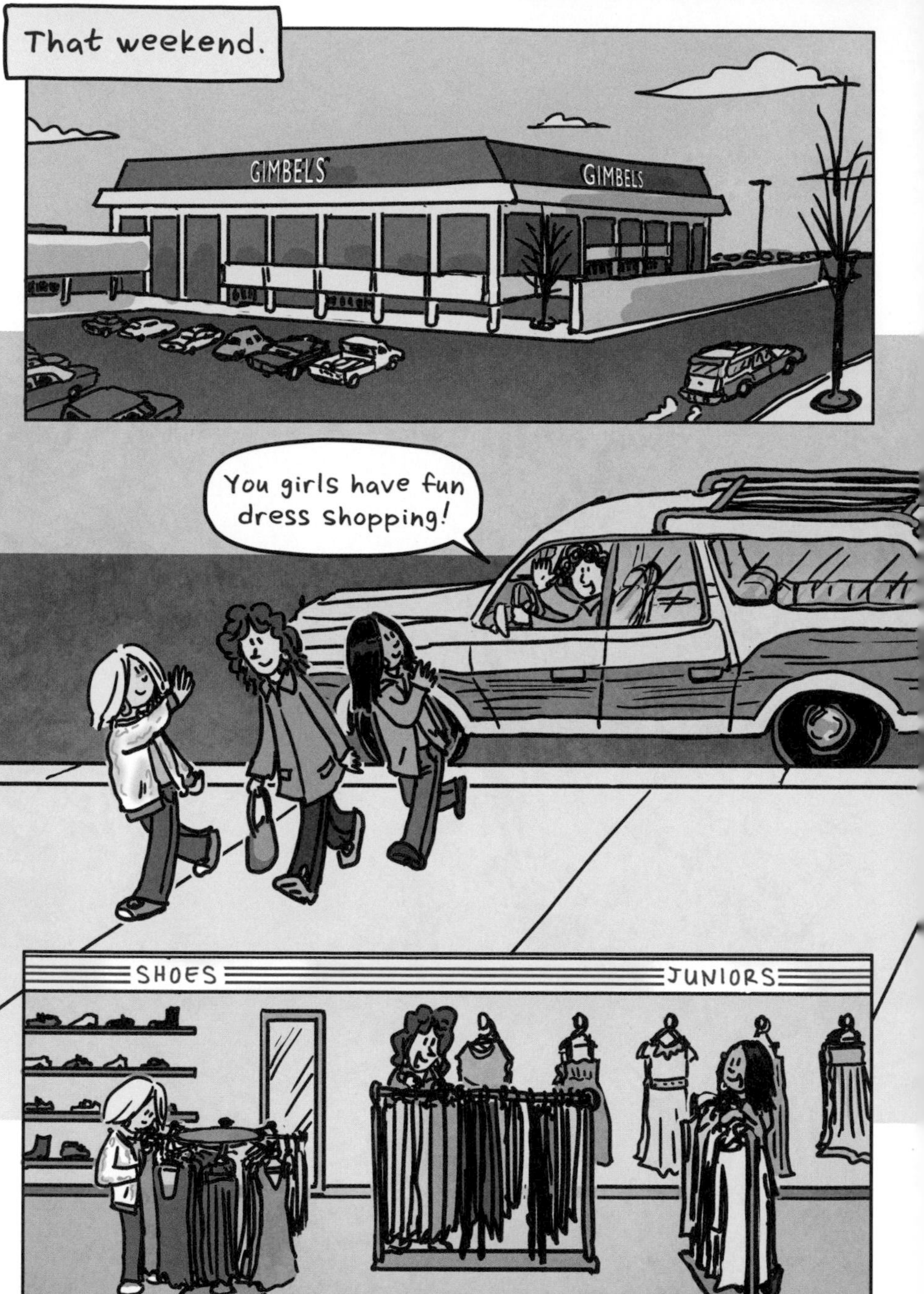
That weekend.
GIMBELS
GIMBELS
You girls have fun dress shopping!
SHOES
JUNIORS

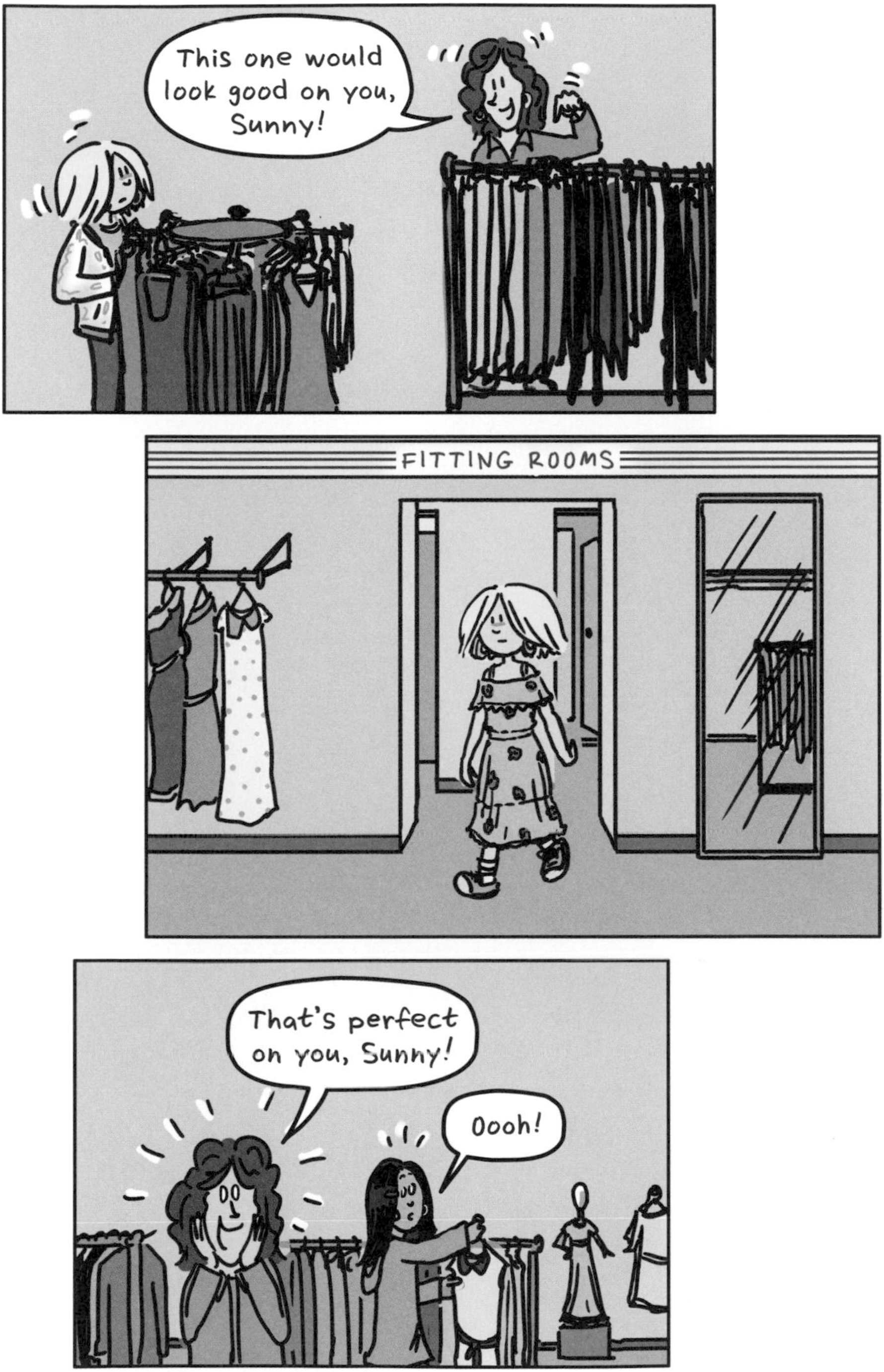
This one would look good on you, Sunny!
FITTING ROOMS
That's perfect on you, Sunny!
Oooh!

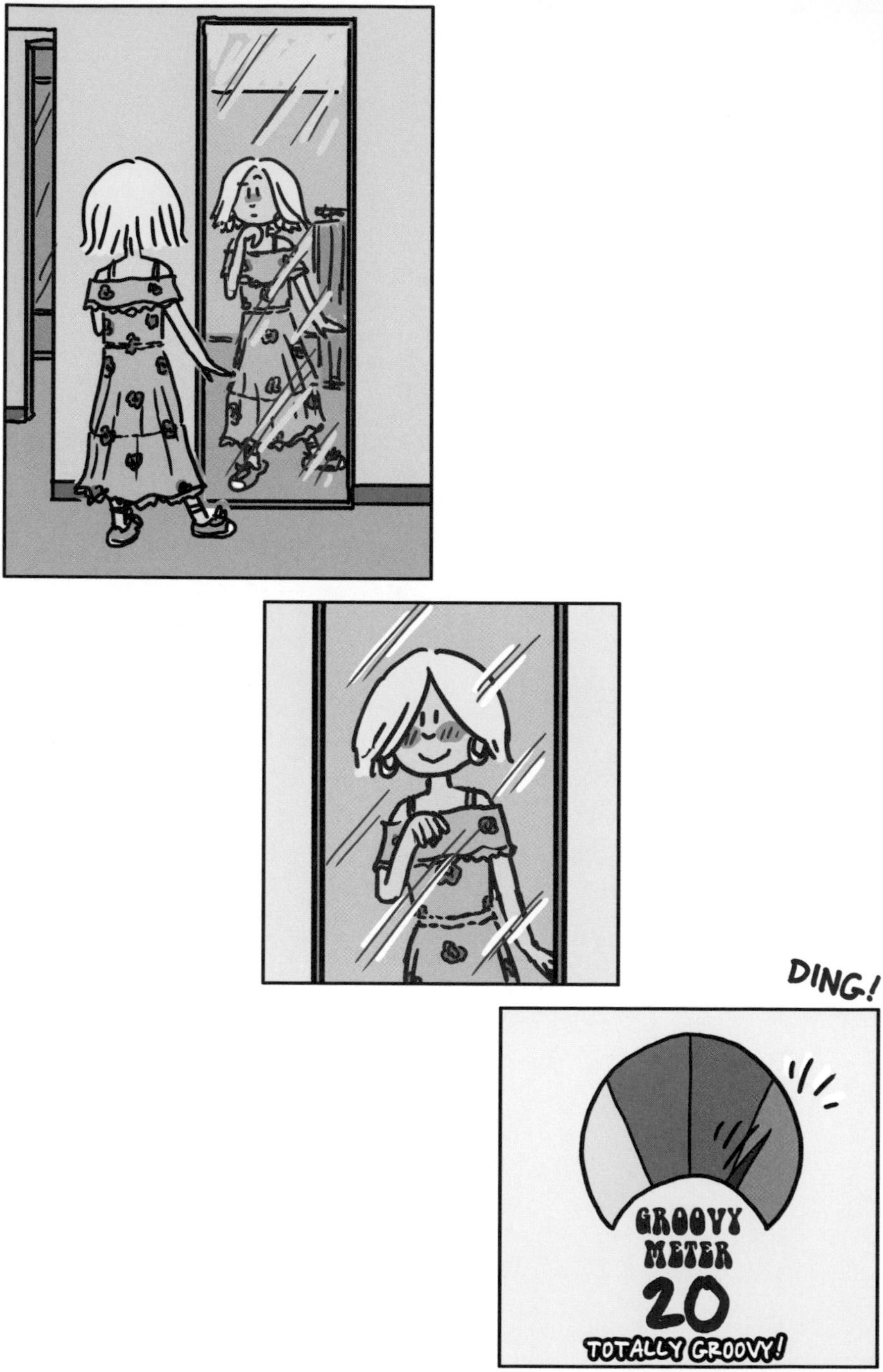
DING!
GROOVY METER
20
TOTALLY GROOVY!

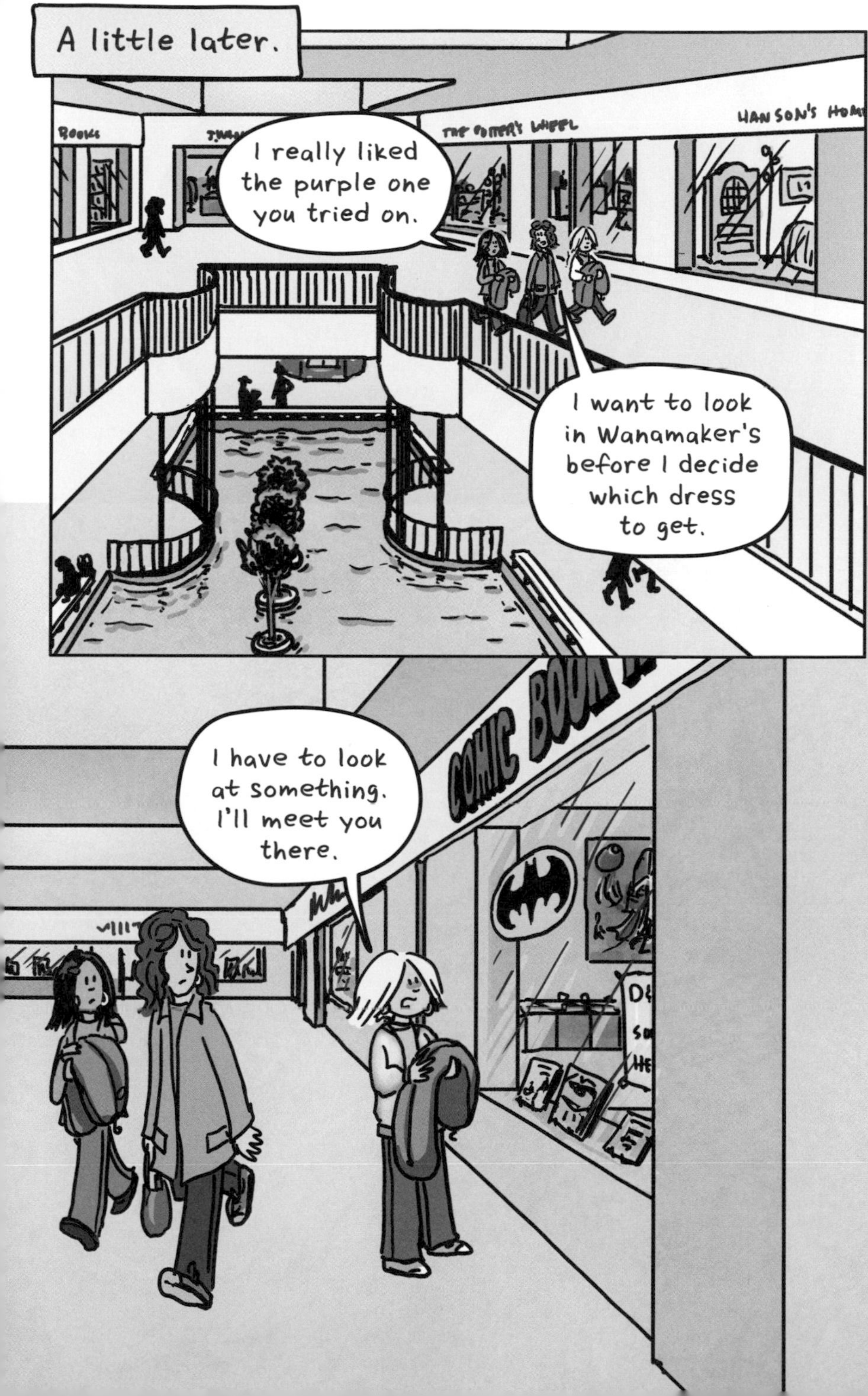
A little later.
BOOKS
THE POTTER'S WHEEL
HANSON'S HOM
I really liked the purple one you tried on.
I want to look in Wanamaker's before I decide which dress to get.
COMIC BOOK
I have to look at something. I'll meet you there.

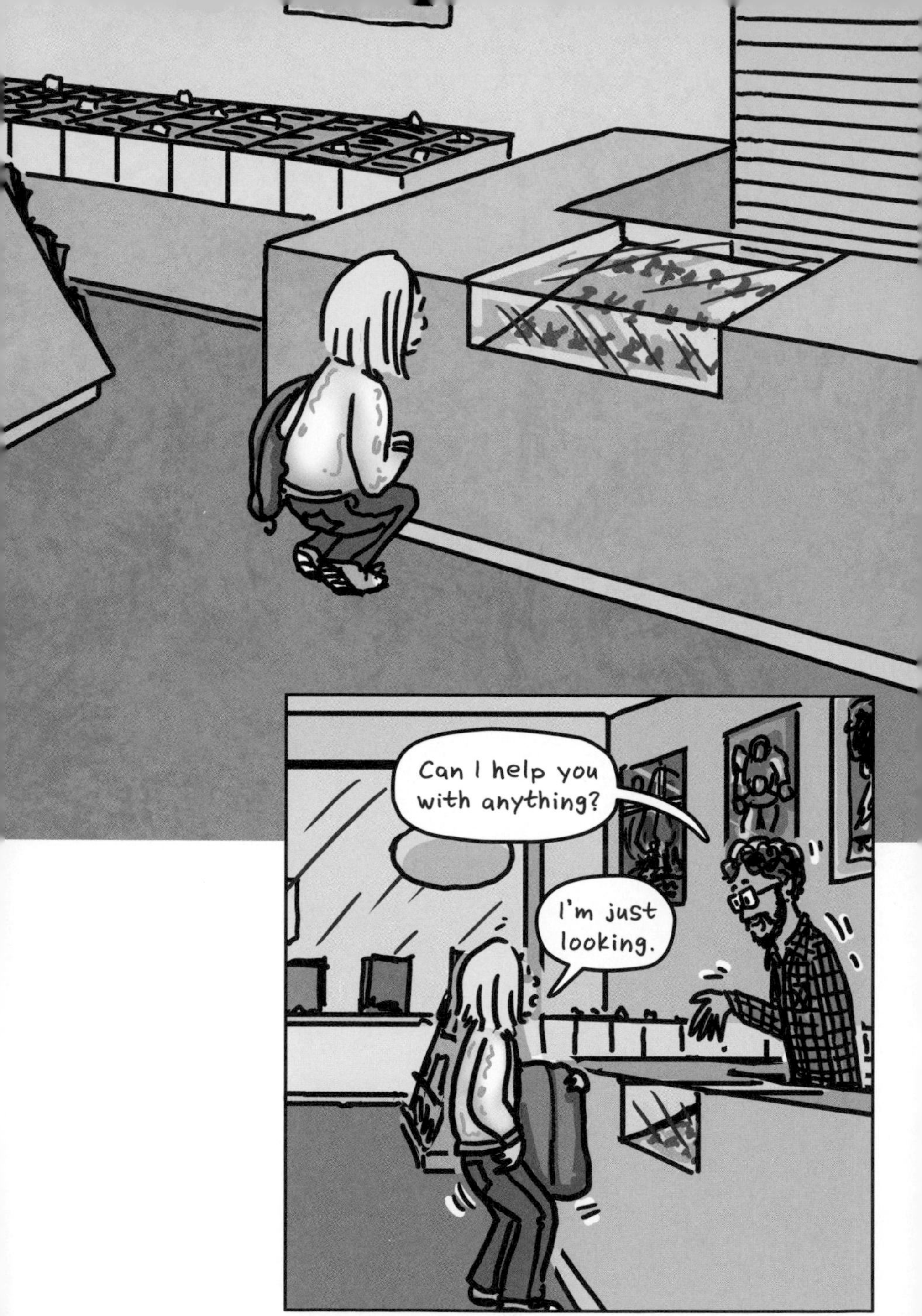
Can I help you with anything?
I'm just looking.

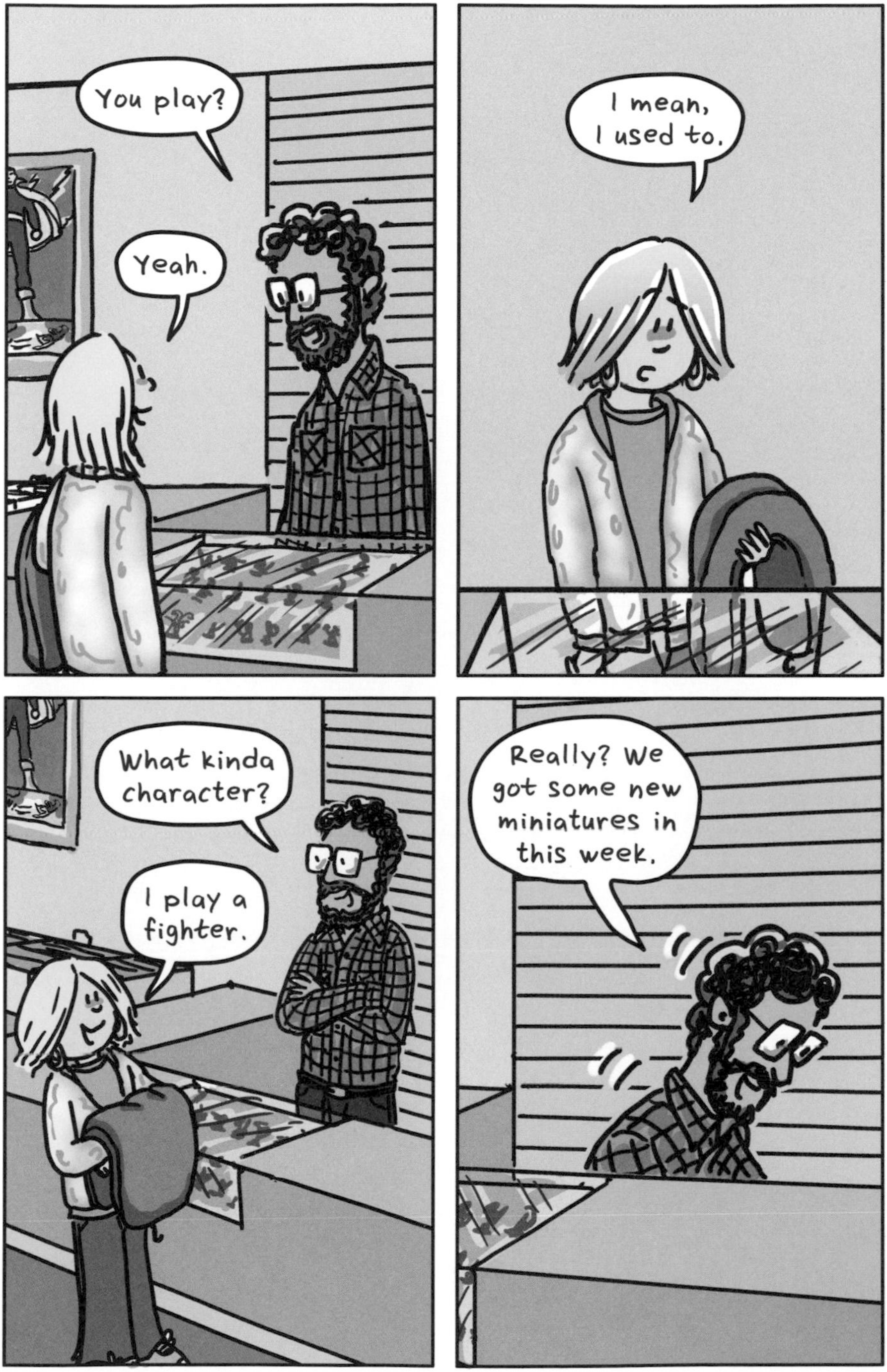
You play?
Yeah.
I mean, I used to.
What kinda character?
I play a fighter.
Really? We got some new miniatures in this week.

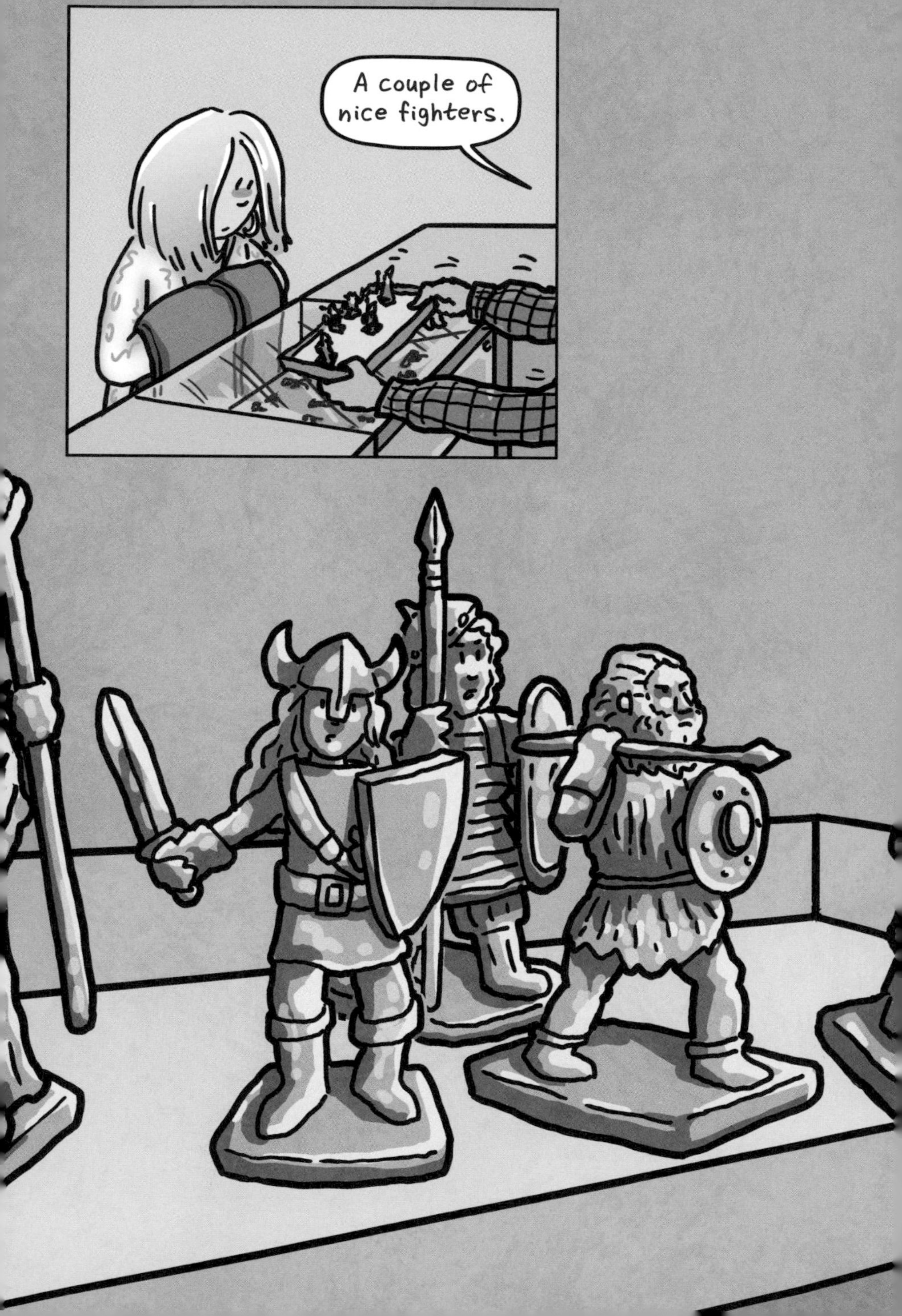
A couple of nice fighters.

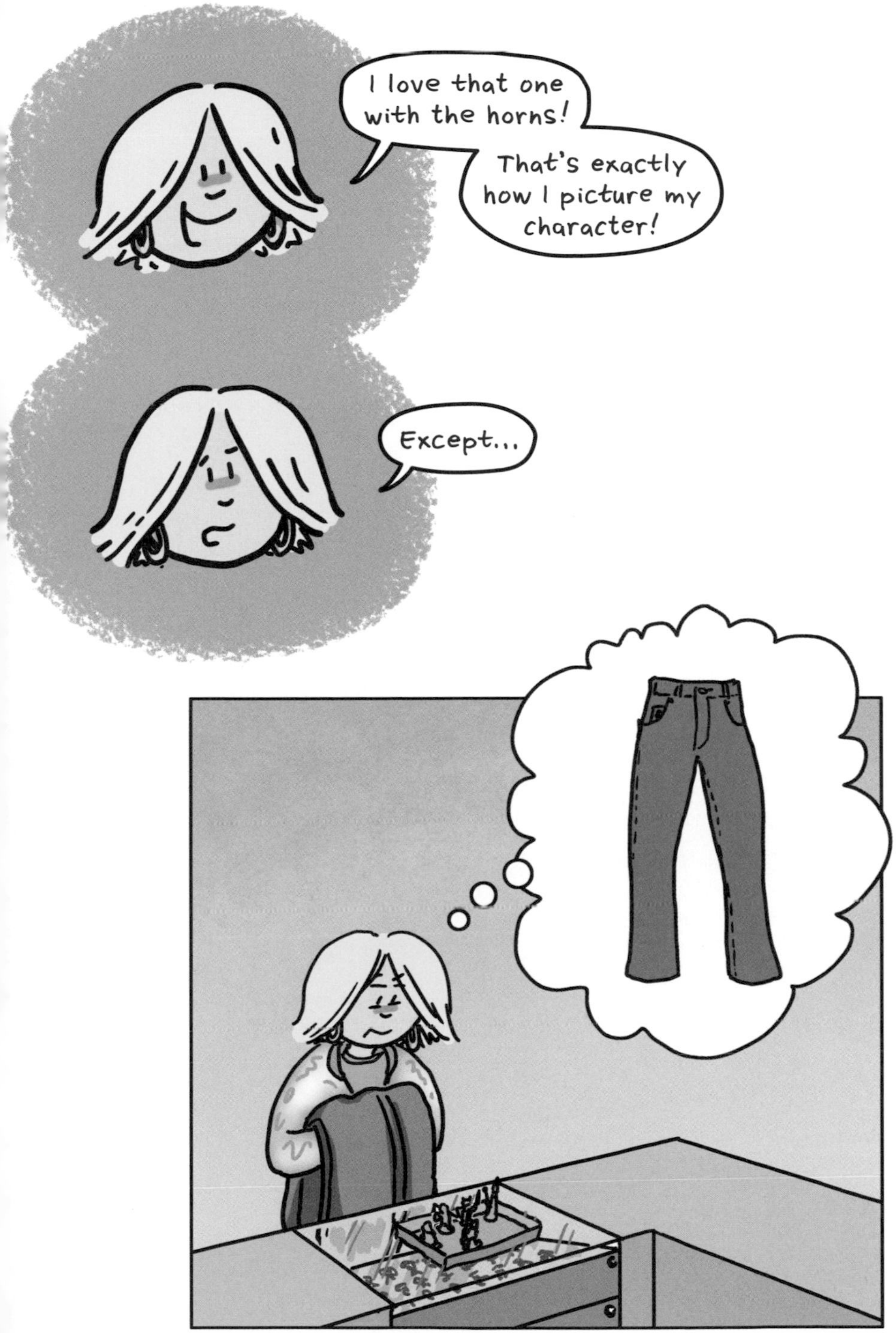
I love that one with the horns!
That's exactly how I picture my character!
Except...

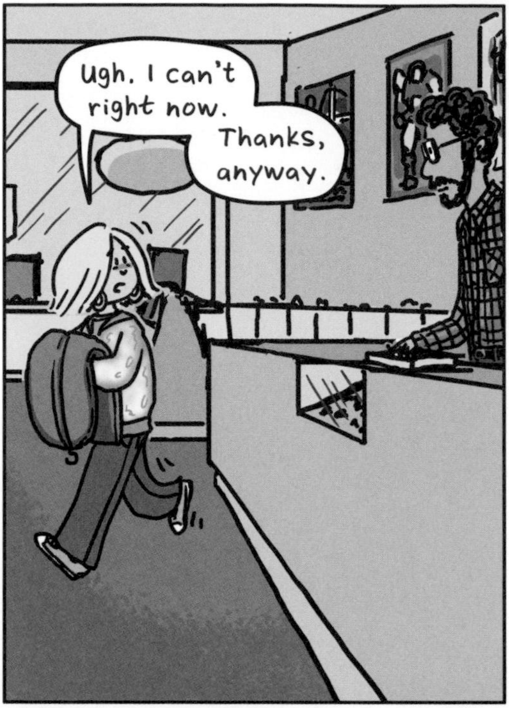
Ugh. I can't right now.
Thanks, anyway.

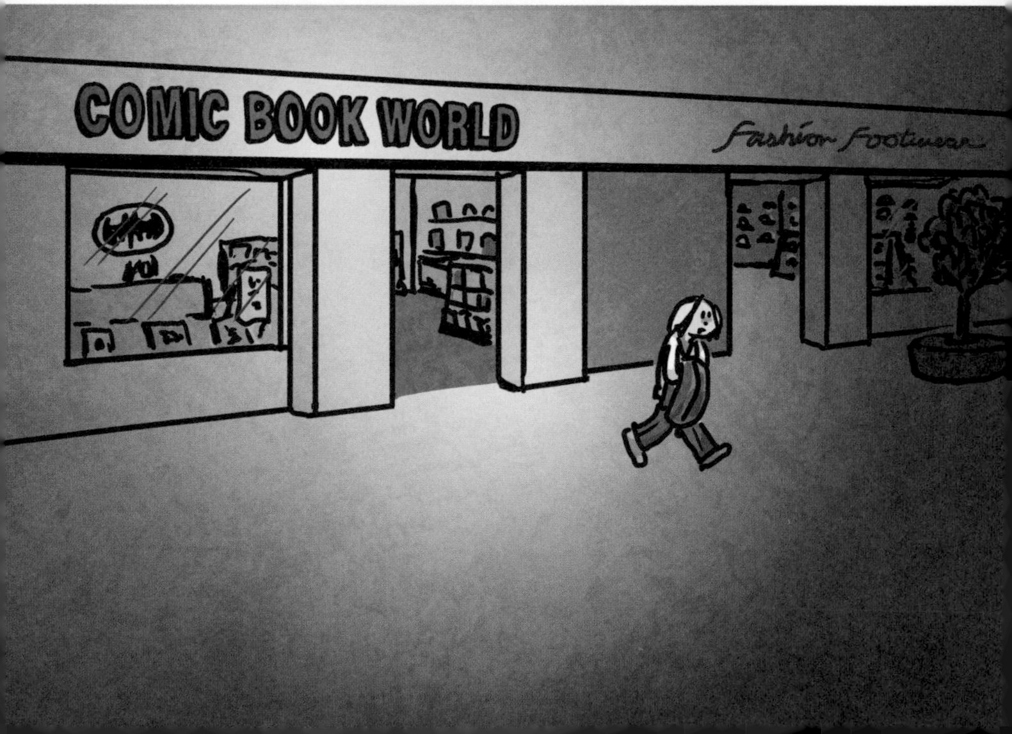
COMIC BOOK WORLD
Fashion Footwear

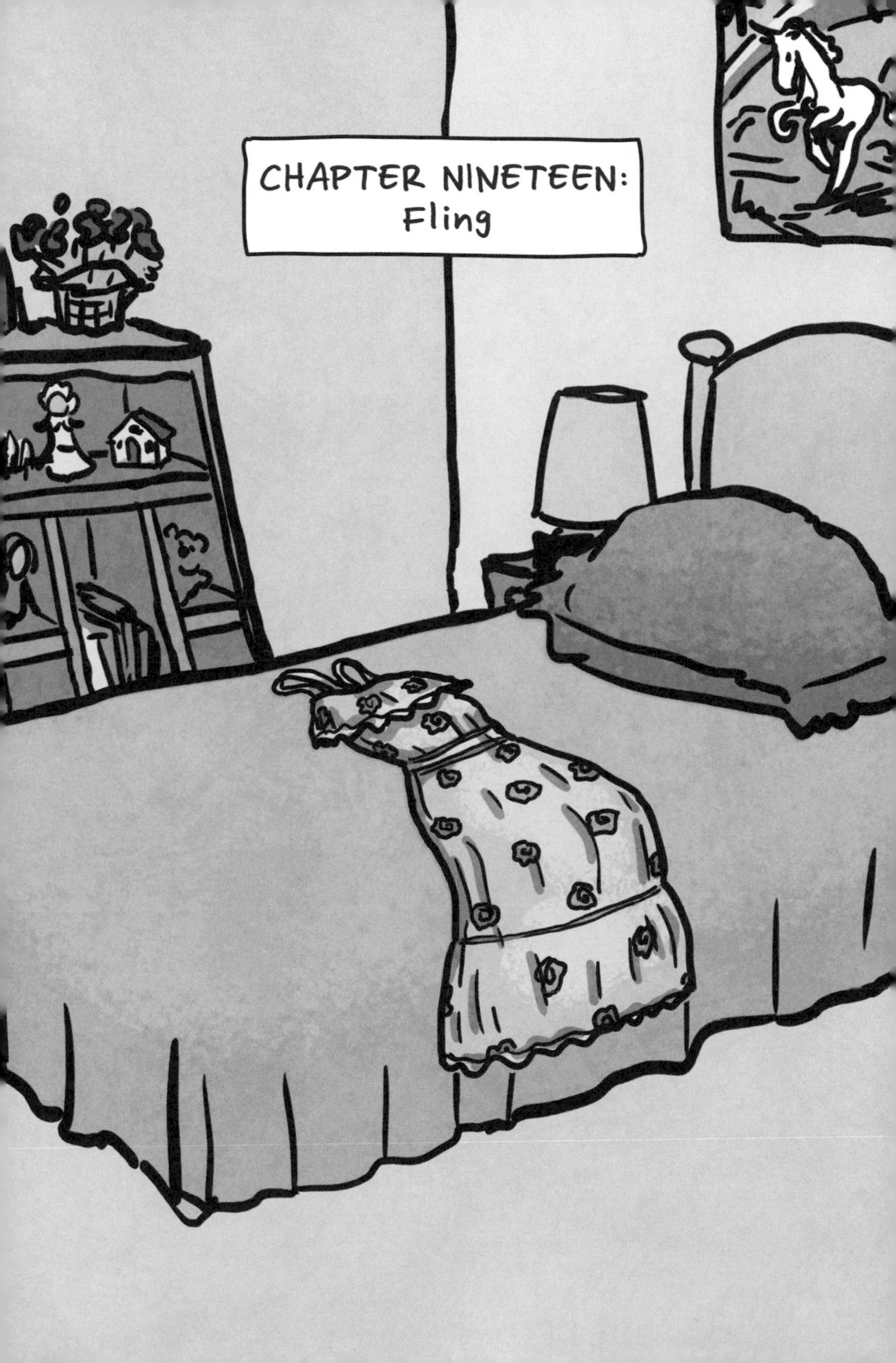
CHAPTER NINETEEN:
Fling

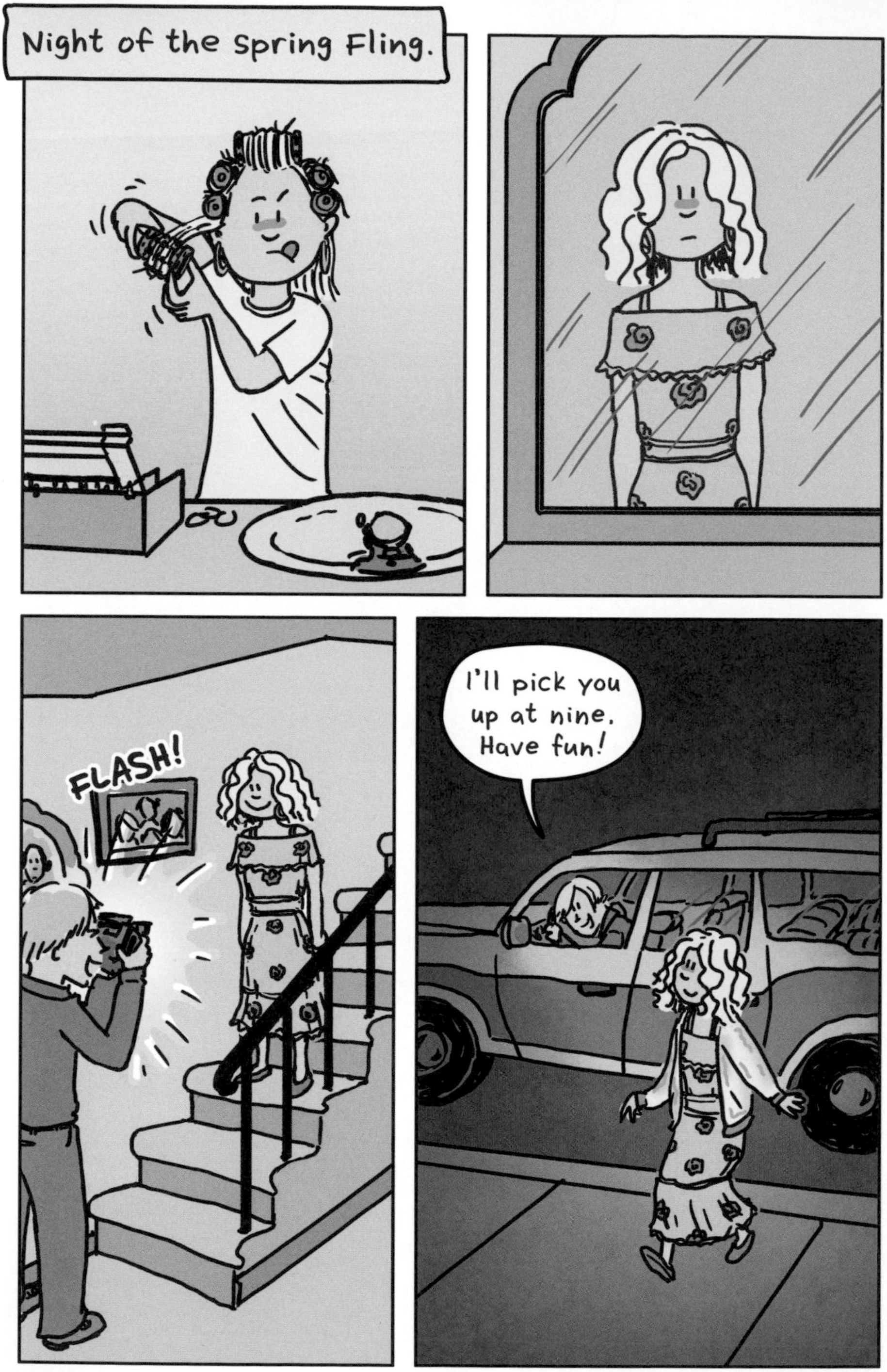
Night of the Spring Fling.
FLASH!
I'll pick you up at nine. Have fun!

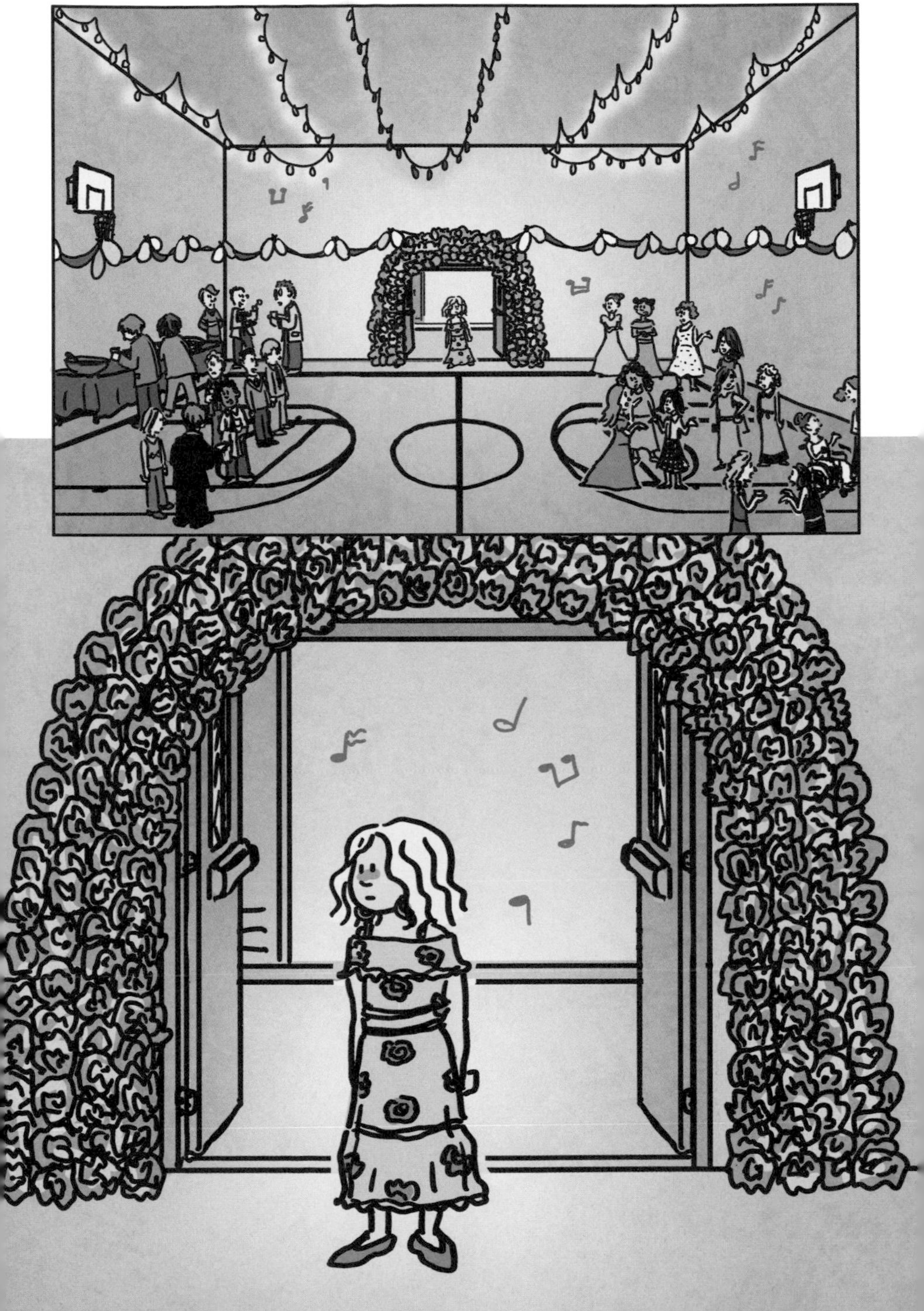

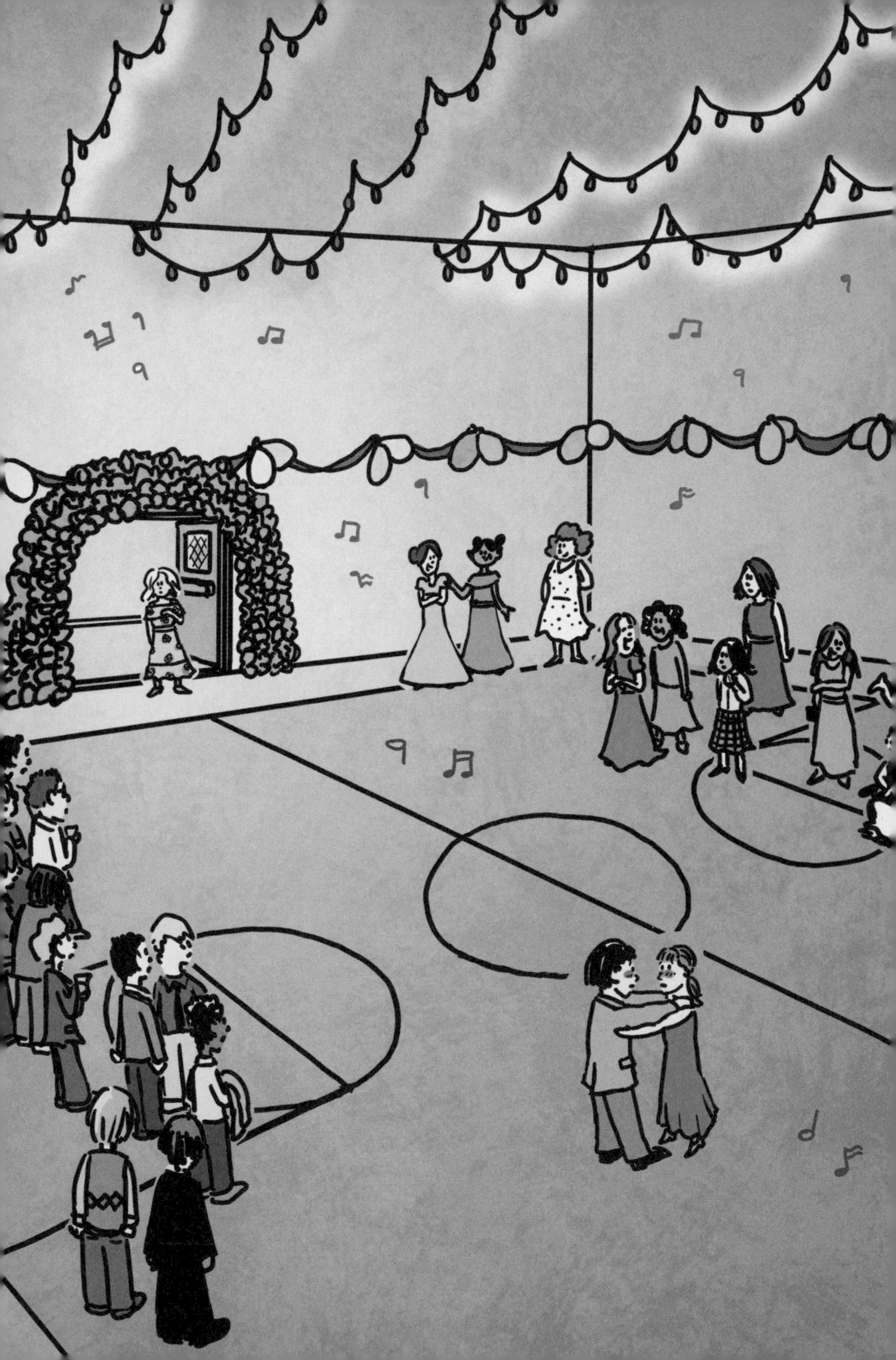

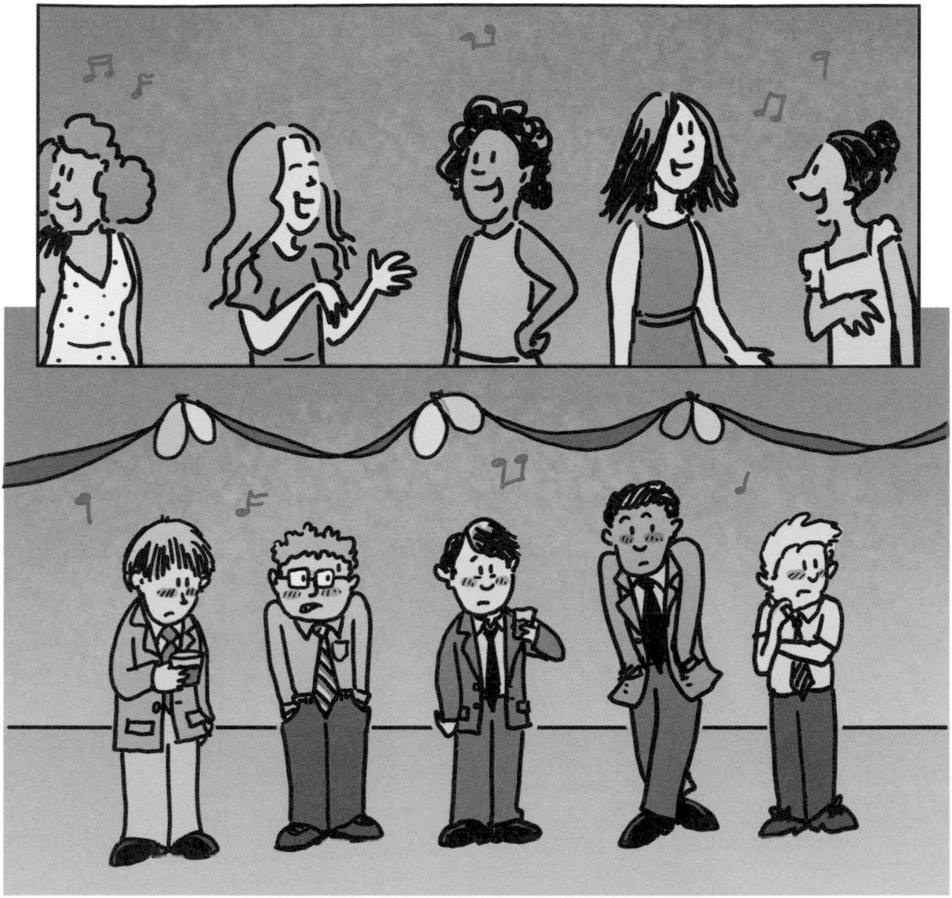

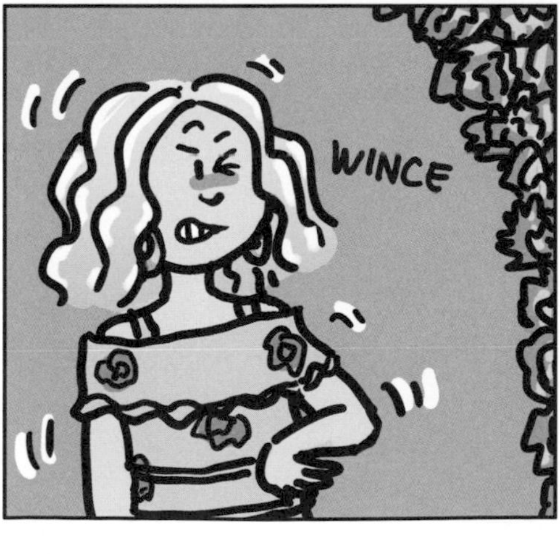
WINCE

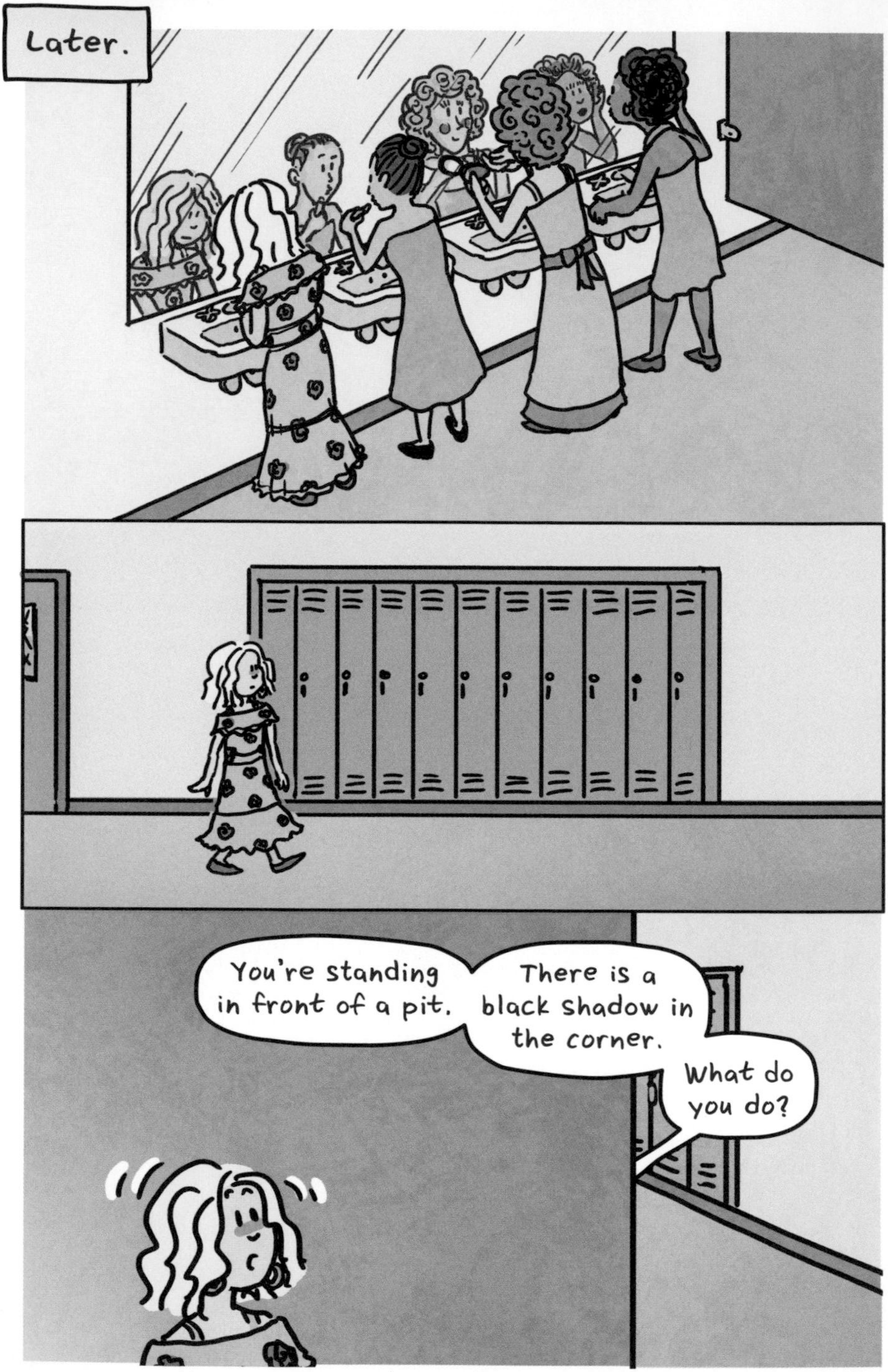
Later.
You're standing in front of a pit.
There is a black shadow in the corner.
What do you do?

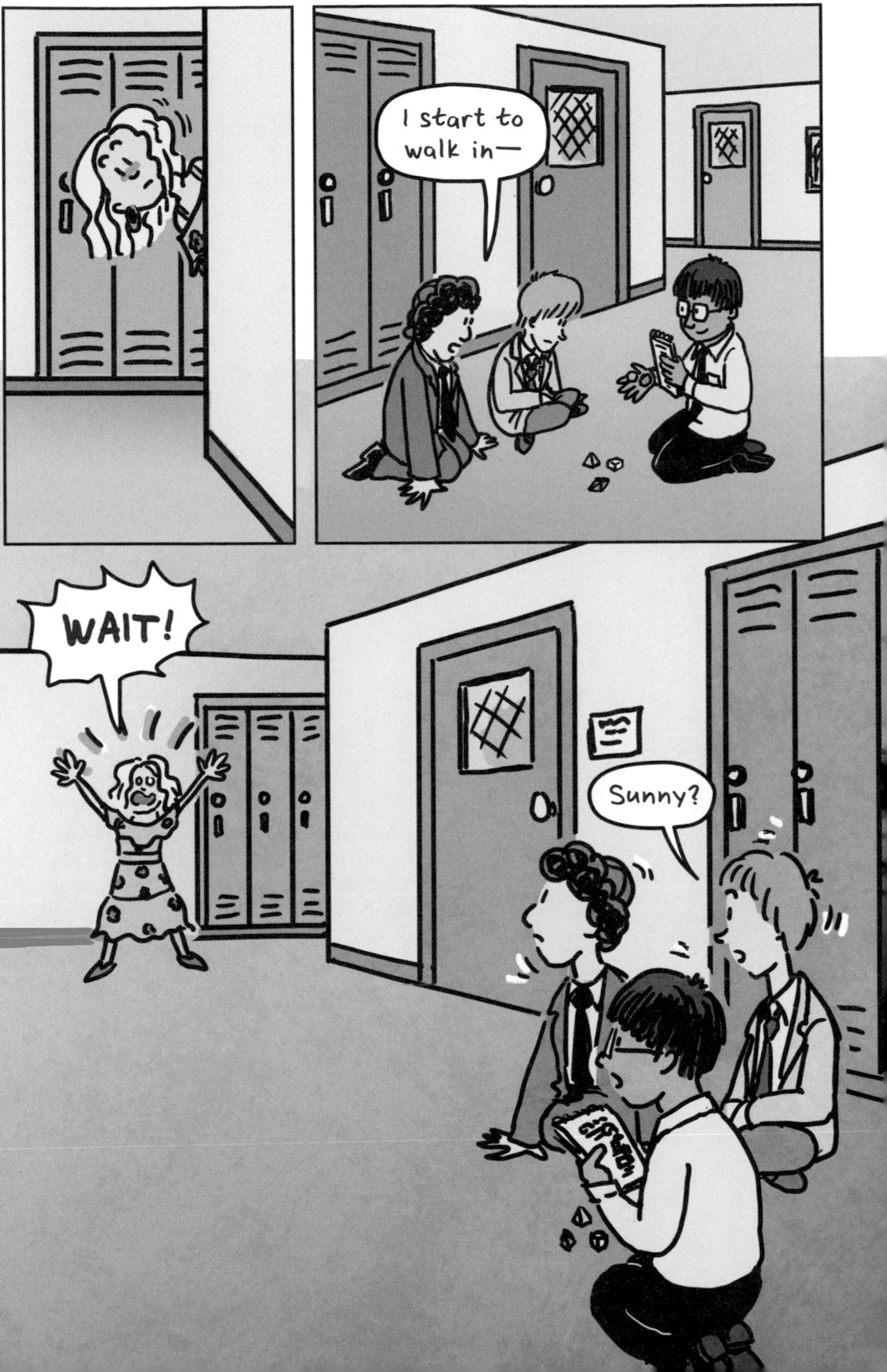
I start to walk in—
WAIT!
Sunny?

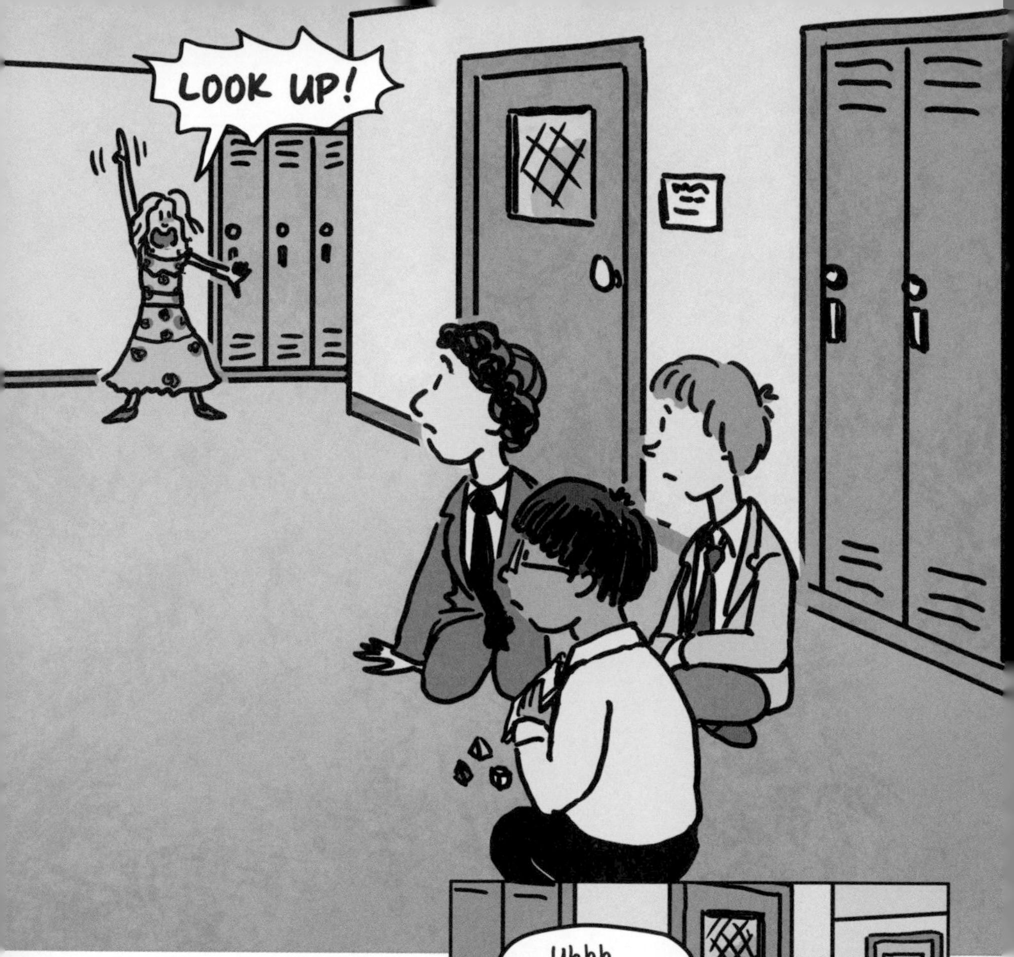
LOOK UP!

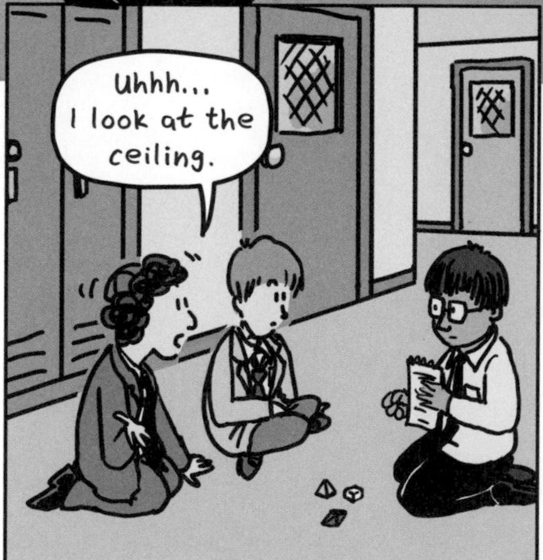
Uhhh...
I look at the ceiling.

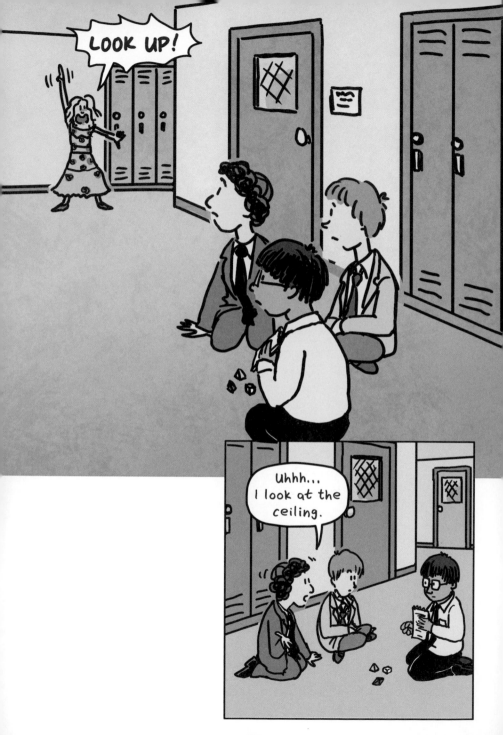

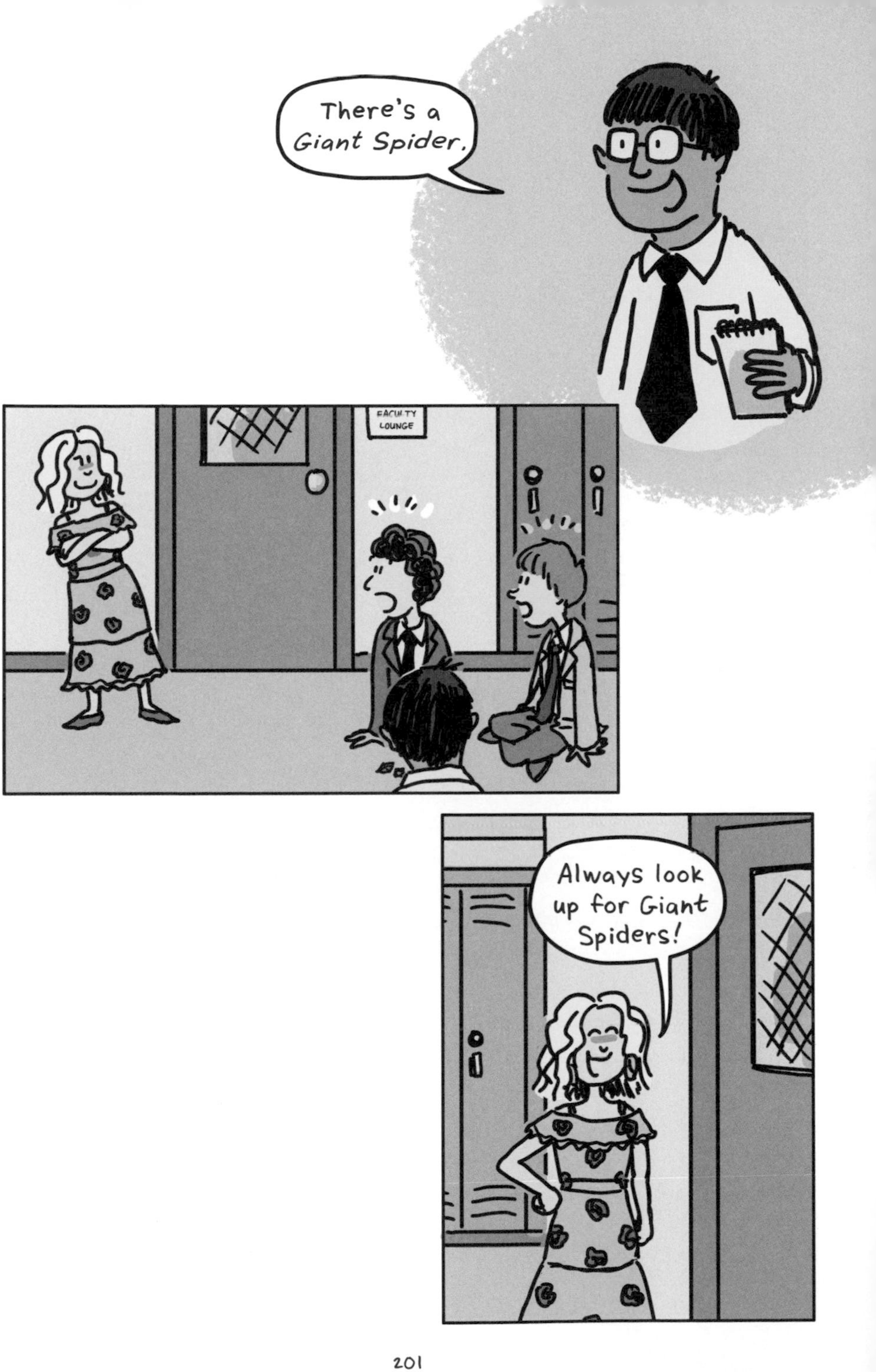
There's a Giant Spider.
FACULTY LOUNGE
Always look up for Giant Spiders!

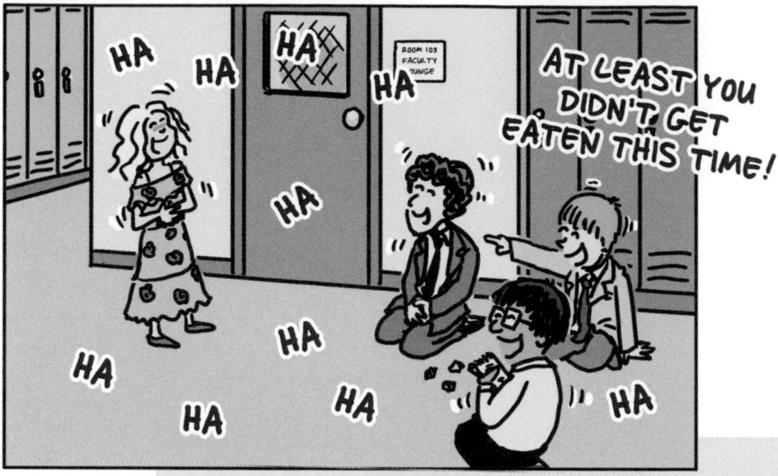
HA
HA
HA
HA
AT LEAST YOU DIDN'T GET EATEN THIS TIME!
ROOM 103 FACULTY LOUNGE
HA
HA
HA
HA
HA
HA

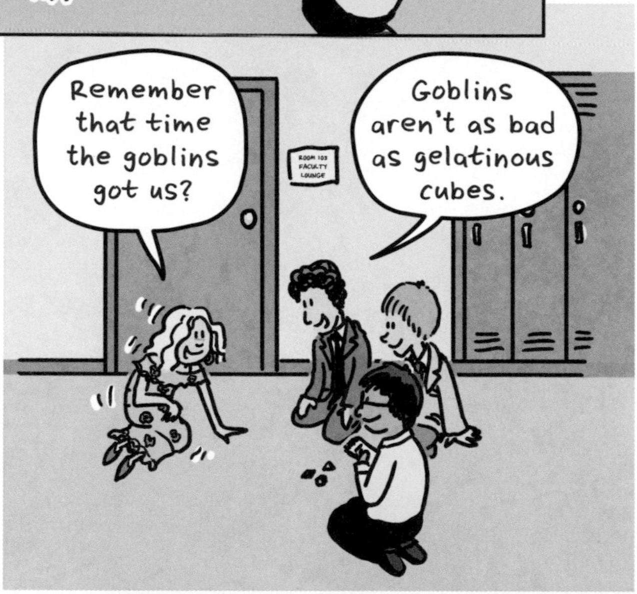
Remember that time the goblins got us?
ROOM 103 FACULTY LOUNGE
Goblins aren't as bad as gelatinous cubes.

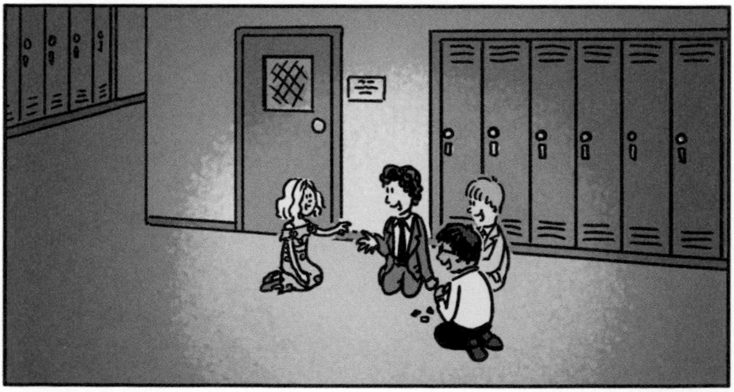

CHAPTER TWENTY:
Saving Throw

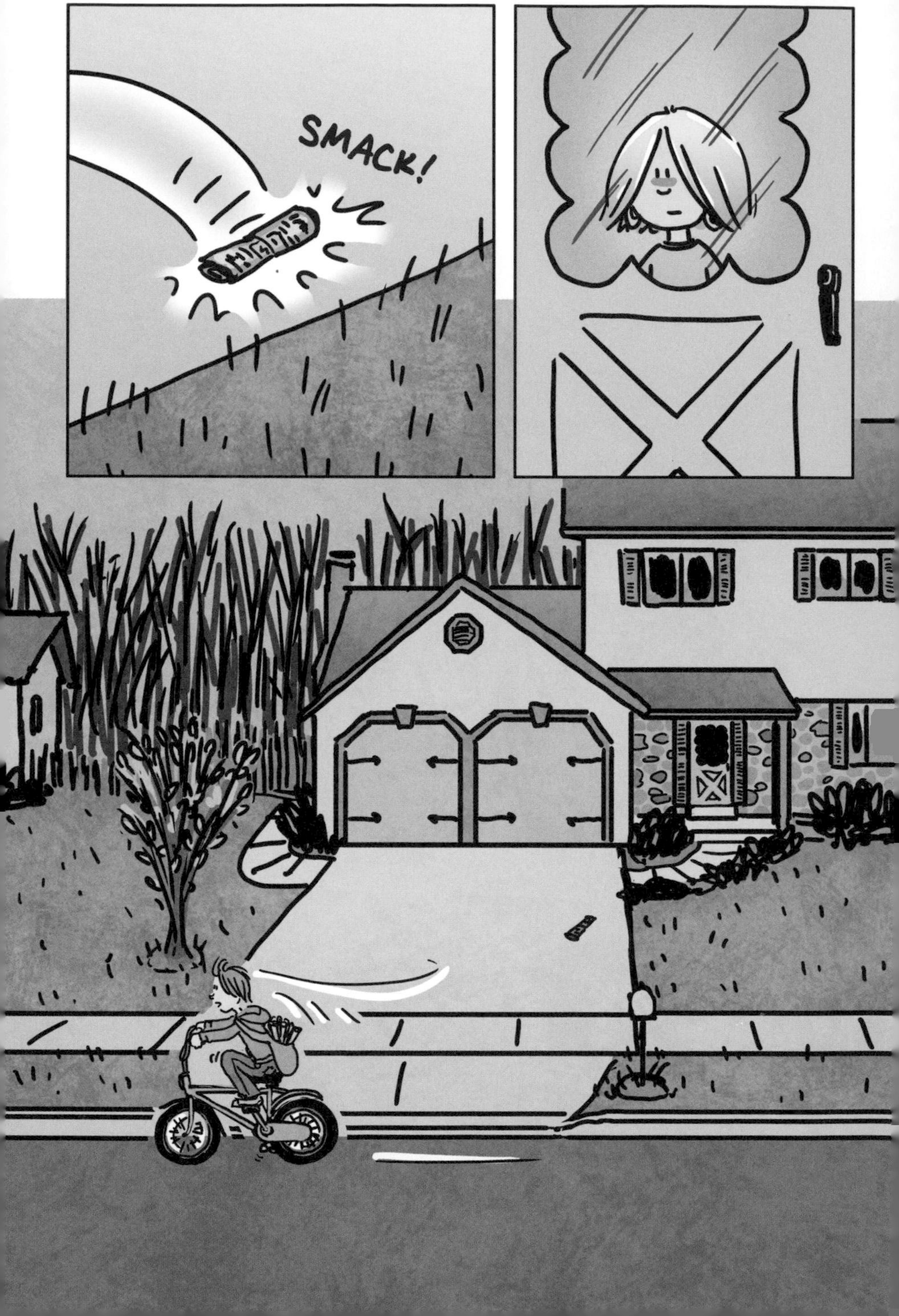
SMACK!

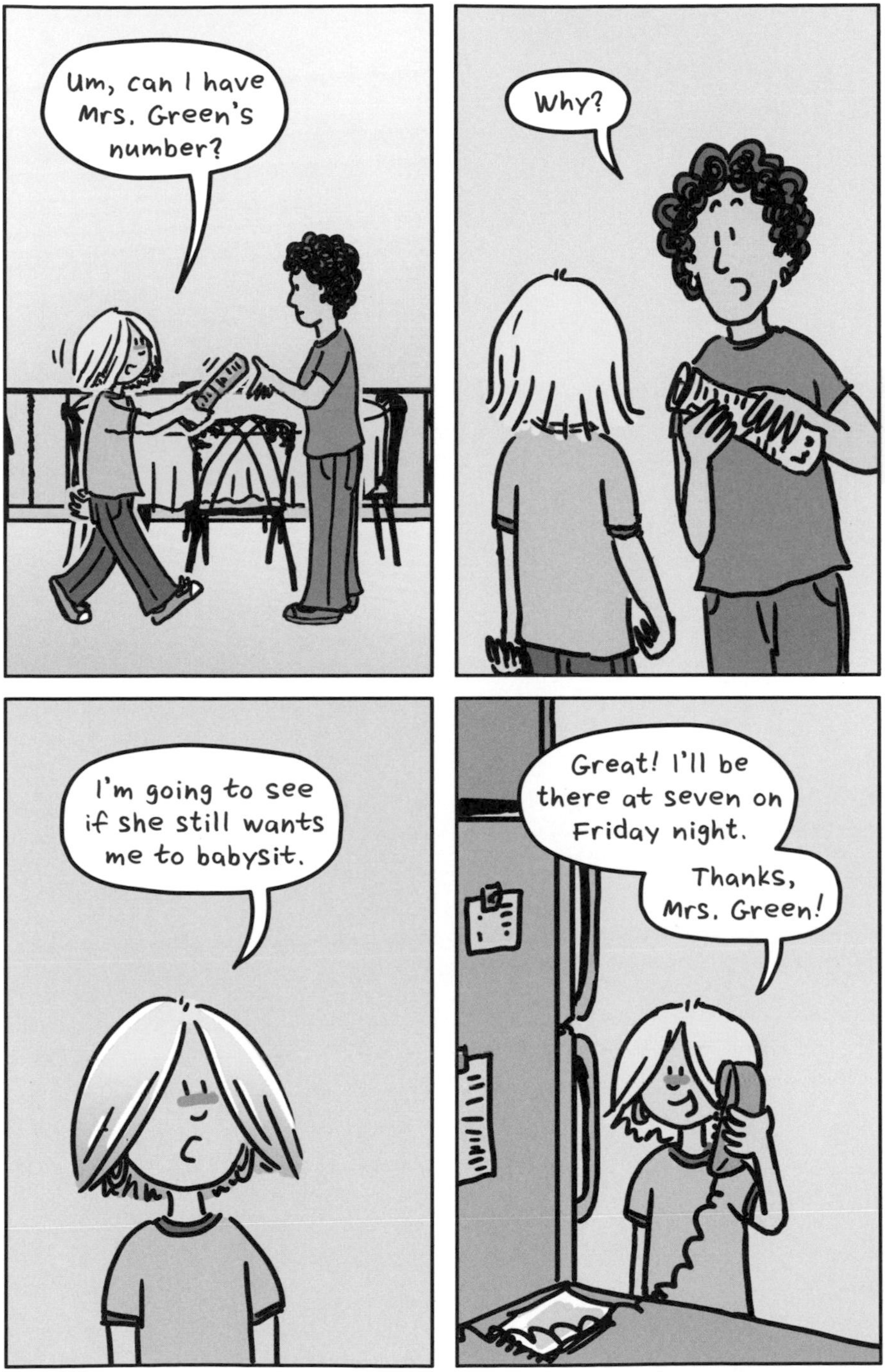
Um, can I have Mrs. Green's number?
Why?
I'm going to see if she still wants me to babysit.
Great! I'll be there at seven on Friday night.
Thanks, Mrs. Green!

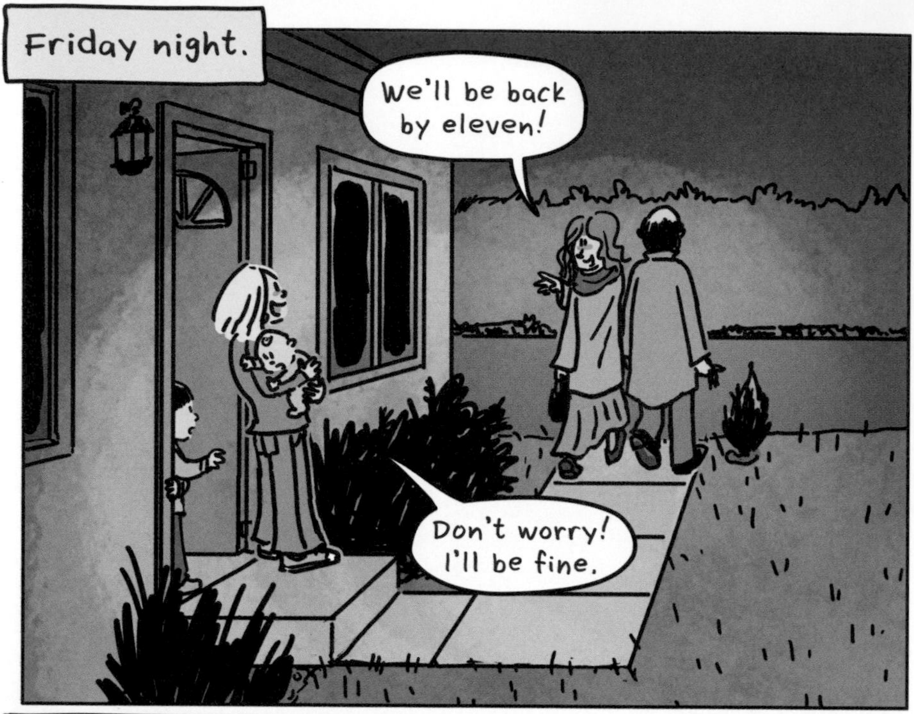

Friday night.
We'll be back by eleven!
Don't worry! I'll be fine.

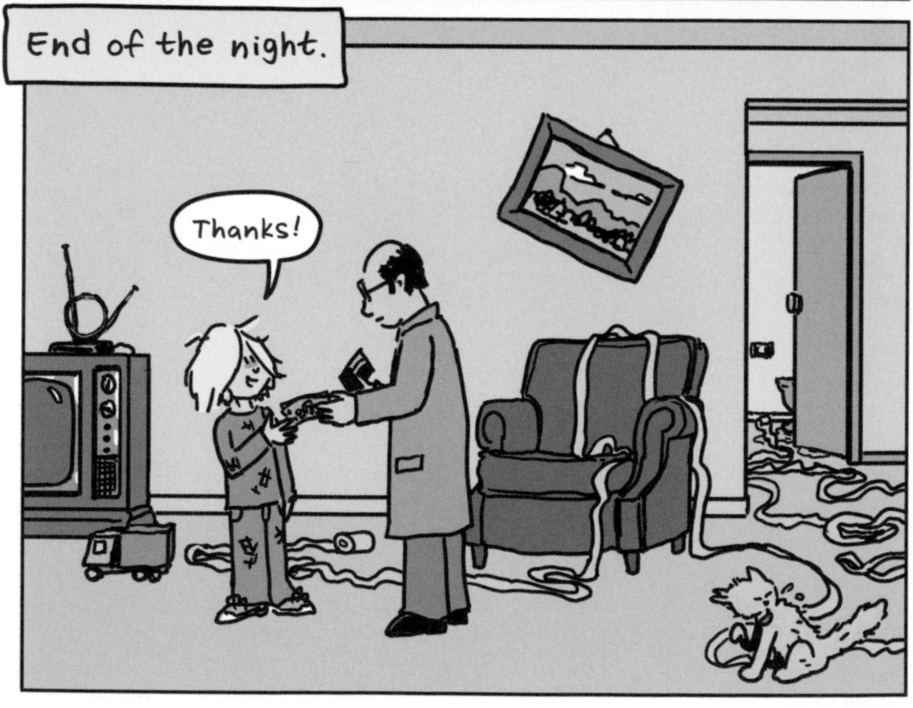

End of the night.
Thanks!

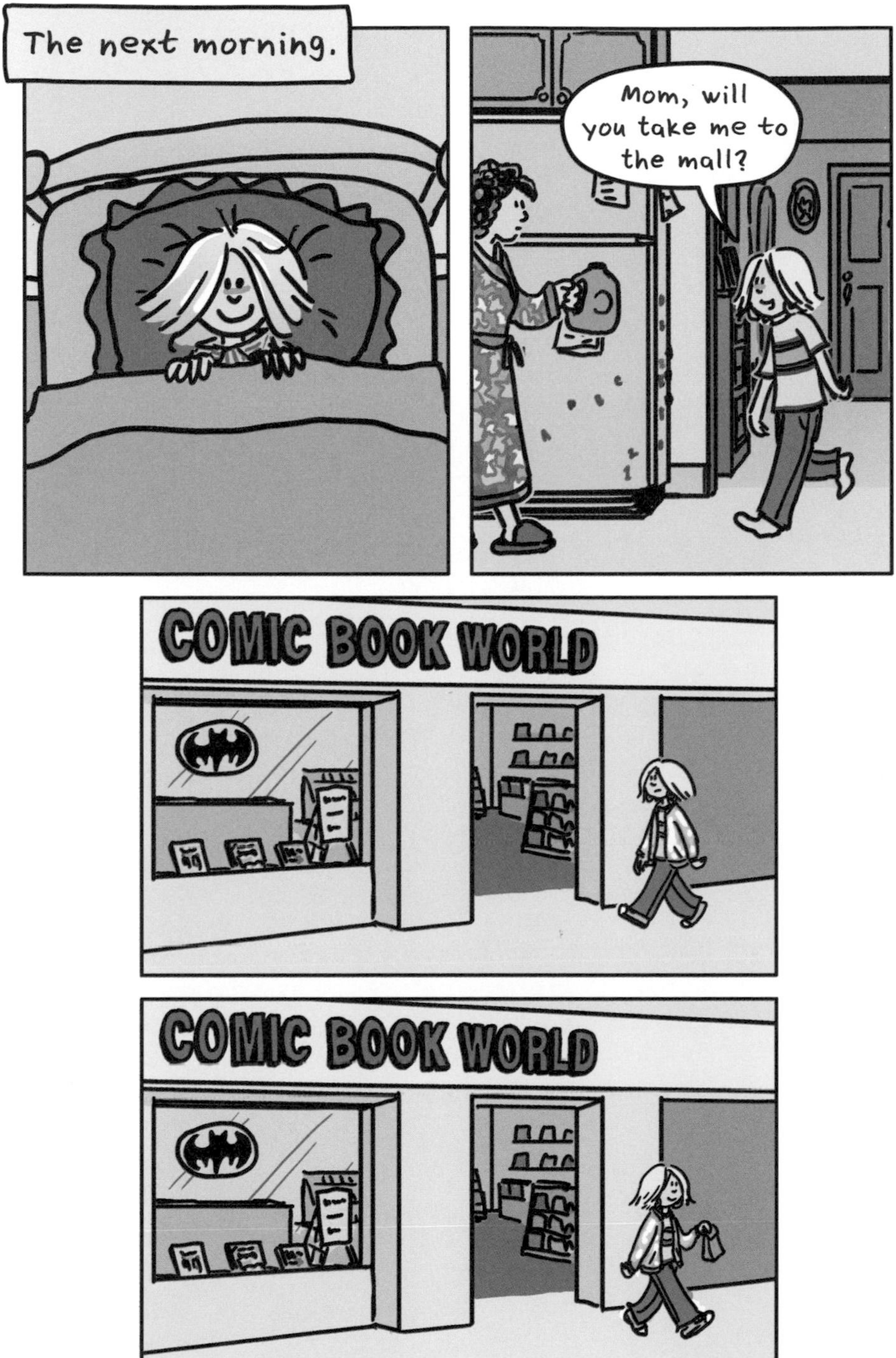
The next morning.
Mom, will you take me to the mall?
COMIC BOOK WORLD
COMIC BOOK WORLD

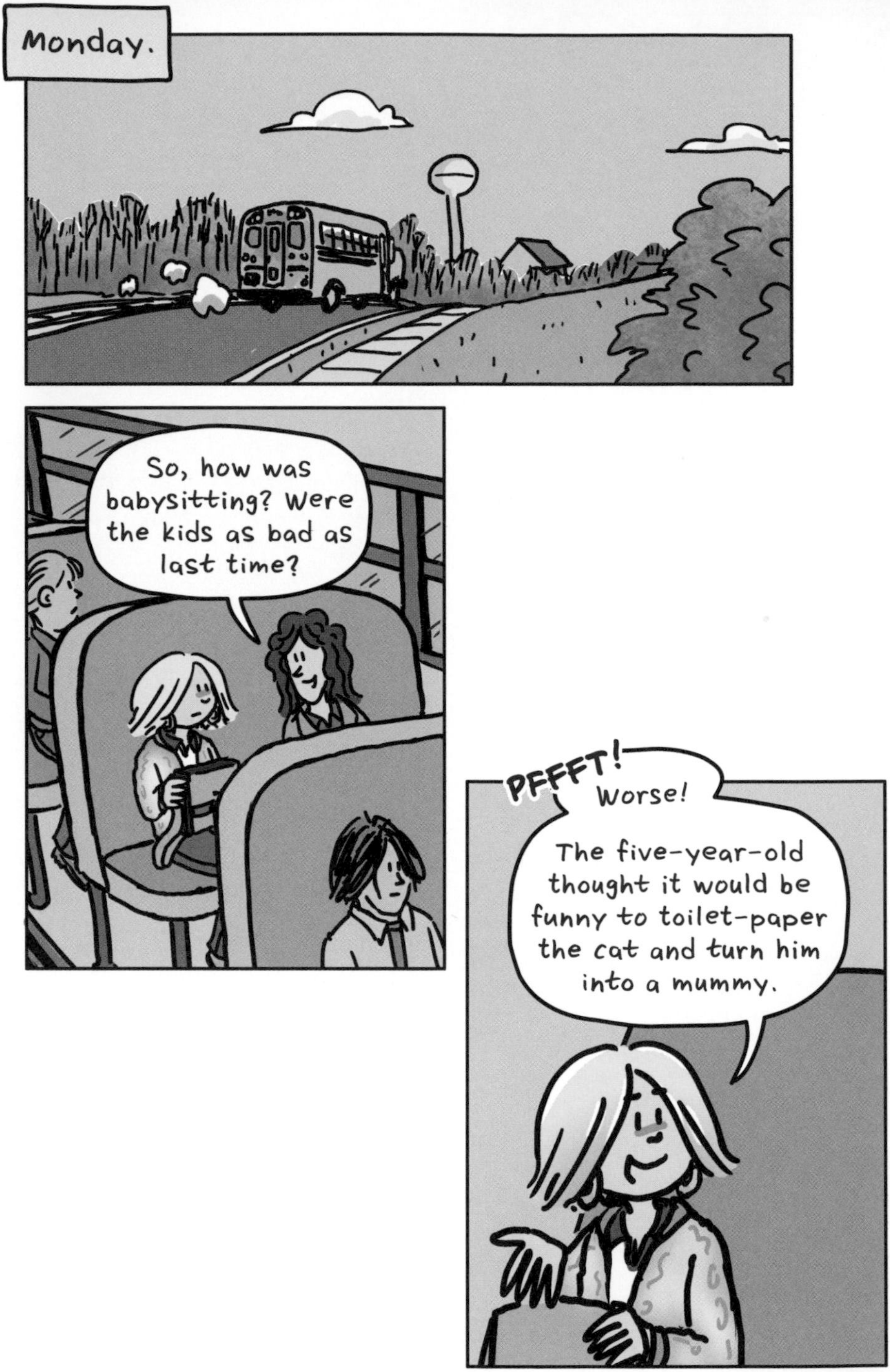
Monday.
So, how was babysitting? Were the kids as bad as last time?
PFFFT! Worse!
The five-year-old thought it would be funny to toilet-paper the cat and turn him into a mummy.

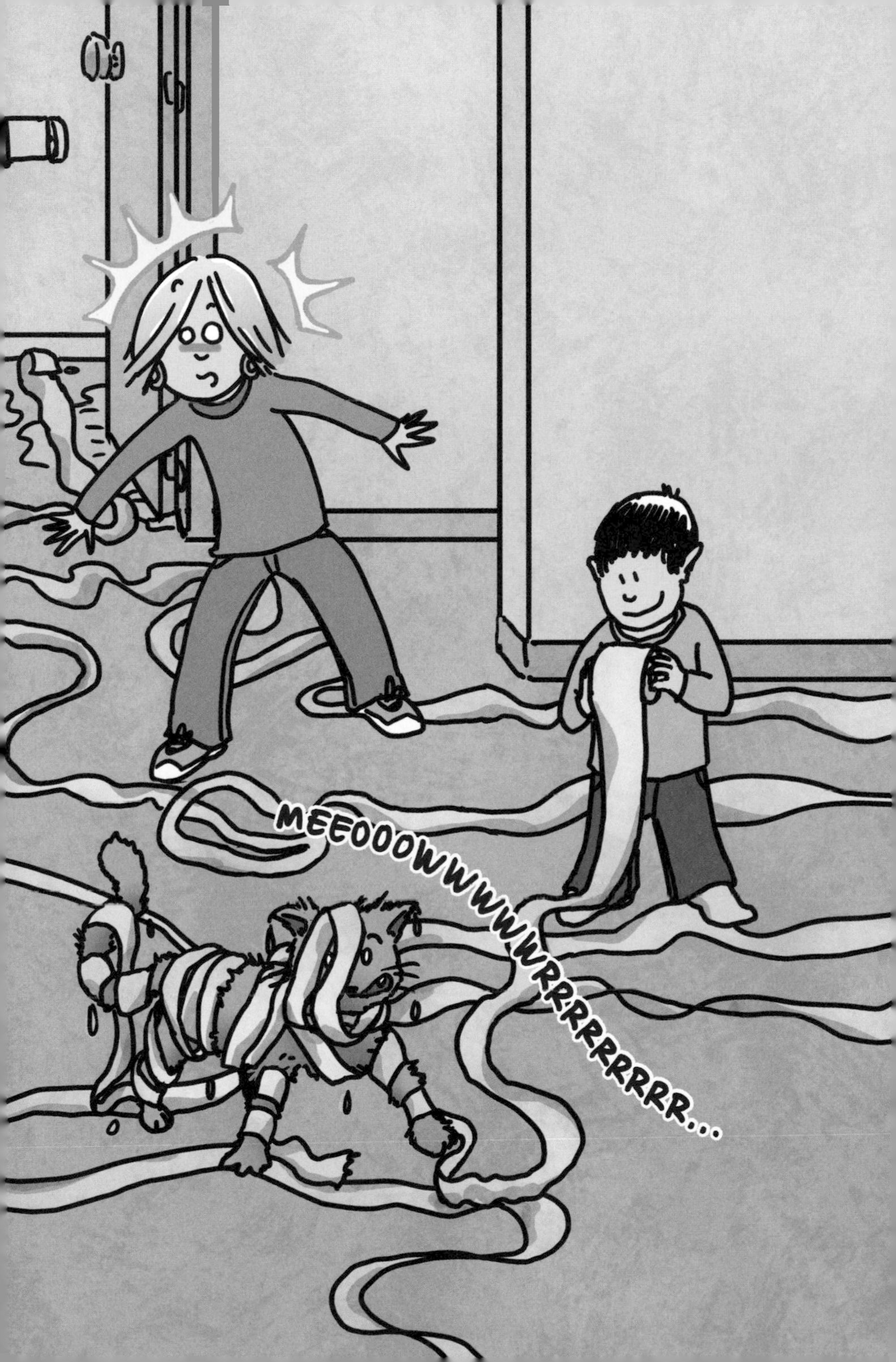
MEEOOOWWWWWWRRRRRRRRR...

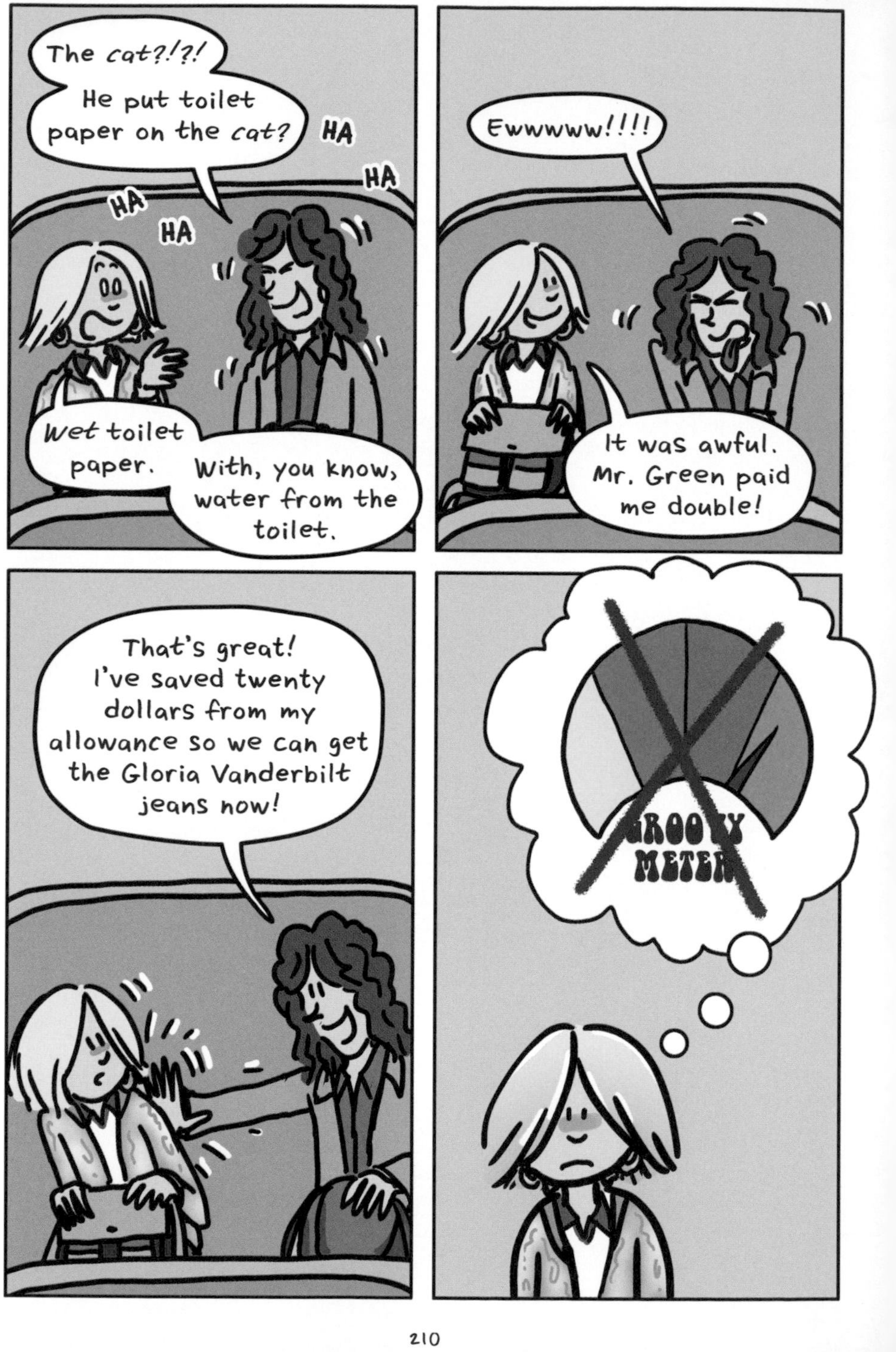
The cat?!?!
He put toilet paper on the cat?
HA
HA
HA
HA
Wet toilet paper.
With, you know, water from the toilet.
Ewwwww!!!!
It was awful. Mr. Green paid me double!
That's great! I've saved twenty dollars from my allowance so we can get the Gloria Vanderbilt jeans now!

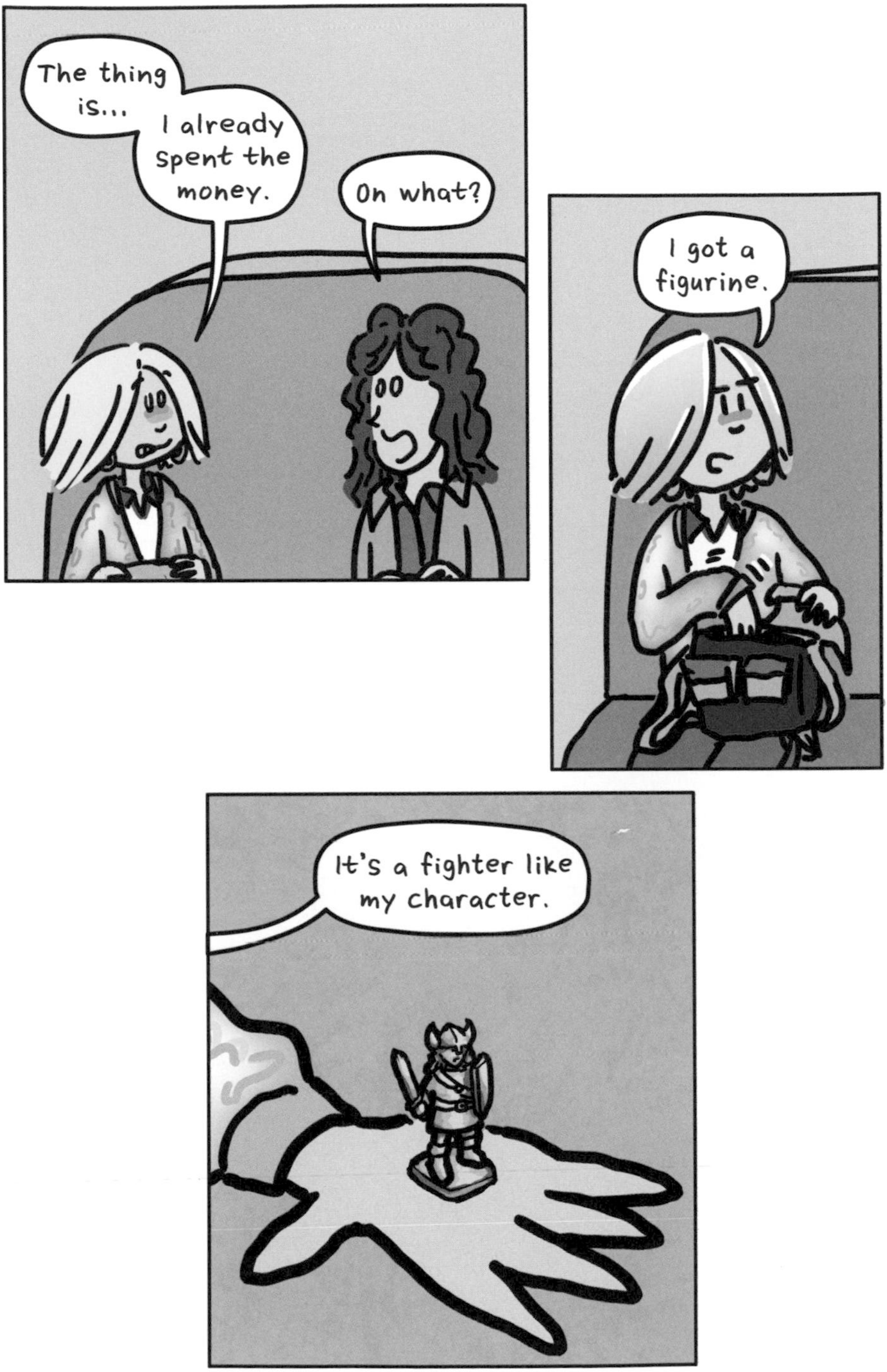
The thing is...
I already spent the money.
On what?
I got a figurine.
It's a fighter like my character.

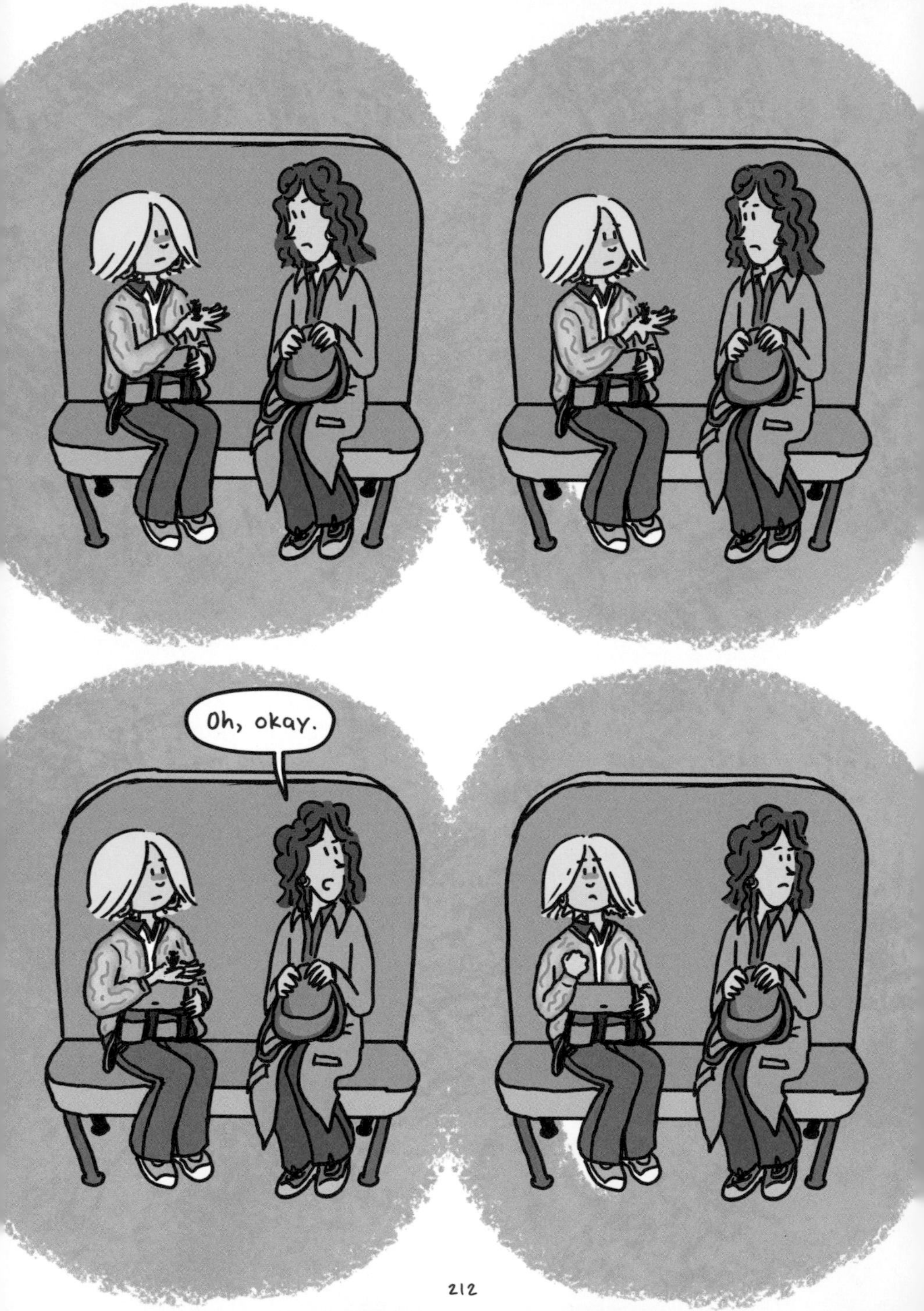
Oh, okay.

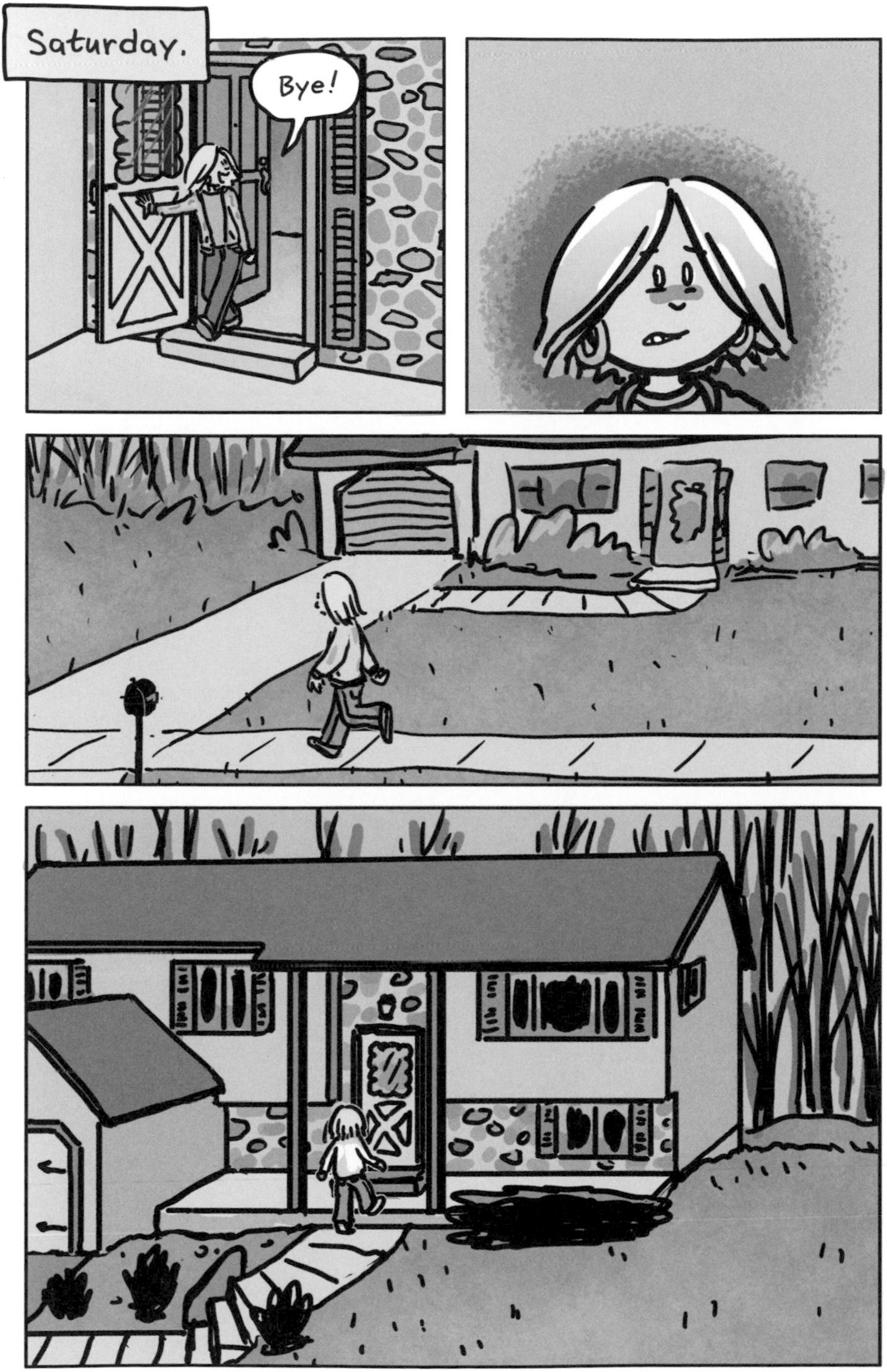
Saturday.
Bye!

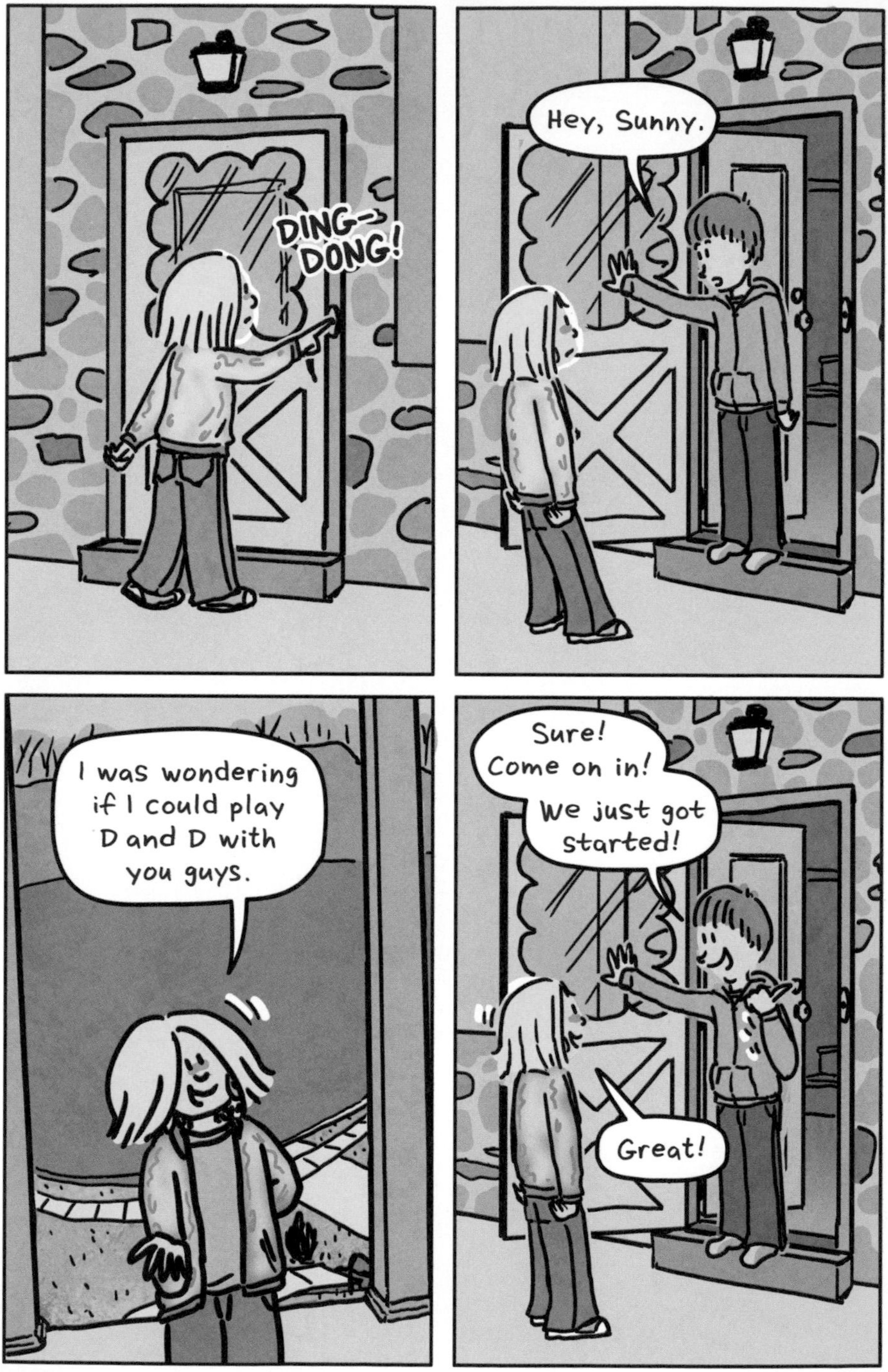
DING-DONG!
Hey, Sunny.
I was wondering if I could play D and D with you guys.
Sure! Come on in!
We just got started!
Great!

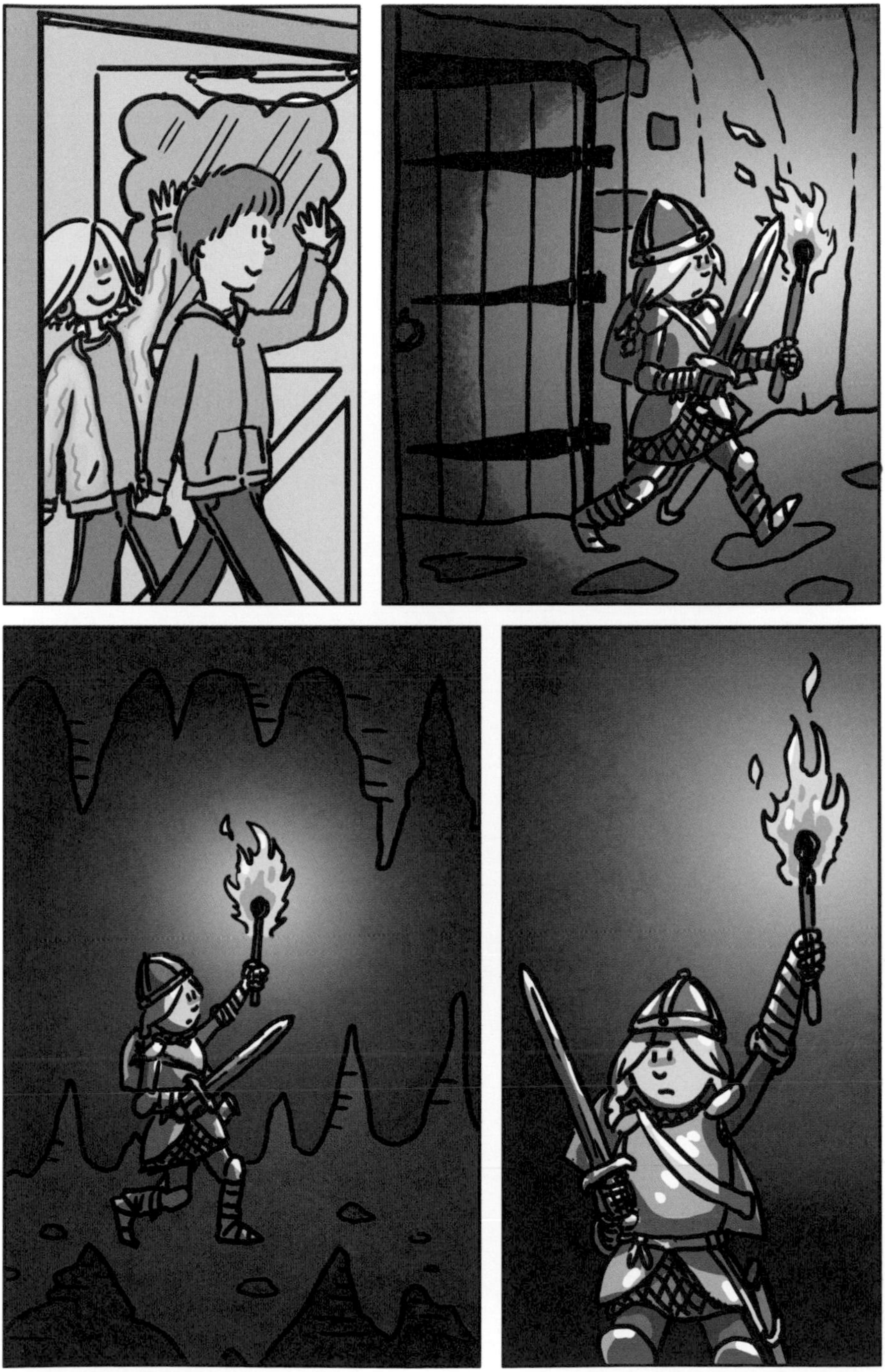

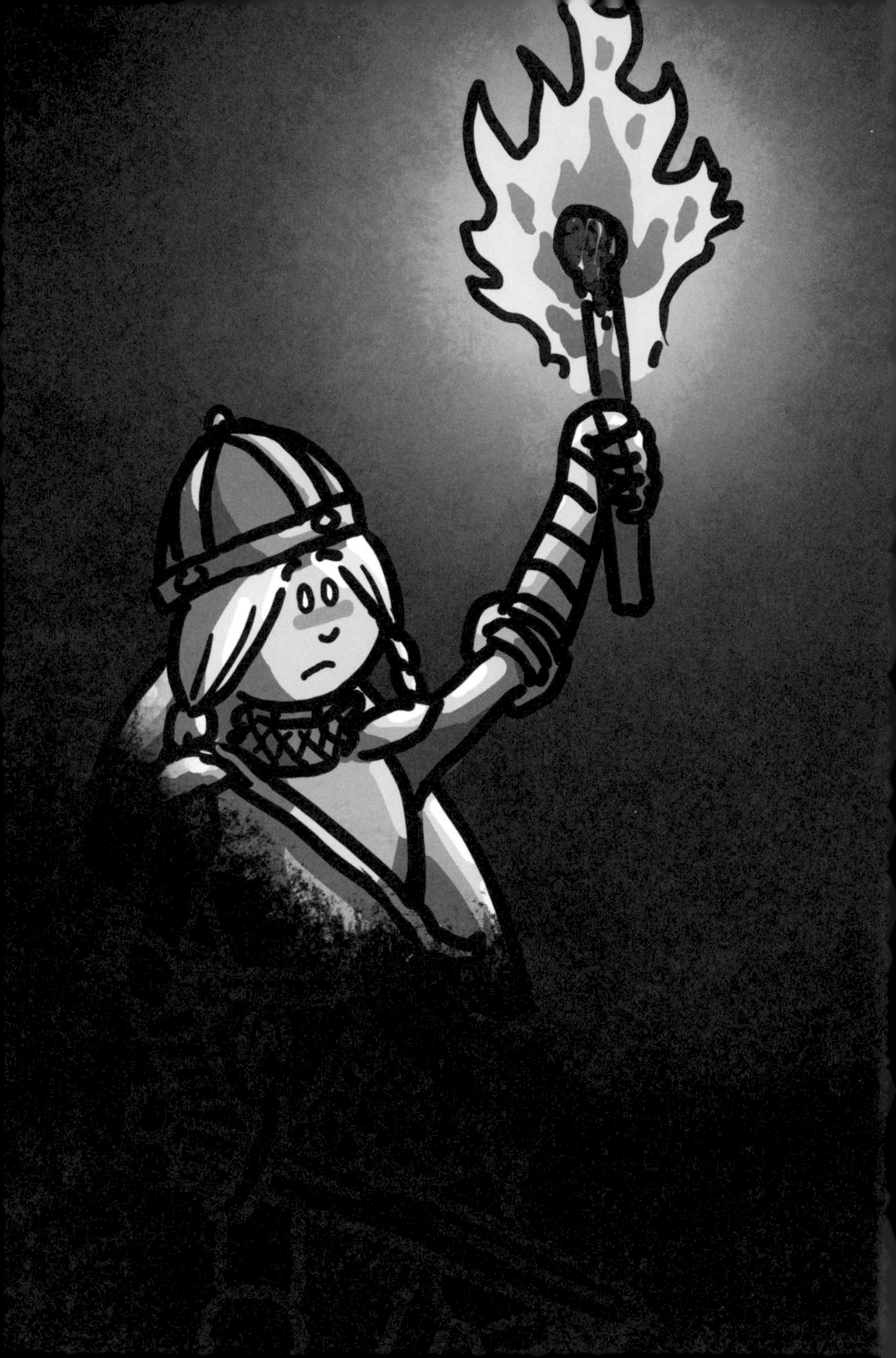

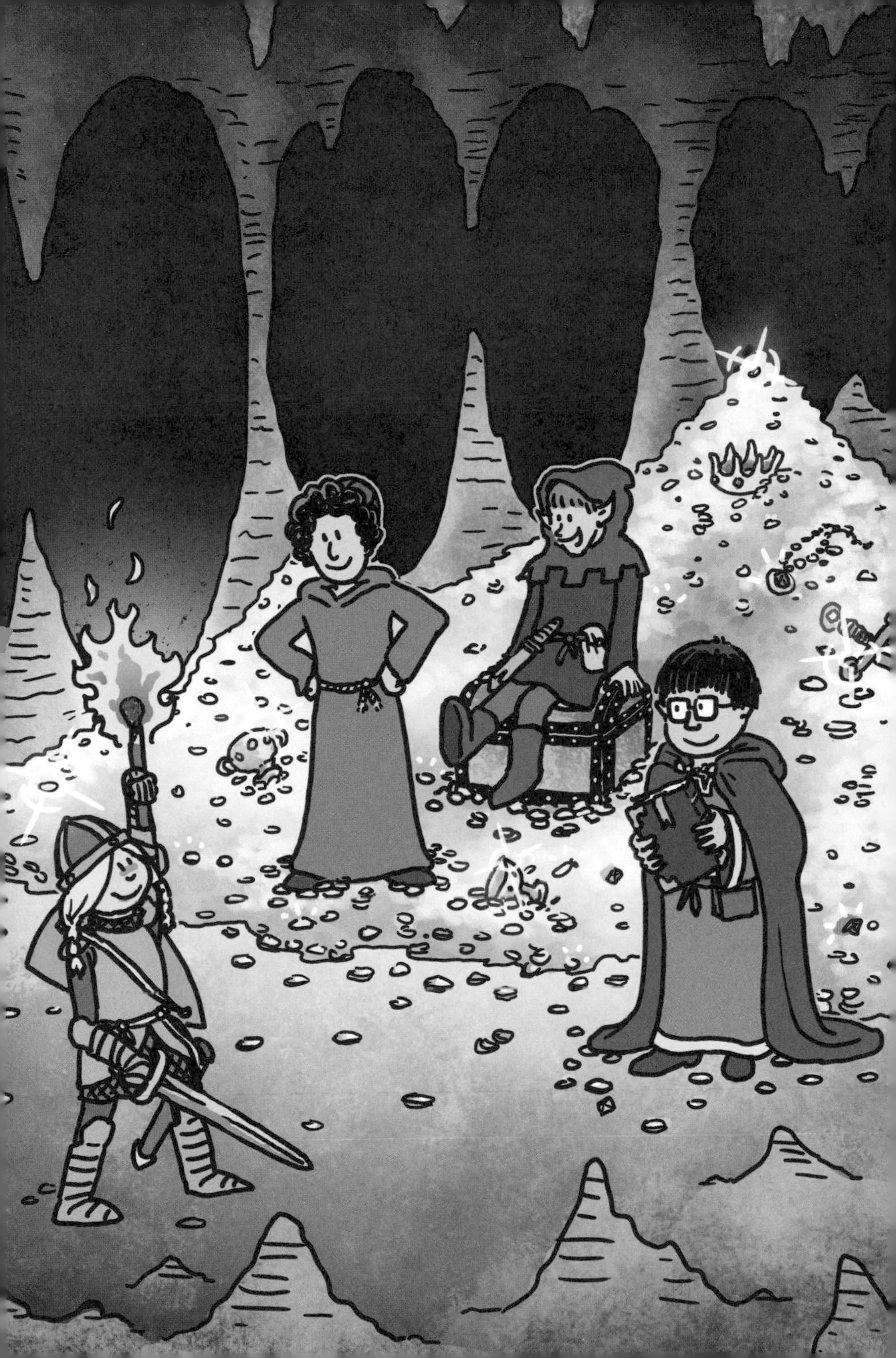

A NOTE FROM JENNIFER L. HOLM & MATTHEW HOLM

We were very excited to have Sunny play D&D in this book. We both spent many happy hours in our wood-paneled basement rolling 20-sided dice and fighting Giant Spiders. If you are a kid who likes fantasy and adventure, you should check out D&D—which is still popular today, even though we played it way back in the 1970s. It's a game that stays with you for life! (By the way, Jenni was a cleric.)

ACKNOWLEDGMENTS

Many, many thanks to our "Sunny Crew" — Lark Pien, Fawn Lau, David Levithan, Phil Falco, Lauren Donovan, Lizette Serrano, and Jill Grinberg. And special thanks to Eric Calderon, Jonathan Hamel, and Cyndi Koon. We would be happy to go on a campaign with all of you!

JENNIFER L. HOLM & MATTHEW HOLM are the award-winning brother-sister team behind the Babymouse and Squish series. Jennifer is also the author of many acclaimed novels, including three Newbery Honor books and the NEW YORK TIMES bestseller THE FOURTEENTH GOLDFISH.

LARK PIEN, the colorist of SUNNY ROLLS THE DICE, is an indie cartoonist from Oakland, California. She has published many comics and is the colorist for Printz Award winner AMERICAN BORN CHINESE and BOXERS & SAINTS. Her characters Long Tail Kitty and Mr. Elephanter have been adapted into children's books. You can follow her on Twitter @larkpien.